Notes from Elsewhere

Also by the author:

Layton, Monique. *Street Women and the Art of Bullshitting* (2010)

Verdun-Jones, Simon, and Monique Layton, eds. *Mental Health Law and Practice Through the Life Cycle* (1994)

Layton, Monique, ed. *Policing in the Global Community. The Challenge of Leadership* (1992)

Boyd, Neil, and Monique Layton, eds. *Crime and Criminal Justice in Canada and Japan: Understanding our Differences* (1991)

Notes from Elsewhere

Travel and Other Matters

MONIQUE LAYTON

iUniverse, Inc.
Bloomington

Notes from Elsewhere
Travel and Other Matters

Copyright © 2011 by Monique Layton

All rights reserved. No part of this book may be used or reproduced by any means, graphic, electronic, or mechanical, including photocopying, recording, taping or by any information storage retrieval system without the written permission of the publisher except in the case of brief quotations embodied in critical articles and reviews.

iUniverse books may be ordered through booksellers or by contacting:

iUniverse
1663 Liberty Drive
Bloomington, IN 47403
www.iuniverse.com
1-800-Authors (1-800-288-4677)

Because of the dynamic nature of the Internet, any web addresses or links contained in this book may have changed since publication and may no longer be valid. The views expressed in this work are solely those of the author and do not necessarily reflect the views of the publisher, and the publisher hereby disclaims any responsibility for them.

Any people depicted in stock imagery provided by Thinkstock are models, and such images are being used for illustrative purposes only.

Certain stock imagery © Thinkstock.

ISBN: 978-1-4620-3649-3 (sc)
ISBN: 978-1-4620-3651-6 (hc)
ISBN: 978-1-4620-3650-9 (e)

Printed in the United States of America

iUniverse rev. date: 11/15/2011

Preface

I indulge here in a type of writing often called, perhaps generously, auto-ethnography. Even though I write about events and emotions familiar to many of us, such as travel, immigration, culture and acculturation, nostalgia, love of language and interest in its pitfalls, remembrance of the past, and thoughts of the future, I do so in a personal way and speak through what is not always an endearing format: the first person.

I shall leave it to Stendhal to make my case. In *Mémoires d'un touriste*, he proposes a justification for those who, embarrassingly at times, will speak or write in the first person. *"Ce n'est pas par egoïsme que je dis* je, *c'est parce qu'il n'y a pas d'autre moyen de raconter vite."* Indeed, rather than an ego trip, it is a useful shortcut to make a point. Who knows better than the teller of the tale or the traveller how it has felt to be there and to do that? It seems to me that what helps in discerning the nature of our journey to various parts of the world and how it affects our life, is the sentiment of dislocation we may feel at times and the various degrees in which disconnection is personally experienced and dealt with—even if it is likely to resemble that of other people. Then, having confronted the particular, we may perhaps be able to aim at the more general.

Like most of us, I wear many hats. The most relevant ones in the context of this book are those of bicultural immigrant, frequent traveller, and cultural anthropologist. Whatever I have experienced in these roles has found an echo here—following a French adage *(Faire feu de tout bois)* that instructs us to make do with any type of wood we can find to build our bonfire. Quilters will recognize patchwork techniques and ornithologists nest building approaches as I make use of any available bit of information and memory while piecing my text together.

When we look back upon our life, I do not think we see it as a well structured and precisely written narrative, all events linked, and their sum total making sense. Rather, we notice and remember the characters that peopled it, the individual events that caused sudden and unexpected changes in its course, the fugitive moments when all was well with the world. What we look for, and hope to find, is some sort of meaning and coherence in what we did and what happened to us.

My French grandmother, the only one I knew, always cooked without a recipe. She just added ingredients until they tasted right to her and, she hoped, to others as well. I also cook this way. And write.

I need to mention that the historical information provided throughout this book is of an extremely superficial nature. It is only intended as a rough background sketch for readers, perhaps to entice them to read further on the subject. This book remains a description of what occurred on my journeys.

Acknowledgments

Most of chapter 3—Meeting Strangers: The Rules of Engagement—was originally published under the same title in the following work:

Loewen, Gregory, ed. *Evaluating the Scholarly Achievement of Professor Elvi Whittaker: Essays in Philosophical Anthropology.* Lewiston, NY: The Edwin Mellen Press, 2010.

    I wish to thank Dr. Lee Southern, Mr. Justice John Spencer, and Dr. Elvi Whittaker for having kindly accepted to read parts of this book and providing thoughtful comments. I also appreciate the encouragements of Eleanor Wachtel, of CBC's *Writers & Company,* and Dr. Patricia Fung.

    My thanks are due to Nicholas Layton, Hunter Elliott and Sarah Elliott for providing badly needed computer assistance.

    Finally, I am grateful to John for his constant support and almost infinite patience. I hope our children, Peter, Stephen, Kim, Nicholas, and Alexandra, find this book interesting.

Contents

Preface..v

Acknowledgments......................................vii

Chapter One
On Being Elsewhere and the Company We Keep on the Journey......1

Chapter Two
"As Canadian as Possible … Under the Circumstances"............21

Chapter Three
Meeting Strangers: The Rules of Engagement....................35

Chapter Four
The Old Moroccan Photo Shoebox (1932–1946)...................52

Chapter Five
Morocco Revisited 1998......................................91

Chapter Six
The Loneliness Beyond the Walls.............................125

Chapter Seven
"The Most Beautiful Land Ever Seen" Cuba, 1992..............148

Chapter Eight
A Paradise of Sorts Seychelles, 1992........................176

Chapter Nine
Abroad in a Bubble 210

Chapter Ten
From Barcelona to Biarritz 1994 243

Chapter Eleven
So, What Next? Cruising to Narragonia? 270

About the Author 279

Bibliography 281

Chapter One

On Being Elsewhere and the Company We Keep on the Journey

We are constantly inclined to isolate ourselves from what surrounds us, as if we were spectators, not elements in what goes on.

—Teilhard de Chardin

We seldom go elsewhere alone. Even if no one walks beside us, we are accompanied by all the knowledge we carry about, whatever its sources and whatever our reasons for being on the road. Some writers may have seduced us and been given permission to shadow us as we progress. Who they are perhaps matters less than what their own influences have been. It is their baggage as well as our own that we carry along the way.

Had Bruce Chatwin not spent years at Sotheby's, would he have seen the world differently? Did Sybille Bedford's upbringing affect her understanding of Western Europe half a century ago? Yes, very likely. I may never know how directly their life experiences have shaped their perceptions, but I need to know something of their progress if I am to spend time reading their books and following them as they proceed, particularly if they proceed abroad, where many of the familiar rules may no longer apply.

Writers usually reveal something of themselves. If they do so unwittingly, all the better, since I do not always want them to tell me explicitly who they think they are, as I would have little faith in their self-assessment. Some thirty years ago, I assisted a sociologist in analyzing the results of a "Who Am I?" test. A number of children at some risk, mostly between the ages of ten and thirteen, were asked to complete ten statements starting with "I am ..." Parents or guardians were asked to complete ten statements starting with "He/She is ..." I particularly remember one of the younger boys hopefully writing, "I am a boy my mom likes." The mother, on the other hand, had written (quite accurately, as it turned out), "He is a little son of a bitch."

I need to know something about those writers if I am to accompany them on their story. What may affect their perceptions? What is their sense of the incongruous? Do they laugh when others do not, perhaps because they see laughter as the only response to the grotesque or the tragic? Are they or have they been happy in love, and has their vision been shaped by tenderness? Do they like animals, seeing them as fitting companions on life's journey? Do they truly appreciate the work involved in keeping little girls in lacy white dresses and spotless white socks for Sunday Mass, when doing the laundry means stretching clotheslines above chickens scratching in the dusty ground?

If travellers retrace the path of Napoleon's *Grande Armée* in the Russian campaign, is it perhaps because they were deeply moved by the telling graph of Charles Joseph Minard (a civil engineer and retired *Inspecteur Général des Ponts et Chaussées*), showing the pathetic correlation between the soldiers' ongoing and compounded decimation and the unbearably cold winter of 1812, when each step on the frozen Russian ground meant yet another fatal French statistic? I would want to know that. If the battlefields of the Great War are their pilgrimage, was their grandfather gassed at Ypres in 1915? I would want to know that too. How old are they, or were they when they wrote—how could we situate anyone unless their age is known? What fads have they gone through? What cultural bugaboos have they had to live with? How many times have we gone around the sun together on our common journey? So many questions, so often unanswered.

It is said (Jean d'Ormesson, in *Presque rien sur presque tout*) that men would be something other than men without Aeschylus and Plato, without Dante, without Spinoza (this is his list, that of a cultivated European; those with other backgrounds might have a different one). That neither Christianity nor Islam would be what they are without the Bible and the Koran. That a whole chunk of history would not have seen the light without Descartes' *Le Discours de la méthode* or Karl Marx's *Das Kapital*. D'Ormesson believes, as many others do, in the word, and more particularly in the written word, as a shaper and conveyor of cultural, religious, and political forces.

In a more modest vein, travel writers help shape their readers' vision of the world through their journeys, imaginary or real, and through the words they use to relate where they went and what they saw. Like other writers with more literary aspirations, they too can base their travels on the experience and the wisdom of the ages. The mythological sources of travel writers include, for instance, the quests of Jason, Ulysses, or Aeneas. In these ancient nautical narratives, the pattern of all travel is clearly established: pains, perils, errors, pleasures, fears, and interference from meddling gods and other powers. In other words, what we all experience abroad with various degrees of exoticism and energy—and, clearly, those are not foreign to what we go through in life itself. Chatwin cleverly points out the semantic closeness—in English, at least—of *travail* and *travel* and its implication: the bodily and mental labours, the toil, the exertion, and the hardships that the former describes and the latter should evoke.

Contemporary travellers' relations reconstruct unfamiliar societies that we recognize nevertheless through the previous works of earlier travellers, philosophers, naturalists, missionaries, or ethnographers, whose writings constitute our basis for such recognition. Obviously, anthropologists will have a different perspective from Jesuits, even when they consider the same cultures, as they sometimes do, particularly in North America. And nineteenth-century naturalists sponsored by the Royal Geographic Society had, in the rush of their breathtaking discoveries, a different focus from that of modern ethnobotanists determined to understand and salvage what they can when there is still a little time left. But, whatever the sources of this baggage, it all adds up somewhere in our reading unconscious.

Who, what, where, when, why, how? *What* travel writers saw and heard; *when* they left, arrived, and left again; *where* their impulses took them; and *how* they travelled, and more importantly, *how* they understood what they perceived: we certainly learn all that in their books. *Why* they went is sometimes less obvious, but their reasons fall mostly into two categories: to write guidebooks or to describe individual journeys. But *who* are they? Travel is what individual travellers make of it, and without knowing who they are, we understand less of what they relate.

Novelists, in theory at least, control the unexpected; travel writers do not. They must adjust to it and how they cope is at the core of their writings. Travel provides us with new environments, new contexts in which to see ourselves by stretching the link binding us to our deep native roots (or to our forged acculturation, if we are immigrants) and to our reality at home.

While I have covered many miles by air, rail, road, sea, and on foot, I certainly would not call myself a traveller. Being a traveller or a tourist (for which roles I am not very well suited, tiring easily and often getting lost), is often a question of attitude and self-perception. By most standards, Peter, our eldest son, was a traveller at some point in his life: camera in hand, recording what he saw and heard on three extended journeys to South America, South East Asia, and later Africa, from Cairo to Zanzibar. I have absolutely no desire to emulate such activity—in fact, it would be quite impossible for me to do so for I would see little point in it. He and I happened to be in Venezuela a few months apart, and without hesitation, we each took the course of action best suited to our respective nature. He visited Angel Falls in a helicopter, whereas I walked through playgrounds in Caracas and watched local news and soap operas in my hotel room. Our impressions of Venezuela undoubtedly bear little similarity.

In the same manner, when I travelled with John, my husband, I was less enthusiastic than he would have wished me to be. We were younger then, and he exhausted me with endless walks, every visit becoming a marathon. He truly thrived on the energy he spent, while I was perfectly happy sitting in the shade somewhere, pretending to watch the world go by, eyes half-closed under heavy lids, but in fact turning myself off.

Notes from Elsewhere

Maybe start the book here

For good or bad, travel changes us by forcing us to look at ourselves carefully since we are usually left to our own devices abroad. It is only through travel that I have discovered my main weakness, one I had been able to overlook until then. I do not travel well and I miss the big picture. I tend to overlook the obvious (myopia may explain some failures of perception, but this may be too literal), and I forget a lot of what I have seen. When sent to work elsewhere, I write upon my return sensible reports that people seem to find useful. Yet, when asked, "Well, what was it like?" I am dumbfounded and as much at a loss as if I had been asked to wade through treacle.

So I resort to short sketches while scrambling for coherence. Details, street corners, reflections on cobblestones under a streetlight in the rain, the smell of spices, the condition of some toilets, what some beds were like, a hairstyle, a sign by the side of the road ("Drive nice!" on the way to San Antonio), those I can talk about. Somehow, a hedgehog rather than a fox, and certainly not an eagle, I definitely seem to miss the big picture. So mostly, I say, "It was interesting." And people think either I am trying to be mysterious or clever, or perhaps I am lazy, or even, who knows, that I may not think enough of them to make the effort. Such a supposition would be unfair, since my weakness is not one of arrogance but of limited vision and scope.

On the other hand, for there is always one, thanks to travel, I have achieved another perception of myself. I have learned to turn my physical attributes (some might say disadvantages) into assets. Being short, female, and no longer young, gives me an unthreatening appearance and facilitates exchanges. A few seasoned wrinkles, so undesirable at home, and a mild expression often mistaken for benevolence, have served me rather well. My status as a mother of five and a grandmother of eleven even carries prestige in some parts of the world. Such fertility, common in the 1950s but now an inelegant anachronism in my own society, can be taken elsewhere as a sign of solidity and experience and be worthy of respect. As I list, in non-Western countries, my sixteen credentials to maturity, I mentally sit back on my haunches and become a Wise Old Woman of the human tribe.

But how do we travel in the late twentieth and early twenty-first centuries? We are no longer explorers or discoverers in search of the wealth of gold, silk, and spices—even if some still look for knowledge in the depths of the oceans, the lushness of the Amazon forest, or whatever the stars can reveal—and, nowadays, we mostly travel for selfish and personal reasons. Tourism has become an important industry, often the mainstay of local economy for countries poor in other natural resources but rich in sun, beaches, and folklore. It is to these countries that we mostly travel, alone or with family and friends, and that we visit in more or less organized groups.

Let us consider the different types of tourists now familiar everywhere in the world. We see them traveling in groups, known as *charter*, but also as independent travellers. We see them traveling and writing about their journeys. Some may also consider themselves drifters. Others may be temporarily "embedded" abroad as consultants or become *expats* of long standing. The mode of travel we choose determines to what extent we may participate in the local life. I try to illustrate through my own travel experience some of those categories.

Charter Tourists
For those, safety and comfort are paramount as they mostly expect to be duly protected from the unfamiliar: abhorrent foods, crude lodgings, rough customs, and unsafe conditions. The origin of this type of travel can be directly attributed to Thomas Cook, a Baptist lay-preacher and supporter of the Temperance movement in nineteenth-century England. He believed that the luxury of leisure now afforded by the Industrial Revolution to a new segment of society—the working and lower-middle classes—created the risk of a potentially unhealthy use of their spare time. The earlier Grand Tour had established the infrastructure for mass travel, and Cook made the most of it to ensure a sober and educational use of this new leisure time. Starting with the first Temperance Society, excursions in the Midlands in the middle of the nineteenth century, he rapidly established himself as a travel promoter and organizer.

Notes from Elsewhere

The success of his first excursions on continental Europe and the subsequent refinement he brought to the organization of group travel established him as the creator of the "packaged" tour. From the continent, he organized tours to the United States, and after the opening of the Suez Canal, to the Middle East and the Far East. That the roaming *Cookites,* as they were known, were not "real" travellers was an accepted fact. In 1875, Lady Isabel Burton described the arrival of a Cook's party of some one hundred and eighty tourists in Syria and the natives' reaction to them: *"Ma hum Sayyáhin: Hum Kukiyyech."* (These are not travellers; they are Cookii.)

Faithful to the same pattern of safety and convenience, contemporary charter tourists still travel in partial isolation from their foreign environment and almost totally separated from the reality of the country visited. Some writers describe them as traveling within an "environmental bubble." In this case, the tourists' own reality is carefully preserved. They are often entertained by fabricated spectacles that recreate for them some stereotypic version of the culture visited, which they are expected to recognize from what they have read in guidebooks or seen on televised documentaries.

These tourists often travel in air-conditioned touring coaches or cruise ships stopping at foreign ports on the way, and while still getting a taste of the exotic, experience little sense of disconnection from their own culture. Thanks to the bubble effect, their social contacts are far more likely to be with other tourists than with local people. "Marjorie and me in front of the Taj Mahal with Ingrid and Sven, a great couple we met on the tour," may be written on the back of a photograph. The photograph will be shown to their friends in Edmonton, and Sven and Ingrid will show it to their friends in Stockholm. This picture, now a formal document, attests and validates that all four have travelled halfway around the globe to meet in Agra.

A rather specialized aspect of bubble tourism is the international conference. The event organizers take those who attend such conferences, usually lasting about a week, well in hand. Tourists are housed, fed, entertained, and have often little latitude for wandering around alone. Their time is rigorously managed, and their activities are intended to allow them to see as much as possible in as little time as can be taken away from the business at hand.

If honest, few of them would deny that they have seen little by the time they leave, and that they have misunderstood or misconstrued much of what they saw. By the time their jet lag has dissipated and they are eager to discover a little of the ordinary life around them, it is almost time to leave. All they are expected to gather is a mere flavour of the place visited. There are, of course, exceptions, and often, someone who has previously visited the city is tempted to gather a small group to organize a private sortie. With luck, some may even have local acquaintances willing to show them around. Even then, they are escorted, protectively cushioned; being the innocents abroad, the babes in the wood, that by any standards, they truly are, these visitors' main characteristic is their willingness, eagerness even, to be led.

A number of years ago, I attended the two conferences I describe here: a very large one in Bangkok and a smaller, more intimate one in Caracas. As well as a significant difference in jet lag (a manageable four hours in one case against a discombobulatingly long one in the other), there were enormous differences between the two continents, cities, religions, languages, cultures, and peoples involved—totally alien in one, almost familiar in the other. The two conferences left me with a vastly different impression, but the nature of the trip was essentially the same. In both cases, the bubble was respected, since we had no independent contact with the ordinary local population, and we remained entirely within the culture of the conference.

Independent Tourists
The other groups of tourists, who travel mostly on their own, are the heirs of those former participants in the Grand Tour. The nineteenth century saw travellers crisscrossing Europe and the Middle East as never before since the Middle Ages, when commerce and religion prompted people to move ceaselessly on well-travelled routes. In that century, travel became the thing to do for the satisfaction of personal curiosity, the completion of gentle folks' education, and the reconnection to classical sources for artists and intellectuals.

Stimulated by books and relations of journeys, reports by surveyors, architects, linguists, artists, naturalists, and scientists of various disciplines (such as those Napoleon took to Egypt with him), long-established connections with the Orient (such as those created by the East India Co.), a fashionable taste for Egypt, Greece, and other such exotic places, swept Western Europe. Indeed, European tourism, as we know it, had started. It was only a matter of time until anybody who was *anybody* simply had to go on the Grand Tour.

From the conventional young woman sketching Italian lakes or touring Egypt with her aromatic vinegars as protection against vile odours to the young and foppish Disraeli touring the Mediterranean and heading for the heart of the Ottoman Empire and the Holy Land, they all set forth and reported on their journeys.

Europeans found it difficult to understand those who did not share their taste for such endeavours. "The Turks," wrote Robert Byron between the two world wars, "have no idea of travelling for amusement." But amusement may not always have been found in actual travel, and for some, the dislocation must have been extreme. Thus, in 1866, Emily Lott describes herself in Egypt as "unaccustomed to the filthy manners, barbarous customs, and disgusting habits of all around me; deprived of every comfort by which I had always been surrounded."

What, then, were the expectations of those travellers who set out more or less on their own? They were no doubt interested in the picturesque, and looked forward to seeing some local colour, genuine or contrived for their benefit. Many might not have known the difference, for few would have been as well prepared as, say, Lord Curzon reading "between 200 and 300 books in European languages and Persian written over the past five centuries" before setting forth to Persia in 1889, his precious Kodak in his bags.

However, what many individuals were to find through travel was a renewal, a new understanding of others and of themselves in the disconnection from their habitual worlds. This was particularly true of those who felt inadequate at home. It was precisely dislocation they sought in order to find their true selves, liberated from the bonds of a familiarity that weighed them down. Women, particularly nineteenth-century women but some closer to us as well, often enjoyed the benefits of a new, temporary life without the conventions of home. Such a pattern, reported in their writings, is worth considering for it proposes the other side of being uprooted: the joy of experiencing novelty and discovering the depths of one's resources, often unrecognized and perhaps unnecessary at home.

Isabella Bird, fighting family responsibilities and ill health while at home, stormed her tough and irrepressible way through Hawaii, the Rocky Mountains, Japan, Persia, Kurdistan, Tibet, and China. "It is so like living in a new world, so free, so fresh, so vital, so careless, so unfettered," she wrote, "that one grudges being asleep." There were, she rejoiced, "no demands of any kind … above all … no conventions."

Gertrude Bell, a polyglot and a mountaineer, among her many accomplishments, could only survive the torments of unrequited love, unbearable at home, through the sublimation of travel. She wrote to the unresponsive and uxorious object of her passion, "I have filled all the hollow places in the world with my desire for you." Those hollow places included, among others, Persia, Syria, Turkey, Arabia, India, and Baghdad.

Jan Morris, having faced the trauma of transsexuality and progressing from accidental man to a woman's full status, admitted, "Only lately I recognized that incessant wandering as an outer expression of my inner journey" and "I have come to see my own life … as a prolonged and fascinating quest."

Dervla Murphy, riding her bicycle in India—alternating between a mule, a pony, and a donkey in Tibet, Nepal, and Ethiopia—and forging ahead through Madagascar, Cameroon, South India, often with her young daughter Rachel in tow, found in travel the escape she needed from a former, emotionally destructive family situation.

No hardships stopped them. We see Clara Bromley, "severely shaken by domestic losses during the preceding years," travelling at a grueling pace through North and South America in 1853 and nursing a yellow fever victim in Barbados. Yet, she wrote, "The year I spent on the other side of the Atlantic was the happiest and most peaceful of my life."

Lady Brown, whose well-researched writings contributed much to the knowledge of the day, when asked in 1924 whether she would do it again, replied, "Weighing the intense thirst and burning heat, the fever and the mosquitoes, the not being able to take off clothes for days on end, even the shortage of food, I can truly say 'Yes'—for I was not the same being—sex had disappeared."

Similarly, Alexandra David-Néel, the first European woman to reach Lhasa in 1924, and a Parisian whose background had not prepared her for walking through Tibet in the depths of winter dressed as a man, described her time and her spiritual quest as "the most blessed existence one can dream of, and I consider as the happiest in my life those days when … I wandered as one of the countless tribes of Tibetan beggar pilgrims."

The conditions of individual travel have certainly changed. Gone are the days of "safe conduct" derived from simply being a *civis romanus*, or a few centuries later, a member of the British Empire in its heyday. Or from belonging to some far-reaching religion (Christianity or Islam, as Ibn Battuta, "the best travelled man in the world," according to Jan Morris, could have attested in the fourteenth century), or even from belonging to the right social class. Most of those privileges have disappeared, and safe passage must now rely on administrative regulations (passports, visas, immunizations) and adjust to external conditions (wars, rebellions, political strife, embargos, floods, famines, epidemics).

The sheer number of tourists abroad has also affected the way in which we travel and the manner in which we are viewed by local people. While still only too easy to spot, the independent travellers are somewhat less conspicuous than the charter groups and are not totally dismissed *a priori* by local people, if only because the latter often have to engage with them in some form of everyday transaction. These tourists may even fool themselves that, shopping for food at a market, sitting on public benches in a little square, tramping along, they are able to blend in.

John and I used to travel with various degrees of independence. We would rent rooms in a small Mexican town, for instance, and ride in buses where, early in the morning, field workers laid down their machetes upon boarding and then picked them up when the bus stopped and dropped them off on a road near fields seemingly in the middle of nowhere. We would also stay at modest hotels intended for local people and eat at little cafés out of tourist paths. In each case, we were forced to cope with whatever prevailed—language problems, ignorance of customs, dislike for our country. We too may even have fooled ourselves that shopping for food at a market or sitting on public benches in little squares and talking to old people nearby, we were perhaps not quite like those *other* tourists. But naturally, we were mistaken.

Significantly, John's family was already well anchored in British Columbia before the province joined the rest of the country in Confederation. He is among those for whom even driving in their hometown becomes the source of so many explorations. A back alley explorer, he will never use the same route twice if he can help it. As for me, not only do I scrupulously follow the same path, I also change lanes, or cross the street if on foot, in exactly the same spot. Anything out of the ordinary might disrupt my constructed sense of familiarity, hence of wellbeing.

I say significantly when describing my husband's origins, because our different backgrounds, his established settlers versus my footloose migrants, more than likely have led to his yearning for travel and to my dragging my feet when forced to leave. And, when made to go elsewhere, from the first day I recreate familiarity. But so do most of us, for we can only bear so much dislocation. Thus, once abroad, even John often seeks the familiarity of the same café ("our" café) where to have the same breakfast every morning and read the newspaper. He too feels momentarily reconnected by talking briefly to other tourists from home or merely close by (in Essaouira, for instance, Seattle may do in a pinch for Vancouver, both being part of the imaginary Western land of Cascadia, the land of common interests). So, even those keen on wandering are not immune from seeking a facsimile of home and recreating a familiar if artificial home base elsewhere.

Travel Writers
For travel writers, travel is conceived from the start as a narrative. Its very essence is to be related. There are two types of travel writers: writers of travel guides and literary writers, who have an essential divergence in their *raison d'être*. It could even be said that their objectives are contradictory. The former try to put themselves in situations likely to be encountered

by potential travellers, their intended readers. Thus, they offer historical background, geographical descriptions, brief introductions to language and culture, advice and directions to make the journey safer and more interesting for their readers, and intended to reduce their sense of estrangement from their home environment. One only needs to mention the Lonely Planet Books, Fodor, Baedeker, Eye Witness guides, Royston Ellis, Rick Steves, and others that fill the shelves in libraries and bookstores. Thomas Cook started the trend by publishing the first travel newspaper, *The Excursionist and Exhibitionist Adventurer* (where exhibitions, naturally, refer to world fairs or trade events). For those shy about venturing on the Grand Tour without guidance or connections, there was *The Gentleman's Pocket Companion for Travelling in Foreign Parts* to facilitate accommodations with the natives.

The second group of writers proposes instead a contrived story line, almost a fictional plot, full of events and characters never to be met by the potential traveller who reads them. However excellent their style and outstanding their travels (and one must think, for instance, of the sophisticated Jan Morris, Bruce Chatwin, and Paul Theroux, the adventurous Wilfred Thesiger, or the irrepressible naturalist Redmond O'Hanlon as he takes us, more daringly, to the jungles of the Congo, Borneo, or Amazonia, where we have no intention of ever going ourselves), their experience is too personal to ever be of practical use to those attempting to follow timidly in their footsteps. Although writing about one's particular journeys participates in the same booming industry as charter and packaged tourism and individual travel, its main interest usually lies in the fact that the journeys related cannot be duplicated and often describe a much more intense level of dislocation than ordinary readers are likely to experience in their own travels.

A third type of travel writers use the satirist's guise, describing the social, economic, and political conditions in their own countries by depicting them as if they existed in imaginary distant lands—or else having them described by supposedly naive visitors from equally imaginary distant lands. In both cases, the writers successfully fuse *here* and *elsewhere* by including them in the same dislocated reality. Thus, the hero of Thomas

More's *Utopia* (1516), a fictional explorer contemporary of Amerigo Vespucci, described how, on his way around the world, he discovered *Utopia* ("No Place") where reason, order, and dignity prevailed. In the eighteenth century, France became fascinated by the myth of the "Noble Savage," as Jean-Jacques Rousseau conceived him. Voltaire, who had read Champlain's writings and the Jesuits' *Relations,* insisted (in *Candide,* for instance) on the nobility and simplicity of the primitive mind; as well, Bernardin de Saint-Pierre was to write the influential, *Paul et Virginie,* which described the innocence of those untouched by civilization.

In a different vein but similarly inspired, Jonathan Swift's *Gulliver's Travels* (1726) and Montesquieu's *Lettres Persanes* (1721), the former more outrageous than the latter but both equally biting, demonstrated that in fiction often lies truth, provided it takes place elsewhere. In such books, dislocation from reality is a *sine qua non* condition for creating the perfect world.

Drifters

In the early 1950s, at the age of twenty, I took modestly to the road, as one did in those days, when borders were easily crossed and unstructured wandering was safer than by today's standards. I left England with a friend, and we meandered our way through parts of Western Europe. Rather than the days often spent in hypnotic walking, particularly in the Rhône delta of Camargue where the long, flat, empty roads seemed to merge unnoticed into irrigated rice fields and flat salt beds *(salins),* with nowhere to stop and nowhere to rest, it is the nights I remember most. Where to stay, with our more than limited means, was always a serious problem. In the country, we sometimes slept in barns with the sweetish smell of cows around us. In Florence, we barricaded ourselves in the upstairs room of a flophouse across from a prison, the lower floor turned over to cots for men working on shifts.

In Rimini, on the Adriatic coast, the owner of a beach café agreed to let us sleep on his tables after he had locked up at two in the morning. It was not a satisfactory arrangement, as we found it difficult to wait, shivering on the beach, until closing time. So, when we met a young German hitchhiker—a printer's apprentice just back from six months in North Africa where he had fared well on olive oil, dates, and bread, well tanned, superbly equipped, and seemingly knowledgeable—and he mentioned having heard of a good place to spend the night, we followed him. It was well after dark. The place, up in the hills, was rocky but offered good shelter, and we slept well and late.

I woke up with his face very close to mine, his hand firmly clamped over my mouth, and I heard his ominous and whispered injunction, "Keep quiet. It's all right." Mostly, I felt shock at having been such a poor judge of character. He whispered again, "Be quiet and move very slowly." I gradually sat up, restrained by his hand on my shoulder. Snakes, sleepily coiled on flat rocks and warming in the morning sun, surrounded us. He then went very slowly to my friend, who must have gone through the same, short-lived disappointment in misreading his character and fearing for her virtue.

When she left to return to England, I continued to travel on my own. Some campers on their way to Alsace offered me a ride, and I joined them for a day or two. This went on for a little while longer. Soon, I knew that I could travel forever, moving as the fancy struck, perhaps for no other reason that, being already on the go, I simply could not stop. There was no more reason to stop than there had been to keep moving, and it was only through an inner sense of motion, perhaps acquired from the very first step, that I went from one place to the next. After a while, it even seemed that these places no longer mattered much. I certainly did not go there to visit them, but rather, going from one place to the next had become its own purpose and created its own momentum. I walked so much, my eyes always fixed far ahead, that after two months, my vision had improved to the point where I no longer needed glasses.

There was an extraordinary seduction to being on the go, from X to Y to Z, walking or riding, without particular rhyme or reason, save serendipity, opportunity, encounters, and perhaps some inner logic too difficult to pin down. I could easily have become a drifter. But having neither the skill nor the nerve for family confrontation, after two months, as expected, I returned to England where I lived at the time.

Since then, I have never travelled in the same manner. Being, I suspect, of a nature rather prone to addiction, I no longer fall into temptation. And many aspects of such travel would no longer charm me: I dislike the heat, prefer clean beds and toilets, and become almost catatonic at the sight of large lizards and snakes. I also find little appeal in the combination of human smells and sweat, shoving, pushing, shrill voices, and exotic hawking, spitting, and belching.

Embedded Visitors
These "embedded" visitors, usually consultants officially under the protection of their hosts, are somewhat restricted in their actions. They generally visit for a definite period, usually several weeks, and are charged with a specific task typically intended to benefit the host country. Mediators are often appointed to guide them through the intricacies of local work customs and probably to screen their contacts. When these people take it upon themselves to make the visitors' personal life easier and their own culture more accessible, they become mentors as well as mediators.

A longer term than a few weeks would constitute a passage to temporary expatriation and involve different techniques of acclimatization. The shorter stay permits an interesting compromise between the alienation of being away from home, often in countries we are just barely discovering, and the comfort of creating for ourselves a new and temporarily familiar environment.

My personal search for the familiar, at its most evident when embedded elsewhere for a few weeks, may derive from having a collector's inclination. Every object is, for me, the beginning of a potential collection; with two, I am well on my way. The same mind-set, I believe, partakes of the ability to create continuity through forming habits in a foreign environment. The same dog seen at the same street corner enjoying his early morning pee at the same time every day constitutes the beginning of a sense of belonging, as does the same old man on his bench, smoking his foul tobacco and taking his usual afternoon sun. Although the dog and the old man ignore us, the sheer repetition of seeing them draws us into local life. We may remember them later and may miss them as having been part of our experience. This collection of similar or related paths, patterns, and experiences helps us create a fictitiously familiar environment in which, in truth, we only participate as spectators.

These host countries are definitely *elsewhere* in the sense that almost nothing there reminds us of anything close to home. Yet, either through the vague compatibility of language, culture, religion, occupation, or through spending time working there, some familiarity emerges, some liking for the country, some sense of the nature of its people, something indeed emerges, which forces us to reassess the depersonalization of being elsewhere and its near transformation into a temporary imitation of home.

This process takes on a temporal dimension—about two weeks in my case, after which a budding familiarity makes me overlook the fact that I do not actually belong there at all. I found Cuba and the Seychelles, for instance, to be such places. I miss certain street corners in Havana and in Mont Fleuri, while knowing that the feeling has probably little to do with the land and its people and more with my having been there long enough to create habits. It is perhaps a fact that all one ever misses is oneself.

Travellers at Home

These, while properly speaking not travellers in the sense of going to a foreign land, form a distinct category, well known to urban anthropologists. Robert Louis Stevenson in *The Foreigner at Home* writes, "It is not only when we cross the seas that we go abroad."

Indeed, some of my most alienating experiences have meant passing directly from family, friends, routine, and work to the strange sounds, smells, sights, and the alien worlds of Canadian jails and English psychiatric hospitals, where my professional activities have taken me. No change of country or even city was required to make that leap—indeed, some of my trips were only a city bus ride away—yet the changes were as strange and confusing as if I had travelled hundreds of miles. A memorable journey took me downtown one year, out of my own suburban, middle-class, and law-abiding culture. First asked by the British Columbia Police Commission to prepare a report on juvenile street prostitutes, I went on to study the techniques of verbal manipulation of street women, prostitutes, and drug users.

Whether on the street late at night, sometimes walking in the company of social workers, or driving with police officers, or talking to streetwalkers, I felt as alien as I would at other times in distant lands. The language was full of pitfalls and references I did not always catch, and even the city, so familiar by day, looked different at night, almost like its own negative in inverted black and white versions. Many doors appeared at night where none had been noticeable by day, and this was equally true of people lurking at night but never seen by day.

I once asked a jailed informant with whom I had got on quite well what I should do if I met her in town after her release. Her expression became distant, perhaps to underline her response, "You don't know me." It was a fitting conclusion to a six-month exchange where our worlds had barely brushed against each other: mine was outside, hers inside—literally, of course, but also inside the cultural framework she had described for me, the outsider. After her release, we would both be once more in our respective and appropriate realities, estranged from each other. She had been, after all, no more than a casual and brief encounter, someone from a different world altogether.

Jails, psychiatric hospitals, and street cultures are extreme environments. But it sometimes takes much less to contribute to the dislocation between the familiarity of our own environment where people behave as expected, at least according to our lights, and the behaviour of some others, whose actions are as alien to our experience as to leave us out of our depth and take us on a different journey.

This happened to John and me while staying overnight at a motel full of ordinary-looking people on the Oregon Coast, twenty-five years ago but still vividly remembered. We had seen a young couple arrive in an old red pickup and walk towards the unit next door to ours. They dressed alike; both wearing Levis and white T-shirts. They were medium build and narrow hipped, their hair bleached the same washed-out blond colour. He wore his left sleeve rolled high and tucked up to store a pack of cigarettes. His arm revealed a tattoo. He carried a six-pack of beer in each hand while she hugged a bag of groceries from which emerged a bright yellow top of a large bag of Cheezies.

Tired after our long drive, John and I were not too happy to recognize the signs of a potentially noisy evening next door. Indeed, some festive sounds were coming from next door when we returned from dinner, and through the thin walls, we heard a gradually increasing noise of music and conversation. Then the mood changed. A few things came crashing down, the man's voice raised, and the woman appeared to plead for quiet. Things got rapidly worse. Every crescendo in his litanies culminated with "Fucking bitch!" repeatedly yelled with venom and out-of-control hatred. Only his voice was heard, hers only an inaudible murmur, humble, and trying to placate.

We decided to call the front desk, unwilling to confront his violence personally and perhaps increase it, but afraid for her. As I reached for the receiver, I heard the telephone ring in their room. He answered it meekly, and he must have made some promises, for after that there was silence, except for the sound of a bath being run. His low-key willingness to comply was as much a shock to me as, mere seconds before, his ranting viciousness had been. He had not been out of control after all. This self-satisfying, gratuitous violence, too, was an alien world.

※ ※ ※

Some of our most alienating experiences may possibly include these forays into what we believe to be known territories, but which turn into upsetting discoveries. Since, after all, we are at home, or at least in an environment whose parameters we recognize, it becomes all the more difficult to accept that what we may witness does not really belong to the world we know, but in fact pertains to something totally estranged from our everyday experience. Our surprise probably comes from too much complacency—and perhaps laziness of mind—in assuming that what we deem to be familiar and evident will prove itself to be just that. Then, to our surprise, we have to admit that it does not conform to our expectations.

We would never commit such a basic error while travelling abroad. Indeed, whether travelling with others or alone, whether briefly passing through or staying for a while, whether merely catching casual glimpses or observing in order to report on what we have observed, we never allow ourselves to be lulled into a false feeling of familiarity and security. Rather, we remain watchful and leery of unpleasant surprises, and we make it our responsibility to being focused on expecting the unexpected.

Chapter Two

"As Canadian as Possible … Under the Circumstances"

Winning entry from British Columbia in the "As Canadian as …" contest run in the 1970s by the CBC radio program *This Country in the Morning*. It has since become a Canadian joke to demonstrate that there is no corresponding Canadian self-definition quite as satisfactory as "As American as apple pie."

My father ran away from his Jesuit college in Budapest at the age of sixteen to join the French Foreign Legion. In 1920, in Sidi Bel-Abbès, lying on all counts, he recreated himself as an eighteen-year-old German under the assumed name of Nicklaus. A scrawl on a document no one believed, and presto! a new man was born. By the Second World War, he was known in England for his perfect manners, his attractiveness to women, his extraordinary Gallic charm, and was often described as a "typical Frenchie." From real Austro (his mother)-Hungarian (his father) to fake German to ultimate Frenchman, it had taken him a mere two decades and a half to achieve this feat of mimesis. What perhaps gave him away to the perceptive observer was that he was better than the original.

Having inadvertently followed a somewhat similar path myself (conceived in Syria, born in France, brought up in Morocco, nearly self-exiled in England once, and implanted in Canada for more than fifty years), as well as having similarly traded countries, nationalities, languages, cultures, and allegiance, I am, however, singularly different from him in that I have never been able to "pass."

Being *dépaysé* means being away from one's usual surroundings or rather, more specifically, from one's country *(pays)*. It encompasses the notion of being transplanted, a hint of alienation, a sense of non-belonging, a lack of communication, and the constant marginality of having come from somewhere else. The latter feeling is of particular relevance to immigrants since it often persists long after those around us have forgotten that we are not one of them. But perhaps they have not forgotten at all, and this may well be another of those fictions we indulge in to ease our way through life.

When people tell me they think of me as being French, I am surprised and disappointed that a transformation or more precisely a transculturation that took more that five decades to achieve should have only resulted in a superficial veneer, easily seen through by others.

This discrepancy reveals another aspect of dislocation, which involves the way we perceive ourselves and how others perceive us. It is the Asian immigrant's Banana Syndrome, or rather that of his children and grandchildren: yellow on the outside, white on the inside, with other derivations for other races (Oreo cookie, coconut, etc.). Such a label, being from somewhere else, may not seem important until we remember that in many traditional cultures, the word for Man is the name they give themselves, to which no other group can aspire, and that everything of social and cultural importance (identity, kinship, marriage, residence, warfare, trading rights, ownership of myths and songs) is defined and regulated in terms of whether one is classified as being within the group or as being outside of it.

This *dépaysement* evokes a vague drifting of the spirit to match the pulling out of bodily roots. It may well speak of bemusement, of unease, but it can also be the prelude to new foundations, and if it is melancholy and weighs vaguely at times, it also holds the seeds of new possibilities. Thus would speak Pollyanna or Candide (to bring my two basic cultures together) and they could well be right.

While the word *dislocation* might perhaps also encompass all these aspects, it does not entirely suit me. This preference may seem a minor detail, but having the word *country* rather than *location* as the root adds an emotional weight necessary to convey its full effect. The country itself, France in this case, has little to do with it. I think that adding the bits and pieces of short stays and holidays, I have not spent more than five or six years there. Compared to the sixteen years I spent in North Africa and the fifty odd years I have lived in Canada, it is really quite insignificant. The culture and its guardian, the language, are what matters, not the country.

❦ ❦ ❦

For newcomers to another culture, the core of dislocation is that the nature of knowledge held by those around us remains a mystery to us for some time. In order to fit in and play the game, it is essential to hold the same cards as the others, or if not, to know how ours differ from theirs. I once attended a seminar on international education where we played a game designed to illustrate the difficulties of cross-cultural communication. The rules were deceptively simple. We formed groups of three players. In each trio, two participants sat back-to-back, each in front of a table on which were piled a number of small wooden blocks of different shapes and colors. One player was to build any structure he liked with his blocks and describe to the other what he was doing, expecting her to duplicate the structure. She could only see her own blocks and had to proceed strictly according to his directions, forbidden to ask questions or seek clarifications. The third participant observed and reported afterwards, explaining where and how the duplication had gone wrong (for it usually did). I do not remember which player I was, but very likely the would-be duplicator, since what I remember most of the game was my intense frustration at not knowing whether both players had been given the same blocks.

And so it goes with cultural blocks: Do we all play with the same elements, is our basic knowledge the same, are our tools equal in value? But in real life, as perhaps in the fiction of that particular game, for we were never told, the coordinates are skewed. Only two things are certain: we do not start with the same worldview, and until we meet the other halfway, no communication is possible. But even before we can worry about whether we dispose the blocks properly, we must be able to describe them and understand. And for that, we need a common language.

Seeing language as an essential agent of belonging must go as far back as when language was first codified. It is a first line of defense against dangers from the unknown. In the time of Herodotus, those who did not speak Greek were called Barbarians and were deemed to be, by that definition alone, despicable aliens.

Language is the agent of belonging par excellence. *Mother tongue* evokes the metaphorical and determining role of the female licking the newborn into physical health and grooming it into family or group inclusion. When we lose our mother tongue, we no longer belong to the group that made us what we are; we no longer have the confidence to open our mouth, speaking familiarly and without hesitation in the right context.

I remember my frustration at attempting to tell a joke and preparing the path to the punch line when I first came to Canada. "How do you say this? And when somebody does that, what is it called? And when this and that happens, is there a word for it?" Then, having cleared the way and secured the keywords, and the punch line being by then painfully evident, I would finally embark upon the formal telling of the joke. It did not take me long to become a quieter person: I am not sure how much I bored my listeners with this painstaking process, but it could not have been more tedious for them than it was for me.

Two or three years later, by then more settled, I believe I acquired among the women of my neighbourhood (those were the days of stay-at-home mothers meeting for morning coffee to discuss measles, recipes, and the shortcomings of those absent) a reputation for being either pedantic or educated (depending on their goodwill) for a peculiar failure of my vocabulary. Often hesitant about the common English term, I would substitute a word of Latin or Greek origin, the one commonly used in French and other Romance languages. Thus, my speech would be peppered with words such as *acerbity, amulet, vehement,* and *perspicacious, cicatrices, hirsute.* This inadequacy, combined with the French preference for the abstract rather than the concrete, gave a decidedly stilted and precious tone to my speech, one I did not have when I spoke French.

We all know there is far more to being *at home* in a language than having mastered syntax and vocabulary. I am not one of those lucky enough to have also perfected the new accent and intonation, so I am a poor judge of what it must be like to be mistaken for a native speaker. On both American continents, whatever language I speak, I am, by the sound of me, an outsider. Even my native language is not exactly the one spoken either by Francophone Canadians or the *Cadiens* (or *Cajuns,* to make allowances for the pronunciation) of Louisiana.

The English I speak tags me as me someone vaguely European. My Spanish intonation and incorrect grammar make me impossible to situate, since I have abandoned the Spanish affectation of the *seseo,* which I had first learned in grade six from the fierce Señora Oyós in Casablanca, and which could have been a clue to some Iberian influence. Finally, whatever rudiments of Portuguese I have acquired in a university classroom do not have the Brazilian cadence either.

Even after so many decades, reconfiguring my tongue and lips to produce English sounds, by now familiar, still does not always feel natural. In times of great stress, my body reverts to a state of greater familiarity; lips, teeth, palate, tongue automatically reposition themselves in preparation for speech as they did in childhood, when language was first learned. The literal (and perhaps Freudian) slip of the tongue is here to reveal a mechanical return to hidden sources of comfort.

For a very long time, the two languages were at constant war within me. But they have gradually diverged into selective affinities. Nowadays, I knit, count, write poetry, and read literary criticism in French. In English, I cook, write prose, do crossword puzzles, read novels and detective stories, and study the social sciences. Against all the rules of custom and linguistics, I translate from French into English and never the other way around (but always with a native speaker to go over the text afterwards).

I even think that I breathed differently when I spoke French, perhaps to accommodate those more elaborate, more rounded sentences. There is an energizing cadence to it, a rhythm, symmetry, a deep purring almost, which owe much to its classical poetry and the French predilection for the alexandrine verse. Nouns always came equipped with three qualifiers when I wrote in French (and perhaps they still do), a stylistic habit I find hard to discard in English. I played with words, never having considered puns a lower form of humour. I was totally defined by my language, confident in it, reassured by it.

Nowadays, as soon as I open my anglicized mouth, I feel psychologically, socially, professionally undermined by my accent. I have sometimes been told, "But it's charming!" usually at parties and often by kind women who wish me well, but they do not understand the need for anonymity craved by those who only want to blend in, unnoticed.

I had a talented, well educated, and multilingual friend, a Finnish ethnographer, who wrote English well. This clever woman had a pronounced accent, and she told me that when people thought she might not have understood them, they repeated what they had said, using exactly the same words but only louder. We both laughed, precisely because it was not funny. Physically handicapped (I use the word advisedly) people probably recognize the feeling. I am aware that the more times I am asked to repeat my words, the worse my accent becomes, and the more incoherent I sound.

I go to extraordinary lengths to avoid certain words. The careless start of a sentence may point me to a verb form I will have difficulty pronouncing or that will call for a word I never stress properly, so midway through, I start the sentence all over again. My English speech is punctuated with backtracking and half sentences. The subtle use of correct prepositions still defeats me and sometimes results in tortuous attempt at reconstructing my sentences. In other words, I resign myself to never speaking gut-English, the way my six-year-old granddaughter does.

I understand that alert stutterers resort to consulting a mental thesaurus, which provides them instantly with alternative words to substitute for problematic ones as soon as they sense the latter coming up. A slight hesitation barely marks the passage from potential danger to rescue. This would also work very well for foreign speakers—but they would also have to contend at the same time with grammatical demands, which are not always evident to them, and with the dreadfully unfair English use of prepositions, which very likely can only be learned with aplomb in an English womb.

Even when writing and supposedly able to guide my words and control the structure of my language, I write in detours. Where English would use separate, shorter sentences, I allow French to take over and enter into a succession of quasi-parentheses, pseudo-dashes, confusing in-text footnotes, and puzzling annotations. At times, it must seem as if another syntax, another language still regulate the delivery of my thoughts after more than fifty decades of transplantation.

However, it is not as if I could go back to French either. My accent is perfect, my grammar still good, but I speak the French of the 1950s. When I hear contemporary French, I become mulishly resentful of the changes I discern and snigger quietly at an improperly used Anglicism.

Perhaps more than the language itself, what we miss when we are dislocated is being steeped in the culture of which that language was an integral part. It is almost impossible to anticipate which translation of thought and context will be easy and which problematic. From minor to crucial, we have all lived through such transitions if we exist in a culturally different environment.

I remember, for instance, being shown how to prepare meal trays to satisfy specific dietary requirements while training in an English hospital. One such tea tray required jam to accompany bread and butter. Any jam we liked, we were told, so why such puzzlement when I produced a jar of orange jam? No, I was sternly told, marmalade would not do, as it was only served at breakfast. Such was the rule, I was told, and anyway, marmalade was definitely not orange *jam*. So, I failed Trays, because of the cultural value attached to one ordinary word.

On the other hand, twice sitting as a juror in a Canadian Supreme Court trial, I had to make the presumably enormous intellectual leap between two systems of law and philosophy: one in which a French accused must prove his innocence, the other where the complete judicial process must prove his Canadian counterpart's guilt. Yet, it presented no problem, since a juror's duty is a purely intellectual exercise, theoretically unmarred by prejudice or sympathy, one in which the basic premise (initial guilt or innocence) is soon replaced by the bare examination of facts alone. In that sense, although radically different legal and philosophical positions were at stake, the process itself was totally culture-free.

I have sometimes wondered whether native speakers continue to appreciate the effect of their words as they say or write them. "Dear Sir," to start a letter, for instance? Do they really mean that the person who will read their letter is dear to them, or even has endearing qualities? For learners of the language (the non-gut version), every word may well mean what it denotes, and unlike native speakers, putting words together may not equate for them a formula where separate components have lost their individual meaning.

Let me give an example. I was at some point in my university career dealing with students wishing to enroll in criminology courses through correspondence. One day, I received a letter from Clifford Olson, the so-called "Beast of British Columbia," seeking admission to our program. I have to assume that every person in my position in all the criminology programs in Canada received the same letter, as well as subsequent ones, often illustrated with cartoons depicting the "fat cat" life he was enjoying in jail. It should be noted that he listed among his favourite pastimes "reminiscing over past events," an entry that sent shivers down one's back.

It was clear that his only interest was in talking about himself, convinced as he was that we were dying of curiosity about his motives for raping, torturing, and murdering eleven adolescents. I had no problem listing for him, in the most detached and academic manner, the prerequisites needed for the program and the registration process, since I could almost turn it into a form letter. What I could not do, however, was to write "Dear Mr. Olson" at the beginning of the letter and knowing he would read those words written by me. The head of my department kindly wrote them for me.

I would like to put my finger on a map and say with authority, "This is where I come from," and knowing the statement to be true. Inherent to this statement would be childhood memories shared with others; facts learned at school and accepted on faith in a national and cultural context; the finesse of common expressions; allusions to fictional characters (others than those depicted in Anglophone literature or folklore) that would be greeted with a smile or appreciative guffaws of recognition. But when I meet French people of my generation, I find we have very little in common. Whole life stories separate us. In fact, I am never as Canadian as when I am in France.

The former French colonial empire understood well the power of common terms of reference. When I was a child, the first history lesson taught to little Francophone Africans, Asians, or Pacific Islanders, started with the words, "Our ancestors, the Gauls," and described how those strong men with their braided blond hair and their fierce blue eyes had only one fear: that the sky would fall upon their heads.

The physical description and the beliefs had hardly more relevance to twentieth-century French children than to their colonial counterparts, but it provided some commonality of references for both. However, such Gallic history, taught as their own to little Asians and Africans, probably made little cultural difference and one suspects they properly heard it as just an ordinary tale, a fictitious story with far less relevance than their own myths. Actually, it did have a tinge of relevance after all. When we all grew up, it became a common joke of colonialism turned inane—our common ancestors, the Gauls, indeed.

It helps enormously, of course, to know what one is. The British-born actress Charlotte Rampling, for instance, steeped in French language and culture from childhood, married to a Frenchman, sharing her time between the two countries and acting in both languages, declared herself to be unequivocally British, even appearing astonished at the question. She did so on a French television show, Bernard Pivot's *Double Je,* which is based on a clever pun, where bilingual and bicultural people examine their dual identity (double *Je*) and their possibly duplicitous one (the *double jeu* of those who run with the hare and hunt with the hounds).

In Canada and the United States, countries made up in great part of immigrants, many of us, of course, even have a triple *Je,* and perhaps more. In my case, I have to contend with the country of childhood and nostalgia, Morocco; the country of language and culture, France; and the only deliberate one, the country of choice, adoption, and family, Canada.

I feel a greater emotional attachment to Morocco, rather than to France in whose language and culture I am powerfully anchored. I recently watched a French television program about people whose parents were born elsewhere and who had immigrated to France with them. "What Is It Like to Live With Two Cultures?" was essentially the topic under discussion.

Several were Maghrébins. They showed the most poignant homesickness. I listened to their evocation of growing up in a place exactly like the one where I grew up. They described the dryness of the land; the sweet smell of the orange groves; the deep, deep blue sky that Winston Churchill never quite succeeded in catching on his painting trips to Marrakesh; the food and its characteristic spices and aromas; the *yoo-yoos* of the women and the henna markings on their brow, chin, hands, and feet; the heat off the dry dusty ground; the music, the smells, and so much I knew so well. Above all, the light, that amazing, incomparable North African light.

Those various Maghrébins, the *pieds-noirs,* the *beurs, and* the sons and daughters of refugee *harkis,* all issued from North Africa with different histories[1] and now living in France. I cannot think of anyone with whom I have more in common, and with whom I could share so intimately the nostalgia of the lost country. Yet, they would disdainfully reject my claim, even though some of them were actually born in France or were very young when they arrived and only inherited their nostalgia from their parents.

While this nostalgia seems justified, I do not feel entitled to share it, I who perhaps knew better the reality of the country they left too young

---

1   *Pieds-noirs,* **the name given to former Franco-Algerians, refers to the black footwear for which they were originally known.** *Beur* **is the name currently used for Algerians and Moroccans living in France. The term** *harkis* **refers to a particularly sordid episode of the Algerian War, where native supporters of the French were abandoned by them after they were forced to leave the country. The** *harkis* **(soldiers) as they were called, were then left to face alone the Algerian forces they had opposed. Pressure at home forced the French government to bring some of those people and their families to France, but is unlikely that they faced a privileged welcome.**

to remember. However, unlike them, I did not grow up in my native land or that of my parents, but in a country where I was not wanted, where my parents and I had lived on sufferance. I had left nothing behind when we returned to France, except that for me, unlike my mother, I was not going *back* to France, since I had never lived there.

I was sixteen by then, and it was too late to be anything but a temporary resident in France, ready to leave again since there was nothing to keep me there—no childhood memories and certainly no sense of belonging. In that sense, as well, I was very much like those people on the television screen.

❦ ❦ ❦

Having more or less successfully undergone the passage from Africa to Europe in my teens, I had taken in my early twenties the next leap to North America. The process of becoming Canadian has not been straightforward. Rather, is has been a long and unconscious one, particularly at the beginning, where a great deal of confusion occurred. To my European identity, achieved through schooling and a few years' residence in France and England, a very thin North American layer was first applied. It was nothing very specific, just a sense of strangeness—Europe and America eyeing each other with curiosity and little understanding at first.

That it should have been American rather than Canadian is easy to understand. The television programs I watched were American, so were the films I saw and the music I heard. I could not see any difference between the two countries, both being equally new to me. However, little by little, like dabs in an impressionist painting, minute Canadian touches were added. I started noticing that American television programs and films bore little resemblance with the everyday Canadian reality I experienced. Then, willy-nilly, progressively, over time, everything around me started becoming more familiar, almost natural.

Often, travelling elsewhere made me realize that I had started comparing what I saw there with what, almost without my noticing it, had become the norm (my norm) in British Columbia. Many of those moments were markers, like signposts along the way, and they signaled subtle differences in my progress, showing that this Canadian elsewhere was gradually becoming my personal place.

Surprising even myself on occasions, I had started interpreting events no longer from a North American perspective, but with a Canadian twist, a bias even.

One such was a rather ridiculous misunderstanding on a visit to Minneapolis in 1981, which could not have happened anywhere but in the United States. Had I come directly from France, Morocco, or England, the event would have made no sense at all, even after having it explained to me. But, after more than two decades in Western Canada, it made an odd kind of sense, since I knew *they* did things *we* would not do, naturally assisted in that opinion by my having watched American television all that time. Television, which had initially provided me with a means for apprehending a new North American context, was now serving to differentiate between the finer lines of two related cross-border cultures.

As our plane landed, a familiar tune filled the cabin. When people around me started humming, I recognized it—the *Mary Tyler Moore Show* theme song. Of course, Minneapolis: Mary's hometown! Once out of the terminal, I sat on a bench and waited for the hotel minibus, my bag at my feet. A very large, young black man leaning against a charter bus was observing me with far more attention than I warranted. Just at the point when I was becoming quite uncomfortable with his staring, he walked over and said something I asked him to repeat, because it did not seem to make any sense. He said it again, "Are you with the Little People of America?" It took me awhile to understand what he meant (to be truthful, I am not sure I actually understood even then). Almost immediately, a flow of real little people streamed through the airport doors herded by a young man walking towards their bus, all on their way to a national convention.

I am five foot one, and I had to admire pragmatic American frankness in pointing out that, as a European woman of a certain vintage, I am actually quite short—something I had never actually thought about before but which, to him, at least in this particular context, was certainly an important and overwhelmingly defining feature.

After all this time living, studying, and working in Western Canada, I naturally feel very much at home here, more so than anywhere else in the world. My children and grandchildren were born and brought up here. I have absorbed the geography, the history, and the political complexities of the land. I feel the equal of all and sundry. Until, of course, I open my mouth in front of strangers.

❦ ❦ ❦

Most of us recognize that the sense of being uprooted we experience when trying to fit into a new culture is, overall, relatively painless, even if it takes time. Even the initial contact, often a cause of anxiety and many misunderstandings, is usually still within a scope we can accept and whose validity we recognize. There are, however, infinitely worse ways of experiencing the introduction to an alien culture.

Years ago, a fellow graduate student in an anthropology seminar, reporting on his fieldwork, described how he had spent what may have been days (he was so disoriented that he could no longer measure time) on the edge of a small village in New Guinea, squatting in the dust, waiting for someone to acknowledge him, to make the first move—as custom required—and approach him. Towards the end of what had truly become an ordeal by invisibility, he seriously doubted whether others were actually aware of his existence. To him, *depaysement* had become a true dislocation between two sets of reality, his and theirs—a rough definition of schizophrenia.

Only an ethnographer would find himself in such an extreme situation nowadays, one of abandonment, alone and entirely dependent on another culture's acceptance. Without this acceptance, he would have had no hope of surviving among them. This is far more than a figure of speech, since being ostracized from the group was the most radical and often fatal punishment in traditional societies for committing severe crimes. Symbolically, it is also the function of excommunication and shunning in some religious groups, where the excluded offender is deemed to be *dead* to the group—until authorized to repent and rejoin the community.

Without belonging to a group— whatever its size (even Crusoe needed Friday)—the social animals we are simply cannot survive. Unlike that ethnographer, we—ordinary newcomers to a strange culture—have many ways of being gradually introduced to it, of finding it possible to function satisfactorily within it, and of easing our thought process into a completely new worldview, even if that culture or society's acceptance is still the final and sole seal of approval.

Canadians and Americans have diverging philosophical, political, and metaphorical approaches to the process of acculturation and acceptance: multiculturalism and its cultural mosaic in one case, rather than assimilation and the melting pot in the other. I have no intention of taking sides here, but as the former holder of the registration number A 160243 of the United Kingdom *Aliens Order* of 1920, I am fairly satisfied that either approach is an improvement over past procedures.

Chapter Three

Meeting Strangers: The Rules of Engagement

For the advantage of some, conversations ought to be so arranged as that they may have the trouble of saying as little as possible.

—Jane Austen, *Pride and Prejudice*

Meeting with strangers is fraught with danger. Territories must be rapidly assessed, limits ascertained from the start and respected throughout, for the rules of encounters are clearly, if tacitly, set out. Each move must be tentative, like an elephant's walk.

It is said that one of the reasons Hannibal was able to cross the Alps is that the elephants went first. They did not plant their feet squarely on the difficult and unknown ground. Rather, each foot hovered slightly, one foot at the time, tentatively, feelingly. The ground secured for that foot, they proceeded in the same manner with the second foot, then with the third foot, and finally with the last one.

Horses and men, reassured, followed without fear into the tracks prepared for them by so much attention to tactile detail and infinitesimal feedback from the ground. It was all guesswork, really, but considered, thoughtful guesswork, based on the nearly intangible, and ready to withdraw at the slightest doubt.

In such manner should people meet and progress, with some appropriate hint of feedback to permit another step forward or, if need be, a tactful return to the fork in the road to engage in another and more appropriate direction.

We meet many people along the way, some more interesting than others, a few more memorable than most. Unlike friends, who matter in themselves and interweave their life patterns into our own, people casually encountered have no existence beyond what we make of them. They constitute one of life's many vignettes, their importance sometimes difficult to pinpoint. Why they, rather than two hundred possible others, stick in our mind?

It is perhaps not so much the individual but the nature of the encounter that matters. This is particularly true when meeting strangers abroad, because the terms of reference vary enormously, depending on the place and the occasion, as much as on the peculiarities and culture of the stranger we meet. The encounter situation must be considered as a whole and not a single element disregarded in selecting a strategy. There are rules to be adhered to and failure to do so renders the occasion difficult for both. To illustrate what I consider the proper application of rules, I will try to describe six such encounters in my life; two I deem very successful, two whose success can only be assessed within their intrinsic circumstances, and two I rate as utter failures.

Two Perfect Encounters

The first one occurred while I was working on a project that caused me to fly to Edmonton during the late 1970s to interview a woman I did not know. We could only manage to meet after work, so I invited her for dinner. We had finished our interview by the time our main course arrived, and as she was not a particularly forthcoming woman, and I have little talent for small talk, I was not looking forward to the rest of the evening.

It was clear that at first glance, we did not have very much in common, apart from being women of roughly the same age and working in the same field. Neither of us wore a wedding ring, so even that small marital clue was unavailable. The few topics of conversation we attempted soon petered out, although I learned that she had a dog.

Then, at some point, one of us must have said something—perhaps introduced some metaphor deriving from a sewing technique or came up with a term specific to a certain pattern—which made us realize that we were both quilters. I have seen sport serve the same purpose with many men, creating a temporary common ground beyond which everything else becomes irrelevant to their encounter.

It turned out to be a delightful evening after all, perhaps because it was so unexpected. Neither of us showed the slightest interest in our respective professional accreditations, accomplishments, or publications, nor did we try to show how clever we were or impress each other in any way, except perhaps (and this, we did mockingly) with the smallness of our stitching.

She mentioned the West Virginia Cooperative and their work, which she admired. I told her of our Amish-style quilters in the Fraser Valley and introduced her to an oral history book, recently published, about quilters and domestic art. We were both, at the time, traditional quilters and talked Log Cabins, Double Wedding Rings, Lone Stars, Trips Around the World, Grandmothers Gardens, Dresden Plates, and so many others, until the restaurant staff started giving a few hints that we were beginning to outlast our welcome.

As we parted, she humorously accused me of being one of those quilters who are sometimes overtaken by the greed to collect fabrics and use quilting as an alibi. I defended myself but remembered that remark the next time I went on a fabric-buying spree.

I had been very impressed by her knowledge of quilting, but perhaps even more by her having actually *listened* to what I had been saying and to the meaning behind those words. Who knows, it may have been a mere conversational gimmick, one she commonly used to facilitate exchanges of little import—telling others something they might think profound because at once unusual and apt—but I had to admit that she had been right.

Until then, I had not realized it was true. Seeing those fabrics aligned by dominant colours, the sheens drawing the eyes, the patterns warming the heart, and all that crispness, actually gave me more pleasure than trying to combine them into a quilt and practicing one of the oldest recycling arts. I kept on collecting fabrics for many years after that, with a special and sensual pleasure, and chose to restore a few old quilts rather than make new ones.

I did this until we had to move into a smaller place. Then, I gave all my fabrics to a neighbour, a non-quilter, who simply displayed them for the sheer joy and beauty of the display. I thought of the Edmonton quilter that day. But of course, we never met again nor have we even heard of each other since.

❦ ❦ ❦

The second encounter took place while I was attending a conference in Albany in 1983. My husband's grandfather having squandered much of his wife's fortune at the Saratoga races, I was curious to see the track. So on a free afternoon, I decided to go to the races. I soon found myself sitting on a bench beside three elderly black gentlemen, sparsely fleshed, scrubbed so clean they shone, their trousers pressed just so. One sensed three, no-nonsense women—their three wives—who, for five dollars each, had got rid of the old boys for the day, to do what they enjoyed most: play the horses. That was the deal: five dollars, once a week, the whole day.

By the time I sat beside the men, their five dollars had gone and their betting was a moot affair. They were absorbed in the racing forms and consulted some printed material. They barely noticed me. After awhile, I leaned toward the one closest to me and asked him politely what he knew about the horses running in the next race. He appeared to be torn between the reluctance to talk to an apparently forward woman (and, this being the 1980s, perhaps the colour of my skin had made the approach seem even more unusual and had something to do with his reluctance) and the pleasure of showing his knowledge. After awhile, reassured that my intentions were honest, he talked willingly, pointing out why this horse or that horse was a sure thing or a loser. The reserve was still there, but it was more in the nature of good manners than mistrust.

Finally, I made him an offer that left him silent for a moment. "What if I give you ten dollars and you place some bets for me? We'll split whatever we make." He waited a little, tempted but cautious. "What if we lose?"

"We'll only split what we win. I'll be paying for your knowledge." He was clearly interested, but no doubt the responsibility of investing someone else's money, two weeks' worth of his own betting allowance, also made him nervous. He then made up his mind and stood up. Formally, he said, "I'm Mr. Brown." I too stood up and just as formally introduced myself. "I'm Mrs. Layton." We shook hands.

Overall, I think we made a two-dollar profit each that afternoon. Between races, we loosely engaged in small talk. We talked a little about British Columbia, since he had courteously enquired where I came from. We talked about his and his friends' weekly outing (the friends never spoke to me and hardly looked in my direction: I was obviously Mr. Brown's find). Finally, they had to take their bus back to be on time for dinner. Once more, we stood up and formally shook hands.

It had been a pleasant afternoon and one I will remember with kind feelings for such a nice, courteous little man. I have absolutely no idea what he had thought of me, but I know that despite what could be seen as my initial breach of propriety in addressing him, I had not offended him any further.

I had initiated that particular exchange, but sometimes events force us to be unwittingly in the middle of the fray. This was the case for the two sets of encounters I now relate, which strained considerably my usual rules of engagement among strangers.

A Peculiar Journey (1975)
Rather than fly directly home from Paris where I had spent a week, I had decided to stay overnight in London to visit a friend. The following day, an IRA bomb exploded in one of the car park levels across from the Heathrow terminal where I was waiting for my flight to Amsterdam, where I would transfer to Vancouver.

Several hours later, I found myself sitting in an unscheduled plane beside a stranger. His English was so clipped as to go clickety-click and I took his accent to be German. He had those bland blond looks where at some distance the casual glance skims over the fawn hair, hazel eyes, and tanned skin, unable to stop anywhere with any precision. He turned out to be a South African of Dutch descent, and like many of us, had been stranded at Heathrow for quite some time. We were both on our way to Amsterdam, in transit for our final destinations of Vancouver for me and Hamburg for him.

I think we flew on some South American airline, but I would not swear to it. I suppose we flew on whatever airline would fly us. The interrupted journey had already gone far too long, and I was tired. I also seem to recall that a bunch of us reached our plane in an open truck that took us to the far end of the tarmac, but I would not swear to that either, since everything had been quite hectic, and my memory now plays tricks with this particular segment of the trip.

All I recall is that in the vague alliances that had taken place during the many hours spent waiting at Heathrow, seven or eight of us, mostly Canadians and Australians, had pooled our last English coins to buy and share four long-lasting beers, one or two sips at a time.

Now I was sitting beside Mr. X, on what I assumed would be a trouble-free, final leg of my journey. We eventually found ourselves alone in Amsterdam, the others having by then scattered towards other planes and other destinations. The Heathrow incident had played havoc with the schedules and reservations of many airlines, and we were both part of a large crowd on standby who were told not to bother showing up until early the next morning. It was then very late and as we had little cash handy (those were the pre-ATM days), and neither of us having planned a stay in Holland in the middle of the night, Mr. X suggested that since the weather was fine, we spend the rest of the night walking around the city. He had been a student in Amsterdam some twenty years earlier and offered to show me the sights.

We must have walked all night reliving his student days. We must also have been thoroughly exhausted, because it seems to me that every remark led to peals of laughter. Surely, we could not have been that funny. Once, we stopped for a beer, followed in his case by the customary shot of schnapps, then walked for what seemed like miles, then a joke would erupt leaving us leaning against a wall, weak with laughter.

I remember very little about him, not even his name. He must have been a few years younger than I was, in his late thirties perhaps. He was either an engineer or a businessman, he too had five children, and he lived in a pleasant suburb of Johannesburg. Out of curiosity, I briefly mentioned apartheid, but since it was obvious that we would disagree, we dropped the subject at once. It was definitely not a night for a serious discussion. So we nattered on about everything under the moon, stopping to guffaw at leisure. It was a carefree and silly night, a full regression into childhood.

What I remember most clearly about Mr. X is something he told me almost before parting, something so personal and so unexpected that it was like a gift. Once, as a young man, he had shaved his whole body, and in a slightly perverse way had enjoyed the feeling of total nakedness it had given him.

I had nothing to exchange for such a confidence, nothing so wildly exotic and louche, so shocking and so strange, so seemingly dangerous even. Would the fact that at the age of sixteen, I had faked an attack of appendicitis to get out of a math test, and unable to backtrack, had actually gone the distance (and being allergic to ether, had almost died under the knife) be comparable? No. I had just been cowardly and fatalistic, not clever and mysterious, like him.

But I should have told him, because the point was not whether we had done something particularly smart or unusual, but whether, like children sealing a momentary friendship, we could exchange a secret. Back at the airport in a dirty dawn, we shook hands, wished each other good luck and safe journey, and went our separate ways.

❦ ❦ ❦

Unable to find a flight to Vancouver, I flew to Montreal instead. I slept on and off most of the way, stretched out across three seats. I was astonished to see so few people on board the flight. A passenger across the aisle said the plane had come from Israel, and because of some rumours, many people had cancelled their flight. "Rumours?" "Yeah, bomb scare." But we were already well on our way by then, and anyway, I had already had my bomb scare for the day. So I closed my eyes and tried to go back to that exhausting sleep that makes you feel worse rather than better. Mostly, I was anxious to get home.

But it was not to be, at least not so easily, as there was no connecting flight to Vancouver. Once more, I found myself on standby until the following morning, and a few of us waited in a rather dark corner of an airport furnished with rows upon rows of unyielding plastic seats.

When we boarded the plane in Amsterdam earlier in the day, in the confusion of our last minute scramble I had noticed an unusual figure also waiting on standby, one actually very difficult to overlook in the midst of the slightly scruffy group we formed. A tall, slender, blond, bearded, longhaired man, immaculately robed in homespun white, stood in silence and serenity. Jesus. The white and gold Jesus of my First Communion pictures, minus the halo, the lamb, and the little birds gathered at his feet.

He was still immaculate and serene when I saw him again in Montreal. We both had to wait for a westbound plane in the morning and would be waiting companions for the rest of the night. I had only a dollar on me and learned without surprise that he had even less. Together, we had enough for a cup of coffee that would have to wait until the coffee shop opened first thing in the morning. So we sat and waited.

We must have made an odd pair. He, as I have described, with a Teflon-like quality for repelling smudges and stains from his white garments, and I, very battered by then and exhausted to boot, unkempt in my leather coat and crumpled jeans, and a bit smelly in clothes I had not changed since Paris, from where I had sent my luggage home ahead of me. He also had, and by a good twenty years, the advantage of youth.

Coming from I knew not where, young boys in their early teens soon started to appear and gather around him. They were local youths who found their way to the airport almost every night in search of some amusement. Gathered at his feet like acolytes, sitting on the linoleum floor amid cigarette butts and discarded gum wrappers, they talked and listened to him, entirely oblivious to my presence.

They talked of many things together, of a vaguely philosophical turn. They drank in his words of Eastern wisdom. Joints started circulating. They offered me one, and so much respect did he command that my refusal (Cesar's wife: I was married to a judge) appeared neither patronizing nor censorious since, having seen us sitting together and talking, they took us to be friends.

I cannot remember his name, but James seems a name noble enough to suit him, so I shall call him that. James, the son of a Calgary businessman, had done his self-owed two years in an ashram in India, was going back to Calgary to settle down and enter his father's business. He would cut his beautiful curly blond hair and his soft wavy golden beard, and in a week or two, don a suit and start work at nine o'clock one morning, briefcase in hand. It was a ludicrous picture he depicted for me with gentle, self-deprecatory good humour, but as sad as the end of summer holidays in childhood. In my weakened condition, I was almost bawling with regret and sorrow on his behalf.

We did have that cup of coffee at the counter together after all, with just a few cents remaining for a tip. His plane to Calgary was due so we shook hands. "Good-bye and good luck," I said lamely. He looked at me, deep in the eyes, and said, "Take care." This was 1975, and I had never heard the phrase before, so I took it literally. I toyed with the words long afterwards, finally homebound to Vancouver. What did those words mean? Take care, because you are a dear person, loved by those around you? Take care, because we would grieve if anything bad happened to you? Thanks to him, I still think there may well be some kind thought and human caring behind the now irritatingly trite expression.

Tea with Strangers (1992)

Only a few months apart, two different women invited me to have tea with them. In both cases, we were strangers, away from home, and I assumed they were pleased to find someone who, at first glance, might have had compatible interests.

They were quite unlike in many ways: separated by nationality, language, upbringing, possibly station in life, dress, and general demeanor. I met the first one in Drumheller, Alberta, and the second one in Bangkok. They are solidly linked in my mind for a curious characteristic they shared.

In the first case, a few of us were to meet at the Royal Tyrrell Museum, a leading centre for paleontological research, on a cool and breezy morning to depart for the digs at precisely eight o'clock. I arrived first, early enough to see the many whistling heads of gophers popping up from holes in the landscaped mounds and berms, bobbing up and down, small bodies erect and standing still to salute the new day. They were constantly appearing and disappearing and it was impossible to count them, but there must have been a good many of these small whistlers, and it was charming to imagine the earth teeming with narrow, furry bodies scrambling through tunnels to take turns at the sun hole.

Five or so people arrived and sat well apart from one another on some benches by the entrance. Then a school bus pulled in and parked in front of the benches, the driver remaining inside. Finally, two or three staff members, probably graduate students working for their summer keep and experience, drove up, parked, and disappeared through the museum door.

We were all dressed the same way, except for a mother and daughter who seemed to be using the time and place as a neutral ground for a tentative reunion or perhaps reconciliation. The mother wore a Tilley hat, the daughter cowboy boots, and they spent most of the day walking the hills absorbed in each other. We, the others, looked much the same: cotton pants or jeans, sweatshirt and windbreaker, cotton hat, comfortable shoes—more or less, as we had been told to dress given the cacti and the insects. We were uniformly drab and sensible. And we waited.

There is still one more to come, said a young woman, who had just arrived and who would lead us into the mysteries of touristic paleontology. So we waited. We'll give her another ten minutes and then we have to leave, she said again. Ten minutes later, raising dust— but perhaps I am imagining the dust to evoke speed and in-the-nick-of-time arrival—a taxi nearly skidded into the curb just as we were filing into the bus. We scattered to our seats, each intent on positioning herself (and the lone himself) as far away from the others as possible, except for the mother and her daughter who sat beside each other but created such a wall of aloofness around them that they would have been safe from contact and interference in the middle of a crowd.

Then she came in. The taxi woman. Our resentful, carefully averted eyes drifted surreptitiously towards her with both curiosity and smugness. She was, quite simply, all wrong. Her bright blue tights molding robustly rounded thighs and a good show of bare calves, her white running shoes over apple-green ankle socks with pompons; above, a very pink fancy-lacy top covered a black skin-tight T-shirt, and topping her bleached white-blonde Heidi braids, a floppy fabric hat displayed three huge red fabric roses at the front. Perhaps a young girl's beach or picnic attire, but even on a beach or at a picnic, it would have seemed quite unsuitable for a woman who appeared to be in her fifties.

Worst of all, she immediately started talking, explaining why she had been late. She had read the ad for the digs only a few days ago, had registered at the last minute, and had taken the bus to get to Drumheller. It had been a two-day journey, there had been something wrong with her connection, but she was glad to have made it in time, and was she ever looking forward to it!

I have sometimes wondered whether my inability to respond to confidences, off-the-cuff remarks, or generally speaking, disturbers of the peace, was an idiosyncratic shortcoming, but if so, I could see that I was in good company that day. The group leader, a pleasant zoology graduate student, made the appropriate comments, as our communal clenched teeth remained firmly clenched.

Then, she—the woman—introduced herself. As we were forced to mumble our own name in response, she affronted us further by repeating our name, obviously to memorize it, asking us to repeat if she had not heard properly. Mine elicited her interest. Where was I from? France or Quebec? We then all firmly turned to our windows and gazed at the extraordinary landscape of Alberta's dinosaur country. Before doing so herself, she vigorously rubbed her bare arms, said she was cold, and cheerfully accepted the driver's offer of the jacket he was not wearing. We, the righteous, all had jackets or sweaters, having been advised to do so.

It turned out to be a great day. The breeze scattered away the mosquitoes that usually plagued the diggers, we were excited by the prospect of digging, and although we knew the site was no longer active, of discovering something of interest. We mapped the site; used our little trowel, pail, and other tools as carefully as if we were performing brain surgery; brushed away dust, and plastered bones with respectful gusto.

About an hour into the dig, I came upon a two-inch-long fossilized tendon broken into three small pieces. Surely, such an insignificant find did not warrant the rush of pride and pleasure I experienced, but it was there nonetheless. After the tendon was duly entered in the record book with its position and description, I received the congratulations of my fellow diggers who had not had the good luck to discover such an important fossil. I felt extraordinarily mollified towards the world at large. The woman from the taxi was the most generous with her praise, and she had often emptied my heavy bucket with her own. Her good nature could not be rebuked.

At noon, the mother and daughter returned from their solitary walk and she did what we could never have done, she asked them about themselves. The nerve, we thought, almost warmly, sitting on boulders and eating sandwiches brought in by the staff.

We returned to the museum in the late afternoon, a drive that took nearly an hour, first out of the black hills surrounding Drumheller, then into the suburbs, where plaster dinosaurs the size of large donkeys sometime adorn front lawns, as do elsewhere plaster gnomes or plastic flamingos. After visiting the back rooms of the museum, we set out to leave, and since the woman from the taxi had no car, I offered her a ride into town. She exclaimed how brave I had been to drive alone all the way from Vancouver. I felt she had been infinitely braver than I would have been if confronted by the unfounded dislike of rude strangers, but did not say so.

When we arrived at her hotel, she invited me to tea. I accepted her invitation, by then quite embarrassed by my earlier surliness. She was actually pleasant enough, once one became used to her costume and her being overly friendly.

※ ※ ※

I met the other woman in a gift shop at my Bangkok hotel. She was obviously French and finding the Thai sales clerk's English difficult to understand. I was feeling particularly vulnerable, having just had my hair cut at the hotel beauty salon and realizing that it would take me at least two months to grow out of the awful cut, so I felt some empathy towards others having language difficulties. I translated the two women's exchange and moved on. But the stranger followed me. She gushed over my kindness and insisted on thanking me by inviting me for tea.

Feeling somewhat out of sorts in Bangkok, I was not displeased with, if nothing else, the prospect of hearing familiar sounds for half an hour or so. The woman seemed respectable, faintly dowdy, middle-aged, and rather plain, but very self-assured. As we sat in front of our tea, the tedious process of becoming acquainted started.

What to say to strangers has always been a heavy burden for me. I remember asking my mother at a very early age what did people do after they were married, and what did they talk about when they were alone together. Tactfully, she replied, "By then, they know each other quite well," which surprised me very much indeed, as it seemed too easy to be true.

So the woman and I sat across from each other and we talked. Is she regretting this as much as I am? I wondered. But she seemed to be enjoying herself, infinitely more adept at conversation than I was. There was little small talk, actually, for she soon plunged seriously into her history. She was true to a certain, well-defined type of bourgeoisie, now perhaps disappearing, and had the slightly sibilant sounds of the well bred and the exaggerated animation that on some French faces passes for charm.

It is not in the Canadian repertoire to engage in such nearly seductive tactics—charm for charm's sake—and I did not respond very well, mostly out of ignorance for what the proper (French, in this case) response should be. Or perhaps I once knew and had since forgotten through lack of practice, but whatever the reason, I sensed my voice getting flatter and my face blanker.

She was not without interest. In fact, her life sounded more interesting than mine was, and there was no ridiculous sense of superiority in my cooler and cooler response to the details of her past. She had spent five years in Indonesia, her husband being something in administration, diplomacy, or engineering and spoke intelligently of it. She had just moved to Bangkok, and in contrast to the futile way in which I had allowed myself to be led about without taking any initiative, she had immediately started looking for an apartment in the city, and after a week or so knew so much about Bangkok and the Thai that I could not help being impressed.

At the end, she offered me her card; I only had a business card to trade. When she saw the PhD after my name, she almost became rapturous. "I knew," she said. "I just *knew* you were somebody absolutely special."

❦ ❦ ❦

Neither of these women seemed to regret meeting me and in fact, both claimed with some apparent sincerity to have enjoyed it. Perhaps, since I had so little to say, they saw in me the perfect listener and an adequate foil for their vagaries. For, once the brief and superficial introductions had ended, both left without transition the beaten path of banal conversation to progress forcefully into far more mysterious realms. It is possible that being away from the normal constraints of home had given them license to stray into unexpected and undue intimacy.

The first woman in Drumheller was fascinated by tealeaves readings, revelations, horoscopes, predictions, numerology, coincidences of all forms, and dream analysis (she may even have read Freud or Jung). The one in Bangkok had studied Eastern religions and the mythologies of the Orient; I do not recall whether she referred to the *Book of the Dead,* but she may have; some Egyptian revelations also held her attention, and perhaps even theosophy and the confused and contradictory contentions of Madame Blavatsky. Neither mentioned Nostradamus, but I think both referred to the *I Ching.*

Their knowledge was arcane and puzzling. Perhaps they were trying to honour me, a supposedly educated individual, with the benefit of their own interests, so we could converse at a level worthy of our respective intellects. Or did they perceive in me a faint streak of the bizarre that would respond enthusiastically at the slightest mention of the occult, the weird, the non-pedestrian?

For, surely, it is not a gambit of ordinary conversation over tea between strangers to delve into the mysteries of their psyche. Perhaps they perceived my unwillingness to continue discussing these topics to be a form of unjustified arrogance. Yet, having said two or three times to the two women that I knew very little about such things, what more could I do?

Their efforts at drawing me into their personal mythologies with very little warning and no indication that I was willing to follow them there really bothered me. I also found it rather amusing that their refusal to take any cue from me revealed that ESP had not yet figured in their exploration of the supernatural.

※　※　※

Mr. Brown at the racetrack had been the perfect interlocutor, reserved but polite, in a situation that was familiar to him and which he tried to explain to me with no false move outside the strict contexts of a racecourse and old-fashioned courtesy. What may have slightly upset him at first was the unfamiliar offer I had made him, but I had spoken mildly and with modesty, and given him time to reach his own conclusion. The most salient aspect of our interchange had been mutual respect and good manners. Neither of us would have dreamed of overstepping the barriers of privacy.

Neither would the Edmonton woman and I have dreamed of stepping outside of what we saw as a well-defined and lighthearted conversation between people with similar interests. It started with quilting and the love of fabrics and it ended there, warmly and with mutual satisfaction.

Mr. X in Amsterdam and James in Montreal had adapted the ordinary rules of interaction among strangers to our encounters in exceptional times and unusual locations, neither likely to occur again—and certainly not with us as participants. We had invented our own nocturnal and less-regulated environment, creating a new, slightly different culture, congruent with the events that had led to it.

Yet, even in this less rigid context, Mr. X's confession could be seen as an infraction to the arms-length rules of interaction among strangers. While the mood had been uncommonly relaxed, such intimacy had not been the norm. Had it taken place at another time than when we were ready to part, it could indeed have put some stress on our passing relationship, but the timing made it acceptable since I had been unable to reply.

The case of the two women with whom I had tea was different, and they could have taken valuable lessons from elephants proceeding through unknown and potentially unsafe territory, something they should have known through their familiarity with the occult. For is it not one of the implications of the unknown that it is potentially dangerous? In both cases, our common life experience, established by the fact that we were women of a certain age, of a certain race, able to guess a little at each other's background, and meeting in very specific circumstances and places foreign to both, that common experience was to provide the sole initial topic of conversation. After that, it would have to be one careful elephant step at a time, not the mad charge of blaring pachyderms tearing up trees and villages in their passage, of which I had been the unwilling victim.

❦ ❦ ❦

But what does it mean that, with one exception, women are treated harshly here and men assumed to be behaving appropriately? It could mean that I am more attuned to the way women proceed in their encounters, thus more critical—and that I egocentrically assume their rules of engagement should conform more closely to mine. Moreover, we had met in the somewhat specific circumstances of women having tea, suffused which mannerly behaviour. The rules of such encounters are codified and well known and those women were blatantly infringing them.

I feel less secure in attempting to define the behaviour of the men, my travelling companions. In their case, the circumstances were such as almost to invalidate preconceived ideas about proper behaviour. Would things have been different if they had been women? I do not know. The fact they were men had imparted a subtle difference to what might otherwise have been a similar interchange. For I do not dismiss the possibility of my having given them more license and of having followed their lead more readily in defining what could be accepted as legitimate in our encounters.

Women of my generation tended to be unquestioning of men's guidance. After all, the voices of legal, medical, religious, and technical authority were all male at the time we formed our sense of social and professional hierarchies. Whether or not this is the case does not really matter, since so many factors influence our perception of relationships.

Some loom large in our consciousness, some are almost imponderable, but all add to the construction of an encounter and to our perception of its nature.

We may be aware of these in ourselves and able to control them, but we can only affect the outcome of an exchange by offering the other, also laden with his or her unknown baggage, enough cues to permit a tentative, painstaking, and mutual progression, one sentence, one smile, or one silence at a time.

Chapter Four

The Old Moroccan Photo Shoebox (1932–1946)

Me voici tout contraint par mon passé. Pas un geste aujourd'hui que ce que je ne faisais hier ne détermine.

I am totally constrained by my past. Each of today's gesture is determined by what I did yesterday.

—André Gide, *Les Nourritures Terrestres*.

I was taken to Algeria at the age of six weeks, but my childhood memories revolve around Morocco where I lived until I was sixteen years old. In 1946, at the end of the war, my mother and I repatriated to France on a Canadian troop ship, the *Betelgeuse*. I felt banished and never expected to go back.

My father left me several books on Morocco, which I mostly enjoy for their decorative value: leather-bound a lifetime ago in the souks of Tiznit, their colours differing at first by literary genre (they bear no title, the binder being illiterate), but having since matured into an almost uniform warm tan. A few of these books deal with southern Morocco in the 1930s. They are obsolete and almost unreadable today, and their authors are not only dead but also long-forgotten.

These books are period pieces. It must be remembered that until 1907, when French troops landed in Casablanca, and 1912 when the Treaty of Fès led to the establishment of French and Spanish protectorates, Europeans had little knowledge of Morocco. Twenty-odd years later, it still elicited much romantic interest, and the lyrical and breathless style of the books was not out of tune with the times.

In 1935, when we arrived in Tiznit, that part of the south had only been recently pacified and the regions of the Draa (the longest Moroccan river and the area where my father worked) and the Dadès were still under military control. In 1935, visitors still needed a military permit and had to report to the military authorities. The few Frenchmen who worked in Tiznit were in the army or worked for the Office of Native Affairs.

Morocco had been an independent nation since the arrival in the eighth century of Moulay Idriss, a grandson of the Prophet Muhammad, and a mere thirty years of French and Spanish presence had made little difference. The southern part of the country, unlike the larger cosmopolitan cities of Tangier, Rabat, or Casablanca, was still relatively untouched by French influence.

Another book of more recent vintage was Edmée Doria's *Sur Les Routes Du Destin* (1976), a memoir written soon before her death by a former military nurse in Tiznit in the 1930s and one of the very few Frenchwomen there. She described my parents at that period of their life, particularly my mother.

> A very pleasant young *bourgeoise,* who ended up here [Tiznit] for the love of her husband, a great vagabond who, after commanding Cherkess troops in Lebanon, was now heading the local corps of engineers.

Literary license at work, no doubt, or failing memory as she was getting on in years when she wrote this. In fact, my father had been in the French Foreign Legion in the Middle East during the 1920s (mostly in Syria and Lebanon) and had never commanded Cherkess troops, however romantic this detail may have sounded. My father was a great charmer, and much charmed by women as well, but I remember quite well how much he and Madame Doria claimed to dislike each other, each having recognized in the other the same pride, self-assurance, and mulish obstinacy they possessed themselves. Everyone, even my mother, her closest friend there, formally called her Madame Doria. My father nicknamed her *la Mère Dodo,* which, had she but known it, would have mortified her.

Children seldom see their parents as romantic heroes, but there must have been some truth to her description of my father, who must have been quite a dashing character with elegant manners, an accomplished horseman, an excellent skier, and a competent linguist. After leaving the Foreign Legion, but still in the army, he had completed his engineering degree. I remember being embarrassed at the beach in Agadir seeing the bullet and knife scars on his body, a Syrian memento of battles fought in the hilly Druse *djebel.*

While less gloriously in a hospital bed in Syria with a broken leg after a fall from his horse, he had befriended a young French conscript suffering from appendicitis, who had waxed so eloquently about his young cousin that my father took a leave in 1928 to pay her a visit in Compiègne, her hometown. Apparently, he still had a Hungarian accent in those days and made her a little uncomfortable. But my grandmother, a woman of little formal education but great insight, fell for him immediately, starting their mutual and enduring affection.

He died a long time ago, and I am now more than twenty years older than he ever was. In a few years, as memories fade or betray even more, he may lose all substance and will disappear completely with me.

My soon-to-be mother eventually joined him in Lebanon and they were married in Beirut upon her arrival.

The chaplain baptized her at the same time, for my grandfather (a petty anticlerical tyrant who, against my grandmother's wishes, had named their two sons Kléber and Marceau, after Napoleon's generals) would have nothing to do with the Catholic Church and none of his children had been baptized. Cranky tyrant though he was, every First of May *(Fête du Muguet,* in France), he would airmail my mother in southern Morocco a little perforated package of lilies-of-the-valley, the stems wrapped in still-moist cotton wool, which he picked for her in the Compiègne forest, riding his old bicycle to get there. Then, one year, he fell off his bicycle and two days later, he was dead.

The newlyweds in Ras al Aïn, 1929

Perhaps the most significant aspect of the sixteen years I spent in the Maghreb is how little I knew about local life. We had servants, to whom we spoke a form of broken French mixed with a few Arabic words. In Tiznit, living in the military camp, we had no Arab or Berber neighbours (Morocco's two racial, cultural, and linguistic groups), and we had nothing to do with local families. Whatever receptions were held that included both Moroccans and French were always formal events, which native women did not attend.

I did not play with other children in Tiznit, where I lived between the ages of five and nine. It is quite possible that efforts were made to find little Berber girls, but I do not remember them being successful, and although I attended the local boys' school for three or four weeks, I do not recall that it led to anything beyond the few hours spent together respectfully listening to the master. I was the only girl and a Christian, so no friendship would have been conceivable with my schoolmates.

I can still count to ten in Arabic and swear a little. I also remember a few basic words, but that is all, and I feel that I have been unwittingly cheated out of much wealth.

It is difficult to conceive nowadays of such a sense of estrangement, particularly in Canada with her British traditions, but France and Britain handled their colonies differently. The tradition of bilingual English children brought up during the *Raj*, with their *amah* as their closest caretaker, was mostly foreign to the French colonialist experience.

For most people—I think particularly of women who stayed at home and usually mixed only with other French wives—ignorance of the culture and history of those colonies was very much the norm in those days, with the exception of Indochina, and particularly, Algeria, where roots ran much deeper.

French colonist families had been established in Algeria for two or three generations, whether as tradesmen, farmers, or administrators. Unlike her other two Maghrébin neighbours, Tunisia and Morocco, Algeria was a legitimate French territory composed of three administrative *départements*. It is those special bonds, after 130 years of French presence, which made the Algerian War of Independence of 1954–1962 the particularly bloody and nasty event it was.

In other colonial territories, including Morocco, French women, whose husbands were mostly in the army or the administration and who only stayed there a few years, usually found it unnecessary to learn much of the countries to which their husbands' career had taken them. They undertook the minimum of interaction necessary for the performance of daily tasks, such as being able to shop and give instructions to native servants.

Children, who would normally hang around servants, even though often ignored by them, were certainly more interested and perhaps a little more knowledgeable than their mothers were. Fathers, naturally, were in a different situation altogether, for much of the work they performed required close contact both with Moroccan *caïds* (chiefs), officials, and native labourers.

My father, for instance, first built roads and bridges south of Tiznit while in the army, then upon the dissolution of the French Army after 1940, worked as an engineer in an anthracite mine near Oujda owned by a Belgian company. Finally, before joining the Free French Forces in England, he directed a salt mine in Taza. All these various positions required him to be politically and historically astute, culturally sensitive, and aware of semantic implications and the small subtleties of courtesy, all skills that simply meant he had to know Moroccans to the extent they allowed themselves to be known.

My mother had a shoebox filled with old photographs, and a few years ago, I decided to put some order into these mementos and help her sort through them. I had not looked at the snapshots for many years and was surprised to see how little the photos actually revealed: bits of ramparts, some palm trees, a minaret, the *Mechouar* in Tiznit, a street corner, two or three dogs, the door to our house, the odd servant standing stiffly, some people whose faces were almost indistinct with the passage of time—a very slim baggage, indeed.

But what also surprised me was how the snapshots came to life. What I saw was not just a street corner, but our street corner, the one where one of the few cars in town had killed our young dog. What I saw was not just a door, but what had happened behind that door. It was like ransacking a dusty attic. Pell-mell, from these photographs, images of my childhood emerged.

The places I had known were all there. Meknès, which I was too young to remember, and where all women were photographed wearing small cloche hats like upside down chamber pots, but so young and gay in their summer dresses, white sandals, and crocheted cotton gloves. Then the cities in which I went to school: Casablanca, Oujda, and Taza. And particularly, Tiznit, a small town on the edge of the desert, which in unguarded moments I tend to call my hometown. Tiznit was a Berber town; Casablanca, the town of my teenage years was almost a French city; they hardly belonged on the same map in my mind.

Other places were there too: Marrakesh, Mogador (now Essaouira), Safi, and Tindouf in the very south near the former Spanish enclave of Ifni. Also, the southern posts of Goulimine, famous for the *guedra* dance, and Foum el Hassan, sometimes hidden behind a wall of sand when the harsh and hot *chergui* blew from the south. The cooler places, too, Azrou in the Atlas Mountain, Ifrane where I saw snow for the first time, and the Tizi N'test in the High Atlas, then farther down the map, Taroudant and her rich carpet weavers.

And Agadir and the large hotel where my parents used to go to the ball—driving one hundred kilometres of rough road in a little two-toned Renault Roadster they had at the time. My mother's elegant navy satin or silvery pink velvet evening dress—homemade but cleverly so—and my father's resplendent uniform were both loosely packed on the backseat beside me, dressed in light cotton pajamas, ready to be put to bed upon arrival.

Snapshot #1 (Tiznit)
The Mechouar-I: Rue de la Joie
Southern view of the Mechouar, *the main square, with the beginning of a small street showing in the corner*

The focus must have been the heavily studded doors of the house to which El Glaoui, the pasha of Marrakesh, head of one of the most eccentric and powerful Berber families, and so-called Lord of the Atlas, had more or less exiled his brother, providing him with a job of sorts in this southern town of little importance against a promise to stay put. The side street, our street, is what interests me.

Our arrival in Tiznit, where my father had preceded us by a few weeks, was memorable. My mother and I had been accidentally dropped off at the corner of the main square, the *Mechouar,* on July 14, 1935 at three o'clock in the afternoon in the middle of Bastille Day celebrations. In Morocco, no real celebration could be conceived without a *fantasia*.

We emerged just as the wild charge of small horses with their flat slicing bits, distorted foaming mouths, furiously snorting nostrils, and bulging wild eyes stopped short at the wall beside us, their riders dressed in white, standing on the broad stirrups, and firing ornate muskets, the closest one only a few feet away, spraying horse spittle on us.

The enthusiasm shown by the *fantasia* riders had a lot more to do with the joy of rushing fiercely on horseback in clouds of gunpowder than with the unlikely duty of celebrating a colonialist country's National Day. This enthusiasm left my mother and me terrified.

Moreover, we had no place to stay the first night save the local café, whose owner, Hajji, a rich man, had made the pilgrimage to Mecca. It made up for what it lacked in bed linen by an abundance of bedbugs and voracious fleas, and I slept wrapped in my mother's dressing gown of tightly woven silk, which prevented their assault. It did not feel like an auspicious arrival, yet it soon became home, and four years later when I could no longer be taught at home and was sent to boarding school in Casablanca several hundred kilometres north, I truly felt I was leaving my roots behind.

The following day, finding out that the house my father was building for us inside the military camp would not be ready for a few months, we rented a house in the *rue de la Joie* (the street of Joy), so called because it was the street of the brothels. We stayed there for a few months, and I keep friendly memories of it. Some of the small attendants to the women next door were girls barely older than I was, and we often met on the adjoining roofs.

Rue de la Joie, **with our guard and a young neighbour**

The prostitutes were part of every public festivity, their presence expected. Veiled and wrapped in outer garments, the black *haïks,* they stood in a group and often provided cheerful *yoo-yoos* as the occasion required. This, I remember well, but perhaps I do not remember as well that they stood around the symbol of their profession, a life-size model of a woman hoisted on a pole and dressed in bright garments, her face hidden by a richly embroidered veil and wearing a profusion of silver jewels, the just reward of their communal activities. I read about it much later, and from some vagueness of memory or imagination, came a faint confirmation that, indeed, it was perhaps so.

Once a week was *toubib* (doctor) day, when they filed away on the street towards the military infirmary, moving on lazy swaying hips. Since they tended to the needs of the *légionaires,* the native *goum,* and the Moroccan *tirailleurs* (skirmishers), they were checked regularly. They walked by with the ancestral grace of those used to carrying heavy jars upon their heads, each one steadying on her shoulder with a hennaed hand, the necessary implements of feminine hygiene: a red rubber tube and a jug of purple permanganate water.

They would hail me good-naturedly whenever I happened to be on the street with my mother, whom they did not greet and who did not see them, with a slightly singsong *Ayaaah Mouniiique,* far softer than the sound of my name in French.

Snapshot #2 (Tiznit)
On the roof with Yamina
I am standing with the maid, our fatma, *near the low wall that separates our roof from that of our neighbours, the houses of ill fame*

Each roof encloses an inside patio. It is a black and white photograph, and a little faded as well, but I remember well the implacable blue of the sky and the blinding glare of the low white walls.

There is no rabbit, so the picture must have been taken on another day. Yamina had chosen the rabbit for the shine and colour of its coat as much as for its plumpness and its anticipated tenderness, since I wanted to make

[Handwritten note: Where are these snapshots?] ❦ Notes from Elsewhere ❧

a little purse out of its skin. We took the rabbit up on the roof to kill it. We often had rabbit for dinner, but I had never assisted at the killing. However, since this time I was involved and I was supposed to cure the skin myself, she had told me to come. She positioned the animal on the low wall, took her big kitchen knife, and started to saw its head off. She had to stop and told me to help hold the struggling animal because the knife was blunt and she needed to sharpen it against the rough side of the wall.

After more desperate struggling, energetic sawing, and the oddest of squeals, the rabbit was properly decapitated and divested of its skin. She showed me how to rub salt into the bloodied pelt turned inside out; the fur now inside it formed a large, plump sausage. Eventually, I made my little rabbit purse, a sporran-like appendage, and wore it for a while despite the long-lingering smell.

I was not duly upset at the time by the sloppiness of the rabbit's execution, and perhaps our *fatma's* matter-of-fact attitude towards the killing of animals had much to do with it. It may also be that it is not in the nature of young children to empathize with the suffering of other creatures.

Snapshot #3 (Tiznit)
The Souk
This very confused picture was taken at some distance and shows small tents, people milling around, and often bent over market goods. Tethered sheep are in the left-hand corner

Looking at this snapshot, you can almost hear the sounds of haggling.

Many souks were a weekly event, distinct from the larger urban markets composed of permanent shops, often grouped by artisanal specialty: skin dyers, leather workers, potters, silversmiths, etc. In the agricultural plains where grain and horses were sold, the souk formally took on both the name of the day on which it occurred and of the nearby villages, often existing because of the souk itself.

A few souks might also be noted for some particularity. For instance, the one in Moulay Idriss, one of Islam's holy cities, took place on Saturday and was not attended by Jews; in Goulimine, the camel souk took place on Sunday *(souk el Had)* and commanded the roads to the desert. I understand it has now been revived after losing some of its importance in the intervening years.

The most famous permanent souk in Morocco is still the one held in *Djemaa el Fna* in Marrakesh. It has so often been described, been so well attended by foreign visitors, and has been photographed and filmed so many times that one does not even have to set foot in Morocco to have a good idea of what a popular Moroccan market is like.

Ours, in Tiznit, although far more modest, was nevertheless well attended. It was held beside the ramparts, and what a cacophony that was, mostly in *chleuh,* the local Berber dialect. Almost every trade and custom was represented. Here, an itinerant tailor, wearing one of traditional robes, a white *djellabah,* quickly ran up loose garments, his bare feet rapidly pumping up and down the treadle of his sewing machine. There, a water seller, a copper cup on its chain dangling on his chest, and the water kept cool in a goatskin on his back, his large brimmed hat adorned with red pompons, shrilly called for attention and customers.

Almost at our feet, in flat baskets on the ground, all sorts of foodstuff: sticky dates, vegetables and fruit, and sugar cones wrapped in dark blue paper. And in clay dishes filled with water, slightly rancid butter shaped in flat sticks with the mark of thumbs still evident. Elsewhere, babouches, the slip-on footwear everybody wore, from embroidered to plain, were shown off in neat rows, and a faint smell of cowhide in the air competed with the wafting scent of spices.

Hennaed female hands, reaching out from under wraps and veils, fingered the cloth offered for sale, of a dark blue shade popular in the south, a cloth that would eventually stain the skin the same shade of indigo.

Away from the main action, sheep stood patiently in the sun and huddled in each other's shade. Still farther away, at the edge of the souk, the tethered dromedaries, one leg bent tight at the knee, snorted, self-satisfied in the knowledge that they and they alone according to legend knew the unknown hundredth name of Allah.

For, located as it was on the edge of Mauretania (the border has been pushed south since those days), this was a market sometimes frequented by the Blue Men, their skin dyed the colour of the cloth which protected their hidden mouth from sand, wind, sun, and spiritual contamination. Once, a veiled young Targui (Touareg, the better-known word, is the plural form) gave me a small gazelle carved in wood and stained deep ochre. My mother, French in the extreme, expressed some sanitary concerns about the tail, made of matted human hair, and the little toy was soon banished from our house.

I doubt those caravans still carried salt across the Sahara in the mid-thirties. Alvise da Cadamosto, a Venetian in the service of Henry the Navigator of Portugal, described in the fifteenth century the active trade between the Moroccan border and Timbuktu and Mali, and the swapping of desperately needed salt for gold, a trade no doubt already centuries old by then. Tiznit, by the 1930s a marginal and almost insignificant town, may well have been an important trading centre in those days, perhaps even the equal and rival of Goulimine, farther south.

During one particular souk, my mother was taking a long time examining meat hanging from large hooks in the open air (slabs of often unrecognizable parts, buzzing with delirious flies, stamped red or blue by the French military veterinarian to reflect the grade of the meat), and I wandered around. First, I probably went to the circle of the storyteller who went on interminably, and for me, unintelligibly, the rhythm seductive and passionate in turns. Soon tired of it, I wandered even farther, well out of my mother's sight, to arrive near another circle of spectators.

I wriggled into the first row. A man sat cross-legged on a mat, a basket in front of him. It took me a little while to understand what he was doing. He had a snake in his hands, the snake's head near his mouth, and then he bit it firmly behind the head, tearing a strip of skin all the way down to the tail, the way one peels a banana. Then his teeth taking another bite at the neck, he started peeling another strip.

By then, hands were holding me firmly, forcing me to keep on watching as I fought to get away. Only my mother's arrival opened up a path for me to escape while they laughed at me. My mother asked what they were watching, but I could not bring myself to tell her.

Snapshot #4 (Tiznit)
Poum the dog
The black and white cocker spaniel sits looking into the camera with his usual grin, pulling its mouth to the left

Poum had a very hard life before joining our family. Its former owner, a French captain, had taught the dog to chew razor blades, a feat Poum managed with great delicacy. Its owner had left him with my mother when he went to France on leave, and on his return, she had refused to give the dog back. Every afternoon, she sat reading in a large armchair, and Poum would lie across her chest, its head on her shoulder. The dog adored my mother, following her with its eyes, whimpering when she was away.

One morning, Poum returned from its first outing of the day, its neck covered with bloody spittle. My mother rubbed its fur trying to find a wound or a cut. Yamina then arrived, full of excitement and gossip. Men armed with brooms and sticks had chased a rabid dog through our street, and as Poum emerged from our front door, it collided with the rabid dog and they both rolled on the ground. The reddish foam on Poum's coat came from the other dog.

As all cases of rabies had to be reported at once, the army doctor visited my mother, and after examining her hands, he noticed a small cut on the right one, between her thumb and index finger. He urged her to remember whether she had moved her hand along or against the dog's fur. Since it was likely that she had rubbed it both ways while looking for a wound, he decided she would have to go to the Pasteur Institute in Meknés for a month of very painful daily serum injections in the abdomen. I would tag along since there was nowhere to leave me.

Poum was tied up in the yard at the back of my father's office, to remain in isolation for sixty days before the rabies symptoms would declare themselves if, indeed, it had been bitten by the other dog. There was no getting out of it, even though no sign of a bite had been found. After two weeks of the dog's crying and refusal to eat, my father had to put Poum down. A vet examined the dog's brain, but my parents refused to know the test results.

Snapshot #5 (Tiznit)
The Mechouar*-II: The School*
In the foreground is the school near the Office of the Native Affairs.
In the background, over the roofs, you vaguely see the minaret

The particular type of minaret shown in this photograph is only found in the southern reaches of the country, near the Sahara, as well as in the Niger and in Mali. It features horizontal perches where lost souls in need of rest can settle for a while.

In the foreground, at the northern end of the *Mechouar* and right beside the café-hotel run by Hajji, stands the local school I attended for a short while. We sat cross-legged on woven palm mats, the boys reciting the Koran while swaying from the waist, very likely a mnemonic device. Around their neck, under their shirts, the boys wore a small leather pouch containing a verse of the Koran.

The teacher, dressed in a Western jacket but wearing the traditional loose pants, the white *saroual,* would sometimes touch with a long bamboo pole—and not always lightly—the head of a boy at fault, a round shaved head, save for a small tuft of hair to make sure it could be grabbed by Allah even if decapitated in battle.

I was always spared, being French and a girl; in fact, my status was so privileged and ambiguous that my parents soon took me out of school. Being a Christian as well, I must have been an extremely problematic presence in the classroom. The Koranic lessons were lost on me since I did not speak Arabic, and the French language lessons were too basic to be of much benefit to me.

The teacher lived in a little house at the back and grew cotton in his garden. I remember that we picked cotton for him that summer and that it was hard on the fingers.

Snapshot #6 (Tiznit)
The Mechouar-III: Aïd el Kebir
A full view of the Mechouar *showing people moving about*

Like the *piazza* in Italy or the *zócalo* in Mexico, the *mechouar* is in Morocco at the centre of all public activities. Ours seemed immense to me, but maybe it was just a small village square.

The photograph is not well taken. I see dressed-up people leaving on the right and others entering on the left. All seem to be moving quickly towards some event out of the frame. Perhaps several pictures were taken in a sequence to show what was happening, but this one is the only one that has survived. It could have been a holiday.

The souks and the feasts are somewhat blended in my memory. Although they served different functions in Moroccan society, they generated the same kind of activity, excitement, noise, and social exchanges. My clearest memory of the various feasts held on the *Mechouar* must have been the *Aïd el Kebir* of 1939, the last I attended before being sent off to boarding school in Casablanca.

The Muslim calendar, as does the Christian one, governs the cycle of religious life and holidays. It officially starts during the month of *Muharram,* celebrating the anniversary of Muhammad's flight to Medina. Its two most famous holidays are the *Ramadan* (followed by the *Aïd el Seghir* that celebrates its ending) and the *Aïd el Kebir,* the latter commemorating Abraham's sacrifice of a sheep instead of his son Ishmael.

Tiznit celebrated these holidays in style, and I particularly remember the celebration of *Aïd el Kebir*. At the centre of a circle of spectators, a few dancers, wearing the skin of freshly killed sheep, twirled and gesticulated, pounced on the onlookers, and scared children with the head of the dead animals thrust at them, the blood still fresh. In the heat, the stench became almost unbearable.

Adding to the confusion and the excitement, others danced as well. The *gnaoua* (Guineans), black dancers and acrobats dressed in resplendent white (who usually danced in Djemaa el Fna, but often made an appearance in Tiznit for such festivities), also whirled to dizziness and exhaustion, furiously playing their enormous iron castanets and whirling the tassel on their cap. That double synchronized whirling—of their body within the circle of spectators, of their heads within this larger motion—the pounding of the drum, the shrieking and laughter of the crowd, set small hypnotic tremors of exhilaration through the crowd.

Snapshot #7 (Tiznit)
The Blind Beggar
He is little more than a human heap near the doorway of a rich man's house. His fingers curl around a wooden begging bowl

His face seems serene, perhaps because he is blind. The Koran orders charity and the poor were seldom entirely neglected in those days.

I do not know why this picture was taken, as he is like so many who relied on the goodwill of others. There is nothing memorable about him, except perhaps his very familiarity: Pierre Petitfour, a neighbour of ours and an obsessive painter of southern Morocco had painted him. Both snapshot and painting are identical. The painting is now in my mother's living room, and we can see the colours that are missing from the photograph—the deep pink walls and the dull brown of the raggedy *djellabah* that covers him.

There was another familiar beggar nearby. He must have been old since most of his offences had presumably been committed at the time when an older justice system prevailed. Having stolen once, his right hand had been amputated. Recidivism was not looked upon with much lenience, so his left hand had also been amputated later, and then one foot, after which he either learned his lesson or had been too incapacitated to pursue his trade. He now dragged himself on the ground to take up his usual position, a wooden alms bowl in front of him.

Justice was harsh, and we sometimes saw chain gangs on their way to work, long lines of men linked together by a rope tied to their wrists, the iron shackles on their ankles forcing them to shuffle along noisily. We would see them later, breaking piles of rocks into small stones to build roadbeds. They wore no goggles, of course, and I assume stone chips flying into their faces must have blinded a good number of them.

Snapshot #8 (Tiznit)
Arkiya

She is dressed for indoors. Under the dark blue gown, she wears a white blouse. Around her neck, she wears the heavy Berber jewels of which she is so fond

We cannot see the henna markings on her face and on her knuckles, but I know they are there. Her attire may well be inappropriate for a servant at work.

Arkiya

She is a tall woman, and another photograph shows her draped in a dark blue *haïk,* one elegant hand holding her veil slightly to the side. One babouche, peaking under her long skirt, shows some embroidery. She is quite beautiful, and as I look at her, a strong smell of patchouli still comes to my nostrils, mixed with spices, an olfactory *petite madeleine,* as I suddenly find myself in my mother's kitchen, Arkiya's domain.

I remember when Arkiya first came to our house after Yamina had gone back to her village; rather, what I may remember even better is my mother telling the story. My mother, in her best broken French-Arabic, interviewed her. Arkiya's answers were quiet monosyllables as she was coolly biding her time.

After my mother had finished her questions, Arkiya had one of her own. In superbly grammatical French, she had asked at what time Madame wanted breakfast served in bed in the morning. Yes, she eventually deigned to explain, she had gone with Commandant X's family when he was posted in Versailles and had spent five years in France. My mother often told the story, humorously making the most of her intended discomfiture. The aspect of one-upmanship implied went far above my seven- or eight-year-old head.

Arkiya turned out to be no better and no worse than other *fatmas* we had over the years (and she certainly had little time for me). However, she always remained elegant and quite superior, even when both the days and the nights of *Ramadan* left her drained of all energy—the former because of the fasting, the latter because of the feasting. No wonder, my mother would say, she has been partying all night again! Apparently, Arkiya's reputation was not as spotless as her appearance, and I believe that is why she left us eventually. Or perhaps my parents' social life was too limited a framework for her talents and training? When she went, much of our domestic prestige left with her.

Snapshot #9 (Tiznit)
Ali and me in the garden
We are grinning at something. He is tall and wearing the customary baggy saroual *and a white shirt, and I, half his size, looking scrawny in shorts. We are both barefoot*

He stands, a gangly youth of eighteen or so. Officially, he was the gardener. Unofficially, he and I spent a lot of time together, and our companionable stance reveals some complicity between us. Although he is twice my age and size, I may well have twice the authority.

I remember the green ribbed cotton top I am wearing with the shorts. It has a little white anchor in the front—it does not show on the black and white photograph, but I remember the top well, as few garments have pleased me as much since.

The house designed by my father had finally been built in the military camp, and it was a nice house. I can trace in my mind every nook, cranny, archway, window, corridor, patio of it. I could draw every piece of furniture he had also designed and I can still hear the all-day twitter of the large aviary on the dining room patio.

I remember well the coolness of the water on my feet in the sunken tiled bath where, in the heat of summer afternoons, I kept shop. Standing in two or three inches of water, I used the thick ledge of the built-in tub made of dark blue tiles to display my wares: pictures cut out from my mother's magazines. It was cool and fairly dark in the room, and I do not think I ever missed having no one to play with.

Ali had given me a large cardboard box, of which I made a little house at the bottom of the garden. He had helped me cut out a window and there I was, like Big Alice, scrunched up in it, my knees bent high up, sitting on a small gazelle skin, the box so small that I was unable to move. As time slowed down to a near standstill, I do not recall what I actually did in the cardboard box, if anything. All I remember is that I was perfectly happy there, enclosed in silence, shade, and solitude.

Whenever a new *Fillette* magazine for young girls arrived in the mail, my pleasure then knew no bounds as I read quietly in my box, sheltered by the largest of the four banana trees. I was particularly fond of a regular Shirley Temple section, and even practiced mincing around with my right elbow bent and my hand dangling elegantly as, no doubt, Shirley herself did in Hollywood.

My only other game may well have come from reading Robinson Crusoe. I used to devise the perfect survival kit. If alone on a desert island, what would I need? I had started collecting bits of string and tying and braiding them together to strengthen into a rope that could hold my weight. To my cache, I also added a penknife and some matches. The game, a persistent attempt at taming an imaginary hostile environment and imposing my presence in it, went on for quite some time.

Years later, when I went into a science fiction phase, the books I found most interesting were those depicting new societies millions of parsecs away or, what in fact I preferred, the reconstruction of our own destroyed environment—tinkering with small tools to recreate social order and organization out of chaos.

There were cement paths in the garden among the banana trees and the numerous plants my mother had tried, not very successfully, to grow in an imitation of a French garden. From her and the nostalgia she passed onto me, a nostalgia not attached to any real memory of my own, I learned to believe that only French roses, soft, floppy, sweet-smelling, and large enough to require both hands cupped to bring them to your face, could make up a real garden. Instead, we had several shades of bougainvillea, marigolds, zinnias, and a profusion of very coarse orange and yellow flowers, much like calendulas, which the French call *soucis* (worries), and which my mother gathered and placed in a cauldron made of hammered copper to rest on the dining room table.

We also had *rats de palmiers*. Those were not rats, but large lizards—much like foot-long crocodiles, not including a long and fat tail—that climbed up trunks of palm trees. They were popular during the thirties: stuffed, they sat as radiator grill ornaments for our cars. Having them demonstrated that you came from the "Real South," the part of Morocco you did not visit without a military pass.

One day, asked to call my father for lunch (I only had to cross the garden, open the back gate that led into the camp, and walk a few steps to reach his office), I was forced to stop. A *rat de palmier,* solidly stationed across the path and blocking my way, dozed in the sun. If I shouted to make it decamp, it would move; something I could not face. What if it moved towards me? It was too large for me to jump over without entering its space. Out of pride, I could not call my mother, and Ali, to whom I would not have had to explain anything, was not around.

I waited a little, finally turned around, and left the garden from our front door on the street side, which required a long detour and reentering the camp through the official gate in order to reach my father's office. Distance and time distort my memory, so I cannot tell how long the walk was or the time elapsed, but it was quite possible that my father had already come home by then, and Ali had perhaps been sent to look for me. I do not remember.

But I know the front garden door was not one I would have been allowed to use alone. Neither, as a rule, would I have chosen to do so, for it held a ghastly memory. One day, just as we came out, a woman afflicted with rabies was being taken to see the camp doctor. Tied to the back of a donkey, she struggled with her bonds, and attempted to chew on the donkey's ears. The memory of the noise, the shouting, the braying, the pushing, and the shoving, was what I had chosen rather than face the sleeping lizard.

My intense dislike of lizards is still there, still irrational. Quite ridiculous, in fact. On Mexican beaches, for instance, my husband had to whisper "iggies" under his breath, as a discrete warning that sellers of long-dead and stuffed iguanas were coming our way and that it was time for me to close my eyes and freeze until the danger had passed.

Snapshot #10 (Agadir)
The Kasbah
It stands on the top of the rocky spur, a white
building, vaguely shapeless in the distance

The Kasbah, traditionally a large family estate built around a granary, was the most noticeable building in Agadir. Built high up and overlooking the town, the road leading to it was the favourite place on which to test new drivers' performance.

Perhaps the snapshot was taken after my mother had been tested for her driver's licence. She had had to drive the tightly winding road up to the Kasbah. Her friend, Madame Weiss, a nice woman who missed her native Alsace, had to drive down the road. Before they took the test, they had been told with all appearance of seriousness that they would have to drive in reverse the whole way. Before obtaining their license, they were also tested on whether they could change a tire, a necessary skill on the roads we had south of Agadir, and recognize spark plugs.

Agadir (the Arab word for granary and fortress combined) was where we went on holiday. Tiznit did not have a beach, being some twenty kilometres inland, and the small fishing village of Aglou, its closest neighbour, provided a very inhospitable access to the ocean. There were strong and treacherous rolling waves along the coast (the famous and forbidding "bar" of the Atlantic) that made swimming perilous. The *gharbi,* a west wind often blowing from the Atlantic, did not encourage picnicking either.

Yet, I remember a picnic at Aglou, an outing to which the entire French contingent had participated, even the military chaplain, who had lost a good chunk of skull during the Great War and was said to be absentminded. (He had prepared me for my First Communion, and although I was the only French child in town, I always had to remind him my name, which he promptly forgot and continued to call me *fillette* [girlie]).

Two young *métropolitains,* Frenchmen freshly arrived from France, accompanied the group, and ignoring all advice, went for what should have been no more than a short dip in the sea. They did not swim very far out but were soon unable to come back. Someone went to fetch the fishermen to push and heave the heavy fishing boats into the water, but that was going to take too long, so some of the men went in after the distressed swimmers. A human chain was also formed trying to reach them.

After what seemed like hours of effort but may have been just a very short time, one of the two original swimmers was pulled back over the bar. The other could not be reached and neither could two of the would-be rescuers.

A fourth victim was added to the count when it was discovered that the young veterinarian, a non-swimmer who had stood in shallow water near my mother, had also vanished, sucked in by the current and the shifting sands. We did not see him go, nor heard him. One minute we saw him there, anxiously watching with everyone the progress of the attempted rescue, but when my mother next turned to speak to him, he had disappeared.

I remember the day, which had started so well, but I probably remember even more my parents retelling an incident that marked so direly the life of the small French community. The second Parisian left Tiznit soon afterwards. None of the bodies was ever recovered.

The tragic picnic at Aglou

So we went to Agadir instead. At the time, it was deemed the last bastion of French civilization in southern Morocco. What it meant was that there were good restaurants, one big and very elegant hotel where formal balls were held, and shops where French clothes and shoes could be bought. The Bata store even had a magic X-ray machine through which children could admire the many bony intricacies of their feet. There were other families on the beach, mostly from Agadir, some with children, but I was not very adept at playing with them.

For our holidays, we used to stay in a very nice little hotel built on a small hill. The windows bringing light to the winding staircase going down to the rooms were shaped like portholes, and to maintain the nautical theme, there was instead of a banister a hard twisted rope to hold onto. My mother would say it was like being on a yacht.

Madame Gauthier was the name of the owner of that very modern establishment. Her garden consisted mostly of juicy cacti and succulents, often in bloom. Her daughter, who inherited the hotel after her death, perished in the earthquake that completely devastated Agadir in 1960, or so my mother told me. The same source had also told her that high up on the hill, the Kasbah had mostly been spared by the earthquake, but that nearly all the old Medina quarters had been destroyed.

Just outside Agadir was the Aït Melloul, a small place on the Oued Souss, where a French couple kept a little restaurant. I learned to swim in their pool, around which they had put small tables and chairs, an elegant and sophisticated innovation at the time. My parents ate lobster *à l'Américaine* to their hearts' content, while I paddled around with my head sticking high in the air.

The Aït Melloul was where I took the "express" bus to Casablanca on my biannual visit to the dentist. My parents would drive me from Tiznit and put me on the bus for the daylong drive. Friends expected me in Casablanca, and then would put me back on the bus two or three days later.

I have little memory of the details of these trips, and I only remember the heat, the boredom, the loading and unloading of baskets, crates, and packages on the roof, and chickens clucking away or the odd little goat with its feet tied up tight. I would try a test of endurance: how long could I keep my hand on the burning metal of the window frame? I was always surprised and disappointed not to see a huge blister, but only a pale redness.

I assume people must have been kind to me (children are used to taking such things for granted) and the driver, in whose care I had been entrusted, must have seen to it that I was fed, watered, and taken to the toilet along the way.

Snapshot #11 (Casablanca)
Institution Sainte Jeanne d'Arc
My first boarding school on boulevard Moulay Idriss

The elegant boulevard is bordered by short trunks of rich palm trees, very unlike the tall, skimpy plumes of the south. The discreet door, barely visible in the photograph, is the entrance of the boarding school. Farther down, there is an even more discreet door, which must be that of the cool and dark chapel, which outsiders could attend on Sunday.

I had spent my early childhood under the fatalistic influence of *Mektoub* (It is written) and *Inch'Allah* (God willing), often accompanied by pleas for divine protection, and apart from a perfunctory catechism preparation by the absentminded chaplain, I had received almost no religious education.

Then, my mother, believing that nuns would be kind, sent me at the age of nine to a convent school in Casablanca, the Institution Sainte Jeanne d'Arc. Some were. Kind, I mean. A few had a slightly sadistic bent to their nature. All but one nun, a motherly and low-ranking nun, were indifferent to me. I may well have been an unprepossessing child. I thought of myself as somewhat retarded and perhaps others did as well.

In that institution, I heard a lot about the original sin, redemption, and the possibility of bailing souls out of purgatory through particular prayers designed to that effect. In fact, these prayers were said to be so well conceived that the number of days of release obtained was shown beside each prayer. One could double the number of days by repeating the prayer. Puzzled, I wondered why one would not always go for the big numbers. Those were only words, after all. My instincts must have been right for I learned much later of the scandalous sale of indulgences: another arrangement with the Catholic church, but so excessive as to become one of the causes of the Reformation in the sixteenth century.

Every Friday a visiting priest heard us in confession. Finding it very difficult to recognize what my own sins could be, since I had not coveted, stolen, murdered, lied, or had particularly voluptuous inclinations, I had to invent a few. So, I mostly confessed to laziness, although with the draconian regime at the school, it was impossible to be anything but diligent and always busy.

I also confessed to greed. Every Thursday, we had mashed peas which, coming after Wednesday's two tiny vinegary sausages, were such a welcome relief that I gorged on them, even though we could not have seconds (gorging is sometimes in the mind). I was unable to distinguish between hunger and greed.

So I confessed my sins, recited my act of contrition, received absolution, and made penance. But I never really felt forgiven, perhaps because I had no sense of having actually sinned in the first place.

None of my memories of the school are particularly good ones. Everything felt extraordinarily alien, and despite my good will, I never fitted in, or to be frank, never really understood much of what went on and what was expected of me. I now realize that what I was lacking was not so much intelligence as the most basic skills at interacting with both adults and children.

Between the ages of five and nine (I do not remember much before our arrival in Tiznit), I had had almost no opportunity to meet people and play with children, and my closest companion had been Ali—and, after all these years, I do not even remember what language we spoke together. So it is perhaps not surprising that I found school and other children incomprehensible.

I must have been thought, with some justification, as being somewhat slow. For instance, I had the mumps in the middle of the term and my German lessons stopped for a while. I never caught up and could only count to ten, sing *O Tannenbaum,* and mumble a few words of a German prayer, but I never, ever, progressed beyond that, as did the other mumps sufferers who readily went on with their lessons and achieved reasonable fluency by the end of the year. At about the same time, I developed the common enough and baseless notion that I was adopted.

Occasionally, friends of my parents took me out, which meant I was sent to the movies with their *fatma,* who would park me in the first row in front of the screen and then disappear, sometimes for several hours. I saw the same episode of *Zorro* many times, to my intense satisfaction. Zorro was, in fact, my second love.

My first one had been a tall German *légionaire.* Every so often, Madame Doria organized a party at the soldiers' canteen with tea, cookies, and music, all terribly civilized but not particularly well attended. The entire French female contingent attended, three or four altogether, officers' wives for the most part, passing cookies around and chatting with the lower ranks.

Suddenly, a young German appeared in front of me and asked my mother whether Mademoiselle would like to dance. I stood up, stunned with joy and bitterly resenting my mother's amused tone of voice when accepting on my behalf, and then he took my hand and off we went. It was not very easy since I could not dance, and being seven or eight, I was less than half his size.

Yet, not only did we dance, but he also spoke to me, asking in poor French my opinion on this and that and even appearing to listen to what, consumed with pride, I was shyly saying to his belt buckle. I later told my mother, gravely, that I would love him forever. I wonder whether he had simply been kind to a little girl with sharp elbows, freckles, and mousey hair, or whether, perhaps barely out of his teens himself, he had found me the only approachable female at the party.

One day, Mother Superior approached us, and with red eyes, told us France had capitulated and that for us, the war was over. Other nuns wept, which caused much curiosity and speculation on our part. The war had not meant very much to me, save for my having to keep quiet as my parents, their ears glued to the radio, tried to receive whatever information they could gather from the French and even German news. It was only later that they were able to listen to the BBC. After entering the convent school, I had probably even forgotten we were at war.

The religious order of nuns who taught us came from Alsace (hence the accelerated German lessons), and it is perhaps because of the patriotism of a province so often torn by war and invaded that we were spared any more news of the infamous defeat we had suffered. However, the next year, when I briefly attended a public school in Casablanca, there was a flurry of pseudo-patriotic activities to which we owed some very pleasant free time.

We raised the flag and sang every day, something I am sure goes against the French grain. What did we sing? Ah, I remember it well! What we sang was *Maréchal, nous voilà/ Devant toi, le Sauveur de la France/Nous jurons, nous, tes gars/De servir et de suivre tes pas.* (Marshal, here we stand/ In front of you, the Saviour of France/We swear, we, your lads/To serve and to follow in your footsteps.)

First, note that we said *Tu* to him, perhaps to introduce an element of simplicity, perhaps because his white hair and mustache made him look grandfatherly and lovable. Second, I do not think it was explained to us that the war from which Pétain had "saved" France was not the one we had just lost but the previous one of 1914–1918. Third, the word *gars*, which seemed to apply to girls as well, injected a healthy rural tone, for those times were to be a return to more innocent days. Formerly obsolete expressions such as *terroir,* an old term for land, and "return to the land" now became part of the everyday vocabulary. The *francisque* was seen everywhere, that nasty Frankish ax that mysteriously reappeared to become symbolic of French roots.

After her defeat, France was to become an idyllic country, where some rural ideal was presumably to transform us all into blond and blue-eyed land workers. Squads of young men, *les Compagnons,* adorned with badges and wearing berets, looking like happy operetta bit singers, were officiously present at every one of the many ceremonies that took place at that time.

Even more pernicious was the creation of a *légion,* where former soldiers would be redirected into new channels. In Morocco, this *légion*—in fact formed by the Vichy government under the secret tutelage of the Germans—was initially understood by men such as my father to be the seed for the constitution of an underground French Army, a new army in exile.

These were very difficult times indeed, full of isolation, misinformation, and out-and-out lies. In Morocco, we knew of the scuttling in Toulon of most of the French fleet, historically anti-British and determined not to join the Royal Navy, yet desperately anxious not to fall into the hands of the Germans. We also knew that the RAF had bombed and sunk the few French vessels that had sailed from Toulon and taken refuge in the Algerian port of Mers-el-Kébir, and much resentment and hostility had resulted.

We heard that a French officer by the name of de Gaulle, of whom we knew very little about at the time, not even that he was a military strategist and expert in tank warfare, was making speeches in London, speeches that suddenly gave hope to those who had not abandoned the idea of continuing the fight.

However, other information remained undisclosed that would otherwise have made it easier to do just that: continue the fight. For instance, we knew nothing at first of a certain Général Leclerc, whose real name, de Hauteclocque, was not revealed to protect his family until the end of the war when both names were legally joined. After escaping from a German prisoner camp, he had fled to London, from where he had been sent to reconstitute French troops in Africa.

This ragtag army of some three thousand, made up of Senegalese *tirailleurs,* a small armoured unit, and some pilots from Brittany who had rallied with their elderly planes, started from French Equatorial Africa, marched quickly from Chad to Tripoli, and met with Montgomery's Eighth Army.

Eventually, other soldiers, my father among them, joined the new French forces in England and, what had somewhere along the way become Leclerc's *2ème DB* (French second armoured division) went on to land at Utah Beach under Patton's command, march on to Paris, and finally reach Berchtesgaden. But in those early days, the future still unknown, men sometimes came to blows as they argued about they knew not what.

Snapshot #12 (Tiznit)
Walking through the olive grove with the minaret behind

I am about ten years old in the picture, which must have been taken during my first school holiday. Behind me, the silvery dusty olive trees seem to be moving in the breeze. Farther behind stands the minaret in the direction of the river where women pounded the wash with large pieces of palm bark over flat stones.

To the side, some horizontal branches low to the ground can be seen. They must have been from an argan tree—and missing from the picture, then, were the goats that climbed it and ate the hard dried fruit from which very fine oil was made. In the foreground, hedges made of Barbary figs (a cactus fruit originally from Mexico but that had adapted well to the Moroccan climate), a form of prickly pear, which once the coarse skin was peeled off, showed a rich, pitted orange flesh.

Much later, I asked my mother why we never ate the fruit greatly enjoyed by Moroccans. I saw them in Vancouver and was almost tempted to buy and finally taste one, but old, unfounded distastes held fast. My mother, who was then more than ninety years old, did not remember, or perhaps never knew why we did not eat the fruit. We just did not in those days, she said lamely, perhaps thinking I was blaming her in some way for our lack of insight or dietary open-mindedness.

She took me every day on what seemed like endless walks right after lunch when everything dozed off in the shimmering heat. Although I usually hated these walks, I did not mind too much the one through the olive grove. It was cooler than the one that took us outside the ramparts, past the vast dump where sentinels—piles of human excrement baked silvery gray by the sun—stood guard, and into the stones of the *hammada,* a rocky desertic plain that disappeared into the distance.

There was no shade anywhere on most of these walks, and like mad dogs and Englishmen, she and I marched on under the blazing sun. Sometimes Madame Doria came with us, and it was even more dreadful. Oblivious to the heat and my boredom, the two of them talked and walked on. I too marched on, but to an internal whine, the faint echo of their conversation.

Yet another of my mother's favourite walks

One day, my mother and I met a young boy mounted on a donkey. The sight was commonplace enough of those four delicate legs hurrying below the overstuffed *chouari,* the huge double basket hanging on either side of donkeys, usually surmounted by a man or a boy.

Commonplace also were the boy's actions. Clicking his tongue, he rhythmically poked the little animal, trotting with such grace, with a sharpened stick used for prodding donkeys into the same open sore, either high on the shoulder or on the hip, neither of which the animal could lick.

I would like to mention in passing—and this is as good a time as any to do so—that as early as 1923, a British woman had founded the Society for the Protection of Animals in North Africa, and my dream to have one day a pampered atonement donkey fed on green grass has been realized by yet another Englishwoman at the Donkey Sanctuary in Sidmouth.

But to go back to that small incident in Morocco. My mother, who also had a soft spot for donkeys, reprimanded the boy. Instead of pressing on as such boys usually did, no doubt to inflict a particularly vicious and resentful series of jabs once out of sight, this time he spat at her and insulted her.

My mother, relating the incident, maintained that the boy's newfound rebellious attitude was a result of Marshall Pétain's reiterated message on the radio that France-Had-Lost-the-War. My mother would then imitate the Arabs' presumed reaction to the message. Aha, they would sneer, so *They* have lost the war, so *They* are not so smart or strong after all, and we can do what we want. Her comments made perfectly good sense to me, and perhaps from then stems my taste for facile and clear-cut politics.

Actually, she had been, unwittingly, quite right in her judgment. It was generally accepted for a long time that the fall of the French colonial empire started with the fall of Dién Bién Phu in May 1954, with the crushing by General Vo Nguyen Giap of the French forces (an army composed mostly of the Foreign Legion and colonial troops) at the Laos-China border. This French defeat, the first major, bloody, and conclusive one suffered by a colonial power, was greeted with great pride everywhere in Asia and Africa, and marked the beginning of the momentous process of European decolonization.

However, many Francophone African writers and thinkers, whose compatriots were part of the Moroccan or Senegalese troops at the front (the famed *tirailleurs* so feared by the enemy) and saw at firsthand the debacle of the French army in 1940, define as the beginning of the end of the colonial empire the French defeat and the Vichy government's shameful and reiterated acknowledgment of it.

Notes from Elsewhere

Snapshot #13 (Oujda)
The Road to the Cemetery

The photograph was taken from the living room window of the apartment we were renting in Oujda after leaving Tiznit. My father stayed at the mine in Jerada, nearby in the Rif Mountain, and my mother and I lived in Oujda where I attended school, and where he joined us for the weekend. The window looked down on a wide avenue lined with trees. We would not stay in that apartment very long, because my father soon had to leave for Taza where my mother joined him, and I stayed in Oujda to complete the year in a boarding school.

The apartment was empty when we moved in, save for a few cardboard boxes of miscellaneous items left by previous occupants. One of the boxes contained several volumes by Leslie Charteris and I was introduced to the Saint. It was a revelation! Such nonchalance, such casual elegance in the performance of dangerous tasks, such devil-may-care attitude to life absolutely charmed me. He also had a girlfriend named, I believe, Patricia or Pamela, who was also very witty and fond of wide leather belts that showed off her slender waist.

He was the third man I fell in love with (somewhere in my personal mythology stands the Romantic Hero—a composite of Zorro, the Saint, and the German *légionnaire*—who embodies what I then assumed to be the virile virtues of courage, intelligence, grace, and kindness, unaware that women could also possess them).

I was around eleven and I suspected my mother would not have approved of such sophisticated readings, so I read in secret, always fearful of being discovered, and I can't remember more delicious afternoons than these.

There were other secrets around as well. My mother had a Spanish or Portuguese cleaner who came two or three days a week. The woman was not young, and we knew she had several children. One day, in the middle of a violent storm, my mother stepped out on the kitchen balcony to secure the shutters and saw on the very small backstairs landing three children, soaked to the skin and terrified at having been discovered. She ushered them in, outraged at finding out that the children had come each time with their mother, only to remain hidden the whole morning outside the kitchen door.

Thereafter, the children came indoors and sat in the small kitchen with the gloom and reproach they tacitly inflicted on our household. Once they came during a weekend when we had been visiting my father at the mine and the children had played in the bathroom, turned on the tap, and flooded both our apartment and the one below. Could their mother have been fired after that? Maybe, and then, maybe not. I would not have been told. My mother soon after left for Taza, anyway.

It had not been a very successful school year since it was interrupted by a typhus epidemic that killed one of the girls at school. We had all lined up and held a flower in our hand to drop into the grave where her small coffin had been lowered. All it meant to most of us who did not know the young girl was that the school would close and we were quite happy about that. Afterwards, my mother and I stayed home as much as possible in that apartment that overlooked the road to the native cemetery.

All day long, as the epidemic worsened, we saw grimly chanting processions following bodies covered with a white cotton cloth, resting on a small platform carried on the shoulders of four men. On and on they went, more numerous all the time. Then the numbers started to diminish a little and one day, we realized they had stopped. I was getting a little bored by then and was quite happy to be going back to school. It was exactly as if nothing had happened.

Another memory I have of Oujda, more fleeting, is that of an afternoon party among women, the women whose Belgian or French engineer husbands worked at the mine, away in the mountain. I was a quiet child, almost silent, and went by unnoticed, a simple appendage to my mother when there was nowhere else to leave me. Why do I never recall other children attending such parties? Possibly because there were none.

That particular afternoon, a young bride, a Belgian girl of no more than nineteen and recently introduced, was playing hostess. Quite beautiful and polished in an old-fashioned way (black chignon, white skin, pearls, lace collar), she had the social and artistic skills of the bourgeoisie and the convent-reared, skills that none of the women present very likely had.

With simplicity, as it would perhaps have been expected of her in her provincial Belgian town, she offered to sing. She sat at her piano, and to compound the offence, sang *Le Temps des Cerises,* a demure, dated choice that showed how little she understood the society in which she had landed. She must have been competent, if not talented—I would not know—but the poor girl had not realized how such a display of good manners would be interpreted. There was no doubt in the women's mind that she had been pretentious and trying to show them up with her attempt at offering a more civilized alternative to local gossip, the usual fare of such tea parties.

I was sitting behind two middle aged women (they all seemed middle aged to me); one whispered to the other, *"Vous avez vu comme son cou est crasseux?"* There was a pale, silvery sheen, a gentle patina on the girl's long neck. True her neck was probably *sale* (dirty), but why condemn her even more by using the word *crasseux* (filthy)? I think the bride, rumoured to be homesick, left Oujda before we did ourselves a few months later.

Snapshot #14 (Taza)
The picture shows an apparently restive horse, tightly held by an anxious-looking young man in front of my father's office. There are some trees in the background, as the office gives out on the city's main square.

It was soon afterwards that the horse disappeared. At least, that was how it was put to me. He was a nasty brute, impossible to handle, and had seriously injured a groom, perhaps even the young man in the picture although, since the grooms changed all the time, it may have been another one. Thereafter, my father rode to the mine on a motorcycle. Once, I rode behind him and it was pure heaven.

Taza is located in a basin sitting tight at the convergence of Morocco's three mountains: the Rif, the Middle Atlas, and the High Atlas. The heat gathers there, giving no respite, and summer nights were so hot that it often required several cool showers to permit a little sleep. I only spent one summer holiday there but bore the worst of the heat. There was not much to do except walk to the swimming pool, a most modern affair built on a hot spring a few kilometers out of town. A Swiss refugee and former European diving champion taught the French youngsters.

No Arabs were to be seen, except those tending the grounds. Even if their hard working life had given them enough leisure to practice such a sport, mixed bathing would have been unthinkable. Moreover, the sight of half-naked European women would hardly have appealed to their sense of esthetics, the fashion already being for women to be thin and tanned, very different from the enchanting white plumpness of the *houris* all good Muslims see as the ideal picture of femininity.

❦ ❦ ❦

It took my mother several years to live down the mortification of the event I am about to relate. The local *caïd* (chief) had invited my parents to dinner. Upon arrival, they were immediately received into the large hall where the *caïd* greeted them with beaming expressions of welcome and bade them sit down among the bulging silk cushions and thick carpets.

A few elderly men soon arrived. They conversed and noisily sipped scalding and very sweet mint tea in little glasses, as custom required. No women attended, as was also the custom, although some female whispering could be heard behind the draperies. The conversation went on at some length, the odd courteous remark addressed to my mother and translated through my father (although, no doubt, most of them spoke or understood French). They waited a long time, seemingly longer than politeness required the preliminary conversation to last.

Finally, a kettle of water to rinse their hands was brought in and soon after the meal was served. Although I was not told exactly what they ate, it must have included the usual delicacies, for Moroccan cuisine is very fine indeed. Succulent mutton *mechoui* cooked in a clay oven and dripping with glorious golden fat; *tagines,* the meat dishes sometimes accompanied by unexpected vegetables and fruit, such as artichokes or prunes; the finest *pastillas* of tender pigeons, subtly seasoned; and always, couscous, delicately eaten with two fingers and the thumb of the right hand, with its accompaniment of poultry, stewed vegetables, raisins, and chickpeas. There would have been *cornes de gazelle* for dessert, shaped like the dainty horns of the small desert gazelles and covered with almond and honey. The large quantity of food left over would then go to the women and children, and then the servants of the household, as custom dictated.

After the last belches had been offered as signs of appreciation and the last *bislamma* had been exchanged, my parents went home. My mother, who had remained uncomfortable throughout the evening, checked my father's agenda and discovered that the invitation had been for the following evening.

One does not apologize in such cases, since an apology would indicate that the guests had noticed something not being quite right with the meal. One must continue to pretend, as had the hosts, that everything had occurred as planned. My father took it very much in stride, accustomed to the Muslim sense of decorum through his many years spent in the Middle East and North Africa.

But for my mother, whose allegiance was sternly to the French bourgeoisie and its lack of flexibility, the incident took on the proportions of a nightmarish impropriety, a grotesque faux pas she never forgave him.

For their host, who knows? Maybe the event was retold as a good joke at my father's expense, maybe it was experienced as yet another evidence of the foreigners' uncouthness and crass behaviour, or maybe it was simply dismissed as an error not worth thinking twice about since it had been smoothed over successfully.

Snapshot #15 (Casablanca)
Place du Maréchal Lyautey
I stand in front of some flowerbed, obviously hating having my picture taken, and not looking particularly pleasant.

I have breasts, which embarrasses me, and all the uncertainty of puberty. By the following year, things will have changed completely. Having for the first time spent a second year in the same school, I will have made friends and indulged many times in the helpless and glorious bouts of adolescent laughter.

I was about thirteen when I came back to Casablanca. The boarding school was full and I stayed with a family of three women, the single male (their husband, brother, and son) being a prisoner of war somewhere in Germany. A few months later, my mother joined me and rented an apartment for the two of us; my father had by then left for England and enlisted with Leclerc's second armoured division. We stayed a long time without any news from him.

It was a very long way to the *Lycée de Jeunes Filles,* and since I was always a little late, the streets were usually deserted by the time I was rushing through them. Once, a man on a bicycle appeared from a side street, stopped by the curb, pulled out a notebook from his pocket, and signaled for me to approach. I was so convinced that he would be showing me an address and asking for directions that it took me a little while to understand what he was showing me.

The picture was of a man standing up and a woman kneeling in front of him. Judging from the man's hair, parted in the middle and shiny with brilliantine or Macassar oil, his thick mustache, his tight coat jacket, and the woman's floppy chignon, plump white shoulders, and stays, the postcard dated from around the Great War.

Those details, obviously, only came back to me later; all I saw at the time was something unthinkable. It is probably hard to believe nowadays that a young teenager would have been so innocent and caught unaware. Yet perhaps not so innocent after all, since I immediately guessed what he was actually showing me, certainly not the details but the essence of it, and it was enough to trouble me deeply, and enrage me as well for having been tricked and having my good intentions of being of help to him betrayed in such a crass manner.

When I was much younger in Tiznit and trailing behind my mother on her walks, I had once or twice been taunted by small boys guarding their fathers' goats. Making sucking wet sounds with their tongue and the inside of their lower lip, they would repeatedly poke their middle finger into the hole made by the thumb and index finger of the other hand. They would call, laughing and sneering, *nick-nick.* I am not sure what I understood, but I did understand enough to be angry at my helplessness in making them stop. I also understood enough never to mention these gestures to anyone.

The photograph in front of the flowerbed was very likely taken at the time of the American landing in Morocco. When guns fired into the harbour of Casablanca, so skillfully as to inflict almost no damage, there was mostly great rejoicing, and a banner proclaiming "Well Come" was stretched across our street. Americans established camps and immediately started distributing chewing gum and nylons. Feeling too old for the former and being too young for the latter, I missed out a little on the general sense of bounty.

These people seemed alien, and the fact that there were blacks among them came as an astonishing discovery. Whether black or white, their language held no resemblance to the English we were studying in school, but even if we could not understand them, they injected an extraordinary element of youth, energy, and wealth into a tired population.

Although I seem to recall people being cranky and complaining a lot about various annoyances since the French defeat, there must also have been a sentiment that our lives had been extraordinarily easy in comparison to whatever else was ravaging Europe, the true extent of which we only found out afterwards. We also felt powerless, and the arrival of the Americans revitalized us.

To provide some context to how we had until then lived the war, I should explain that since Morocco was not a French colony but a protectorate, it had not been subjected to German occupation. Instead, there had been an Armistice Commission in some evidence, which had been actively resented even if its members had been "correct" (a favourite expression at the time, by which the French meant that the Germans minded their manners).

A concentration camp, which bore no resemblance whatsoever with what we later learned other concentration camps to have been, was also run for inimical aliens (a few Britons living in Morocco at the time) and European Jews, mostly French, who had been running successful businesses—among whom, a friend of my parents.

Local Jews apparently remained undisturbed. Casablanca contained a large *mellah*, (the Jewish quarter in Moroccan cities), and Jews, either Berber Jews established since ancient times and living mostly in the interior of the country or descendants from Spanish Jews, constituted a substantial population in Morocco.

I looked at two or three more photographs, feeling more and more hesitant all the time. The snapshots did not reveal much, really: just some apparently anonymous walls, a few people long gone from our lives, all shadows of a past only my mother and I (with all the distortions of childhood) still remember. She has already forgotten some of the past and since, as an only child, I have no one else with whom to share and reminisce, most of the memories are dying with me. None of this is probably worth preserving.

Although we lived in several Moroccan towns, Tiznit remains the anchor of our memories. Edmée Doria wrote that the four years she spent in Tiznit before the war were her happiest. For my mother, Tiznit also represented the best part of her life. My father certainly did some of his most productive work there. The bitter winter of the 1944 campaign in France robbed him of his health and he was a changed man after that, but there must still be a bridge or two in southern Morocco where his initials are scratched in the concrete arch to show that he had passed that way.

Succession of bridges over the Oued Draa

For me, it held all the sounds, smells, anxieties, and daydreams of childhood. To this day, one part of my pluralistic notion of home includes the dry smell of scrub, the sight of the *bled* and perched goats munching on the fruit of the argan trees, all of which I left in 1946.

Chapter Five

Morocco Revisited 1998

Ne désire jamais, Nathanaël, regoûter les eaux du passé.
Never wish, Nathanaël, to drink again from the waters of the past.

—André Gide, *Les Nourritures Terrestres*

In 1998, I finally went back to Morocco, fifty-two years and one month after leaving it. The trip was my husband's idea. On my own, and by instinct, I would never have gone back. My mother, who had several opportunities to return as a tourist, never did either.

Naturally, this was not the same country I had left. From a French protectorate, it had become once more an independent nation, a kingdom, since Hassan II had abandoned the title of sultan. The currency was no longer the *franc* but the *dirham*. The map had also changed, as the country's very borders had expanded to reflect Morocco's desire to dominate the western part of the Sahara after the Green March of 1975, and the cities I had known as Mogador and Mazagan had been respectively renamed Essaouira and El Jadida.

Yet, I could look at the new map and feel pangs of recognition. It was like a barebones travelogue of childhood memories as I traced on the new map the familiar routes between Tiznit and Casablanca or Marrakesh, or the one to Oujda and the Algerian border, now closed.

Each stop on these routes meant something to me. In Taroudant, my parents bought the Berber carpet that eventually followed me to Canada, and I was given at the factory a thick carpet sample, barely a square foot, which I had used as a cushion in my little cardboard house at the foot of the garden. In Marrakesh, what I remembered was the magnificent medlar tree in the garden of family friends with whom I once spent a week's holiday. The list could go on but would only be meaningful to me.

John and I landed at the Casablanca airport on October 17, 1998. My husband was full of curiosity, this being his first visit to a Muslim country (and he has enough English blood in him to make him hold his breath at the thought of dromedaries swaying through the desert), and I was full of hope and apprehension, Casablanca and Tiznit being both on my hit list of potential disappointments.

Casablanca

Casa, as she is usually known, the largest city and port of Morocco, is an important and modern commercial centre and may probably disappoint those in search of the exotic. But her past belies her matter-of-fact appearance.

The city of Anfa (now a suburb of Casa) had been a Berber capital and stronghold until the Almohads conquered her in the twelfth century. However, the inhabitants soon reasserted their independent and enterprising spirit and turned very successfully to piracy. The Portuguese did not take too kindly to these activities and attacked the city on several occasions. Finally, deciding to deal with it once and for all, they stormed the territory, occupied it, fortified it, and renamed it Casa Branca. Unfortunately, the same earthquake that destroyed Lisbon in 1749 also destroyed most of Casa Branca and signaled the end of the Portuguese influence in Morocco.

What was left of the city declined for a while, but the developing European industrial nations were soon looking for new commercial developments in North Africa. Casa Branca happened to be located in a fertile plain that could provide all the grain and wool necessary to those countries and the city, now renamed Casablanca by the Spaniards, became the centre of a brisk trade with Europe.

The early nineteenth century saw some very serious conflicts in the area. Natives and French troops clashed, and in the violence that erupted all over the land, several thousand Jews were massacred in their *mellah*. The Treaty of Fès in 1912 put an end to the struggle and Marshal Lyautey became the first *Résident Général* of the French Protectorate. He immediately set about to develop Casa and make of her the commercial success she has been ever since.

I chatted with our cab driver on the way to the hotel and asked what had become of the two schools I had attended. The Institution Sainte Jeanne d'Arc on Boulevard Moulay Idriss, where I had gone straight from Tiznit, had naturally been renamed and was now an elementary school, and the school I later attended was still the main secondary school for girls. He offered to take us on a tour the following day and I took his card. We thought of calling him in two or three days but, in the meantime, we intended to spend that time walking about the city, as I was hoping to find unchanged what I remembered of Casa.

The *Place du Maréchal Lyautey,* the core of Casa during the French presence there, had become something else, but under what name? I was not even sure where the new *Place des Nations Unies* was in relation to the new *Place Mohammed V* and which one might once have been *Lyautey*. All the names of old boulevards around it had changed and since so many new ones had been built, I had to give up the task of orienting myself, as the map of the city did not raise a flicker of recognition.

It is not surprising that city maps elicited no memory. My knowledge of Casa in the 1940s was not derived from looking at maps, but directly through the pounding of my feet on the boulevards and side streets, and through eyes attuned to familiar sights. I remember vividly the street corner where, to my almost unbearable humiliation, I was "goosed" at the age of fifteen by a passing man in flowing white robes, but even then, I could not have found it on the map.

However, when we went looking for the apartment of my parents' friends and the dress shop they had owned, where the *tout Casa* shopped for cashmere, silk, and linen clothes imported from Paris, we were in luck. In a manner of speaking, actually, for what had been the true centre of sophisticated shopping in Casa had become a very run-down district, with stores cut in half and offering every cheap object or service available in poor cities all across North Africa. I did not even bother to cross the street to peer inside the windows. Yet, the seamstresses in the atelier above the shop had made most of my dresses, and I had fond memories of two of them who had greatly admired my small waist.

These friends' second floor apartment must have been subdivided among several families, judging by the amount of laundry now hanging on the balcony, which seemed partitioned. It used to have large rooms full of soft, yellow leather and dark mahogany furniture endlessly polished by Larbi, the old manservant who looked after them and was always very kind to me. From its wide balcony and large window, light poured onto the copper frame of a painting by Majorelle, who had already started his rise to fame. The late afternoon light reflecting on the metallic frame extended the golden scenery at sunset depicted in the picture. I remember the comments full of admiration and the frame far more than the painting itself.

Only later did I realize how luxurious it had all been, but it really did not mean very much to me, either then or now. The sight of its decadence would have affected my mother far more than it did me. Obviously, business had shifted to other parts of town, and the building showed its age. But it was a natural process and there was really nothing to regret. Even on the second day, I would already have found it difficult to deny that the past only existed in my memory with little substantiation from the present.

We walked nearby along a large street covered with arcades, which had also been a place central to the life of Casa. There were enough decorative tiles remaining on the pillars that one could still guess at its former elegance, but everything was in very poor shape. Naturally, I recognized nothing until, in a small run-down alley opening into the arcades, I saw the cinema where I had watched the Zorro movies that had entranced me so much that I would even forget to scratch my fleabites (the walls were originally covered with grass matting, which harboured permanent colonies and generations of relentless fleas).

Notes from Elsewhere

The cinema was closed. In fact, the whole alley seemed more or less condemned, with detritus piling up against its walls, but its last function had indeed been that of a movie theatre, since we could see the glass showcases now empty, where pictures of movie stars and film posters had been displayed. Instead of depressing me as most of the other sights had done, this one filled me with pleasure, because I certainly had not expected to see it again, and would not even have thought of looking for it.

It was one of the few exceptions to what I had started to realize, that nothing corresponded anymore to memories of my childhood, that I was now a tourist, and that I might as well accept it. Until we went to Tiznit, of course, where everything would be different.

The following day was a Friday, the Muslim day of rest, and we walked and walked, somewhat aimlessly. By early evening, we decided to have dinner at the restaurant where our breakfast croissants had been deliciously buttery. The building stood across a large boulevard, and there was a thick traffic of cars, buses, and trucks to contend with, so we looked for an appropriate pedestrian crossing.

We suddenly realized that we could barely see anything on the road below a foot or two off the ground. My asthma had already alerted me that the pollution was quite severe, but even John was amazed to see to what extent the unregulated gasoline emissions coming out of so many vehicles had engulfed everything in a thick cloud, made all the more visible by the neon lights. We did not cross the street, but turned away from the main arteries and found instead an indifferent little eatery. The following day we took the train to Fès.

Fès

A proverb states that "Fès is the key to Morocco," and it is said that successive dynasties first had to ensure the city's acceptance in order to rule the rest of the country.

Fès has been since the thirteenth century one of the four imperial cities of Morocco (Rabat, Marrakesh, and Meknès being the others). Idris II of the Idrisid dynasty founded her in 789. By the ninth century, her population was substantially boosted by the arrival of eight hundred families fleeing Córdova and two thousand families fleeing a rebellion in the Tunisian city of Kairouan; these newcomers gave a distinctive Arab character to Fès. Other groups continued to arrive, Muslims from all across North Africa, the Middle East, as well as the Moriscos of Granada taking refuge from the Spanish Reconquest.

After Marrakesh was forced to relinquish the position of the capital of Morocco, Fès took over that function. It had long been the country's intellectual and artistic centre. Her university, Quaraouiyine, is the oldest running university in the world. Famous for its library and its *madrassah*, it is still one of the leading spiritual and educational centres in Islam.

With the arrival of the French, who sensed the city's rebellious nature, Fès was replaced by Rabat as the capital, but the city retained to this day her intellectual, religious, and scholarly predominance. She regularly hosts the Festival of Sufi Culture, attended by people of all faiths and all nationalities, a festival dedicated to poetry, music, and philosophy in the best Sufi tradition of seeking communion with God.

Fès is also famous for the quality of her artisans. It is known that 124 ceramist shops existed by the thirteenth century, and Leo Africanus, in the sixteenth, described with admiration the ancient tradition of their work. The tradition has endured and Morocco's tiles are still among the best. The same is true of her other artisans, such as silversmiths, copper workers, weavers, the all-important guild of tanners (which already numbered one hundred in the thirteenth century), dyers, and the associated trades of leather workers and makers of saddles, babouches, and the ornate pouches worn by men.

Most still reside in the ancestral *medina* (the name refers to the holy city where Muhammad gathered his disciples at the beginning of Islam, and now designates the historic part of all Muslim towns).

Great concern has been expressed for some time about the preservation and renovation of this ancient place, now declared a World Heritage Site by UNESCO.

The late king, Hassan II, had already sent a message to the world to help save the dilapidated houses of the old *medina,* and it is one of the priorities of the current government to ensure their preservation and rehabilitation.

Fès also had the characteristic in 1998 that street signs were only in Arabic. Some cities, more attuned to touristic needs and perhaps having had in the past closer dealings with the French, had bilingual signs. Not so in Fès, and we spent an inordinate amount of time getting lost—it is after all also known as the City of the Thousand Alleys.

After dropping off our bags at the hotel, we went to the souks. The ones in Fès are well known for their timelessness. It is often said that nothing has changed since the Middle Ages *(our* Middle Ages, that is, a European concept), and this is probably true. It is also true that many *Fassis* look somewhat different from other people in Morocco. Some are even reputed to have blue eyes.

I must admit to disliking many things about souks, in particular butchered animal parts, live chickens strung up together by their feet and always held upside down, small donkeys straining under loads sometimes large enough to fill the whole width of narrow alleys, none of which would have bothered me in the least in my childhood.

What I also disliked was the pressure of people trying to sell us something, anything. Soon it became impossible to simply look at an object and ask its price. The response, since it was then implied that we were interested in buying it, was to be immediately urged to name our own price. We would then be expected to haggle, a transaction during which the fate of the seller's children would hang on our offer, his mother's medical treatment would depend on our being sensible about the price quoted, etc., or so it was in my childhood.

It is possible that people are nowadays in too much of a hurry to engage in full-fledged negotiations. After awhile, the tedium is such for those disinclined to play the game that they avoid touching and even looking at anything with more than a passing glance.

Now for the other side. It is part of the Arab culture that once initiated, a deal must be concluded (this is perhaps why Arabs are such superb debaters). Tourists should understand that they may look and admire but must not ask the price unless they intend to engage in a proper exchange of offers and counteroffers, eventually leading to a purchase in which both parties will find satisfaction. Shopping in an Arab souk requires diplomacy, patience, artistry, and above all, a clear intent.

Our Western process of showing what is taken as interest, asking the price, then debating, most often internally, whether the request is justified and whether we can afford to meet it is deeply antithetic to the serious, elaborate, formalized, conclusive exchange expected by Arabs. When halfhearted discussions result in aborted sales, Arabs see the entire transaction as an insulting waste of time and a lack of respect for customs.

After years of witnessing tourists ask for a price, declare, "No, it's too expensive," turn away, and walk on despite being urged to engage in a sensible discussion, Arab sellers still pretend to deeply resent this incomprehensible behaviour, as if experiencing it for the first time. The least offensive response may be to say, when solicited, that one is only looking *"pour le plaisir des yeux,"* (to give pleasure to the eyes), perhaps an acceptable formula recognizing craftsmanship but denying any interest in a purchase. Or perhaps not, since the same sentence is sometimes used by these very shopkeepers as an initial step towards further negotiation.

Some bronchial disorder, to which I am predisposed and that had not improved by breathing the air of Casa, had started once more, and I had to stay in my room wheezing and coughing for the rest of the day. We arranged with the hotel concierge to find a sensible English-speaking guide to take John around the souks, particularly the souk of the leather dyers and tanners, which were reputedly quite a sight (and a stench as well), while I sunk into a despondent sleep. In a wifely way, my last words to him were, "Don't buy anything without me!"

He was apparently well served by his guide, enjoyed every sight and smell (I am thinking here of the spices) of his visit, and did not buy anything—although, pressed by the guide, John brought back a piece of cloth for my approval. I did not approve and the guide's nose was apparently out of joint since, by accepting to show me the fabric, John had indicated some potential commitment on our part.

After I recovered enough to accompany my husband, we wanted to visit some of the museums recommended by our guidebook, and found ourselves searching for Dar Batha, which we knew to be near Bab Bou Jeloud, the entrance to Fès el-Bali, the original *medina*. With no help from street signs and having gone around its approximate location for some time, I decided to ask someone for directions. I chose an official-looking building, assuming that someone inside would speak French, and I spotted a man in Western dress and carrying a briefcase coming out of it. I walked towards him and immediately noticed how uneasy he was about my approach. I looked back and saw that John had gone to drop off something in a garbage bin, leaving me apparently alone. So I started my sentence with, "Excuse me, Monsieur, my husband (and I pointed to John doing his civic duty in the background) and I are looking for …"

Everything went swimmingly after that. The man had never been to Dar Batha but decided he would find it for us. We piled in his small van and drove around, within the same two blocks it seemed, still unable to find it until some passerby pointed him in the right direction. He was most pleasant—with the type of pleasantness that in the olden days would probably have secured an invitation to have tea at his house—and upon parting, gave us his card.

I made sure to send him a postcard from Vancouver to thank him again for his help and recommended Dar Batha to him in the most flattering terms. I felt sure that had I been alone, he would have politely informed me that he did not know where Dar Batha was and left it at that, not even offering to enquire further on my behalf.

My postcard to him was truthful. Dar Batha was a delightful little museum with beautiful examples of the most intricate woodcarvings and some of the finest blue pottery seen in this part of the country. The only problem was finding it.

Rabat

Like many Moroccan cities, Rabat has enjoyed enormous ups and suffered equally enormous downs. From a small ancient settlement occupied by the Romans, to a fortress built in the twelfth century by the Almohads as a naval base from which to attack Spain, to a decimated town following political shifts in the sixteenth century, to a revitalized city with the arrival of the Moriscos fleeing Spain in the early seventeenth century, Rabat has had many faces and many functions.

Finally, in the twentieth century, thanks in part to the French Protectorate (1912–1956), she became the administrative capital of the country, a decision that was upheld by Mohammed V after Morocco regained her independence.

We took the train in Fès on our way to Rabat, where we intended to see the Mausoleum of Mohammed V, the white onyx tomb surrounded by old men reading the Koran, which could be visited silently and respectfully, even by non-Muslims, from the gallery overlooking it. Situated opposite another landmark, the Hassan Tower on the Yacoub al-Mansour, the mausoleum holds not only the tomb of Mohammed V but also those of his two sons, the late king Hassan II and his brother, prince Abdallah.

In our train compartment was a woman on her way to Casa, to whom we introduced ourselves. She was a very well to do Jewish woman, who shared her time among Fès, Paris, and Casablanca, and was not shy about expressing her views on many subjects, particularly the poverty of the land and the laziness of servants, of whom she appeared to have many. She was overtly racist and happened to be elitist as well, being clearly astonished when, speaking of our respective children, I mentioned that one of our daughters, now in her thirties and with a degree in criminology, had just gone back to university to train as a teacher, an elementary school teacher to boot. "A teacher?" the woman said, barely believing her ears that one should actually choose such a lowly profession when one had the choice of doing anything else.

She revealed that she, too, had been a teacher for a short while, and simply could not wait to do something else that would reward her with more money and prestige. So she had started a business, had married very well, and now travelled among her houses, leaving lazy servants in charge when she was away, and resenting it.

I only mention her because she brought to me an astonishing realization, perhaps one of my greatest revelations on this journey in fact—I did not know how to say "thank you" in Arabic. I had to ask her. After spending sixteen years in North Africa, fourteen of which in this very country, still remembering how to go through the polite forms of greeting and a number of words and expressions, I realized that I had probably never said thank you, at least in Arabic. *Shokran.* Thank you is *shokran,* a word to remember and use frequently.

We said our farewells as she was continuing towards Casa and we left the train in Rabat. Every city has her mood, and Rabat revealed at once her orderliness. She was not modernly bustling like Casa, austere and teeming like Fès, or as we found later, lush like Marrakesh, down-to-earth like Essaouira, or touristic like Agadir. She seemed orderly and spacious, as was appropriate to a capital city, a function she retains under the present monarch, King Mohammed VI.

We stopped at the France Hotel in the Medina, described in our guidebook as "cheap," but it was perfectly adequate and even had banana trees in the patio. In fact, we had always been quite satisfied with our accommodations, which were usually on the modest side. Our main problem was that, old-fashioned and elderly Canadians that we were, we always wanted to dine at an ungodly early hour, usually opening the restaurant and often dining in an empty room.

Marrakesh
An imperial city founded in 1062, among the oldest in the western part of the Islamic world, Marrakesh was the capital of Morocco during the rule of two dynasties, the Almoravids, and the Almohads. At the time, Youssef Ibn Tachfine, her founder, reigned over an Almoravid kingdom extending from northern Spain to Senegal (and for those also interested in Spanish history, he is noteworthy for having been defeated in battle by *El Cid Campeador*).

He is, however, far more noteworthy for having built the extraordinary irrigation system, the *khettarats,* underground canals similar to those of ancient Mesopotamia, that brought water from the foot of the Atlas Mountains to Marrakesh. The arid land then became livable, sustaining a large and prosperous city, and would eventually become the site of some of the most beautiful gardens in Morocco.

The next dynasty, the Almohads, promptly destroyed much of what the Almoravids had built—creating from the ruins brought by that destruction the Palace of Stones, which actually resembles a cemetery full of large tombstones. However, one of their main accomplishments was to build the Koutoubia, the imposing mosque still standing as one of the symbols of Marrakesh. Both dynasties had strong connections to Spain and the Koutoubia was obviously inspired by the mosque in Córdova.

Their second accomplishment was to improve significantly the *khettarats* system. The canals, the large reservoirs also built at the same time, and the gardens that were soon created, strengthened Marrakesh in her position of capital of the country and continue to make of her a uniquely attractive city. One of the largest reservoirs, the Menara, is at the centre of ninety hectares planted with olive trees. It is often either unknown or overlooked that two thirds of Marrakesh are devoted to historical gardens.

With the arrival of yet another dynasty, the Merinids of Berber origin, Marrakesh lost to Fès her status of capital city. However, with *La Reconquista*, by which Spain finally ended the Arab domination in Iberia in the sixteenth century, many Arabs returned to Morocco, and those who found their way to Marrakesh revitalized the city to the point that she became once more the capital.

I do not wish to bore readers with too much information on this complicated and fascinating country, or too many details about the history of this city, so I will only mention two more facts about one of her most interesting rulers. Sultan Sidi Mohammed ben Abdallah, Mohammed III, who reigned at the end of the eighteenth century, gave each of his four sons a magnificent garden as a wedding present.

One son, Moulay Mamoun, was given the garden where was later built La Mamounia, one of the most luxurious hotels in the world. Salam Garden, given to another son, Moulay Abdelsalam, reputed to have been a poet and a philosopher, has since also become renowned as a "cyber park," where visitors are connected electronically to the rest of the world and where world-class art exhibitions are routinely held. The other two sons' gardens, while not as well known, still flourish and are part of the wealth of the city.

Another unusual fact about Mohammed III is that he was the first foreign ruler to recognize as an independent nation the United States of America in 1777.

Eventually, like everyone else, we ended up in Djemaa el Fna, the tourist souk par excellence. Some writer claimed that piles of false teeth could be found there. I had no doubt anything could be found in Djemaa el Fna, which had never been one of my favourite places. What could be found mostly was junk of all sorts. There were also the usual people: the black performers (the *gnouas,*) the water sellers, the storytellers, the snake charmers, the gawkers, the tourists snapping photographs.

I should also mention that Djemaa el Fna, the centre of what is deemed an essentially oral and popular culture, sits in the shadow of the Koutoubia and its extensive and scholarly library famous throughout Islam.

Djemaa el Fna probably has its good and its bad days, and John was disappointed, so we soon left and found nearby a pleasant little café, dark after the blinding sun outside and very cool, with a handful of men smoking and noisily drinking mint tea out of small glasses.

We walked endlessly in Marrakesh, the thousand-year-old Red City with her pink ramparts pierced by eighteen gates (*bab*). There, John saw, just outside the ramparts, his first dromedaries. Ungainly though the animals were, it was love at first sight. Of course, he had seen them numerous times on film and in zoos as well, but there, in the flesh, profiled against the red earth of the ramparts, a palm tree close by, it was the real thing at last. And they did not disappoint, as real things so often do.

John's first sight of dromedaries in Marrakesh

Finally, we went to visit La Mamounia (mostly to see the garden, which did not disappoint either). La Mamounia Hotel, one of a handful of superior palaces in the world, opened in 1923. Always in search of improvement, it has undergone four total renovations since then. We were not to see the latest one, in 2006, which cost 120 million euros and did away with the previous art deco look of the earlier decor, the one we saw.

We decided afterwards to have a very modest meal on one of the terraces. The chicken sandwich we ordered was horribly overpriced, which we had expected, but what we did not expect was how dry and tasteless it would be. The people around us, it must be admitted, were of an infinitely grander type than we were, since for some reason we always look slightly rumpled (even at home in our usual habitat), and perhaps better service and better meals were available to them.

But La Mamounia, which I remembered from childhood in the 1930s as a lovely, luxurious palace, with an allure worthy of the *Thousand and One Nights*, seemed to have become just an overpriced luxury hotel. It rated more stars than any other hotel in Morocco, and catered to rich tourists whose manners, from what we could see, were not always worthy of the surroundings. But perhaps one should not judge too rashly based on a very short visit.

After all, Winston Churchill used to reside there for months at a time and no fewer than five American presidents have been its guests. Not to mention the endless succession of glitterati, starlets, and rock stars whose manners, we all know, leave nothing to be desired.

We had decided to visit the painter Majorelle's famous garden, and started walking in, presumably, the right direction. The garden had seemed fairly close on the city map, but more than an hour later, we were still walking, having by then lost all sense of direction. We asked, but nobody had heard of it. The last person we asked looked at us as if we were seeking directions to the moon. We said thank you just the same and raised our eyes to see, amazingly, the very entrance to the *Jardin Majorelle*, in front of which we had been standing during that conversation. Perhaps they only knew it as *Bou Saf,* its other name, which I found out afterwards.

Majorelle bought the house when he first arrived in Marrakesh in 1919. Suffering from tuberculosis, he had been seeking a dry climate, and as an artist, he had been drawn to the beauty of the land. He was an avid gardener as well, his second passion after painting, and a dedicated collector of exotic plants.

His father was a good friend of Marshal Lyautey who, it is said, used his connections with the French Navy to ensure that war ships cruising in exotic places would bring back choice specimens for Majorelle. It is also said that he had occasionally exchanged one of his paintings for a rare and perhaps unknown cactus. Proud of his garden and wanting to share its beauty, he had opened it to the public in the 1950s.

After Majorelle's death in 1962, the house and the garden were more or less abandoned until, eighteen years later, threatened by urban development, they were saved *in extremis* by the couturier Yves Saint Laurent and his friend Pierre Bergé. The garden was resurrected and the artist's studio then became a small museum devoted to Moroccan arts and crafts. Yves Saint Laurent was buried there in 2008 and Pierre Bergé is now a discreet occupant of the house, while the garden and the museum are once more flourishing and visited by thousands of tourists.

The garden was as beautiful as we had expected it to be, and the museum, with its intimate look (it is, after all, not a very large place), permitted a close view of the artifacts on show. It had been well worth a visit, despite the long and sweaty walk to get there, which, of course, we had to repeat on the way back.

The Bus from Marrakesh to Agadir

We either had misread the schedule or just missed the previous bus, so we had to wait for quite some time at the station. We sat on a hard bench surrounded by families with bundles at their feet, or the old-fashioned cardboard suitcases I had not seen for decades.

A young boy, six- or seven-years-old, in poor clothes and a smudge on his cheek was there too, looking alert and curious. A server holding a tray with leftover food crossed the waiting room, and when the boy asked, the server gave him a good chunk of bread, which the boy wolfed down. Boys of that age always seem hungry, but this one appeared hungrier than most.

He came and sat beside us, while everybody else had given us a wide berth. We had only two bananas with us, so I gave one to John and the other to the boy, who impressed me by saying *shokran* and getting up to put the peel into a garbage bin. He came back to sit beside us, obviously looking for more. We tried to talk a little, but his French being equal to my Arabic, we did not get very far. At one point, I felt his hand, small, and none too clean, trying to sneak into my pocket. I shook my head and quietly said, *"La,"* a rebuke he took quite cheerfully.

He was a charming child, beautiful, and good-natured. A man had been discreetly observing us all the while, and I felt somehow tested in my handling of the boy. Finally, our bus arrived and we got on it, no doubt breaking in so doing all sorts of tacit rules of undetectable etiquette.

Sometime later out in the *bled,* the backcountry, driving across a small bridge spanning a dried up *wadi,* I saw halfway down the embankment a dead donkey. For some reason, it was a shocking sight, and I remembered having seen something similar (perhaps also a burro, perhaps not, but certainly a domestic animal of good size) in Mexico years before. Some unexpected feat of memory—not usually my forte—made me recall a detail I read in a book, which I looked up upon my return.

Gerald Brenan, in *South from Granada,* described a custom of southern Spain, where no one in the village he was visiting "ever killed mules, or donkeys, or cows." Pigs, certainly, were slaughtered, and lambs, and kids, but other domestic animals, when hurt or with broken limbs, were "either thrown down the ravine or tied to a post till they starved to death." Such was the custom as recently as the late 1950s.

The action may seem cruel, but the reason given had to do with a perverted sense of delicacy. It seemed intended to spare some sensitivity on the part of the owners, for "one could not kill animals that had been brought up in the house." This was not merely a metaphor to signify the tameness of the animals, since I remembered that in Tiznit, donkeys and cows did indeed live on the ground floor of the houses, the earth trampled solid under their hooves.

The dry scenery was familiar behind the closed windows of the bus; I knew its smell. In that context, at least, I was home. To John it was probably reminiscent of some arid parts through which our Mexican bus had once driven on the way to Cuzco in the dry season. The vegetation was different, although all probably of the same thorny family.

The bus was comfortable enough and the road in good repair, but the sharp swinging at every turn started churning stomachs after awhile. One of the two young women sitting in front of us started to heave and vomited noisily in her hands and in her friend's lap. I then remembered how it used to happen every time I took the bus to Casablanca on my visit to the dentist. It was somewhat deflating to realize that my feelings of familiarity with the country were more related to the evocation of people vomiting on the bus and to the state of toilets at bus depots than to almost anything else, as they provided a sense of continuity lacking elsewhere.

At one of our stops, always plagued with insistent beggars who barely allowed us to get off the bus, I once more looked for toilets. It was a matter-of-fact and discreet affair, very unlike a similar quest in Mexico where our entire busload had cheered me on, pointing in the right direction. The present bathroom was reasonably clean when I found it, the cement footsteps on which to position myself were dry, and its access was free, while the Mexican one had been filthy and some attendant had asked me for five pesos for its use. However, faced with the evidence that the loose change in my pockets did not amount to more than twenty *centavos*, he had been pleased to accept them. Moreover, I was not entirely convinced that the Mexican busload's encouragements had been all that good-natured—the tourist being an unlovely comic object, almost by definition—and the whole thing had been something of a circus.

Across the aisle sat a young couple, probably husband and wife, or perhaps brother and sister. He was an ordinary young man, rather well dressed in neat Western pants and shirt, and sat very close to the woman's side. More than half a century ago in the part of Morocco where I came from, women used to dress modestly with their faces partly covered for outdoors, but one could still see a hand and a bare foot in the babouche, and even half a face could be seen, particularly when haggling at the market.

Less traditional women even allowed more of themselves to be seen. But this woman, in 1998, was covered from head (her black veil only revealing the eyes strictly cast down) to hands (black gloves) to feet (white silk socks in her babouches). She wore an elegant pearl gray *djellabah* and neither spoke nor moved during the entire trip, except when we stopped and he bought her a bottle of pop that she drank modestly under her veil. She was making an extreme statement, very likely an extremist one; probably an uncommon one as well, at least for the company in this bus, since the other travellers, all Moroccans, also looked at her discreetly but with some curiosity.

In Agadir, we had time to have some tea before switching bus stations on our way to Tiznit, the end of the road where all childhood memories would come alive, where the ramparts would open up to let me in and enfold me like a prodigal daughter finally come home.

At the bus station, there was the same bedraggled crowd one always sees in such places. Perhaps even more bedraggled than usual, as this was a local route frequented by local people going mainly to the suburbs of Agadir. An old man squatted by the door of the office with a tray on his knees holding loose cigarettes; a young man approached him, hesitating between buying one or two, finally settling for one.

Tiznit

We were, as usual, the only Europeans on the bus, particularly travelling on SATAS *(Société Anonyme des Transports …* but I could not remember what the final AS stood for), which was much less comfortable—now, as sixty years ago—than CTM *(Compagnie des Transports Marocains),* but had more frequent runs on shorter trips in the south. I was strangely comforted by the fact that SATAS was still operating and still slightly rundown, hoping that little else might also have changed.

This hope did not last very long, as the route I once knew so well was no longer at all the same. The suburbs of Agadir went on and on, where once there had only been scrub. To my amazement, we found ourselves at the Aït Melloul (where I had learned to swim) without seemingly having left Agadir, an Aït Melloul I would not have recognized either, being now the typical sprawling Third World stretch of poor shops, overloaded donkeys, and cars of barely remembered vintage.

Tiznit, my so-called hometown, because it holds all my childhood memories, is a walled city. Her ramparts have fifty-six towers and five gates, some of which appear rather dilapidated nowadays. Although the ramparts are somewhat reminiscent of those of Essaouira and look respectably old, Tiznit is actually a rather recent city. From a large *douar* (traditional village), she was built up as a garrison town in 1881 by the sultan Moulay Hassan to deal with the dissident Berber tribes in the Souss region.

Then, in 1912, the rebel El Hib attempted to overthrow the French who had just signed the Treaty of Fès, and tried to establish himself as the Sultan of Tiznit. His attempt did not end well, and Tiznit became a French military zone, which it still was when we arrived in 1935.

But this was now 1998. We arrived in Tiznit and the bus stopped in the *Mechouar*. I had not entirely given up hope, for I still had to look for the house my father built. I had entertained nostalgic thoughts, whereby I would stop at the front door and ring whatever bell might be there (usually in a little niche carved out in the thick adobe wall). Someone would come, probably a servant, who seeing a European might call her mistress. I would explain myself and would be invited to come into the garden (the trees planted by my father must be huge by now) and perhaps be given permission to visit the house.

I realize now, realized even then, the little likelihood of such an encounter actually taking place, but I was still hopeful. I was also curious about the people living there since the house, although built around a patio, was not at all like the typical Moroccan house.

John and I had decided to walk around Tiznit a little that evening and postpone our search for clues to the past until the following day. The *Mechouar* was still there, of course, and seemed smaller, perhaps simply because it had been mostly empty in my childhood, whereas a good part of it was now taken over by arriving and departing buses and the large number of passengers milling around.

John and I were in two different moods. He was interested and looked around curiously, since it was his first experience of a non-touristic town and the closest he had been so far to seeing ordinary Moroccan life and activities. I felt anxious and deeply regretted having come back, but still hopeful that the following day could bring something that would have made my return worthwhile. For I was still thinking in terms of a "return."

Walking back to our hotel outside the ramparts, we spotted a very unpretentious little café where the owner invited us in and served us an excellent *harira* (that most adaptable soup originally intended to break the fast of *Ramadan)*, which John had quickly learned to appreciate.

Next door to the café was a building under construction. The workers, barefoot and without any protective gear whatsoever, climbed on high shaky scaffolds, wielding hammers and saws. I asked the café owner whether there had been any accidents, and philosophically, he said that, yes, there had been some. Broken limbs often, deaths sometimes. But the hotel they were building was to be a five-star establishment backed by a German company that would, they all hoped, finally bring Tiznit into the touristic loop.

So far, most regular tours to the south only included Agadir and Taroudant, or went directly into the southern cities of the desert, and totally bypassed Tiznit. So they all had great hopes for an improved life once Tiznit finally took in some of the foreigners' wealth.

We wished them well, but we had too often seen on our travels the dubious improvement of newly discovered towns. We were glad that our trip had taken place now rather than next year when the hotel might perhaps be completed. It surprised me to see how soon I had gone back to the habit of mentally adding *"Inch' Allah"* when expressing a wish or a probability.

The following morning, we set out on our systematic search. The *Mechouar* had changed remarkably little, except for the noise and pollution of having been transformed into a bus depot. But the buildings were much the same, if not their function.

On one side, the palace of the Glaoui seemed completely deserted, and oddly, put to no use that we could see. Given the former alliance between his family and the French, it was not perhaps surprising to see it so ostentatiously condemned nowadays. At the opposite end, the former

French administrative offices had been taken over by the army, for we learned that Tiznit was still a military post.

We went along a little street to the left, past these offices, but what once was a familiar way to our house, had disappeared. At about the level where our street and our house should have been, was a public garden, then a hospital. New streets had sprung up everywhere. I could not even be sure we were in the right place anymore, while the day before I could have traced, I believe quite accurately, the map of that area. The honourable part of my mind knew that a public garden and a hospital were infinitely preferable to a military camp and an old house, but there was that insidious, bitter, mortifying little voice in my head that cried foul.

I think John felt a little sorry for me, and understood perhaps why I had not really been enthusiastic about the trip. We walked back to the *Mechouar,* where, to my amazement, I saw the school. I cannot say it had not changed, for obviously the teacher's house in the back as well as his garden had been appropriated to enlarge the building considerably, but the facade was the same. The doors were open and we saw two rows of children, both boys and girls in separate lines, waiting to go into their classrooms. When they saw us watching them, some started singing "Frère Jacques."

Later that day, we saw some boys in the *Mechouar,* possibly from the school, who asked us for pens, whether to use or resell we did not know, but they were polite and pleasant when we told them we did not have any. John and I found the children attractive and well mannered, and back at our hotel, I asked for the school director's name and address. I knew women were emancipated in modern Morocco, but was still surprised to hear that the director was a woman.

After our return home, I wrote to congratulate her on the good manners of the well-spoken children we had met, and included some *dirhams* we had left unspent (roughly $50–$60) to use for whatever supplies or activities the children might enjoy, or for some special event of her own choosing.

The Moroccan *dirham* (like the Cuban *peso,* the Thai *baht,* the Seychelles *rupee,* or the Venezuelan *bolivar,* as I had already discovered) is not a currency easy to change at a local Vancouver bank, so I sent cash rather than a money order. Perhaps the school director was offended, perhaps she did not receive the letter (although it had been sent registered mail), or perhaps someone else received it first, but we never heard anything from her. It was disappointing, because I would have liked to continue with some regular connection to the school.

What we found without difficulty was the *rue de la Joie,* now a street of little shops, the prostitutes having long gone (at least from this site, but Tiznit was still associated with the military, so there may have been some discreet relocation). I found, within a block, the place where our first house had been.

But what was puzzling was that there were now houses and shops on both sides of the street, while I only remembered one side, and an old photograph had indeed confirmed that the left side of the street used to be a solid wall. However, the formerly solid wall was that of the Glaoui's palace, and the latter may have been more or less gutted to provide room for a commercial expansion on both sides of the street, only leaving the facade on the *Mechouar* as a reminder of its past importance.

We visited a few jewelry shops where the intricate designs had not changed over time. Fibulae, necklaces, and ankle bracelets were on display, still clunky and beautiful, and so were the silver filigrees for which the region was famous. Everything was quite pricey and credit cards were accepted, so I doubted the shops were intended for local people. At the hotel, a German visitor had explained that he had come for the day to buy Berber jewelry, and according to recent interior design magazines I had seen, it would appear that it has now pride of place everywhere, displayed in cabinets, particularly in chic New York lofts or European apartments.

As a walled town, Tiznit used to be completely contained within her ramparts. The approaches to the city still showed these to be in reasonably good shape, although modern edifices (banks, two-storied office buildings, etc.) were now on the outside by the main road. Indeed, this would appear to be the business centre of modern Tiznit, plunked in the middle of nowhere beside the old city. Barely a hundred metres away from one of the modern buildings, an old man, sitting in front of his skimpy goatskin tent with his donkey tied to a scrawny tree, looked stubbornly incongruous.

On the other side of town, where businesses had not flourished outside the ramparts, were poorer houses. There, many of the older gates and adjoining walls were reduced to rubble. We clambered up over one, and as we emerged over the debris on the outside, an old woman severely veiled, her back very straight and sitting on a donkey, came into view. John, almost as a reflex, aimed his camera at her (she was indeed something to behold, right out of the old Maghreb) and I whispered harshly, "Don't!" But it was too late, as she had already pointed her index and little finger at him, giving him the devil's horns, the evil eye.

Naturally, John had not intended to offend her and would not have aimed his camera if he had remembered in time. First, one does not take pictures of old Muslim women, and second, one should always ask permission to take a photograph, even if the culture permits it. The whole incident lasted less time than it took me to write about it. John seemed somewhat shaken having just been curious, and certainly had not deserved to be cursed, probably forever. However, one could only hope that the bad luck would not last that long. *Inch'Allah!* Or, with a fatalism he might not appreciate, *mektoub* (It is written ...).

I was sorely disappointed with all the changes I had seen, and we felt there was little point in staying much longer. However, we should have gone and visited the famous spring, Lalla Tiznit, where a local prostitute had once been martyred and where people reported still seeing her. I was quite familiar with it as my mother and I often went by on one of our endless afternoon walks. I should also have taken John to see the distinctive Saharan minaret. But unfortunately, we did none of those things and decided instead to leave for Essaouira, farther north.

When we bought our tickets, we were told that the SATAS bus on its way to Agadir was scheduled to arrive at 5 a.m. at the junction of our hotel. In Agadir, we would once again change to the larger and more modern buses of CTM on the way to Essaouira. We arrived a quarter of an hour early, in the dark, unsure of where to stand.

A couple was waiting a little farther up from us. At ten to five, we saw headlights approaching, and a bus stopped near the couple who climbed on. Carting our two bags and rushing to get there, we realized as we approached, and luckily too late, that the bus was going in another direction. The bus looked very much the worse for wear—local public transportation taking people to work.

At five to five, two somewhat stocky, powerful-looking men running in concert, obviously in training and wearing white T-shirts, white shorts, white socks, and runners, appeared on the other side of the road. Arabs, not Berbers, I felt sure, even in the very faint light of a very early dawn, even across the road. An incongruous sight, those jogging men, I thought, until I remembered the garrison nearby. At five o'clock, our bus arrived. Whatever means of transportation we used in Morocco—train, CTM, or SATAS—we were always picked up and delivered on time.

In the early morning light, we saw along the way a few small *douars,* those dusty hamlets built of mud and straw. They appeared the same as in my childhood and as they probably had been for centuries, except for the flimsy, black plastic bags caught on every shrub in sight, sometimes miles away from any habitation.

Nowhere did I see a trace of those threshing wheels to which a donkey and a camel or an ox used to be harnessed together. Perhaps it was not the season, or perhaps they had disappeared altogether. However, we did see a trio of agile goats perched on an argan tree, a sight I had promised John since our arrival.

Essaouira
Essaouira (The Well Designed), known for many centuries as Mogador (The Well Defended), is a very windy city, whatever name she goes under. It was only in 1957 when Morocco regained her independence that the city acquired this new name, as a formal sign of disengagement from French influence, even if the name of Mogador had nothing to do with France.

She was designed in the mid-1760s by Théodore Cornu, a French architect, perhaps a prisoner of the Moors at the time, whom Sultan Sidi Mohammed ben Abdallah, the same Mohamed III we met earlier, ordered to draw the plans for the harbour and the fortress. The idea was mainly to build a naval base for a fleet of corsairs that would sail south to Agadir and punish the inhabitants who had rebelled against his authority. It took

Cornu, inspired in part by Vauban, the famous military engineer, three years to complete the task.

Built on a small peninsula below sea level, the city is worthy of her two names, the well defended and the well designed. Large bronze cannons abound, facing the sea, set on a forbidding wall protecting the city. As to design, one only needs to look at the souks, which unlike the usual meandering and tortuous narrow lanes in most other cities, are made of wide and straight streets, cutting at right angles and bordered by little artisan shops.

※ ※ ※

The city's prosperity had been largely due to the presence of her Jewish population. By the first half of the nineteenth century, Mogador, as she was then, was in the extraordinary position, probably never found elsewhere in the Arab world, of having more Jews than Muslims—roughly 15,000 Jews to 10,000 Muslims. This prosperity was mainly due to the active commerce they generated and rested of the willingness of the Arabs to accept this cohabitation.

Such a peaceful cohabitation was in sharp contrast to what had happened in other parts of the country, and the Jews had not fared so well in Fès, for instance, where several thousands were massacred in 1465.

Treatment of the Jews has always been ambiguous in Muslim countries, even if they often fared better there than under Christian rule. As anyone who has travelled to Spain can attest—particularly in Andalusia, but also evident on our trip to Toledo— the three faiths, Christianity, Islam, and Judaism have lived side by side in the past without too much turmoil.

Martin Gilbert, who wrote a history of Jews among the Muslims, indicates that the positive side of this association is usually based on economic reasons (as we have just seen in Mogador/Essaouira). Gilbert believes that from the time of Muhammad until today, "Jews have often found greater opportunities, respect, and recognition under Islam than Christianity." *The religious history is interesting*

On the other hand, he also recognizes that "they have ... been subjected to the worst excesses of hostility, hatred, and persecution." This may well happen when other sources of national unrest translate into inner religious tensions and result in massacres, as we have seen throughout history, whatever the ruling religion at the time. To keep a sense of perspective, as we consider the treatment of Jews under both Christian and Islamic rules, we should probably accept the reflection of Bernard Lewis (quoted by Gilbert) on fourteen centuries of Jewish life under Islam that it was "never as bad as in Christendom at its worst, nor ever as good as Christendom at its best."

Even daily life in times of peaceful cohabitation was not always free of humiliation. When living in the past under Muslim rulers, both Jews and Christians were given an inferior status, that of *dhimmi,* which allowed them to practice their faith but certainly did not make them the equals of Muslim citizens. I also remember from my childhood in various Moroccan towns, that the Jewish *mellah* was always deemed a separate part of everyday Moroccan or French life, and probably slightly despised by both (if childhood impressions can be trusted).

❦ ❦ ❦

Essaouira is nowadays a city of crafts, arts, and music. She is not large and everything one needs is close by. Interestingly, the hippies put her on the American map in the late sixties when they discovered Mogador and her laissez-faire attitude to just about everything. They settled in a small village nearby and soon became involved in the artistic life of the city.

The souks are teeming with all the crafts of a rich culture: traditional silversmiths and goldsmiths, weavers, workers in the famous thuya wood, carvers, and so on. There are also several modern galleries and many artists, both local and foreign, live and work there.

Music is another artistic resource of the city. While Marrakesh has cornered the movie industry market with her many locations depicted on films and the well-known Marrakesh Film Festival, Essaouira has the music. She hosts the *Festival des Andalousies Atlantiques,* where all forms of music are celebrated: classical, folk, jazz, flamenco, and more specially, the *gnaoua* music.

Because of its origins—music made by black slaves moving north with the caravans—it has sometimes been compared to the American blues. It is different in the way it sounds and in the traditional instruments it uses (large metal castanets and deep semi-cylindrical guitars), but it is equally loved as a sound connected to the historical and cultural roots of the country.

I shall note in passing that Essaouira claims as one of her sons David Levy Yulee (1810–1886), an American politician and the first Jew elected to the US Senate. He added to his name his father's ancestral Sephardic surname; hence, the connection to what was then Mogador.

We took our breakfast every morning on the main square, where mostly French and German were spoken among tourists. John, with his casual, laid-back gait and his even more casual clothes, was often mistaken for an American, which is not always an advantage in some parts of the world. And I, with my colonial past, might not have been *persona* terribly *grata* either, had people known about it.

However, to go back to the café we patronized for our morning croissants and where every morning we were treated to the same scene. Two middle-size dogs, hackles raised and balls the size of peaches, would start towards each other from opposite ends of the square. They were pampered dogs, probably belonging to foreign residents, since there was such a colony in Essaouira; they were not the native mongrels whose fights only revolved around food. The dogs, evenly matched in size, were combative—exuding an aura of dogdom—and there appeared a definite sense of entitlement about them. Somewhere in the middle of the square, they would meet, and the fight would start, ferocious, noisy, legs flailing in all directions, jaws snapping at whatever they could grab.

At some point, a man with a large stick would come and beat indiscriminately at the rolling mass of fur and growls and curse them as well. The dogs would eventually pull apart under the blows, their hackles still in full display, their snarling lips curled up over their fangs. Then they would turn around and return to their own side of the square after a job well done, sometimes with a faint limp. We never noticed even a hint of real damage. Most of the fight was for show it would seem, for the glory of it, or

These are good stories

as the French put it *pour la galerie*. We, the gallery, were duly impressed and looked forward to the encore performance the following morning.

Another recurring show was that of a "mad" woman. We could not be sure of her status. Perhaps she was actually mad, perhaps only slightly so and simply allowed to go on because she was harmless. She would appear in front of the café shouting and shaking her fist, apparently insulting all and sundry until two police officers would appear and take her away. The next day, the scene was repeated. We were prepared to see it as a more or less indulgent treatment of people who did not quite fit in, a treatment accepted by a society not hostile to its poor and afflicted members, and even at times benevolent in its treatment of them, until we accidentally witnessed a far more unpleasant event.

Another character frequented the same square, a man, obviously mentally deficient, who regularly begged for food outside restaurants. He was shooed away by waiters, usually with a great deal of impatience, since he was obviously a constant thorn in their side. One particular restaurant had a terrace where people took their meals. One day, the man reached out, grabbed some food from the plate of a tourist, and stuffed it in his mouth. Admittedly, it was not an appetizing sight as the man was utterly filthy, but he had not been threatening, just desperately (or pathologically, who can say) hungry.

The restaurant manager, a well nourished and well muscled young man, rushed out, grabbed him roughly by his torn *djellabah,* and dragged him across the square to a side street. Had they moved another step or two into the street, we would not have seen him throw the beggar to the ground, punching and kicking him as he might have kicked a dog.

Once more, we did not think it impossible that the same spectacle would occur again the following day, but there had been no "entertainment" in that vicious attack, no local colour meant for the tourists. It had certainly not been intended for the gallery, as the "gallery" remained uncomfortably silent afterwards. Because of where John and I sat, I believe we were the only ones to have seen the conclusion of the forceful removal of the food beggar. What had affected us as much as the brutality of the attack was its having taken place so very carefully out of sight.

One afternoon, sitting on the large terrace of a small café dispensing soft drinks, tea, and coffee, near the port and facing the sea, we saw a heavy wooden fishing boat arrive into the harbour, all sails deployed. Then another arrived. Still another. And more, until there were seven boats. These were not hasty arrivals, but stately ones. And stately was the circle they made, like a formal dance.

Fishing boats are not as a rule particularly elegant vessels, but those white sails and the slow motion charged their dance with unusual grace. I asked the waiter who was standing by and also watching, the reason for what looked very much like a ceremonial display. And it was indeed exactly that—a ceremonial display. Some important visitors had arrived in town, and the circling of the fishing boats was by way of welcome. We learned that there would also be other ceremonies later, with lots of feasting and music in the evening.

When we arrived after dinner in the square by the harbour, a crowd had already gathered around a platform on which a modern band was playing with amplifiers shaking the old ramparts. The mood was relaxed with people moving idly about, many in Western garb, some girls even wearing jeans. We sat on a low wall at some distance looking around, three young women in traditional dress sitting beside us. It was rather dark, as night was falling and all the lights were aimed at the stage.

John was looking at everything with interest, even at the young women beside us, until I poked him sharply in the side. One of them was breastfeeding a baby, so modestly that he had not even noticed the child. It is sometimes difficult to know what, precisely, will offend, but a male *roumi* (the old-fashioned name for a European) thought to be ogling the hint of a native female breast would definitely have qualified.

One evening we decided to go to a restaurant we had spotted right beside the ramparts—those ramparts, which were being repainted thanks to some international cultural funding agency, probably UNESCO, but no one could tell us for sure. It looked like a never-ending job. Repainted is not the right word, since it looked more like a pink wash slapped on with reasonable energy.

The restaurant was more elegant—tablecloths, candles, and chairs upholstered in red velvet—than most places where we usually took our meals. The few couples around us were all dressed up, quiet, and mostly foreign. We noted once more how well behaved and non-offensive all those tourists were that we had seen in Morocco (we had not been to Agadir yet), probably owing in part to the unavailability of alcohol in public places.

Our salad arrived, and since the restaurants had its pretentions, the dressing was made with argan oil. I rejoiced, having bragged to John about its exquisite taste. It must have been an acquired one, now forgotten, because the oil left an awful aftertaste (the taste before the aftertaste was not all that great, either). So another childhood myth exploded, but I was getting used to it by then.

Argan oil and its by-products are another source of wealth for modern Morocco. They are now sold worldwide as a panacea for both health and beauty. It is essentially women's work to collect the seeds from the thorny argan trees and make the oil. When I was a child and women pressed argan oil from their trees, it was said that the fruit had to pass through goats first, as an initial step in the process of domestic production.

Women nowadays operate in cooperatives and no goats seem to participate in the production. The largest one near Essaouira is called by the Berber name for "beautiful flower," the *Ajddigue* Women's Argan Cooperative, started in 1997. There are now some 140 such cooperatives, producing oil and products for clinics and beauty shops all over the world, where they are available at huge cost. However, I remember watching a joint French-Moroccan documentary a few years ago showing that, being now so popular, many products labeled as being made of argan oil were tested to have an infinitesimal percentage of it, the rest being olive oil. Olive oil is also an excellent product and will certainly do no harm, whether ingested or applied to the skin, so who am I to condemn whoever profits from the credulity of those intent of pursuing beauty and youth at all costs.

We sometimes walked around the harbour when men on the fishing boats unloaded their catch. The fish were large Atlantic fish, many unknown to us living on the Pacific shore. One fish in particular made us stop in our tracks, so dreadful was it. The fishermen laughed at us. We walked away. John may be made of stronger stuff, but I was quite shaken.

Two weeks later in Paris, I asked a friend what the fish could have been. She thought it might have been a *murène,* always seen without its head in

French fish markets, because it is "too horrible to look at." In other words, a very large moray eel. I had barely glanced at it, but John confirmed that it had indeed been a nasty sight, "long and green and ugly." The Romans were particularly fond of that particular fish and kept Mediterranean morays in tanks. Caesar is reputed to have required two thousand of them for a particular feast, a true vision of hell.

Before leaving, we bought a few presents for our children and some friends: boxes and small picture frames of thuya wood, a tree that only grows around Essaouira, but bears some resemblance to the arbutus or madrona of the Pacific Northwest coast. Objects made of the gnarly roots are more desirable and expensive than those made of the trunk, but all are characteristically "old Mogador."

When visiting a small factory where artisans manufactured objects of marquetry, I saw, unchanged through the years, the exact thuya bookends I still have at home in Vancouver. Those odd glimpses and minute details of the unchanged nature of the country no longer elicited any nostalgia in me. I had finally realized that my Moroccan past was definitely just that: merely a thing that belonged in the past.

We only had a few days left in our trip. Since our flight back started from Agadir, we once more boarded the bus and were on our way south. By then we had realized our journey had not been very well organized, and rather than design a proper visit to Morocco that would have included a trip through the High Atlas, a visit to Ouarzazate, and going farther into the south, we seemed to have more or less followed the thread of my past, as I selectively remembered it. It had been a self-indulgent journey on my part, and one I had unthinkingly imposed on John.

Agadir

[handwritten annotation: This seems to be the common thread of the book]

Agadir is a new city, almost entirely rebuilt after the earthquake of 1960. I had not expected to recognize anything, so was not surprised when I did not, although I was pleased to see that the old Kasbah was still there.

The city was overrun with German tourists, most of them staying in luxurious hotels near the beach. They seemed to be there only for the sun, the beaches, and the fact that hotel staff handled all their needs efficiently; they appeared to ignore the local people, the reverse being also true. Usually large and tanned, they circulated in the touristic part of town, seemingly invisible to those Moroccans who were not paid to make them feel welcome and cater to their needs. Certainly, they were not interested in making concessions to preserve the local sense of decorum and propriety.

On a wide boulevard, somewhat removed from the beach, a German family ambled: large father, large mother, abundantly rounded teenage daughter. The girl wore very low shorts exposing her navel and hips, and a skimpy little bra, two tiny triangles really, barely covering the nipples of her overflowing breasts. She was all naked flesh, and I took offence with what would have been blatant ignorance of common rules of courtesy and decency anywhere else in the world. And here in Morocco, it was such an outrageous flaunting of societal values and religious rules. Any of the prostitutes on the *rue de la Joie* in Tiznit, going for her regular medical checkup, would have been mortified to expose accidently one tenth of the skin displayed by that European girl. The Koran requires women to be modest. So does common sense in lands ruled by the Koran. Tritely, I wondered what the parents could have been thinking.

As we continued on the same boulevard, we reached a mini-mart with a few necessities, although it seemed more oriented to tourists' needs (aspirin, Pepto-Bismol, band-aids, orange juice, pop, ice cream, and packaged slice bread) than to ordinary people. It was also in the wrong part of town to be catering to local folks. A young boy in his early teens was in charge of the shop.

Being my usual Canadian and good-tourist-self, I simply could not help showering him with *"S'il vous plaîts,"* and *"Mercis"* until his hatred of us became so obvious that even I could not go on with the charade. Looking at our purchases, pointing to the cash register, and taking our money, he did not say one word to us. His eyes and the grimness of his mouth spoke for him, and it would have been difficult not to get the message. He was evidently more honest and obvious than most, but I did not believe him to be an exception.

Even John, who speaks neither French nor Spanish and thus does not always catch more subtle signs of disdain or resentment as we travel together, had been struck by it. He put it down to our being taken for Americans at a time of strong anti-American sentiments among Muslim nations sympathetic to Palestine and Iraq. It was probably true, but there was very likely more to it than that. Simply being foreign in a society whose economy needed us and who hated us for it, in a country whose customs we outraged daily through ignorance or indifference, did not help much either.

The bronchitis that had bothered me since our arrival had flared up again and I felt unwell. We had done most of our shopping in Essaouira, but I still wanted to buy some spices for a friend we would be visiting in France and for myself, and had delayed this purchase until the last minute. Our hotel was very close to the souk, so we went looking at the colourful mounds of so many spices.

For me, the spice market was always the pinnacle of my visit to souks, but not this time. I selected the few spices I wanted to take with me but did not have the strength to haggle and bring down the inflated prices that were asked as a first offer on the way to achieving a compromise that would satisfy us both. The young man handling the transaction seemed both disappointed and embarrassed to be paid exactly the price he had asked. He could see that I was unwell, so he offered us tea, then concocted a mixture for my cough and my asthma, for which he had the good grace not to charge me.

On the way back to our hotel, we stopped at a little restaurant right by the ocean. We could see the sardine fleet a few hundred feet away, so I ordered grilled sardines for my last meal in Agadir, so fresh they were almost still wriggling. Or perhaps not so fresh after all (at least one of them which, upon reflection, had tasted a little different), for I was violently sick afterwards, and I spent the last day of my Moroccan pilgrimage in bed with every symptom of food poisoning.

John, who could not do anything for me, went to the beach one last time, and perhaps regretted having been afflicted throughout by my personal soul-searching on the way to the past. Being a nice man, he did not once complain, but it was clear that we had two vastly different agendas during our trip. Perhaps the dwindling resources of my immune system throughout had been a physical metaphor for some other failure, one I did not really want to delve into.

But it was time to go home again. The real home, I mean, not the fantasized one—the one made up of children, friends, familiar houses, one's own bed, well mannered dogs, well fed cats, frequent soft rain, and new memories constantly in the making. The following day we flew off from the beautiful new airport, small and all tiled in blue, quite delightful but looking like something from a movie set. No doubt, the German tourists must find it very picturesque.

Chapter Six

The Loneliness Beyond the Walls

Walls are antithetic to travel, yet they sometimes contain worlds more alien than any foreign land. The walls I refer to here were intended, as walls usually are, to define and encompass two different spaces. But unlike most walls, these were equipped where they met at the gates, with locks, safeguards, and sometimes weapons, so that passing through them was a dubious, often dangerous, sometimes impossible task. In approximate and relative terms, they separated the mad from the sane and the guilty from the innocent (in chapter 9, I describe a third aspect of protected enclosures: those that separate the poor from the rich).

The two experiences I describe here have been forays into different worlds and have allowed me to move into the other reality of powerless people confined with their shouting and their silence in their distinct incarcerated cultures. In England, I was a student nurse in a psychiatric hospital and in Canada, a folklorist collecting graffiti in the solitary confinement cells of a penitentiary that had just closed down.

In these guises, I went in and came out of these otherwise forbidden spaces with no difficulty, being officially authorized to do so. But I found passing through the gates, standing behind the walls, and moving however briefly into the walled-in cultures an uneasy process, even after the inmates had gone, since so much of their anguish was left behind.

In the mental hospital, untrained young girls and temporary visitors that we were, we complied with rules and guidelines that shaped our conduct and reinforced the distinction between "them" and "us." As student nurses, our ignorance of the patients' diagnosis and treatment prevented us from getting too close to them and preserved the appropriate sense of distance without which our initial sense of disconnection would have been perhaps too extreme to bear.

In the solitary confinement cells, the worst part of the empty jail, we examined how men, now long gone, had expressed their passage and what their graffiti revealed of their thoughts, their fears, their hopes, their despair—and most of all, how powerful was their desire to share them.

Looking for the Way Out
Barming Heath Hospital, Maidstone, Kent, 1949

> *Here in this bare dormitory that had no door, here on the narrow cot, clothed in a numbered nightgown, she lay with women who were insane and she was one of them.*
>
> —Mary Jane Ward, *The Snake Pit* (1948)

"*Barming* Heath Hospital?" said the man at the French embassy in London where I registered and gave my future address. "How appropriate!" Still uninitiated to the mysteries of English slang, I failed to catch the allusion. I understand that the Kent County Lunatic Asylum, Barming Heath, has since been renamed the Oakwood Hospital, Maidstone, Kent.

I was nineteen, freshly dropped out of a philosophy class after answering an English advertisement in a French newspaper, and had absolutely no idea what I was getting into. I had probably not even realized that I had signed up with a psychiatric hospital. "Lunatic asylum" had certainly not appeared in the ad, and even if it had, I may not have realized what it entailed.

Mary Jane Ward's *The Snake Pit* had recently been published, but I was not aware of the novel. Both the book and the film by the same title offer a very accurate description of life in English mental hospitals in the late 1940s, as I was then able to discover.

Faced with my first day on the wards, surrounded by smells, sounds, and sights unthinkable a few days earlier, I felt some sympathy for what must have been my sixteen-year-old Hungarian father's sense of alienation in 1919, on his first day in Sidi Bel-Abbès, after enlisting in the French Foreign Legion.

However, unlike his French at sixteen, my English at nineteen was quite good. By that, I mean I had always received first or second prize throughout the seven years I studied it. Ever since my first lesson *("**zuh** rabbeet, **zee** elephant")*, I had shown some affinity for the language. However, I could neither speak it nor understand it when spoken. At school, we studied dead and modern languages exactly the same way: straight from the grammar book.

On the strength of that discovery, Sister Tutor—for this was a teaching hospital, and since the next class would not start for another six weeks, I had to be put to work in the meantime—sent me to report to a tiny Irish ward sister. The latter was entirely toothless (her ill-fitting teeth in her pocket, since she only put them in when speaking to Matron or Doctor) and ruled over a ward where it did not make much difference whether the patients understood me and I them.

"Go in there, nurse," she said as soon as I had reported and introduced myself, "and clean that up." *There* turned out to be a padded cell, its floor and walls covered with a rubber-like, washable material. In one corner was an old creature, naked save for the coarse linen jacket holding her arms across her chest, her wild white hair and meek blue eyes the only spots of colour, as her thin, bony body was otherwise fish-belly gray. There were brown crusts of some substance all over her legs, the floor, and part of one wall. The smell, although some disinfectant also wafted, clearly indicated that the substance was in fact dried shit.

After my initial shock, I did my best to clean. Having scrubbed everything and washed her as gently as I could, I attempted the no-mean task of brushing her hair. She grunted occasionally, but overall had been quite docile; evidently, whatever crisis had led her into that cell was now over.

When I gathered up my cleaning tools to make my exit, she grumbled something through her toothless mouth (I was to see quite a number of those mouths, this being after all England only a few years after the war), which I heard well enough but did not understand. Convinced that what she grumbled was unspeakable—but what could I have done wrong—it took me some time to dare ask someone what it meant. She had said, "Nursey, you're a brick!" *A brick*, a good guy. Nursey, you're a good guy, she had said.

To my recollection, apart from that nice Dutch woman who used to swallow her wedding ring and could not stay away from the safety of the hospital, it was the first and only time someone addressed a kind word to me on the wards during the eleven months I stayed at Barming Heath Hospital in Maidstone, Kent.

Barming Heath was very likely neither better nor worse than most mental hospitals operating in the British Isles in the 1940s and early 1950s. Irish girls constituted the majority of the probationers, as student nurses were called, psychiatric training being for many their way out of the hardships of home and eventually a ticket to the lucrative job market in the United States, where British-trained psychiatric nurses were well rated. They, whose formal education was quite basic, took their work seriously, studied hard at school, and worked hard on the wards.

We, the foreign girls, Danish and French, had taken what we assumed to be the least offensive job to which our work permits entitled us. We were known not to stay very long, barely worth our training in fact, and it was not deemed necessary to prepare us for a career we would never properly enter. Most of us considered that year in England as a sort of self-supporting finishing school to perfect our English before going to university or decently paying jobs at home.

Six of us started, three of each, but one of the Danish girls was found weeping and crawling on all fours in the corridor of the nurses' residence a few weeks into our training, so we remained five, three French and two Danes, for nearly a year.

Although we worked in separate wards, for the Danish girls could actually speak English, we took our meals together and spent some of our spare time together. I got on particularly well with one of them, Birte, from Copenhagen, and for several years afterwards, I was sometimes mistaken for a German, because of some residual inflections and hard consonants I had adopted during this close association with her.

The Danish girls were also financially better off than we were, so Birte was able to attend a Frank Sinatra concert in London. "They were all fainting around me," she reported afterwards. "I tried too, but I did not manage it."

Towards the end of my stay at Barming Heath, I was assigned in quick succession to the admission/observation ward (I remember none of the formal appellations and simply name them by function) and to the pre-release ward. In some cases, it was not long before some recently released patient was readmitted into the observation ward to have the cycle begin all over again. Although I mostly remained attached to the little Irish sister's ward, I had so often been assigned elsewhere for a few days at a time that, by the time I left, I had probably seen most, if not all, of the female wards.

I helped wash, change, and feed GPs (general paralysis patients, as we knew them), their heavy, inert bodies an awful weight to roll over. The interesting and puzzling part was our perception of two old GP women in adjoining beds, trapped in the same immobility and completely devoid of expression, equally voiceless and unresponsive to our voices—so, what was there to distinguish between the two? There must have been some subliminal signal, for we had unanimously decreed that one was nice and the other was not. We rushed one patient through her paces, getting a little impatient with the way she pushed her food out of her mouth with her tongue (stubbornly, we thought) when we fed her, while gentled the other through the same process, wiping her mouth patiently and calling her "Dear."

The only difference I could see was that the Nice One had fuzzy pale baby hair and a soft pinkish complexion, and the Annoying One had coarse gray hair and skin. So, our attribution of character traits may simply have been based on esthetic considerations. But what extraordinary powers were implicitly given to us, untrained young women, and not necessarily kind.

I also assisted in ferrying and attending patients undergoing shock therapy treatment. We were quite unaware of the concerns that led to the later reevaluation of the treatment's benefits, and in those days, doctors appeared to apply shock therapy here and there with great frequency.

I should also say that we, the probationers, knew absolutely nothing about our patients. Ours was to bathe, clean, fine-comb for nits once a week, make beds, lock and unlock doors, receive abuse with a reasonable amount of equanimity, clean, clean, bathe, bathe, lock, unlock, make more beds, clean some more, and learn how to leave a room without turning our back on anybody, a curious knack that takes awhile to unlearn.

Not only were we never told anything about the patients we took care of, but also we were unambiguously discouraged from trying to find out about them. Questions about what was wrong with Mrs. Y who, despite having what we assumed to be two perfectly good legs, never went around except on her knees. Ditto with Mrs. Z's eyes and her claim that she could not see, and why was So and So picking at herself so viciously, were not only ignored, but also deemed entirely inappropriate.

I understand now that it made perfectly good sense not to share diagnoses with us, since even very little knowledge would have confused us even more, but I suspect that perhaps only Matron and Sister Tutor would have been able to answer these questions. The little Irish sister only knew what she needed to know to keep everything clean, tidy, and under control. But this may be an unfair assessment.

After eleven months at Barming Heath, we had not even sat for our Preliminary State Examination, Part I, of the Nursing Council for England and Wales, something regular hospitals whipped students through in no time at all. Perhaps there was something in our character or attitude that did not seem positive or perhaps the simple fact of keeping us at that untrained level meant that we could not move to a general hospital, I do not know. But there was no doubt our written English was good enough for the test, and unlike some, we did not have to think of the Welsh politician Aneurin Bevan, much in the news at time, to remember how to spell *aneurism*.

However, before leaving Maidstone to spend another year at a small and highly specialized hospital in London (the Royal National Ear Nose and Throat Hospital, off Gray's Inn Road), a bijou sort of establishment where I immediately sat for the examination, I reflected on my year. I had to admit that overall, the Barming Heath experience had been a useful one, since I discovered how to appreciate very simple pleasures.

I had enjoyed taking solitary walks along the riverbanks in that charming part of England. I had also very much enjoyed the small comfort of coming from the night shift in the gray of the early morning on my way to the bakery to pick up a fresh bun through the open window, the floury baker waiting for us straggling up the road, often through a heavy mist and only guided by the enchanting aroma.

I had also seen my first naked man there, not immediately aware that he was dead and in the process of undergoing an autopsy. I had taken him for a model made of whitish plastic. It would have paid to understand English a little better and been prepared for the experience, rather than wait for the slushy sound as Sister Tutor rummaged through guts in his belly to realize my mistake.

I had seen acts of great kindness as well as unchecked spiteful actions. I had seen people abandoned by their families, but I had also seen an old husband who after twenty years was still coming once a week to sit by a whimpering little body with trapped eyes, crying in silence at the sight of the little twigs of her arms, loosely restrained yet severely bruised. It had been a finishing school in many ways.

※ ※ ※

Two patients saddened me more than most. One was a Dutch woman, so kind and motherly, so normal that I acutely resented what I saw as her unfair hospitalization, closer in my mind to real incarceration. This was, of course, the danger of not knowing anything about our patients, that tendency to espouse their causes, because we had no understanding of the nature and symptoms of their illness. Much later, I realized that she had only looked normal because of the contrast she presented with those around her, for she was indeed on one of the worst wards. She helped, she cleaned, she comforted, she hugged, she protected, and she listened; she was a remarkably kind woman, a good woman.

Learning that I would be going through Amsterdam during my holiday, she gave me her sister's address with a message and what seemed reasonable instructions. The following day, having suddenly gone through a cyclic phase of her illness, she was sent back once more to an even worse ward. It almost broke my heart, so much had I believed in her near-sanity and her future release.

The other one was actually part of a duo. She was a very large woman, huge in fact, and always addressed as Miss and her last name, which was not always the rule. She had been a housekeeper in a physician's house. Like everyone else, she wore the type of little cotton print dresses in washed-out pastels, entirely shapeless, in which British institutions used to attire their inmates. She also had a little girl's haircut (bangs and straight across at earlobe level) that was de rigueur for many decades. In winter, she wore the brown rabbit fur mitts, like soft bear paws, that the lucky ones were given in the same institutions.

The second member of the duo consisted of a tiny woman, almost sparrow-like, who appeared to be the leader of the odd couple they formed. She too wore the cotton dress and had the same haircut. In fact, they would have been identical in appearance, except that one was easily two or three times the size of the other.

Wherever they went, the large one meekly followed the little one, her guide to the Way Out. "Nurse," she would say, politely but anxiously, "please could you show me the way out? I am late and Doctor will be waiting for his supper." Like two moths seeking the light, bumping against locked doors, one leading the other, they sought the way out, persistently, irresistibly.

For years, she had asked, "Please, could you show me the way out?" For years, the little one had tried to help her. On and on they went without respite. They seemed to have no other memory or purpose. Neither was young, and I have occasionally wondered which of them went first. But in such intimate symbiosis, it probably did not make much difference, and the other one, whoever she was, must have followed soon afterwards, both having finally found the way out.

✥ Notes from Elsewhere ✥

Writings on the Walls
Solitary Confinement Cells, 1980

Very few men are capable of estimating the immense amount of torture and agony, which this dreadful punishment ... inflicts upon the sufferers.

—Charles Dickens
American Notes for General Circulation (1842)

When a Canadian federal penitentiary for men sentenced to serve a term two years or more, located in British Columbia and scheduled for demolition, closed its doors in 1980, I obtained permission to collect graffiti on the walls of those empty cells. I went with Elvi Whittaker, an anthropologist at the University of British Columbia, as well as two of my children and a graduate student who were to take photographs and help us copy some of the hundreds of statements written on the walls.

Canadian inmates were no longer held in solitary confinement by the time we visited their cells. They were placed in dissociation or in adjustment units, also known as segregation. For the prisoners themselves it remained *the Hole*. They were put in dissociation under three categories: punitive dissociation, administrative segregation, and protective custody. Whatever the reasons for isolation the cells were usually the same, but the devastating psychological effects of dissociation mostly applied to the first two groups.

Why wish to go and examine these dirty and often vandalized cells? I am interested in folklore. It may be assumed to be the lighter side of anthropology, but it is not. One should appreciate, for instance, the part played by games, stories, riddles, and proverbs in the socialization of young children. Proverbs, particularly, form such an inherent part of traditional and peasant societies that in the fourteenth century a German legal document instructed judges thus: "Whenever you can apply a proverb, do so because peasants like to shape their opinions on proverbs."

Of all forms of folklore, I am particularly interested in proverbs because of their complexity, equaled only by that of riddles. Indeed, proverbs are metaphorical expressions whose structure is so open that they can only be understood in context—not only the context of their application to a specific situation, which is by far their primary function, but also the context of the culture from which they are issued. Let me give a brief example of both in the proverb, "Rolling stones gather no moss." It can be understood in two opposite ways, depending on the cultural value attached to the two antithetic key words *rolling* and *moss*.

In England, France, or Spain, for instance, it means that someone who wastes his time and cannot focus on a task *(rolling,* negative value) will not achieve prosperity *(moss,* positive value). But in Scotland or Finland, for instance, it means that an active and enterprising person *(rolling,* positive value) will not be hindered in his progress by old ideas or old habits *(moss,* negative value). For almost every proverb there is one of opposite wisdom, and the wisdom of each is often debunked, because nothing is simple in popular thinking, where each truth has developed over time its own contradiction.

Folklore is a rather elastic field, and I was satisfied that including all the poems, stories, newly coined proverbs, imprecations, drawings, and profanities written in these cells would constitute a perfectly adequate and appropriate corpus of work. If it is true that folklore lives by the strength of its function, as folklorists often maintain, then the function of this folklore had to be examined through the various forms scrawled, etched, penned, drawn, or even dug out of the plaster of these walls.

Unlike most of the folklore held in common by individuals in unified groups, this particular one (graffiti) had a unique character in that it was shared in absentia and that the voices were unidirectional. Inmate #1 wrote something, which was read and answered by inmate #2, which in turn was read by inmate #3, who may then have responded to either inmate #2 or #1. It is possible that inmate #1 would eventually occupy the same cell again and then participate in the "conversation," but it is equally possible that he never would.

The walls were seldom repainted and the accumulation of these solitary statements by men who ignored one another's identity created a conversation of sorts. The ensuing circulation of "truths" known in jail and the wisdom imparted by the statements constituted the nature of that very special folklore.

By their very nature, graffiti are solitary pronouncements. Whether in prison cells or on washroom walls, their dual function is to express the writer's personal views with the freedom of anonymity, as well as elicit a reaction and give the writer a sense of community affiliation. Graffiti do not have to be profound to elicit a response. I remember a washroom stall in one of our university departments where the three coils of an old-fashioned radiator had been numbered 1-2-3 by an anonymous hand. The next writer had renamed them 3-2-1. This change of orientation had given rise to two groups of later occupants taking sides, pen in hand. Man being a social animal par excellence, it seems as if an anonymous opinion is regarded as a challenge and demands a response in order to initiate a dialogue.

It is difficult to find the proper term to qualify those statements on the wall. They are hardly exchanges, since only the last occupant (and Elvi and I, later) could appreciate their scope. They built up, one author at a time, until their entire cumulative essence could be fully perceived. Although I call them "dialogues" and "conversations," for lack of better words, they were strictly *individual* contributions, lonely voices that did not know whether they would be read and understood. Yet, they definitely constituted communication and created a strong link, one curse, one drawing, one joke, or one calendar at a time among anonymous men, all suffering from the same sense of deprivation while waiting for their release.

As we read the various statements, we saw they complied with all the rules of the more familiar folklore. They served to strengthen the bonds among those who lived within a certain community, often by demonizing those who were outside of it—in this case, not only the *pigs* and the *rats* but also *The System* itself. Hence appeared all the stories of bad treatment, violence, injustice, settling of accounts, and promises of revenge.

Being anonymous, they also allowed a less boastful and sometimes more tender voice to emerge, one that spoke of hope and nostalgia and the desire to see loved ones again. Their authors being inmates, they were also understandably concerned, if not obsessed, with the passage of time.

What they did; however, and one did not have to be an anthropologist to see it, is speak of desolation and loneliness.

❧ ❧ ❧

It was not the first time I had worked in a prison. A few years earlier, I had witnessed the other two types of penal isolation: administrative segregation and protective custody, while interviewing small-time female prostitutes and drug users in Oakalla, a provincial jail since demolished as well. Having trained in a discipline that sees itself as not overly judgmental, I had been exempt from the more "preachy" labels of social workers and psychologists and had got on reasonably well with my informants.

It was during one of my regular visits to Oakalla that I witnessed something both puzzling and disturbing. It took place in the female protective custody unit, a separate building, where all three women had agreed to talk to me. They occupied the upper transversal part of the T-shaped building, extended with a fenced-in outdoor "patio" to which they were very attached, their only complaint being they were not allowed to sunbathe topless. As it was, they elicited their good share of attention from the male inmates working nearby in the vegetable garden.

In the longer part of the room (the vertical part of the T), at right angle to the space used by these three inmates, seventeen Doukhobor women were lying on their beds. Like most people in British Columbia, I knew about the Doukhobor sect of the Sons of Freedom. Known as Spirit Wrestlers, a sect of Russian dissenters, they had immigrated to Canada and arrived in Saskatchewan at the end of the 1890s. Guided by their leader, Verigin, they finally settled in British Columbia in 1908. I also knew of the women's weapons of predilection in their struggle with the government: arson, fasting, and nudity.

Arson in the community had led them to the prison, arson within the prison had led them to this room, and fasting was their retaliation for both measures. Before that day, they had been to me nothing more than newspaper items, fewer and fewer of them, in fact, since the seventeen women there were part of an old guard gradually dying out. These women had recently torched their own section and had to be temporarily housed in protective custody, the only fireproof building then available.

Thus, the three ordinary inmates—prostitutes, drug users, small-time traffickers, and petty thieves—had become the willy-nilly neighbours in seclusion of the seventeen fire-setting Doukhobors. Arson was always on their mind, and they acted as unofficial watchdogs, terrified of being caught in a small burning building, like "rats in a trap," as one put it, a trite enough expression but made powerfully vivid by the sight of steel bars and heavy locks.

My introduction to the three inmates in protective custody, my new informants, was a scene worthy of a Buñuel film. They had invited two prison wardens and me for lunch. As we entered through the door located at the very bottom of the longer section, nothing had prepared me for what I saw. The long and narrow room looked like a chronic hospital ward. Nine beds were on each side of the central aisle, where fasting, haggard, ashen-faced, elderly women rested, their gray hair uncombed or covered with a kerchief, some with their eyes closed, and others weakly sipping water through a straw.

At the horizontal end of that long room, and fully visible from the beds, a table was set somewhat festively. Our three hostesses were busily frying onions and sausages in preparation for the feast. We made our way through the richly wafting smells of fried onion and fried meat, between the rows of nearly starving women. I chose a seat with my back turned towards the fasters; we sat down to our meal, and ate. The onion smell lingered on my clothes and in my nostrils for a very long time. The extraordinary image stayed with me even longer.

※ ※ ※

But back to solitary confinement in the men's penitentiary and its silence. The super maximum-security unit consisted of four tiers with eleven cells each; they were eleven feet by six and a half feet of solid concrete, and bordered on one side by a steel door with a five-inch square window. The units were furnished with a low cement slab covered by a sheet of plywood and a foam pad and used as a bed, as well as a table-chair combination and a sink-toilet combination. Prisoners were given a cardboard box for their personal effects, letters, and books. A light burned continuously overhead, slightly lowered at night. Each day, the men were allowed out for half an hour to collect their food and exercise in the corridor in front of the cells. A radio, controlled by the guards, was often tuned to a station where music often alternated with static.

A Canadian study by Cohen and Taylor (1972) quotes an inmate.

How the hell do you cope with loneliness in a godamned cell 23 1/2 hours a day with the light burning on you. How do you cope with sanity? I've been down away [from solitary confinement] for twenty days and I can still see that goddam light.

Later studies showed that after the closure of this penitentiary many conditions improved in the new location, but that others remained unchanged and some even deteriorated.

The cells from which we transcribed the graffiti were bare of all furnishings; some looked as if they had been the sites of a riot, with toilets sometimes ripped off the wall. The only proof of previous human occupancy was the hundreds of graffiti and several drawings we collected from the filthy walls.

A typical conversation would run as follows, the different handwritings and spellings attesting to separate identities:

- All these pigs are all suckers jam tarts.
- Jam tarts? How about assholes, cocksuckers, no good for nothing, slimy rotten bastards! But jam tarts? Must have been a skinner trying to express himself.
- Agreed! Fully agreed.

Elsewhere, another conversation took place:

- Love and hate give no reason.

- Everything has a reason for happening whether it be human or natural or unnatural as some people like to call certain happenings. If one looks deep enough he or she will find a reason.
- Untrue/Very untrue

concluding with the ubiquitous: "Rat."

Boasts, in particular, had to be slammed down by either bigger boasts or sheer contempt, as it does not pay to pretend to a higher status that one is entitled to:

- J. M. 9717 smashed all the windows in the pig's lounge at Mission [another jail]
- So what, I smashed all the Pigs faces at Mission.
- BIG FUCKING DEAL!

More disturbing were the graffiti expressing the fear of madness, the oppression of boredom, and the frustrations of loneliness. There again, we felt that anonymity allowed a greater sincerity without fear of being thought weak for stating their pain:

- (Solitary violence) trust no one. Hate (disturb). Relate to people, manipulate (reject).
- BC Pen is a NIGHTMARE. END SOLITAIRE
- SOLITARY IS TORTURE.

Two poems illustrate the sense of despair we felt everywhere:

(1) My Belly's A cravin
There's a shootin in my head
I feel like I'm dyin
And I wish I was dead
If I live till tomorrow
I'll be a long time

(2) When you live in a Place
Full of Flashing Knives
where there's cold contempt
for human lives
The Cement around you
The steel and stone
Kind of gives you the
Feelin that you stand all alone.

Some graffiti were also illustrated: "I'm crazy and I don't give a Fuck!" said one under a drawing of a skull and scythe. Another piece next to a horrifying drawing of a distended maw with black fangs, shouted: "PLEASE HELP ME I CAN'T TAKE IT NO MORE THE END IS NEAR."

Obviously, time was an important consideration since, after all, the inmates were doing time, not spending it, or passing it, as people on the outside might. Moreover, being in solitary confinement (for whatever reason: punitive dissociation, administrative segregation, or protective custody), it could be said they were doing time within time. In the case of administrative segregation, the inmates did not always know how long they would be segregated and this uncertainty added enormously to the duress of their confinement.

Social scientists have often noted the difficulty inmates experience in measuring the passage of time, how they invent obsessional rituals to mark the days and even hours. Elvi discovered in her literature search very few studies dealing with graffiti in solitary confinement. Among those, the most interesting ones showed that victims of religious and political persecutions imprisoned in the Tower of London in the sixteenth century experienced the same obsession with time. One Thomas Salmon, for instance, described himself as being a "close prisoner 8 months, 32 weeks, 224 days, 3576 hours."

On the walls we studied, time was also measured. In one cell, an elaborate drawing of a sand timer was titled, "Time passages." Elsewhere, time was shown as being static. A prisoner had created a fictional sentence for himself: "1000-1 year," another had written a mathematical statement: "365+365=730" with seemingly little hope of reprieve. Others made lists, which although called "calenders," were in fact diaries:

Thurs. 12: Canteen and court day
15: the day I go down
Jan 4: Kind of boring, fair day; no smokes
Jan 3: Not bad, was high
Jan 31: Big Day!

Occasionally, meals, which often constitute a central preoccupation in jail—providing sustenance, continuity, and variety—were also used as time markers. One prisoner had counted the number of meals left to be eaten until his release; another recorded menus, real or imaginary (my own experience of meals in jail is that they were varied and plentiful, if not particularly tasty, so the list could be a faithful menu for those ten days):

8 Sunday Pork chops
9 Monday Roast Beef
10 Sausages
11 W. Stew
12 T. Liver
13 F. Sandwich
14 S. Steak
15 S. Turkey
16 M. Steak
17 T. Chicken
18 W. Liver.

As we progressed in our transcribing, categories started sorting out. The most common one consisted of standard statements, expected in these surroundings and somewhat meaningless: "PIG, fuckin' pig, rat, rats suck, death to all rats," etc. Some holes in the wall graphically illustrated the use to which "assholes" could be put, particularly in relation to "pigs."

The word God occupied a fair amount of space, the graffiti being as varied as the moods and psychological health of the inmates who wrote them—again, we felt that anonymity permitted a greater freedom of expression:

- Believe in God as you understand him. A Power greater than yourself
- Soon I'll have the power of god
- Worship the devil/Fuck God he sucks/I know He's given me head before
- God maid me do ALL this I will KEEP in good HEALTH. AMEN

There were also a few rewordings of old biblical passages:

- For I am the meanest/Son of a Bitch/ever to walk the valley of Death.
- To tell you the truth unless a man is born of water and the spirit he cannot enter the kingdom of God.
- Do unto others before they can do unto you.

Given the number of First Nation inmates in Canadian jails (varying between 10 and 40 percent depending on the regions, a very large proportion since they constituted less than 4 percent of the total population), we were surprised to see how few graffiti reflected the writer's race. One suggested, "RED POWER. Not that we don't like you white guys but why don't go back to Europe and England?" And another, tenderly, "AYO OSHINI/Beloved One/AJ I DISH JOI The Heart Speaks."

Apart from these and two impressive drawings of an austere mask and a ferocious raven/salmon, executed in the Haida style, nothing could be specifically attributed to Native inmates. I remembered a Tsimshian woman I had interviewed in jail who referred to "her people," meaning street people and not Native people as I had first thought. Membership in other groups seems somewhat superseded by the jail experience.

The two most important functions of these graffiti; however, were first to establish who the enemies were, how strong, how evil, and what dreadful fate would befall them, and second, to set the record straight. The first were graffiti of revenge and hatred:

Thinking of the day
When they will pay
Floating downstream
While I cream.

A dripping knife accompanied the wish, "May the blood that drips this here knife be that of Pigs very own LIFE!!"

Elsewhere, one of the "conversations" ranted:

- Fuckin Pigs/shit/Shit Eating Swine!!
- You fucking pig/Suck this cock/in your mouth Blood & guts/Pig Guts
- Save us from these Mongrels in Blue!!
- To shit on a Pig would be Putting the icing on the cake!

But the prison guards were only the manifestation of what the inmates were really banging their heads against and its very symbol, "The System." Many inmates must have felt like quasi-political prisoners—victims of unfair powers over which they had no control:

- Justice is a word not reconiced by the Establishment
- Who Ever wrote the Criminal Code should be Procuted & killed
- Using an atonom for the word torture we can say the Canadian Penitentiary System!
- Abolish Solitary Confinement
- The whole damn system SUCKS !!!!! Sign up here is you want to change the system [signed, in succession, Ziggy, Rick, Moose, Billy, Darren, Siggy, Steve]

- When you are in Jail You are striped of your freedom in this place, you are striped of your humanistic instinck! You are animal! So you must behave like one!
- ATTACK!!
- HELP the inmates over injustice. Help the pigs to their Grave!

Setting the record straight gave rise to longer statements, usually couched in precise language. One such testimony was titled, "The truth and nothing but the truth," and gave every single detail of what really happened, where, how, and with whom. It was dominated by the desire to obtain justice.

Another related in resentful tones the following event:

We did a peaceful demonstration that on the day of January 19th on PCV Tom X … was punched in the mouth by what you call PIG in my dictionuray. So he Brick the Pig's nose we had a what you call a PEACEFUL DEMONSTRATION to show we were not going to take his bunch of bull-shit anymore, so the pigs end up smashing everything in the cells and we do the time for it.

Not only must records be set straight, but also accounts must be settled: "Ask J. P. about the K. P. riot then see how solid he is," insinuated one. Another challenged:

Who I will not be hiding behind but it you are a Clark Parker *[Clark Park had a bad reputation in Vancouver and a few rather small-time gangs used to frequent it at the time]* or a follower and you are a pice of ?? Just ask *[name scratched out]* I will make arrangements to meet you one on one if you are man or woman enough.

Frustration and unhappiness also translated into drawings, some simply frightening, others made powerful through the symbols used: a rearing horse with a star on its haunch, a machine gun, a chopper. The latter drawing illustrated a poem evoking the bad boy biker's good life and freedom on the road, in romantic defiance of the very four walls that now contained him:

A true TT, I ride alone
Every bit a biker, Right to the bone
I do what I please, write my own code
Anywhere I crash I call my abode
I love to live and love to ride
My whole world I see on a glide
I break the laws of every and
Run my machine through mud and sand
I rob and steal, rip off dope deals
My gateway is made on two wheels
Once I am gone, never to be back
My goodies are packed in a Harley Sack
Shady ladies, downers and gold
Crystel "T", magic mushrooms I've sold
Mixing whey and mese, with L.S.D.
A speedy trip-that's for me
China white too slow me down at night
A jug of bingo makes me fight
I carry a shiv and pack a rod
Mainlike tracks lad me to hell
I enjoy this like I think it's swell
There isn't a day I don't knock my bride
You know I'm married to a super glide.

As alienated as some statements may sound, the writers shed some of that strangeness when we started finding touches of humour, flippancy, and whimsy:

- We're here for a good time, Not a long time!
- Hi, my name is *[blank]*
  This is a recording
  recording
  recording
- If Rock is Gourmet cooking Disco must be MacDonalds

- *[above the door]* Restricted - Rated X
  No Admittance to Persons under 21
- USA Here I come
  Right back from I started from!
- Kelloggs Rice Krispigs,

Or the anonymous "O.K." in response to the no less anonymous, "Let's Fuck!" A few even showed ironic self-deprecation: "I'm smart/I'm in the B. C. Pen," or under the cartoon of a man wearing a T-shirt marked B. C. Pen, "Mr. Cool!!!"

There were also nice touches and friendly thoughts, which we found a welcome relief after so many hours spent transcribing all the dirt, pain, and anger of these men's writings.

There were wishes: "Happy birthday, Eleanor." Greetings: "Hi #0701 Yours truly #02345." Aphorisms: "Never be cruel to a Heart that's true to you," and complimentary opinions: "The Nurse, Mrs. O'C., sure is nice."

There were hearts decorated with initials and flowers, which spoke of remembered connections: "I still love her and always will deep down inside." On one wall was a woman's body, shown from her round breasts to her knees, each pubic hair precisely—and one would be tempted to say lovingly—drawn. Elsewhere, a man expressed his impatience to be reunited with his wife and child:

> When it comes to love is so, so big & beautiful. I have a 4 year old son who I got to know for the first time when I maried me wife Mo. I'll tell you it sure is going to be a very big beautiful tripe when this B. C. Pen tripe is over come early February.

What struck me the most was not so much the silence in these empty cells, but the absence of the sounds that should have been there. After working in a psychiatric hospital and doing research in a women's jail, I was almost anticipating all the familiar sounds: the clinking of keys, the banging of fists, the rattling of bars, the clattering of turned-over chairs, the angry shouts and curses, the bits of disembodied songs, the shuffling of feet.

There was none of that, yet there was no silence either, and an ir sound seemed to be coming from somewhere. It took me some realize what it was and that it came from the graffiti themselves. This may sound like a literary conceit, but I am simply reporting how I felt at the time. If one believes in the power of the written word, it should not be too difficult to believe that these words were sonorous, clanging with outrage and loneliness, shouting for some corresponding echo, tearing at the mute blankness, and hopelessly feeding on themselves.

Elvi and I thought for a long time about writing an article about these graffiti. She came up with a possible title, "Reasserting the Self: Graffiti in Solitary Confinement Cells." I believe she even wrote a paper to present to an anthropological conference in 1991 as a work in progress. Yet, somehow, something always escaped us. Perhaps, simply, the time had passed to let those voices speak up now, when they had not been heard then, or perhaps we felt unable to convince anyone, least of all ourselves, that all those selves had been reasserted.

Dickens held solitary confinement's "slow and daily tempering of the brain to be immeasurably worse than any torture of the body," and upon visiting an American prison, wrote in 1842 of the "torture and agony" inflicted and endured. It took 133 years for this statement to be read in a Canadian federal court in support of discontinuing the "cruel and unusual punishment" of solitary confinement. Some changes (including the change in terminology noted at the beginning) resulted from these efforts, but men and women are still held alone between four walls for a considerable portion of the day.

I leave the last word to one of those men, the one who had written, high up on the wall, just below the ceiling, in letters so small that I had to climb on a stool to read them:

> "If you are close enough to read this then you must be very lonely."

Chapter Seven

"The Most Beautiful Land Ever Seen"
Cuba, 1992

> There is a sort of disease of the eyes called retinoris pigmentaria, which manifests itself by the loss of lateral vision. All those who have carried away an optimistic view of Cuba are quite sick. They see directly in front, never from the corner of the eye.
>
> Sartre, *On Cuba*, quoting the Minister Oscar Pinos Santos's speech on July 1, 1959.

> We want Cuba to have the image of an earthly paradise.
>
> Fidel Castro, 1994 Conference on Tourism

"The most beautiful land ever seen," or so, according to my guidebook, said Christopher Columbus on October 27, 1492 upon reaching the northeastern shore of Cuba, the largest island in the Caribbean. To which he promptly added, "Where there is such marvelous scenery, there must be much from which profit can be made."

Some twenty years later, the Spaniards' incipient greed had been fully confirmed. According to the same guidebook, an Indian chief by the name of Hatuey, who had already fought the Spaniards on Hispaniola, warned his compatriots:

> These Europeans worship a very covetous sort of God. They will exact immense treasures of us and will use their utmost endeavours to reduce us to a miserable state of slavery or else put us to death.

Notwithstanding, the political bias of the sentiment (the guidebook, published in Cuba in 1989, also described the Catholic Church of Cuba as a "bulwark of slavocracy"), history would agree that the pronouncement was certainly prophetic enough, particularly for Hatuey, who was burned at the stake soon afterwards.

Population Then and Now
The fate of the quite civilized Taino Indians, who had so instinctively mistrusted the Spaniards at the end of the fifteenth century, was cruel. Equally so that of the somewhat more primitive Ciboneys—not to mention that of the even more ancient aboriginal peoples, the Guanahatabeyes—who had all been wiped out from the surface of the island in very little time. Many tribes had in fact speeded up the process of eradication by committing mass suicide; the rest was exterminated in a process that took only a little more than three decades.

In 1992, exactly 500 years after Columbus's arrival, all Latin American countries discovered by him and colonized by the Spaniards, and where native populations have survived and *meztizos* prevailed, were urged by their governments to celebrate the momentous event. One did not detect in Cuba, once known as the Jewel of the Spanish Crown, any of the ambivalence so strongly expressed in those other Latin American countries. Alone, and by default, Cuba, on that count at least, seemed at peace with herself.

In early 1992, I arrived in Havana in the late evening. A few people from the university met me at the airport to welcome me and clear me through customs and the visa check. Lisa, whom I met in Canada and who was to be my mentor and mediator, was among them.

While in Vancouver, I had been asked, since I speak Spanish, to take to lunch two people from the University of Havana who would be waiting for me at an appointed time and place. Influenced by some odd notion that all Cubans looked more or less like Desi Arnaz, perhaps adorned with a pencil-thin moustache and much machismo, I expected two light-skinned males. I saw no such persons. I had momentarily dismissed offhand two individuals, yet so obviously foreign, so obviously waiting, because one was a woman and both were black. This could uncharitably be construed as a sexist and racist bias on my part, but having never met any Cubans before, I had simply fallen back on some unconscious stereotypes deriving from old Hollywood movies and television shows.

A few days later, coming upon them unexpectedly, I observed once more with some surprise that they were indeed black. Being by then completely familiar with them and having fallen under the charm of Lisa's warm personality, I had ceased to notice such physical details. Once in Cuba, colour and racial origins had actually so little effect on me that later, back in Canada, I would have to think carefully about someone's appearance when asked, "Did you meet the director of such and such? A tall black guy with a gray moustache?" The colour of the moustache, rather than that of the skin, would have been the significant distinguishing characteristic.

The racial mix of Havana is evident in streets, offices, and everywhere else. Some 66 percent of the Cuban population is white, about 33 percent either black or mulatto, and the remaining Cubans are of Chinese origin.

The whites are mostly descendants of Spanish colonial settlers, mainly from Andalusia, Galicia, and the Canary Islands, who came on the heels of Diego Velázquez, the founder of Havana, and his 300 conquistadors. They also include later immigrants.

The blacks and mulattos are the result of several waves of Bantu, Dahomeyan, Congolese, Mandingo, and Yoruba slave shipments. They were first brought to the island in 1524 to work in the Jaguar gold mine. Then Haitian slaves, brought by their masters after the Haitian Revolution of 1791, came and finally a steady flow culminating with the 600,000 brought in during the sugar boom of 1821–1831. (Sartre called Cuba "the diabetic monster.") During the late 1830s, blacks almost matched the white population.

Finally, some 130,000 Chinese "coolies" came with work contracts to Cuba in the nineteenth century. Many stayed and their descendants constitute about 1 percent of the present Cuban population.

Hotel Vedado
After going through airport formalities in Havana, Lisa and her husband drove me in their little Lada to the hotel Vedado near the university where I was registered. As a guest of the university, I had no say in the choice of a hotel. My status must have been fairly low, since other colleagues who had been there the year before had been much more comfortably housed. At first sight, the hotel was quite dingy and poorly lit—I did not yet know that this was the rule everywhere in Havana to save precious electricity. But the room seemed clean, so I said nothing.

In fact, by Cuban standards in 1992, the Vedado was a perfectly suitable hotel, catering to local people rather than to tourists, although I believe there were two or three Mexicans and Brazilians staying there. Two years later, I was rather amused to read the following description of his accommodations at the Vedado ("a small, three-star hotel") written by the assistant travel editor of *The Globe and Mail*.

> A dingy room with a lamp that didn't light, a television that wouldn't turn on, a toilet without a seat, and wooden shutters that opened to a close-up view of an exterior wall.

In other words, he concluded, "the world of grunge," which he was glad to leave when assigned elsewhere by Cubanacan, Cuba's travel organizers. Well, what did he expect? It is also possible that conditions had deteriorated since my visit. Or, perhaps, he did not have the right connections (unlikely, for a travel writer under the wing of Cubanacan), because I did have a toilet seat, my room did overlook the street, and the shower did have sufficient hot water. What I did not understand was why he was directed to the Vedado in the first place.

The small lobby was plunged in darkness in the evening, and there would have been nothing there to do or see anyway. Soon after I arrived, a man called me on the hotel telephone, rather hesitantly suggesting the usual services offered to "rich" lone female tourists. I declined politely and my refusal was accepted just as politely. Once, I went into the tiny and smoky bar of the hotel to have a bottle of mineral water opened and, even if I had been so inclined, that bar was not a place I would have had a drink, especially on my own.

Lisa had strongly advised me not to go out alone at night, and indeed, I had heard elsewhere that the Malecón, the wide avenue along the sea, was no longer safe and that one should definitely not venture there alone in the evening. So I stayed in my hotel room, resenting once more that lone women travellers who are not looking for adventure have a less easy time of it than men, and by force see much less of the local life.

So I stayed in, and when I was tired of reading by the poor light, watched television. The short program usually shown in the evening had actually given me an erroneous idea of the technical quality of Cuban television. It was not until Lisa invited me for dinner during my last week that I discovered colour television indeed existed, that there were more than two channels, and that the reception was not bad at all.

We watched two of their favourite programs: some reruns of *Flipper* from the 1960s, and a dubbed Brazilian soap opera full of machismo and female abuse. I asked Lisa how Cuban women, in so many ways the equals of men through their contribution to the revolution, viewed this type of show. She shrugged, meaning that it was only entertainment.

In my room, however, I was regularly treated, through the snow on my screen, to excruciatingly boring documentaries produced in Spain and entirely devoted (or so it seemed) to endless and mind-draining depictions of people climbing mountains or buildings. The evening would usually conclude with a cartoon reminding sleepy little children that it was time to go to bed.

There was one regular show I quite enjoyed. It was an interview with various workers, sometimes a supervisor of a cleaning crew, sometimes people who worked in a bicycle factory—the latter being very topical. Cuba had just started a large bicycle production project, and clunky objects that they were, they nevertheless gave rise to almost poetic descriptions of their strength, lightness, speed, good value, and most of all their Cuban-ness.

The "talking head" interviews were done without any frills and with great awkward dignity on the part of the people interviewed. Indeed, one felt strongly the honour bestowed upon them as contributors to everybody's wellbeing, in the same manner as the common appellation of *compañero* and *compañera* applied to all levels of society never seemed perfunctory to me. But perhaps, I am just naive.

One evening, unable to read and irritated by the television vacuum, I went to a neighbouring hotel considerably more elegant than mine was, although still modest by Canadian standards. I sat for ten minutes or so in the well-lit lobby beside a little souvenir shop, soaking up the wealth. Plunged back into an atmosphere reminiscent of home, it was probably the only time when I wondered what I was actually doing in Cuba.

This was very unfair to the Cubans, and to some extent to the Hotel Vedado itself, where the staff was likely doing their best in those difficult circumstances. There was even a large woman in the dark lobby by the door of the elevator, whose main function, it seemed to me, was to discourage a succession of young women from going up with one particular Brazilian tourist. Another of her functions was to bang on the elevator door to keep it going.

One Sunday afternoon, Lisa and her husband had very kindly taken me to the beach. Here, I must rave about the famous sand on Cuban beaches, smoothly pale, fine as silk, and according to *Condé Nast Traveller*, "soft as a baby's bum." I am sure the couple had better things to do with their very limited free time, but hospitality and generosity prevailed, and they insisted.

Back at the Vedado, I realized I had lost my key on the beach and was sternly reprimanded since, as it bore both the name of the hotel and the room number, the lock had to be replaced. It was done within ten minutes of my return to my room, a grudging efficiency I had not met so far.

My feeling of security was ambiguous. Although the woman guarding the elevator was vigilant enough, my room was totally unsafe, being the last one in a long corridor, right by the open door of the fire escape that provided much needed ventilation, but also opened freely into a back alley. However, I had discovered that the bathroom door and the closet door, facing each other in my tiny hallway, could be effectively interlocked, creating an impassable barricade. No doubt, it would also have been a formidable obstacle in case of a fire, particularly at night.

When I told the emotional senior psychologist (more on her later) that I was staying at the Vedado, she beamed. She had apparently spent her wedding night there, and it had remained for her a lovely place to remember. It may well have been a very nice hotel before things got a little too tough for everybody in Cuba.

The University of Havana

That first night, after dropping off my bag at the hotel, Lisa and her husband invited me to stroll along La Rampa, Havana's main artery, and get acquainted with my new neighbourhood. It was January and the bitter winter I had left in Montreal the day before made me appreciate even more the mellowness of the night. I paid careful attention as they showed me the route I would be taking in the morning and led me along little side streets, by a school, a general store, and a number of old, apparently derelict houses, on the way to the university.

The following morning, having discovered by daylight the somewhat grimmer look of the street, I arrived at eight o'clock for my first meeting. Climbing the dilapidated steps leading to the main entrance of the university, I saw clearly for the first time what was going to become so familiar: the combination of past elegance with contemporary decrepitude.

The oldest Spanish-speaking university in the Americas, the University of Havana was established in 1728, by royal and papal decree from King Philip V of Spain and Pope Innocent XIII. To reflect this dual sanction, it was then called *Real y Pontifical Universidad de San Gerónimo de la Habana*. Then, keeping the king but dropping the pope, it became a secular institution in 1842 under the name of *Real y Literaria Universidad de la Habana*.

Finally, when Cuba became a republic, the king too was dropped and the university acquired its present name, *Universidad Nacional de Habana*.

Notwithstanding its poor physical condition and its lack of the most basic resources, it would be a good university were it not for its Marxist-Leninist ideological orientation, which renders the study of the social sciences or the liberal arts somewhat problematic.

On my first morning at the university, I was to meet the research group from the *Fiscalia General de la Republica,* the prosecutor general's office, who were already gathered around the table, the only vacant seat left at the head obviously reserved for me. Except for one woman wearing a tight orange dress, whose pinched face never relented, the group was delightful and their friendly, clever shining faces seemed like so many sources of welcome. We struggled through my awkward Spanish, whose deficiencies I found useful in partially hiding my inability to satisfy their pressing demands for information—they needed an economist, a sociologist, a political scientist, an historian, a physician, all rolled into one.

This group, which had been meeting informally for discussions and legal research for the last five years, was composed of jurists, psychologists, economists, and one philosopher. Those with advanced degrees had obtained them either in East Germany or the Soviet Union. With the failure of the USSR to continue bolstering their economy and their departure from Cuba, the interests of such people I was meeting here were now turning to other influences and sources of information, either by force, or perhaps through some new inclination, for these were obviously highly intelligent people full of intellectual curiosity.

After the meeting, a young man addressed me in halting English, something that would often happen. While the official part of every meeting was always conducted in Spanish, people sometimes acknowledged later, during less formal exchanges, that they had some knowledge of English. However, visitors were usually expected to struggle in their hosts' language, even if both sides were equally matched in their respective lack of fluency in the foreign tongue.

Often we did quite well by each speaking our own language. But where I spoke English slowly, articulating carefully, I was riddled in return with the Cuban machine-gun delivery of Spanish, eliding many consonants on the way according to local custom. Although I normally have little difficulty communicating with most Spaniards and Latin Americans, the peculiarities of the Cuban speech often defeated me.

One of the deans, who knew no English and was physically or psychologically unable to slow down his delivery, gave me the greatest difficulty. When asked to repeat something, he repeated exactly the same sentence, word for word, only faster and louder. Lisa, on the other hand, who studied in East Germany and was aware of the difficulties of having to live and work in a foreign language, always found other ways, other words, to impart the same meaning if I missed it the first time.

Her patience and kindness were admirable, particularly given the awesome workload she carried. Not only was she teaching law full-time with some administrative responsibilities thrown in and working in conditions deemed insufferable to North American academics, she was also a part-time municipal judge. Moreover, she spent, as did all her colleagues, one week every semester working "in the fields," this term being somewhat flexible and adapted to individual capacities, but the civic duty nevertheless having to be performed.

I had been given an office, vacated for my benefit by one of the administrators. The room was kept in perpetual semidarkness, the blinds drawn, and the windows painted some dark blue shade, as in wartime. After awhile, I got used to writing and reading in the dim light of a weak electric bulb, but never quite figured out why it had to be so. Not that working conditions were much better elsewhere and maintenance left much to be desired everywhere.

The women's bathroom, for instance, located above the staircase leading to a basement shelter (perhaps a bomb shelter? I did not ask), was far from luxurious. Several toilets were usually out of order, but I did not quite figure out what that meant since they did not flush automatically anyway. Instead, there was a large barrel of water with a long-handled pan used to carry water to the toilets and flush, actually a reasonably efficient way to proceed. A badly rusted sink, with no soap and no paper towel, and a small wall mirror badly cracked, completed the amenities. However, the bathroom was as clean as it could possibly be.

The university closed in the late afternoon by cutting off the electricity. Most of the basic resources were lacking in every government and university department I visited. Academic and professional Cubans were well aware of their present deficiencies, and they imagined that even the modest facilities they may have seen in East Germany and the Soviet Union paled in comparison to what the United States and Canada had to offer.

No doubt, the fact that my department was collecting old computers for them and that some of my Canadian colleagues never went to Havana without suitcases full of photocopy and fax paper, books, and basic office supplies, contributed to this sense of inferiority felt—in these matters alone—by our Cuban colleagues. Perhaps it did not occur to them that the situation was equally embarrassing for us.

Almost every day Lisa would take me to visit various officials, leaving me after an introduction, only to pick me up later. My guess was that these meetings were mostly intended to elicit goodwill and much of it was window dressing. Nevertheless, she introduced me to different sets of people and situations, some of them quite unexpected, most of them pleasant. The elderly president of the Supreme Court (Labour Division), for instance, wearing an excellent if very ancient suit, entertained me with great charm and a good knowledge of Quebec and the Canadian separatist issue. He also graced me with the usual Cuban hospitality—a glass of water and a tiny cup of the strong and syrupy sweet coffee to which I never got used.

I also visited the staff at the Medico-Legal Institute and was very much taken by the ironic wit and good looks of their gray-haired assistant director. I also met one of their technicians, a physical anthropologist who had become famous in Latin America for his reconstruction skills. Delighted at finding a visitor interested in those skills, he treated me to a guided tour of his rather grisly collection.

There was obviously a foreign feel to Cuba, but not an alien one, and at a superficial level, meeting colleagues in Havana felt rather like running into distant cousins fallen on hard times. I do not imagine that this benevolent feeling was necessarily mutual, since there was too much ease, too much material ownership, too many years of comfort in my own background to be thought of as an equal.

There was perhaps some envy at my material circumstances—but mostly, I would suspect, the sense of superiority and pride perhaps felt by such self-perceived elite groups as ascetics, police officers, war correspondents, disaster survivors, and obviously, heirs of revolutions, when dealing with those whose life is just too comfortable, too safe, and too conventional for them to have proven their mettle. The land I came from was much too fat, and my feelings had the delicacy of those unreasonably spoiled (the fate of the dogs of Havana, for instance, affected me profoundly). However, even in my sissified ways, I felt comfortable in Cuba.

※ ※ ※

The Hotel Vedado offered three meals a day, and I had vouchers entitling me to those. However, I had tried the evening meal on my first day, but it had been tasteless and much too plentiful. I felt embarrassed at eating only a small portion of what was obviously my ration. Since the meals were expensive and charged to the university, I decided to skip everything except breakfast (orange juice, coffee, a hard-boiled egg, and a variety of sweet buns) and manage otherwise.

I told the people at the office that I preferred staying at work during lunchtime and would not be returning to my hotel. I mentioned being quite satisfied with a roll and a small piece of cheese for lunch, so this became my daily fare: a glass of orange juice, a roll, and a small piece of hard cheese. By the third week, I would sometimes smuggle out my daily ration, unable to face it yet again, and sneak out to the *Habana Libre* (the former Havana Hilton) for a sandwich.

However, whatever I received was always given with generosity and kindness, and certainly, the low quality and scarcity of the food provided had nothing to do with my colleagues' sense of hospitality. I had hoped that Lisa would take me at least once with her to the cafeteria to see whether my juice, bread, and cheese compared well or not with her own fare, but she never did. She was probably looking forward to that time away from me as a respite from her mentoring duties.

I believe it went against the grain for Cubans not to be courteous and friendly, and they found shame in their inability to be hospitable. There was warmth in their attitude and their rapports among themselves—at least superficially and in public—and with their guests that was quite endearing. I was received everywhere with great cordiality.

I should mention that my status was quite modest, and there was little practical reward expected for showing me friendship. In fact, there were times when I might have wished a little less of it. My second week was made quite miserable by a severe cold. Whether started by Lisa or by me, our regular morning hug soon caused us to share it, probably a small price to pay for the daily affectionate greeting. We also shared my supply of Halls cough lozenges and soon exhaled the same mentholated breath.

Desde-el-triunfo-de-la-Revolución

As I walked along the streets of Havana, I could see placards and slogans everywhere. They were much like those I had seen a few years earlier in Mexico City, along the streets on which Pope John Paul II was expected to drive during his state visit. They had been neatly lettered, expressing correct sentiment of piety and welcome, but lacked the erratic spelling and artistic flourish of spontaneous graffiti; there had been something fixed and a little too well orchestrated about them. The slogans in Havana had the same flavour. All extolled two convictions: the triumph of the revolution and the need to continue the struggle.

Naively, I wondered why one should continue struggling when the battle had been so obviously won thirty years earlier. Of the latter, there was no doubt. Many Cubans, at least when speaking with foreigners, did not simply say "since the Revolution," but "since the-triumph-of-the-Revolution" *(desde-el-triunfo-de-la-Revolución),* as if it were a single word. I was then unaware of Castro's latest speech, which had preceded my arrival by a day or two, stating that the country would devote all available resources to solving domestic difficulties.

Indeed, it did not take me long to understand that what the slogans preached and urged was the application to the *economic* revolution of the same principles of solidarity and dedication that had led the *political and social* revolution in previous decades. The few television programs I watched in the little time allocated to them in the evening were certainly dominated by a strong message of being-all-in-it-together.

Even a visitor could feel the power of the argument for people steeped in the hardships undergone in the name of a revolutionary cause. In the face of those new and different hardships and the quickly increasing economic crisis then facing Cuba, it was easy to believe that the survival of her revolutionary ideals depended on the Cubans' ability to survive also their looming economic disaster. Following the massive changes undergone by its old socialist friends and allies, the USSR and East Germany, it was obvious that Cuba was struggling with the formulation of potential new alliances, while still in the process of reformulating its old ones.

Cuba's often violent and tragic history is full of leaders of uprisings and revolutions, who often lost their lives in appalling circumstances—Indians, blacks, whites—they all figure prominently in the long-established Cuban pattern of rebellion. Most of these rebels were young and died young. During contemporary times, Jean-Paul Sartre was struck during his 1959 visit to Cuba by the youth of the Cuban revolutionaries. Guevara and Raul Castro were barely thirty and the other followers of Fidel were even younger.

> No old people in power! In fact, I did not see a single one among the leaders. The fathers don't make themselves noticed. This island has the most discreet 50-year olds.

For Sartre, the reason was obvious.

> The young people had nothing to lose. They saw their elders treating tyranny with respect and thought, 'It's our misfortune to which they're resigned.'

In every office I visited, there was at least one large photograph of Fidel, often flanked by his less imposing brother Raul, both taken when the men were considerably younger. Cuba had the cult of her dead young heroes, such as the idealized Ernesto "Che" Guevara and José Martí. Castro, still alive, had become what they would never be—incongruously old. He was the anomaly in that gallery of heroic young men, the surviving exception. Still, with his beard (the consequence of a revolutionary vow), his uniform, and his charm—for by all accounts, he was still a charming and charismatic man—he remained the symbol of the revolution.

Whatever one may feel about Castro's politics (and I do not wish to minimize in any way their appalling aspects) and the impact of the Cuban Revolution, one should look at what it has done for many individuals. The leader of the small discussion group I have already mentioned, a senior psychologist with advanced training in the Soviet Union, had the dual title of Professor at the University of Havana and Principal Researcher with the Prosecutor General's Office. By contrast, to make ends meet and support her six children, her mother sewed clothes in her kitchen on an old sewing machine that often broke down.

This psychologist painted a cliché for me, one of the conventional success stories often told by post-revolutionary propagandists; however, what was not the least a cliché, were her sincerity and emotion. At the end of my presentation to the group on my first day, she hugged me warmly and gave me a number of books, poorly printed on brown sugarcane paper, one of which was a biography of José Martí, which with tears in her eyes she urged me to read.

For her, and surely for many of her generation, the revolution had been a true liberation of all their potentials and their gratitude seemed unflinching. Things were different for young people, for whom the revolution was a *fait-accompli* and who had not experienced first-hand the conditions in the Batista era in their island. They were hankering, at whatever social and political cost, for the same American luxuries and fashions available everywhere else in the world.

Political scientists, economists, sociologists, psychologists, historians, philosophers, and so on no doubt spend much time weighing the often-humanitarian dire price paid for political and social revolutions versus the individual energy released and the personal accomplishments thus permitted. I certainly do not know enough about such things to comment on them, reporting only what I (untrained in those disciplines) observed in 1992, but in the case of Cuba, I felt both fear and hope for her as she faced inner rebellious turmoil, hostile external pressures, and dire economic prospects, all presumably working towards some unavoidable convergence.

Restrictions

It was impossible to miss or ignore the economic situation. Signs of it were everywhere: in the emptiness of the shops, in the ill-maintained buildings, in the slogans on the walls, in the apologies of the people. Cubans adopted a certain tone of voice when mentioning to foreigners the "difficult situation." A pained, distant, and slightly embarrassed tone and expression as if they were reporting on the health of a relative stricken by a mysterious disease or on some family scandal only referred to in veiled terms and whispered allusion—a tone we could not help also adopting in sympathy.

I experienced none of the difficulties undergone by those around me, the group of well-educated people with responsible jobs, in fact very much like my Canadian acquaintances at home. Indeed, life was relatively pleasant for me in Havana. However, I saw the severe rationing of gasoline (in a city where public transport was both unreliable and uncomfortable), meat, milk (except for children), and food and clothing I would personally not define as luxuries but as necessities.

Only fruit, coffee, orange juice, and sugar to assuage the Cubans' chronic sweet tooth, were abundant and reasonably priced. Pizzas and *hamburguesas,* the latter apparently bearing little resemblance to what they presumed to imitate, could be obtained without rationing, but the long line-ups in front of the shops selling them during the lunch hour were discouraging.

The reason for this extensive shortage in Cuba in 1992 was that all resources were devoted to supporting the development of tourism. The most obvious difference between my Cuban colleagues and me was that I could buy a sandwich at the *Habana Libre* any time I felt like it, and that such modest luxury was not available to them. I had American dollars and they did not.

In this economy under siege, Cubans were not then allowed to own American currency. It is only at the end of 1993, some eighteen months later, that in an effort to encourage the flow of American dollars into the country, it became legal for Cubans to own that currency and buy goods from the shops reserved for tourists, the *Tiendas Intur.* During my visit; however, only tourists could spend American dollars—in fact, it was the only currency allowed them. Exceptionally, a handful of pesos was given to me upon my arrival, but I never found an opportunity to spend them.

What this situation did was create two parallel economies and societies, where the American dollar bought nearly everything and the Cuban peso almost nothing. As a visitor, I had access to goods my local acquaintances could only dream of having. Lisa once said wistfully that "Cubans liked them too," as we saw large baskets of crayfish wheeled through kitchen doors of a luxury tourist hotel by the beach. Upon presentation of my passport, I could buy for her car almost unlimited amounts of otherwise severely restricted gasoline.

When I took Lisa and her husband to one of the excellent and expensive restaurants in Havana, we were surrounded by similar groups of foreign guests treating their local hosts to an elegant dinner in an ambience probably reminiscent of prerevolutionary days. Also found there were couples that were more dubious; male tourists, often Brazilians or Mexicans, escorting very young Cuban girls to places no local man could have taken them. Lisa frowned reprovingly at the sight of such couples; apparently, prostitution, which was said to have more or less vanished from Cuba, had not only reappeared but was now flourishing.

The dual economy, intent on acquiring American currency for Cuban coffers, together with the priority given to increasing tourism at the expense of local consumers already so deprived, had started creating some resentment against well-to-do visitors. Luxuries were severely banned for residents, although I was told that honeymooning couples were allowed to spend their wedding night in one of the better tourist hotels, a small privilege that may well have rankled the following morning when they had to leave.

From a few clues inadvertently given, I also had some notion that a good number of people were tired of the regime. I do not mean those who were politically and violently opposed to it and committed to its downfall, since they would obviously not have confided in me, but ordinary citizens who had to live with substantial constraints and economic deprivation. However, despite this, there appeared to be unanimous pride in the progress made. Three different people told me, for instance, that all children went to school and all wore shoes.

While this may smack of party line, it was nevertheless a fact that all children in Havana did wear shoes, along with neat uniforms, at least when they went to school (as I could see every morning when walking by a small school on my way to the university). All children did go to school and must do so until the age of seventeen, which is no mean accomplishment in Latin America.

Cubans also were—and still are—justifiably proud of their outstanding social and medical services. For instance, partly due to the focus on preventive and family medicine, the infant mortality rate in Cuba still stands roughly between the US and Canadian figures, with infinity fewer resources. As well, Cuba physicians are well recognized the world over, particularly in poor countries and in times of crisis. Their skills are one of the few exports that Cuba can rely on.

However, conditions had worsened, as described by a Canadian colleague who became ill in Cuba a few weeks before my visit and was hospitalized in Havana. It was generally agreed by then that medical care in a hospital could barely satisfy anything but the most basic needs. I could well believe the remark made by one of my local acquaintances that if you were not a child in Cuba, or old, or sick, or mentally incompetent, then you really did not have very much.

Cuba in a Ibero/Latino-American Context

Coming from Canada, I felt it difficult to gauge the place of Cuba among other Hispanic and Latin American countries. We knew, of course, of her previous reliance on the former USSR and to a lesser extent East Germany, where many of her scholars were trained. We also knew of her limited association with Africa, where she sent medical doctors and from where she received and trained students. Mostly, we knew about the US embargo and Cuba's love-hate relationship with the US dollar. Finally, we were aware of the political influence of the Miami group of Cuban exiles. But how did she fare elsewhere?

I can provide a very small clue to this through two personal experiences, illustrating the somewhat marginal position of Cuba among other Spanish-speaking nations in the 1990s. My sense was that, although everyone was aware of her economic plight, not much was actually known about what went on in the country. I would not presume to guess whether many were interested, except in a superficial manner.

In 1994, two years after my visit to Havana, I happened to be in Spain during the fourth Latin American meeting of the chiefs of states and governments taking place in Colombia. I doubt the event would have been extensively covered by the Canadian press and I might not even had read about it, but the Spanish newspapers followed it closely and gave a different perspective on Cuba from the North American one and an opportunity to appreciate her awkward and ambiguous position within Latin America.

"No data," reported the chart on Cuba, while all the other countries had provided economic indicators (GNP, inflation rate, national debt, etc.). Information on Cuba was scant and mostly speculative and anecdotal. The press reported the steadily worsening economic situation in the country and confirmed the effort made by the government to initiate talks with Cubans in exile. Finally, it quoted some Cubans who had taken refuge in the Belgian and German embassies in Havana as pleading for visas to enable them to leave "this hell on earth."

Castro, who attended this conference in Colombia, ranted in his speech against the USA and Bill Clinton. He was particularly incensed at Cuba's recent exclusion from the Summit of the Americas, which had been held of all places in Miami, a hotbed of anti-Castro Cuban exiles. Although he was heard with some sympathy in Colombia, he was also urged to spread democratic reform and to start a second revolution. Not surprisingly, having failed to obtain stronger support, he did not consider the 1994 conference in Colombia to have been a success.

Actually, Cuba's most unexpected contribution to that meeting appeared to have been the sight of Castro in mufti for the first time since 1959. *"Fidel, del caqui a la guayabera,"* gasped one of the headlines, and his symbolic discarding of khaki in favour of the traditional white shirt received almost as much coverage as his desperate pleading for assistance.

In Barcelona, *La Vanguardia* speculated at some length on the meaning of the gesture. Was it an indication of a desire to relax Cuba's position or was it simply a publicity stunt to draw attention to the economic situation of the island? The shift of interest in the press from the serious to the frivolous certainly did not address properly Cuba's somewhat desperate situation.

❧ ❧ ❧

Still in 1994, I had another opportunity to view Cuba in its Latin American context. I was attending a meeting in Caracas on cooperative higher education and training programs in the Americas, where the plight of Cuba had been discussed with sympathy but no sentimentality. There was an agreement to make certain necessary financial concessions so Cuba could be accepted as a working partner, but also an insistence that she be made to pull her weight in other ways (again, medical training or services were mentioned). They were not giving anything away and if Cuba wanted in, she had to contribute fairly.

It had struck me as a realistic (as well as generous) understanding of what future relations between Cuba and other Latin American countries might become. Whether there would then be a role for Castro, even wearing the traditional *guayabera*, would be anybody's equivocal guess. As difficult as the economic constraints and everyday hardships within the country must surely be the fratricide conflict with extremist exiled Cubans in Florida. They never relented and probably never would, Castro being vanquished meant they could return. However, there had been some good indication in the early nineties that *Cambio Cubano* in Miami, a moderate movement formed against the extreme right views of the Cuban American National Foundation (a staunch supporter of the US opposition on Cuba and to its boycott) was gaining ground among exiled Cubans. But that positive effort lost much ground in August 1994 with the US immigration department's reversal of its disposition on Cuban refugees.

The Everyday Face of the Law
One afternoon, Lisa had to attend a meeting with her colleagues at the tribunal and parked me on a bench at the back of a courtroom where a trial was in progress. I am not sure what I had expected, since I was well aware of some darker aspects of Cuban justice, but what transpired was simply

that a young man, the accused, had created some sort of disturbance in a public place.

His girlfriend, his brother, and the brother's girlfriend were there, subdued and telling the judge and the other two required officials sitting at a table beside him that this young man was, really and ordinarily, quite a good young man, and perhaps he had had a little too much to drink that day.

The court reporter was seated at a small table with an ancient manual typewriter where, pounding haltingly away and stopping occasionally to change the paper, scratch her leg, retrieve things she had dropped, or stretch her arms, she took notes. The matter was dealt fairly, and with a computer or recording machine replacing the old typewriter, it could have taken place with few changes in Kalamazoo, Pouce Coupé, or Avignon.

❧ ❧ ❧

The other experience appeared a little more troubling. Across from my hotel was a small apartment building, four stories high, with two apartments on each floor. Used to assess housing by Canadian standards and forgetting the very small range of salaries in Cuba, I had assumed that the people living there were in very modest circumstances, and was surprised when Lisa told me they were probably schoolteachers and government supervisors.

This was again a useful remainder that we should forget our preconceptions when elsewhere. In Cuba, people were at the time mostly employed by the State and their salaries were modest as well as offering very little difference between jobs. On the other hand, there were free education and health care, and heavily subsidized housing, transport, and basic foods. Those neighbours of mine in Cuba could just as well have been my neighbours in Canada too—appearances to the contrary.

I looked into their windows, past their small balconies usually hung with drying laundry, into the main room with its adjacent kitchen. The rest of the apartment probably consisted of one or two small bedrooms and a bathroom. They were mostly young couples, sometimes with a small child or two, one with a dog afflicted with a particularly irritating bark. Sometimes in the evening, I would see in the street below my window a young man bouncing a ball against the wall, which seemed to be his sole entertainment.

Early one morning, a Sunday, a puzzling incident took place. It was about five o'clock and the street was quiet (during the week people would already have been lining up for the bus at that time). I was awakened by the shouts of a woman. I got up and looked through the shutters. A middle-aged, heavily built woman was standing at the street corner shouting and cursing at the top of her voice. From the little I could gather, she was cursing Castro, urging him to take everything else since he had already taken so much. She made some reference to her son that I did not catch.

The woman was obviously in great distress. She made a move to go, then came back and started shouting and cursing again; this time, she also started to disrobe. At that point, two police officers came along on foot pushing their bicycles. They spoke to her, calmed her down, and as she readily followed them, led her away.

The interesting thing during this incident, after all not uncommon in large cities—and we certainly have our share of shouters and cursers in Vancouver, particularly since patients in mental facilities have been mainstreamed, and they too are sometimes led away by the police—was the reaction of those who witnessed the scene. Two men who had been walking separately on each side of the street simply turned back and disappeared at the first intersection.

The people across from me in the apartments did one of two things. They either turned on the lights and stayed inside, hidden from sight. (I wondered what that meant. That there were potential witnesses?), or they kept their lights off and moved cautiously onto their balconies, keeping in the shadows and peering down at the woman (I wondered what that meant. That there were in fact unseen but real witnesses?).

Coincidently, during my visit to the Medico-Legal Institute earlier the same week, the arrest for such cases had been described to me. A number of police officers in Havana had recently been trained to deal with what were judged to be "mental cases" (were anti-Castro sentiments perhaps included in this category?) and take them for psychiatric examination, where their condition would be assessed and their fate determined. I was also told a number of safeguards had been built into the process, but they did not disclose them to me.

The two police officers slowly led the woman away. She had slipped one arm around the waist of one of the officers and rested her head on his shoulder, while the other one pushed the two bicycles. One of the two men who had vanished earlier now reappeared, and he stood at the corner and observed them as all three walked slowly up the street.

Across from me, the lights were turned off, and in the apartments that had been left in the dark, people went quietly back inside.

Touristic Havana
I would leave the hotel early in the morning, averting my eyes from the starving dogs with their loose skins hanging from ribbed skeletons. Cubans were not hard-hearted, and indeed, I saw several who owned dogs and treated them well, but there was no control of stray animals. Moreover, there was not enough food to go comfortably around for people, let alone for stray dogs, and their obvious starvation on the streets was just one of those many things Cubans had to put up with. It is also possible that they no longer noticed the dogs.

At the beginning, I tried to pocket some of the rolls I had for breakfast, even slipping half a smashed multivitamin tablet into bite-size portions to combat the more horrendous cases of mange and whatever else afflicted them, but soon abandoned my ridiculous attempts and simply averted my eyes.

I would occasionally see a recently dead dog on my path in the morning, so thin when alive and now flat as a pancake, and find it reduced to almost nothing by the evening when I came back, seemingly sucked into the ground. Despite their weakness and exhaustion, some still managed to copulate and—judging by the sight of a few skeletal bitches with deflated and pendulous teats—reproduce.

After work and during the weekend, I usually went for a walk, exploring different parts of town. Although people did not look at me, I did not feel invisible, in the way short and middle-aged women are in our city streets. Occasionally, when I stopped to look at a monument or a statue, young boys, some still in their school uniforms and carrying their books, would approach me and shyly ask me the time in hesitant English, and I would engage them in nearly monosyllabic conversations. They were charming, polite, and so pleased to be speaking English that a slow blush would sometimes creep up on the peach of their cheeks.

One weekend, somewhat to my embarrassment as I knew how little time Lisa had to herself, she insisted on showing me around Havana. She and her husband drove me around to see the usual sights: Morro Castle and its lighthouse, and la Cabaña, a fortress facing the harbour with apparently plans to convert it into a hotel, an odd choice since it had been a famous execution site for Cuban rebels during the fight for Independence. We saw the cathedral and the historical museum, a charming eighteenth-century building with a balconied patio, first used as the residence of the governors and presidents, then as city hall, which is open to visitors. Finally, we visited the *Plaza de Armas,* a nobly proportioned square, where it seemed that most official functions took place as well as Castro's famously long-winded speeches, as well as the forbidding church and convent of San Francisco, whose tower once served as lookout for pirates.

Morro Castle, Havana

We also drove along a wide boulevard, well treed and lined with luxurious houses once privately owned but now taken over by government services and lacking some of their former well tended look. Foreign embassies were there as well, the former USSR building sticking out like a sore thumb and looking forbiddingly like a fortress or an electronic bunker. I also noticed that Canadians did well by her diplomats abroad, as both the embassy and the ambassador's private residence attested.

We also walked together in the older part of Havana, which I had already visited on my own, exploring at random to get a sense of the city. In the little tortuous streets, looking up to the upper windows of the once elegant houses, I had seen something that had greatly puzzled me at first: a high-ceilinged room divided, not vertically with makeshift partitions or curtains, but with a horizontal partition instead, separating living quarters below from sleeping space above.

Most buildings were badly run-down, and it was sad to think what a beautiful and elegant city it must have been at its best. Although UNESCO had declared Havana a World Heritage Site, little work had been done in 1992 to restore the lovely but derelict buildings seen everywhere or at least stop further deterioration. I understand that nowadays, extensive work is being done to bring back many buildings to their former glory. Things are definitely improving, mostly due to the influence of tourism, but in 1992, most of Havana was a sorry sight.

On that afternoon, we saw two young men talking to a girl in an open doorway. After a casual look in their direction, we slowed down and looked again, surprised to see so much greenery inside the building. The men invited us to visit, and having said good-bye to the girl, showed us around. The place was a seminary and the young men explained about their studies while they showed us a number of small rooms around a lovely little garden in the courtyard. In my previous wanderings about town, I had noticed that the cathedral was in comparatively good repair and wondered at the official status of the Roman Catholic Church in Cuba (that old "bulwark of slavocracy"). The courtyard was surrounded by columns and arches sheltering a small gallery where cheap plastic seats and armchairs styled in the 1950s made a stark contrast with the beautifully proportioned architecture.

Some of the older buildings badly needing repair, Havana

The young men also proudly showed us the garage and the bishop's car. I had only seen three types of cars on my visit so far. There were Ladas of those few Cubans who could afford to drive and whose future was now as uncertain as Russia's ability to provide parts for them. I had also seen the old American boats of the 1950s, now sadly on blocks but which, until the gas rationing had immobilized most of them, had been a testimony to the quality of Detroit's manufacturing and Cuba's mechanical resourcefulness. Finally, there were the few modern cars reserved for tourist use. The bishop's car came as a surprise: a recent, large brown Mercedes that spoke of prestige and wealth.

Lisa and her husband drove me a little way out of town one day to visit some friends. It was a nice little house with a large vegetable garden growing around a tamarind tree, and one certainly did not have the same sense of deprivation as in the city. I was astonished to see the range of electronic equipment of their teenage son; his room would not have been out of place in any North American house. Even Lisa and her husband's countenance changed during the half hour spent there, and I could guess how they would look if they went on holiday.

On my last weekend, I decided to experience the touristic Cuba and went to spend the day in Varadero, a beach resort town some two hours away by bus from Havana, which used to be the weekend retreat of rich Cubans at the beginning of the century.

Nowadays, a number of co-ventures between Cuba and Germany, Spain, and other interests, had turned Varadero into the Mecca of foreign tourism (Cayo Coco, an island off the northern coast, so far uninhabitable, was the next target for tourist development by a Spanish company, with plans for eventually 6,000 rooms).

The drive to Varadero on the *Via Blanca,* a well managed scenic road along the coast, took us past some of Cuba's oil fields, with many wells idle despite the country's inability to meet her needs. We went past neat-looking army barracks, past teams of oxen doing the work previously done by tractors, and finally past Lenin Park and Pioneer Headquarters, a large playground for Havana's children, usually catering to hobby clubs, and where children from Chernobyl regularly spent some time in the summer.

Varadero was undistinguishable from similar resorts anywhere in the tropics, and because of the familiar language, I felt transported to Mexico where we often used to go on holidays. The hotel where I had stopped for lunch was full of French Canadians on an Air Canada holiday tour package. They struck me as being discreet, quiet, and extremely well behaved (I can only speak of what I saw that day), and I saw no hairy beer bellies hanging over skimpy bathing suits, which is the way our "snowbirds" are sometimes described by supposedly long-suffering Floridians.

Their tour included a trip to Havana, dinner at one of the better restaurants, and a visit to the Tropicana, a nightclub of which Cubans are very proud. I would have thought that such an obvious leftover from the Batista days, when Havana was a gambling and prostitution centre run by the Mafia, would have been abhorrent to them. But beautiful girls, music, and dancing are an integral part of Cuba, so the Tropicana simply continues the tradition.

I spent my last day in the anticlimactic act of buying a stuffed fighting cock requested by the head of my department. My husband had warned me against trying to bring it back home, assuring me that Canadian customs would pounce on it, since stuffed animals were a habitual hiding place for drugs. I had seen the fighting cocks in Havana's two tourist shops and found them revolting, their plucked thighs dyed red.

In the same shop were, of course, the lacquered blown-up frog and toad orchestras complete with tiny guitars, sombreros, and serapes, which Latinos seem to think appeal to us, gringos. I had seen the identical ones in tacky shops all over Mexico and would see them again, more surprisingly, in the expensive Hilton Hotel gift shop in Caracas.

The cock was mounted on a heavy piece of wood, and I did not see how I could carry it back in my luggage, a small bag. The stuffed rooster also looked very fragile. I had it boxed at the shop, but the box was not tall enough and it only came up to its neck so its head stuck out as I carried it, beadily glaring at me, eyeball to eyeball, back to my hotel.

Despite my request that I take a taxi to the airport, Lisa and her husband had insisted on driving me at dawn the following day. After many hugs and kisses, Lisa and I parted and I was left alone, starring at the silly bird in its box, which I had to take with me as cabin luggage while relinquishing my unlocked bag to the hold. I rather admired the nonchalant style of the *Cubana* flight attendant who pointed a vague and somewhat desultory finger to a seat, somewhere over there, roughly in that corner that may or may not have been my own and where, meeting no challenge, I sat with the rooster on my lap.

As to the bird, naturally, it was detained. The customs officer in Montreal could not understand at first what I meant. *"Un coq? Vivant?"* She asked to see the box, and then thoroughly disgusted, called her supervisor. Agriculture Canada was not entirely satisfied, it appeared, that the bird was safe and they wished to have it undergo certain tests. They did not specify and I did not ask.

It did arrive in Vancouver, eventually, looking as belligerently stupid as ever and unaffected by wear after a few days spent in Montreal. I would see it later in the director's office. It had started to molt a little and its red thighs had paled as well, and as time went by, I started feeling a reluctant benevolence towards it. As it kept on deteriorating, now relegated into a corner behind a chair from its former top-of-the-coffee-table place of honour, it seemed to have developed the raggedy, anxious, and somewhat dignified look of homesick exiles.

Chapter Eight

A Paradise of Sorts
Seychelles, 1992

Ah, les mélancolies du voyage ....
—Gustave Flaubert

When I arrived in Mahé on a sticky summer day in 1992, all I knew about the Seychelles was the little I had read in various travel books. Between 4º and 11º south of the equator, they are islands of spectacular beauty, with a tropical climate and vegetation.

Of the 115 granitic islands that constitute the Seychelles archipelago, three include most the total population of approximately 70,000: Mahé (the largest island where Victoria, the capital, is located and where I would be staying), Praslin, and La Digue. Mahé itself is located some 1600 kilometres north of Mauritius and east of Mombasa; somewhat closer to the south lies Madagascar.

First spotted by the Portuguese in the sixteenth century, the islands were visited later by such French navigators and corsairs as Surcouf, Labourdonnais, and Bougainville during the first French circumnavigation of the world in the eighteenth century. The latter named the two main islands: Seychelles, after Monsieur de Séchelles, a friend of the Bougainville family, and Praslin, after the Duke of Praslin, his patron.

The islands remained virtually uninhabited until a little more than two centuries ago, thanks to their isolation in the Indian Ocean. Then, escaped African slaves, European adventurers—mainly French and English—and Asian traders sparsely populated Mahé. The two main influences have been those of France, who claimed the islands in 1756, and Britain, who took over in 1814. Linked with Mauritius throughout history, the Seychelles were granted the status of a British Crown colony in their own right in 1903. From that date until Independence in 1976, the only remaining link with Mauritius was through the judiciary.

The Seychelles opened to international influences with the construction of a US satellite tracking station in 1960 and an international airport in 1971. Strategic and commercial factors have also stimulated the interest of several foreign countries, and tourism now competes with tuna fishing as the country's major industry and source of income.

By the time I arrived, the place, already overrun with working expatriates, had become a favourite destination for Italian honeymooning couples, thanks to a direct flight from Rome. At the airport, most signs were not only in Creole, English, and French, but also in Italian, which puzzled me until I visited some of the luxury hotels where the said couples were found in splendid, topless, and well-tanned self-absorption.

A man was waiting for me at the airport. He did not introduce himself, and smiling, simply took my bag. I had no idea who he was and he gave no explanation. At first glance, and without means of comparison, a neat white shirt and well-pressed gray pants do not give too many clues about rank, particularly in an unknown country. I even wondered briefly whether he was not M, my local contact about whom I knew nothing.

Then, the man, one of the ministry's drivers, as it turned out, handed me a note from M asking that I drop by his office at my convenience. I had left Vancouver more than thirty hours earlier and had caught by then my second, third, maybe fourth wind, so I asked to be driven directly to M's office.

I made small talk on the way. He was very cordial, smiled a lot, and agreed monosyllabically with everything I said, which made me suspect he did not understand me very well or that he may not in fact speak

English at all. This was indeed confirmed the following day, and was the rule rather than the exception with the lower-ranking employees who only spoke Creole.

I also found out that he had waited three hours for me at the airport, because of our long delay in Dubai. The airport being about twenty minutes away from the *Minister Ledikasyon ek Kilitur* (Ministry of Education and Culture, where I was loosely based), I was a little surprised that he had not simply returned to work and picked me up later. However, M told me that the driver's afternoon had likely been spent playing cards most pleasantly with his cronies at the airport, and had been no hardship on him.

The distinguished Egyptian writer Nawal El-Saadawi describes in *My Travels Around the World* a visit she made to the Seychelles in the summer of 1977, barely twenty-two years before my arrival.

> The plane landed in middle of the road, on an island in the middle of the ocean called the Seychelle Island, a strip of green land set in the midst of the water, waves and rock.

Reading this book some time after my return from the Seychelles piqued my curiosity. In 1977, this landing on the island of Mahé (there is actually no single island called Seychelle or Seychelles) must have taken place almost in M's backyard, the same backyard that became part of the new airport where the landing strip was extended after her visit.

There was no mention made in her book of the truly remarkable and luminescent turquoise colour of the sea around several of the islands. But reading again the passage, I realized that her visit must have been in the nature of a quick landing and takeoff, perhaps even at night, on her way from Dar es Salaam to Madagascar. She described the light reflecting on "white robes (What could those Arabic garments have done in the Seychelles?), and the whole island being "enveloped in a sort of magic and behind the beauty was the smell and intrigue of smuggling."

"Magic" and "beauty" would safely apply to any island in the Indian Ocean, while the reference to smuggling was a direct allusion to the history of the Seychelles, described in every guidebook. Nothing there had the ring of personal experience. The seven and a half lines covering Dr. Saadawi's visit to the Seychelles made me nervous, for here was someone whose writings were eminently respectable, yet who had made those very elementary errors. For the clincher, was her astonishing description of the Seychellois "unintelligible dialect" as a "mix of Swahili and Arabic" (but more on that later).

I am not knowledgeable enough to criticize to the same extent her contention that "the features of the people were a mix of Arabic and African blood," but I have my doubts that the blood mix is quite as uncomplicated as that. In fact, the population is usually described as made up of blacks or mulattos, whites (defined mostly in social and historical terms, as *Grands Blancs, Vieux Blancs,* and the picturesque *Blancs Rouillés),* Indians (Lascars and Malabars), and a small percentage of Chinese. I wondered whether I would fare better myself as I described my own experience of the Seychelles.

I was staying in the Victoria suburb of Mont Fleuri, on the airport road, just around the corner from the *Zardin Botanik,* at the Sun Rise Guest House. A Chinese-Seychellois woman ran it almost exclusively it would seem, for the numerous expats working in Mahé.

Madame was unwilling to accept a Visa credit card. I should have been prepared, because it had often happened to me in other countries, but my faith in plastic money seems undiminished. So from the start, I was quite worried that my remaining cash and travellers' cheques would not see me through. Everything was far more expensive than I had expected, and every night, I counted my rupees like a miser. My first question when shopping was not how much the goods cost, but whether the shopkeeper accepted credit cards, which was seldom the case.

Breakfast and dinner came with the *pension.* Breakfast was taken between seven and nine in a large garden annex with an adjacent kitchen where, under Madame's close supervision, two maids prepared tea, toast, and eggs, and served them in silence. This silence was pleasant and seemed to come mostly from the inability to communicate in either French or English, as well as from the respect due to guests.

There were two tables for four, where most of us sat, and a longer one that could accommodate eight, where sat sometimes several Chinese physicians with whom grins and bows were exchanged, since their speaking neither French, nor English, nor Creole somewhat impeded normal conversation.

Everything was scrupulously clean, but the decor was somewhat odd, a combination of plastic tackiness and minimalist sobriety. Through the windows, one could see Madame's glorious garden.

Madame's garden should really be seen in colour

The bananas we ate came from her garden and the jams, so exotic as to be unidentifiable, were made from the fruit she grew. The fact that we could see an abundance of bananas on the trees did not mean they were plentiful on the table. Madame was not one to go overboard. However, the food was sufficient. People arrived, greeted one another, and ate, but the mood turned to the working day ahead and conversation was held to a minimum. By eight o'clock, few remained to linger over their cold tea.

Dinner was quite different. It was taken at Madame's house, in her dining room, and one had to confirm that one would attend. Those who arrived a few minutes early would sit in a row on the seats Madame had lined up on her balcony and make desultory conversation, sometimes watching the rain pelting down.

By seven, the half-dozen people eating in that night would sit with some formality around the table. They were mostly residents of long standing. Madame had few competitors in the area; the hotel was at some distance from the centre of town and public transport minimal at night, so only social engagements or desperation drove us to eat elsewhere.

Madame (it should be clear by now that I never knew her name) had many qualities, not the least of which was the strong hand with which she ruled her household and her business. The maids were well trained, efficient, and could even be quite pleasant—not always the rule in the Seychelles.

None of Madame's talents, however, extended to the quality of the food, which was unadulterated Chinese, a bit greasy peasant food actually, with only a few concessions to local resources. The quantity, too, was modest, which did not strike me as being such a problem; however, some of the guests were large young men and they appreciated my offer of extra rice and potatoes or my share of the sweet, gelatinous dessert. Madame, observant and efficient as ever, soon substituted a banana for my dessert, an improvement for which I was grateful.

After dinner, a few of us would sometimes adjourn to her living room to watch the news on television, as there was very little else to watch. Madame's living room was somewhat reminiscent of her cooking: Chinese, yet with a few concessions to local resources. The room was spotless, but with just a bit more decorative plastic than one was used to seeing.

The social part of the evening never seemed to last very long and soon after eight, everyone went back to their room, a fifty-second trip across the path often long enough to get thoroughly soaked by the evening rain.

On the landing of the sleeping quarters, we sometimes met an ancient fellow whose functions were unclear to me until Lucy, my neighbour, explained he was the night watchman. She showed me the slightly greasy mark on the wall about a foot from the floor where he rested his head in his sleep—a mark, despite Madame's vigilance and the maids' scrubbing, forever renewed. It was also an explanation for the puzzling sound often heard at night, for the old man snored abominably.

The rooms were reassuringly clean, with fake marble floors and a spotless, modern bathroom. There was plenty of hot water for showers and sufficient towels as well, and a large cupboard with a lock. But the greatest luxury of Madame's rooms was not, as one might think, the efficient air conditioning, although that, too, was a welcome treat, it was the spacious work area consisting of a good table, a solid chair, a pitcher of drinking water, and a decent lamp. Lucy believed that Madame's son, an engineer trained abroad, was responsible for understanding and meeting the needs of people who had come to Mahé to work.

In the course of my first week there, I met:

A bearded man from the Smithsonian on his last day there. I did not find out what he did in the Seychelles, because as soon as he spotted the Patrick O'Brian book in my hand (most appropriately, the *Mauritius Command*), he became so enthusiastic that the conversation never went farther than the attractions Captain Aubrey and Dr. Maturin hold for their many admirers.

A very charming and equally bearded Italian doctor, a specialist in tropical medicine, who was to spend the next three years between Mahé and Mombasa.

From him, I learned that the Seychelles were singularly blessed in that there was nothing malevolent on the archipelago apart from some minor intestinal parasites that infected more than 80 percent of the population and transmitted either through the drinking water or by walking barefoot. I also learned that there was no malaria on these islands, despite the plethora of mosquitoes.

Two pleasant Réunionnais craftsmen and art teachers there for one week, who spoke French as if they came from some town in the Loire Valley where the purest of French is reputed spoken.

They were just back from Madagascar and could not get over what they described as the dreadful conditions and state of demoralization. Someone else around the table, also recently in Madagascar, confirmed their impression.

Once again, I had to wonder at Dr. Saadawi's report on her visit to that part of the Indian Ocean. Comparing Madagascar to Zanzibar, she opposed the latter, which she saw as an "island of Sadness and Slavery," to Madagascar, an "island of Smiles and Joy, [where] girls danced the flower dance around the lake, smiling, their dresses fantastic colours." Could a mere fifteen years have sufficed to transform what she described into what the Réunionnais saw, which was not a momentary, if critical, economic crisis but an absolute rending of the social and cultural fabric?

A middle-aged gentleman from Nairobi with gray hair and a gentle brown face, whose English I found so difficult to understand that I could not figure out what he did and why he was there.

The seven young Chinese physicians I have already mentioned, who bowed courteously but spoke nothing anyone could understand. I had no idea what they were doing in Mahé.

A recently arrived white South African man, strongly built and handsome, who was teaching First Aid and spent all his spare time scuba diving and exploring the undersea at Beau Vallon.

And, last but most certainly not least, Lucy, a Canadian health planner by trade and a linguist by training. She was what Anne of Green Gables would have called "a kindred spirit," an unfortunately fleeting one, of a type one is sometimes lucky to meet, however briefly, in travel and in life. A comfortable expat, she had already spent three years in Mahé and was waiting for the renewal of her contract.

In Madame's cosmopolitan guesthouse, I recognized the rules of some boarding schools I have attended where seniority, even by two or three days, counted for much. It was enough to initiate newcomers and introduce them to the ad hoc culture of the expats.

I was not one of them, so little effort was exerted for me apart from common courtesy, as very sort stays (about four weeks in my case) discouraged any attempt at forming bonds. I wondered how long was long enough to make acceptance worthwhile. I should have asked Lucy, with her long experience of seeing people come and go, but I did not wish to appear indiscreet, or worse, anxious for friendship.

It is probably an unspoken rule that people are guarded in their attempt to achieve balance between a natural need for companionship and cautious self-protection in the process of recreating a temporary, always shifting society. Sexual convenience and convergence may be another matter and indeed probably occur on the understanding that it will likely be short-lived, but this is not what I am referring to.

I would have liked to spend more time with the Réunionnais, if only to reflect on the light in which I perceived them. We had planned to go to La Digue together the following week, but I had to excuse myself, having received in the meantime an invitation to dine on the same day with the minister, an important step in my project.

I thought them actually more French than me, although they had never set foot in France. But perhaps their perfect command of the language deluded me, and the close familiarity it evoked may have created an imaginary bond. Their daily experience was entirely different from mine; their national and personal history bore no resemblance to mine, yet I am sure that the pervasive French culture provided some real bond between us. Those Réunionnais could have been anything: brothers, cousins, or strangers behind familiar masks.

While all else was new, one pattern was certainly familiar to a Canadian from British Columbia: the prosperous evolution of Madame's family. Starting from modest beginnings with a tiny grocery and fabric store, they now owned modern buildings all across Victoria, among which this guesthouse to which the original store was still attached. Both children had been educated abroad. The son, a structural engineer, worked next door in a small office building also owned by the family, and the daughter, a public servant, was associated with one of the ministries. My impression was that his success was in great part due to Madame's personality and single-minded determination.

※ ※ ※

The island of Mahé is of almost formidable beauty, a monstrous granite rock very likely dating back millions of years to Gondwanaland. One had to marvel that trees grew and that houses were built on so much rock, on which drying laundry was often draped. The Seychelles are blessed that they are located outside the cyclone belt. The little houses I saw everywhere must have been built on extremely flimsy foundations. In fact, I discovered later that these constructions were even flimsier than I had thought, as the traditional Seychellois method for building small houses consisted of stonework pillars supporting wooden frames built on ribs of the raffia palms.

The country was undergoing substantial expansion. New buildings for the Polytechnic had recently been completed at Anse Royale, new hospital wings were currently underway in Mahé, and a very large and ambitious national library was shaping up rather impressively at the edge of Victoria with the African Development Bank expected to provide funds for its contents. I assumed the economy was good and people did reasonably well. All the cars, mostly of Japanese make, were very recent despite a new tax that had hugely increased their price.

The vegetation and birdlife were mostly unknown to me, and seldom did I suffer more from my inability to name things, one of the few real powers we seem to have over nature—that urgent human desire to impose upon the world the fallacy of arbitrary naming and the fictional point where poetry and science intersect.

While I was familiar with bougainvillea, hibiscus, and banana trees, almost everything else was foreign to me. I saw my first breadfruit tree, my first gigantic papaya tree, my first tea plant, my first flamboyant with its strange orange flowers and pale green fern-like leave (I believe it is a Poinciana tree), my first sweet-smelling frangipani, and at least another hundred trees and shrubs I could not identify. I missed not having the least brushing of botany and ornithology. The only bird I recognized—in a country that boasts the world-famous Bird Island in its archipelago—was the most common: a ground dove, a very pretty little gray bird scurrying everywhere on tiny, mechanical matchstick legs.

I found the heat quite bearable, thanks to an almost constant cooling wind, often accompanied by violent showers. The well-dressed Seychellois usually carried an umbrella, and some small children were often seen propelled by some bigger than themselves. When I say that I found the heat bearable, it is perhaps not entirely true, since I must mention the humidity prevalent on the island.

Stepping out of the Mahé airport, I had felt minute droplets of humidity on my face, but looking up, I saw nothing but the intense cerulean depth of the sky. Within minutes, I was used to the water condensation in the air and the sensation had dissipated. However, from that point on, I created my own source of humidity wherever I went.

On my way to meetings and walking under the hot sun at my usual fast pace, the same revolting liquefaction occurred as soon as I arrived. While being introduced, I would discreetly wipe my hands on my pants or skirt before offering it. Then, sitting down and trying to converse sensibly, I would melt in an outpouring of sweat, a total sloshing of liquidity. Leaking from every pore, my armpits drenched, I would stick to my chair (often with a plastic seat to make matters worse), and give vent, so to speak, to a dreadful, squishy, farty noise to accompany every uncomfortable shift of my sweaty rear end.

I would look at my hosts' composed, cool faces politely ignoring my repulsive display of bodily fluids, and I would feel painfully inferior. After two weeks, I had learned to walk more slowly and I soon became accustomed to the humidity, but I never quite recovered from my first humiliating performances.

The thirty-two hours I spent travelling from Vancouver via London and the long stop in Dubai, as well as the eleven-hour time difference, resulted in the travellers' usual miseries: constipation and insomnia. On the third day, I went to see an Indian chemist who reluctantly sold me five pills. I had refused to buy a bag of some five hundred pills he wanted to sell me—they came loose in a big jar, like old-fashioned candies, and one could presumably purchase as few or as many as one chose—so I insisted on buying only five. Without belabouring the point, Seychellois must have serious digestive problems if what I took was regarded locally as a mild laxative.

As to the second problem, because of frequent housebreaking in Mahé, everyone had several dogs, not as pets but as guard dogs. And they barked all night. I had read about this problem but did not quite believe it. However, I could now vouch for it—the dogs barked *all night*. There were also a large number of roosters, and they, on the other hand, crowed all day.

Victoria, the capital, was about half-an-hour's brisk walk from the guesthouse in Mont Fleuri. During the week, it was extremely busy, but quiet on Sunday. The town seemed to me very functional, with little imagination wasted on making it beautiful. It was a town in good repair, which seemed to go about its business in a no-nonsense way.

I found it a rather plain town, for it is difficult for buildings to compete with such wonderful displays of nature. The monuments were of modest proportions. Much was made locally of the sculpture by Lorenzo Appiani to celebrate the nation's bicentennial, but it looked to me like three unfortunate birds whose nosedive had not been very graceful. However, the little garden around it was quite lovely with a luxuriance of red flowers.

Appiani's bicentennial sculpture, Mahé

Another monument, somewhat more graceful and surrounded by fountains, represented leaping dolphins and was said to depict the ethnic origins and cultural influences of the country.

The dolphin fountain, Mahé

The most noteworthy landmark, because of its location in the centre of town, was *L'Horloge,* a silver clock seemingly equipped with tentacles and bizarrely adorned with little electric bulbs, like some leftover Christmas decoration. It had a slightly tinselly look about it and was much less impressive in reality than pictured on many postcards. However, like many landmarks, its reputation had little to do with beauty, and through sheer familiarity, one could probably grow rather fond of it. It is reported to be a replica of the clock tower at London's Vauxhall Bridge, but since I do not recall having seen the original, I cannot comment on the accuracy of the copy.

On the other hand, a few official buildings erected in the style of a past era of Creole elegance, were lacy, airy, and cool. Before leaving the island, I was given a superb book of photographs and architectural drawings of old houses in Mahé, and I was much taken with earlier styles and the sophistication of local artisanship.

Indeed, the National Archives *(Arsiv Nasyonal)* were making a determined effort to save the lovely old houses and had started registering them. By 1986, eight houses had been classified as protected monuments on Mahé, five proposed on Praslin, thirteen proposed and one classified on La Digue, and one each on the islands of Silhouette, Curieuse, and Farquhar.

Any lover of wood would have been entranced. Most of the timber traditionally used bore names I did not know. Of course, I knew mahogany, teak, and rosewood, but what of dragon blood, sere wood, albizia, casuarinas, or violet wood? Pillars often consisted of the robust trunks of the *coco de mer,* polished a dark brown, and floors were made of the same precious woods used in the construction.

The typical Creole houses had the traditional harmonious Seychellois roof, ventilated through venetian blinds usually overlapping with the veranda eaves. I admired them on Mahé and later on the smaller island of La Digue where they were fewer and built on a more modest scale.

Another of Victoria's rather pleasant traits was the number and variety of its places of worship despite the large Catholic majority of the population. While meandering from shady side to shady side of the street on my way to the market, I would pass within a few blocks a blue arch of a small Catholic church, situated cheek by jowl with the police station. I would also see a green roof of the discreet mosque in slight retreat from the street, only to stop at the pleasant gaudiness of the Hindu temple enthroned in a recess by the open-air market. At first glance, they all looked sensibly companionable.

Victoria was full of very tiny shops, some barely wider than their openings onto the street. There was a great mixed bag of things, bric-a-brac of objects, some of which I had not seen since my childhood in southern Morocco half a century earlier. The faint spicy smell was also reminiscent of souks, and I would not have been surprised to see sugar cones wrapped in deep blue paper. A few shops catered to tourists, prices on the high side and goods of little distinction with the exception of two or three elegant boutiques with unaffordable prices.

Two local tourist exports have achieved some fame. The first are very attractive watercolours and batiks, a few of the local artists having apparently acquired some reputation in Europe. The other was the famous *coco de mer* (sea coco, also called *coco-fesses* or buttock-coco by the French), a fruit from the island of Praslin. The sea coco can weigh up to 200 pounds and cost up to $1200. Inasmuch as natural things could be thought obscene, this one certainly can. It reproduces female genitalia in every realistic detail, right down to a tuft of coarse hair strategically positioned. Sale of the *coco de mer* is rigidly controlled and one must obtain a permit to take it out of the country.

Government officials indicated that I would have no problem obtaining a permit and would receive advice on where to get a particularly nice *coco de mer* at a reasonable price. Being a person of little imagination and perhaps not as broad-minded as I thought, I could not conceive of anything I might want to do with it nor anywhere I could display it in my house. I pleaded weight and cost as prohibitive reasons for not availing myself of this once-in-a-lifetime opportunity. There were all sorts of imitations, including cheap trinkets such as plastic key rings, all lacking the puzzling realism of the original.

The market was somewhat disappointing. There was little meat and only a few chickens, but the fish display was somewhat more impressive. I looked at the fish, fresh and colourful, and compared with some longing the culinary possibilities they offered with the memory of Madame's past meals and the anticipation of her future ones.

Fruit and vegetables, most of them familiar, came in modest quantities and were usually wrapped four pieces at a time in plastic. Many were imported from South Africa and the prices were exorbitant. Thinking I had perhaps miscalculated in converting rupees into Canadian dollars, I checked with Lucy, who confirmed the prices.

A few days before I left, Lucy had obtained her own small house and invited me to visit her. I purchased two pears, four oranges, and a pretty little basket for my offerings. Such a paltry housewarming present almost amounted to my self-imposed meager daily allowance. I did not see how ordinary people on a modest salary, the majority obviously, could afford to buy such produce.

Naturally, they could not, but since Creole diet consists mainly of fish and rice prepared in quite tasty combinations, it was possible to get by simply on these two staples. The price of imported rice was controlled and local fish was abundant and relatively cheap; hence, a diet of mainly fish and rice. And bananas. And what bananas! There are twenty different sorts of native bananas in the Seychelles, from coarse-looking plantains to the delicious *bananes mignonnes,* about two inches long and sweetly flavoured beyond description.

So it was not a grand market, after all, but one with precious little produce and poor displays, and I never saw the crowds one often meets at market places. Perhaps I always went at the wrong time of day. Perhaps the Indian shops, one of them a true mini-market, offered too much competition. Perhaps a tree or two in the backyard gave all the fruit a family needed and could trade. Or perhaps transactions took place elsewhere, by the water for instance (part of the Seychelles wealth deriving from tuna fishing, but on a grand industrial scale with international fishing rights filling the government's coffers).

I usually find great pleasure in shopping in local markets wherever I travel, but I always left that little market slightly depressed, my four tomatoes, and a small loaf of bread in a thin plastic bag.

People were multicolored, but mostly on the dark side. Unless one worked with them, they were not particularly friendly. Occasionally, I asked for directions in town. I usually picked youngsters, mostly to test their ability to speak French or English. I was not always sure they understood me, although they seemed to fare better in English than in French, despite the resemblance between Creole and French.

There were pleasant surprises, however, and once a pretty schoolgirl with those doe's eyes one reads about but so seldom sees, actually offered to escort me to where I wanted to go. She was dressed in a simple cotton wraparound printed in a sophisticated and original combination of colours and wore it with an innate sense of style. Anywhere in the world, I would have found her outfit original and elegant, and I congratulated her on it. She said she had made it herself, and I wondered how the world of high fashion could possibly discover her in such a distant island. Its loss, no doubt, as it was unlikely it would.

Perhaps I should explain the linguistic complexity prevalent in the islands. The country's basic language is Creole Seychellois *(Kreol Seselwa),* whose origins are French. One of the unusual aspects of the Seychellois education system is that children are expected not only to study Creole, English, and French, the three official languages, but also to study *in* Creole, English, and French at various levels and in various subjects—which they do with variable degrees of proficiency.

As a Canadian passably conversant with linguistic and cultural controversies, I examined this system with considerable interest. However, I had been hired by one of the Commonwealth organizations to focus on the feasibility of providing post-secondary education and training at a distance throughout the islands, so linguistic considerations were only of marginal interest, since I was only to concern myself with English as a working language—for which limitation I was quite thankful.

I soon realized how many errors of etiquette I was committing, preferring for instance to walk up to 200 yards, despite having access to a car with or without a chauffeur, and particularly walking to town, usually in the heat of the day, or opening my own doors, or wearing pants, etc. Few errors were serious but all showed me as being quite uncouth by local standards.

Invited to dinner by the minister, I went as far as wondering whether I should actually buy a pair of shoes for the occasion, rather than wear my comfortable sandals. This matter seemed to me worthy of some consideration after noticing that even the women who swept the side of the road with desultory swipes of their palm leaf not only wore shoes, but that those shoes, which had certainly seen infinitely better days, had sometimes fairly high heels.

On my second day, a Saturday, I managed to go swimming for an hour since I had to go to a tourist hotel to cash a traveller's cheque. The beach, in front of the Coral Sands Hotel in Beau Vallon was holiday-wonderful, the stuff of which travel posters are made, but the bus trip across the island and over those narrow, hairpin mountain roads had had its white-knuckled moments. One glance at the driving (on the left, to boot) had made me reject the offer of a car. Lucy, who worked in the hospital, said there were usually several driving casualties during the weekend.

My social life, such as it was, as well as my professional activities, were soon taken over by M. As a representative of the former *Grands Blancs* land owners (all dispossessed in 1976) and the bearer of an aristocratic French name, he presented an interesting mixture of cultural influences.

The links with his French culture had been reinforced, not only by obtaining a doctorate from the Sorbonne, but particularly by his choice of this most French of writers, François Mauriac, as subject for his dissertation—a dissertation he gave me to read and through which I was briefly recaptured by my own cultural past. I found it was far more unsettling to read Mauriac in the Seychelles than it did in my familiar and far less exotic environment of British Columbia, where middle-class France could be perhaps more readily evoked.

One of the endearing aspects of M's already unusual personality was that he treated his dogs as pets. One was silly, one was daring, the third was cowardly, but it was very pleasant to have friendly dogs around again. Since there was no commercial dog food on the island, he fastidiously prepared special dog mush for them. However, it was only mush and they had nothing to practice serious chewing on, so I promised to send them a large box of dog biscuits from Canada. We wondered whether, after they had seen Paree, so to speak, he would be able to keep them on the farm. I saw M two years later in Bangkok, and he told me that my care package (the shipping cost had been ridiculously out of proportion with the cost of the biscuits) had brought endless grunts of delight from his happy mongrels.

Obviously, M and I spoke French, but most of my work was otherwise conducted in English. The question of language was, like everywhere else in the world, mostly a political one. Two days after my arrival, I heard Z, the principal secretary, make a speech at a function for which no background was provided for me and whose point I found at first difficult to grasp. The speech was in Creole and Z, a handsome mulatto who spoke elegant English, articulated with precision. Being familiar with what politicians and senior public servants usually talk about (integrity, objectives, programs, social development, education, national pride, etc.), I more or less caught the gist of his speech.

Much was made of that at a reception at the French embassy the same evening. Somehow, my "understanding" the speech was deemed a sign that the mother tongue had literary and international value. I sheepishly bleated out that had it been anything but a political speech, I would probably have understood none of it, but I was firmly ignored.

At the same party, a young and very pretty French woman in a clingy yellow dress (Barbie herself with brains to match, I had assumed and am embarrassed to confess) told me she had long been intrigued by the evolution of the *Kreol Seselwa*. It had apparently progressed from an oral dialect to a written language subjected to grammatical rules, as Creole gradually assumed its full political function.

She had cleverly based her study on an ideally consistent text: the political speeches made during the last twenty years by the president, hence using the same speaker, the same subject matter, and the same context—the only variable being the evolution and standardization of the language. So much for Barbie dolls.

She then left to refill her glass, and as she undulated away, I looked around with curiosity, not having much experience with French diplomats abroad and the parties they gave. We did not go inside since in these idyllic climes it made sense to stand in the garden near the sea and later watch the sun go down.

A table, shaded by unknown trees, held the drinks and canapés, the former poured by a white-clad servant, the latter prettily passed around by the ambassador's young children. Madame *l'Ambassadrice*, informally yet fashionably attired, spoke intelligently on any topic one cared to bring up. I was impressed, truly, quasi patriotically (on such occasions I remember that I was once French myself), enviously impressed, my own range being infinitely more modest. I hardly spoke to Monsieur *l'Ambassadeur* and could not form an opinion on whether he was worthy of his wife.

I did not really understand the Creole spoken on the street, but when it was formally spoken on the television news, for instance, I could manage to grasp its essence. It was almost a language heard in a dream. I recognized the words but did not necessarily grasp the whole meaning. And, sometimes, the reverse was equally true. Overall, I could guess the general tenor of the speech but would certainly have found it very hard to translate literally.

On the street, I often stood in front of political placards left over from the recent election and soundlessly mouthed the words several times before suddenly discovering the meaning. The breakthrough came when I realized that *Seselwa* was not the name of a candidate but the local word for the language and the nationality: Seychellois.

Written Creole is purely phonetic, and as one must also account for local idiosyncrasies, it is not always easy to get the first time. The necessity to sound out the written word in order to recognize it can be illustrated through the following examples, which are evidently French: *Oli mon lacklé? (Où est ma clef?); Keler i été, silvouplé? (Quelle heure est-il s'il vous plait?); Konbyen mon dwa ou? (Combien je vous dois?); Komanyer pwason i apelé? (Comment s'appelle ce poisson?).*

Throughout my stay, I was puzzled that Seychellois did not seem to find French easier to understand and speak than the English language. This puzzlement was purely of a linguistic nature and did not overlook or misconstrue the political and economic advantage of English over French for the Seychelles.

I was also struck by the lack of effective communication among the different government services, as it was often reported to me. In our parts of the world, we delight in finicky bureaucracy and it was very possible that I simply did not recognize the existing patterns and administrative infrastructure there. However, many of the people to whom I spoke were often frustrated and offered their criticisms spontaneously.

There was, I was told, no system of professional reward: no career path, no job qualification structure, no perks (at least none built-in), no or little recognition for job experience, and the salary remained the same after twenty years as it was after two years. I asked, "No unions?" Nobody seemed to know for sure, but suspected not.

The apparent vagueness and inconsistency that transpired (if it was indeed accurately described to me, which I had no way of checking) seemed to be a function of growing too fast in too many directions and without the time, the experience, or resources to establish the proper underpinnings for it. I was pleased that my task did not involve delving into these matters and that the information had come only as a by-product of my work, and a very marginal one at that.

Unlike most expats and consultants around me who dealt with well-defined topics, such as the *creolization* of the education system, professional training abroad, plastic arts (the Réunionnais), intestinal parasites (the Italian doctor), first aid (the South African), or health planning (Lucy), my own terms of reference, although based on the provision of academic and professional education at a distance, could be taken somewhat loosely because of the variety of fields it involved (nursing, police, teaching, social work, trades upgrade, etc.). In fact, this openness allowed me to examine, albeit superficially given the time allocated, almost everything that piqued my curiosity, including the various technical, social, and political infrastructures that would support the delivery of programs at a distance.

During my second week, I became slightly more familiar with life in Mahé and at the guesthouse. Among other things, I found out what the man from Nairobi was doing there. He worked for the Commonwealth War Graves Commission and oversaw the condition of Commonwealth graves (and possibly those of the Commonwealth enemies as well), wherever the need arose. I found it profoundly reassuring to know that he was spending three weeks in the Seychelles making certain adequate aggregate was poured on some old graves (nearly 300 of them, mainly sailors washed ashore) and that they continued to be looked after. He said that only in France, Italy, and South Africa were Commonwealth graves well kept.

I was deeply touched when I gathered that he firmly believed all those dead young men *knew* they were being looked after through his good offices. Two years later, I immediately thought of him when I read that just weeks before the fiftieth anniversary of D-day, the British government had cut by the equivalent of over two million Canadian dollars its share of the upkeep of the more than 23,000 gravesites in 145 countries. I felt sad for him and for his dead young men.

I also thought of him still later, while visiting the war cemeteries near Caen—Canadian, American, German, the victors and the vanquished, of such radically different moods and influenced by such different philosophies of war and death. I often wondered what his graves were like. Perhaps like the Canadian ones we had seen, which the British and the French tended and which had something of a gentle English garden feel to them, but with different vegetation? It would not be a bad place to rest for eternity, I thought, watched over by a caring old man.

Commonwealth (Canadian) cemetery in Caen, France

One evening, I invited Lucy to dinner at Marie-Antoinette's, reputed to be the best Creole restaurant on the island. It took us nearly an hour to walk there. We were constantly solicited by very direct Seychellois men, which took a bit away from the charm of the evening. Walking through town at night (it was after eleven when we came back) was not something I would have done on my own but Lucy, a veteran of three years, maintained it was perfectly safe.

The meal was as good as the service was surly. I gave a tip and wished I had not, so miserable was the waitress. Uncharacteristically for these parts, where women usually have good features and a nice bearing, she had cheeks like buttocks, black currant eyes, and a slovenly slouch. She quite obviously resented us. And I, whose wealth and status were presumably beyond her wildest dreams of ever achieving for herself, very quickly started resenting her back.

Lucy thought that Seychellois were historically still very close to slavery and much could be explained by that fact. I hoped my irritation was more likely to have come from being tired, hot, and weary a good part of the day, as well as frustrated by constant interviews where much of the information gathered one day sometimes contradicted the information received the day before or the day after. Nevertheless, I must admit that tipping in the Seychelles made me cranky. The manner in which surly servers swept away my tip without the slightest acknowledgment irritated me. Since tipping was neither required nor customary, they likely considered that I had my own reasons for doing so, and that those reasons were really none of their business. What probably irritated me the most was my own pettiness and total loss of cultural perspective.

Anthropologists have discussed at length the concept of reciprocal exchanges of goods and services, seen at its best in egalitarian societies, with nothing bought or sold, with goods and services fairly traded. In such societies, nothing is owed. This brings us to tipping. Marcel Mauss and Marvin Harris, among others, have studied this phenomenon and Harris comments that whether or not people say thank you illustrates whether their lifestyle is based on reciprocity or something else. He maintains that in truly egalitarian societies it is rude to acknowledge gratefully the receipt of material goods or services. If such is the case, there is little doubt that the Seychelles have a far more egalitarian society than, for instance, North America.

In the fear that I might perhaps commit a gaffe and embarrass both the minister and myself, preparations for our dinner together had been tightly organized. I had received a formal written invitation, then three telephone calls regarding the plans for the evening—the first to remind me of the engagement, the second to inform me that we would be going to a different hotel than the one first proposed, and the last to confirm the change. Since the rooms at the guesthouse had no telephones, all calls were taken in public either in Madame's dining room or in the backroom of the general store next door run by her husband. These calls went a long way to enhancing my prestige with her and her staff.

The chauffeur picked me up at the appointed time in a Toyota still smelling spanking new, and we drove to the minister's house to pick her up. Her teenage son also came for the ride and dinner and ate at a separate table with the chauffeur. He sat beside the latter in the car and spoke to him in Creole throughout the trip; a few attempts on my part to engage him in small talk did not go very far, as his command of English was minimal. This was a common problem: while instruction usually took place in English after the third year of schooling, even teachers spoke Creole after class was dismissed. His ambition was to become an airline pilot, so I suggested that fluency in English might be an asset in his choice of career. (I have an unfortunate tendency to state the obvious, for which nobody ever thanks me.)

As soon as we arrived at the Barbarons Club, a Meridien chain resort catering mostly to rich Italian honeymooners and apparently local dignitaries, the French manager hurried to greet us and sent over a bottle of champagne; waiters and servants rushed about, and short of chewing our food for us, did about everything else. The experience was luxurious and exotic, and I got on well with the minister. She was no doubt at her political peak, a pretty and elegant woman in her early forties with dark skin and very pink palms, married to a well-to-do local businessman who sold air conditioners. A smart woman, I thought.

I also remembered how the South African instructor at the guesthouse had complained that his students, particularly the young women all mostly in their twenties, were extremely childish and giggled constantly. Rather, I believe that giggling is culturally designed to deal with embarrassment or new situations, and has little to do with childishness; it could even have something to do with courtesy and be a form of polite self-effacement. The minister did giggle a little when one met her socially and I found it a little unnerving at first. However, during later meetings with her staff and me, she was very much in control, and I suspected she did not stand for much nonsense.

※ ※ ※

One afternoon, I escaped from my notes and my computer and went back to Beau Vallon on the northwest coast of the island, where I had cashed a traveller's cheque on my first weekend and had gone by bus. Overall, buses ran at reasonable intervals. They were also cheap and clean, but getting on them was not always for the fainthearted. I walked to the bus terminal in Victoria and observed the boarding techniques. Much shoving seemed the rule, all done in deadly silence.

I let two or three buses go by before I gathered the necessary nerve, but finally succeeded in climbing on board. I tended to think the run-of-the-mill Seychellois a rather sulky bunch, but in all fairness, I was not familiar enough with them to understand their public behaviour and countenance. Beside, my being there probably affected their exchanges even though no one paid overt attention to me. On board, nobody ever gave up his or her seat for anyone else; however, it was common to have someone drop a parcel on the lap of a person sitting down, without a word from either party. Lucy even saw a woman dump her baby on a man's lap, then pick the child up later, in total silence and without a single glance from her to him or him to her, despite the fact that the baby howled throughout.

So I went to Beau Vallon Beach across the island intending to feel and behave like a tourist and partake of the Coral Sands outdoor buffet. The water would have been wonderful, had it not been for the nearly invisible hydroids nibbling away at us. There were the usual paunchy middle-aged, very tanned European tourists on the beach, and a smaller number of youngish and nice-looking ones, probably the honeymooners. The women were mostly topless, and many would have been better advised to cover up a little more.

There were also two hugely muscled men, not Seychellois since they spoke another kind of English to each other. They were the two best-built and blackest men I have ever seen, a purplish African black, very different from the range of colours commonly seen in the New World. They were showing off with a Frisbee and very poor skills (any dog on any Vancouver beach could have taught them a thing or two) and making a nuisance of themselves. One had modest dreadlocks and the other a more stylish, almost girlish hairstyle of miniature hair curlers in various bright colours. Neither had intended to get wet, so whenever the Frisbee landed in the water, which was more often than not, some good-hearted swimmer retrieved it for them. I do not recall hearing any thanks afterwards on any of these occasions.

Farther along, away from the hotel, some local youths and children played a little on the beach but did not swim. They appeared indifferent to the eccentricities of the tourists and behaved with far more decorum than did anybody else in sight.

Tourism in the Seychelles extended far beyond what I saw when I visited. Huge international interests are building exclusive and luxurious resorts and retreats for millionaires all over the smaller islands, several of which are privately owned by foreigners, a trend that has increased in the last ten years. This restricted tourism is said to be ecologically sound, in the sense that the Seychelles have established adequate guidelines for the use of the land.

However, it is hardly tourism since the beneficiaries of the land's extraordinary beauty are the very select few who can afford the superlative costs of privacy. It is difficult to imagine them having much to do with the locals either, apart from the invisible servants, since all they seek is paradise on earth with no one else in it to spoil it for them.

※ ※ ※

By the third week, the sense of novelty and wonder, normally overwhelming during the first few days in a strange place, had somewhat abated and was replaced by something halfway between boredom and impatience. It was different from just being fed up and irritated because of the constant delays, the lack of adherence to schedule and structure (I have noticeably martinet tendencies), sticking to my seat when attending meetings, and Madame's boring meals.

I had, I believe, reached the point where, because a certain superficial familiarity now existed, dislocation was at its peak. Routines and habits were established, but as they did not correspond to any real belonging, they simply served to underline more clearly my real transience.

In addition, I was extraordinarily tired. My appointments from the start had been totally disorganized to the extent that I could only leave my hotel during lunch hour to remain more or less on call. And I usually had to dash across town after receiving such urgent messages as, "You're meeting in half an hour with the chief of police," usually at the other end of town. The chief of police was very pleasant and displayed the *RCMP Gazette* on his desk, but his office was still at the other end of town.

It was perfectly reasonable for my hosts to assume that my time was flexible and that I could fit their schedules, and that I would be receptive to last-minute arrangements. That had been perfectly true at the beginning, but those last-minute arrangements now tended to be tiresomely the rule.

I also knew that I had gathered enough information to write a reasonably coherent report. Any additional information would either be repetitive and simply confirm what I already knew, or point me in other directions, which would only confuse matters since I would not have time to explore them further. Just being aware that they existed and mentioning them was enough.

The heat and the humidity were also affecting me. Moreover, I had small red spots all over, like miniature blood blisters, very colourful and rather decorative, but annoying all the same. It turned out to be a strong allergic reaction to sand fleas.

After two final unplanned interviews at opposite ends of town on the same afternoon, I decided that I needed a break. So I went to reserve a seat on Air Seychelles for a flight to Praslin, and from Praslin take the boat to La Digue. The idea was to spend my last weekend on La Digue and return in time for my flight to London and then home to Vancouver.

Everything went as planned, and I was rushed in a Jeep to the airport to catch my flight to Praslin, after a lunch given by the principal secretary for a number of local officials, an elderly English couple engaged in some health or education consultancy, and me. The meal, quite a banquet in fact, took place on a patio of a wind-swept restaurant with a postcard view. Altogether, it was a most congenial meal hosted with great style and elegance. It included many local delicacies with which I was unfamiliar (considering Madame's predictable fare), in particular, curried fruit bats. The secretary sitting beside me whispered that it would be all right if I wanted to skip that dish.

The flight from Mahé to Praslin in a Twin Otter was uneventful, but once in Praslin, I found it difficult to find transportation from the airport at Grande Anse to the pier, some good distance away. I finally asked a

Frenchman if I could share his taxi. He reluctantly agreed and did not address a single word to me during the trip, chatting instead with great animation with the cab driver, a woman he knew. From their conversation, I gathered that he spent half the year in France and the other half in the Seychelles, apparently a matter of taxes.

The route took us through the primeval forest of the *Vallée de Mai* National Park, a UNESCO World Heritage Site, where I would very much have liked to stop and take even the briefest look at the astonishing specimens of trees. Among the trees were very ancient *cocos de mer,* some 4,000 of them, as high as thirty metres and as old as 400 years. However, we pressed on, they conversing, I with my head hanging half out of the window. The Frenchman also stuck me with most of the cab fare.

The boat crossing from Praslin to La Digue was very choppy but quite pleasant, and the arrival everything the two Réunionnais had described upon their return three days earlier. The taxi stand, consisting of two ox-carts (the oxen with a thick rope strung through their nose) for guests staying at the few hotels, and a long rack of heavy bicycles for hire, both being the only means of public transportation on the island.

The "taxi stand" in La Digue, Seychelles

I asked for directions to my guesthouse, *La Citronelle,* named after the local lemon grass tea. Nobody seemed to have heard of it. The receptionist at Air Seychelles in Victoria had done the booking. "On the beach?" I had asked. "Oh, yes," she assured me. "You like it. You really like it." I could not find it anywhere in the travel brochure, but she said it was quite new and very nice. Still, nobody seemed to have heard of it until, finally, somebody pointed me in the direction of a path that disappeared into a forest and said it was about a ten minutes' walk away. After about twenty minutes of brisk walking, because the night was falling fast, all I saw were chickens scratching in the dirt.

Finally, I saw a few huts and talked to someone who said he did not know the house, then to someone who said he did and that it was about ten minutes away, which I took to be the Seychellois general method of assessing distance. And, indeed, I reached the guesthouse after another half-hour. It certainly was not the Ritz. Not even a regular guesthouse, actually, just a room, and a bathroom tacked onto a hut. However, it was too late to go back to "town" and the owner seemed nice enough.

I was actually quite amazed at myself since it was totally out of character for me, cautious as I usually am, to venture at nightfall into the forest towards an uncertain destination. Yet, for some reason, I had refused to turn back the two or three times, and I had started wondering about the wisdom of the expedition. I was curious to see what was at the end of the road and instinctively felt quite safe.

Before dinner, I walked around the "village" of a few huts where I befriended a young dog that, misunderstanding my intentions, became passionately attached to my leg. My attempts at, and final success in, repulsing its amorous advances were duly recorded by a few spectators, but without the slightest change in their facial expression. A cold bunch, these people, I thought. But who knows, my efforts may have later become a hilarious tale, and only sheer courtesy prevented the guffaws with which my performance could have been received. I probably deserved what I got, because why would anyone want to chat up a *Seselwa* dog?

The ceiling of the main room was brown with geckos during dinner, two being uncommonly large, real *lizards,* actually. I also saw something in the bathroom that I mistook for a very small rat but it was likely a huge cockroach. (When nature called thereafter, I made a lot of noise before going into the bathroom in the dark.) There was not much one could do about it even in a clean house, as this one was, with the forest on its very doorstep. There were noisy chickens everywhere outside and a few pigs that sounded to be in much distress.

Out of sight, a fight broke out between the owner and some drunk. Between that and the pigs, it was a rather noisy meal, which I took alone. My hostess then asked me if I would be interested in joining her and her two teenage daughters for an evening in town. I accepted gratefully. The night was very dark, totally unlike the nights I am used to in cities, and the deep forest made it even darker. She had a small flashlight, which showed us the way between the ruts and the puddles, and after an hour or so, we arrived at a sort of community centre, huge and quite elegant.

All ceilings are very high and open in the islands to provide good air circulation. Seychelles, as I have mentioned, used to have magnificent and very rare types of wood, which one still seems to find in some of the churches. Because of this architecture and the use of satiny woods, even the smallest church looks like a miniature cathedral. This hall, with its upward sweep, had the same feeling of airiness.

The show consisted of songs, dances, and skits by local girls, accompanied by a professional band from Mahé, which later played for the discotheque. The huge room was packed solid, with, very likely, the tout-La Digue in attendance. Two or three hundred people were sitting, and certainly as many standing, often in front of those who were sitting and good-natured enough not to object. That mass of bodies pressed together was not in the least offensive, since the Seychellois are finicky about their hygiene. In fact, the only unsavory body in the whole lot was probably mine, still sweating away, although by now somewhat more accustomed to the climate, I suppose I had become a slightly less objectionable presence.

Most of the young women and girls on stage were dressed like slightly bizarre prom queens from the 1950s, but barefoot, perhaps for folkloric effect, for women certainly did wear shoes in La Digue. The singing went on *forever*—each individual song, that is, and the concert as a whole. The singing was strangely monotonous, which was not helped by the fact that the singers constantly shifted from foot to foot creating a hypnotic effect. Each singer was armed with a microphone and sounded energetically loud and tinny.

I recognized some French folk songs, reworked almost beyond recognition in their Creole version. The rest sounded very African to me. In fact, heard at a distance and as a background noise, I could vaguely understand why Dr. Saadawi might have mistaken it for being partly Swahili. After three interminable hours, the pleasure of the show had somewhat palled for me.

The dances were a different matter altogether, particularly the local dance, *la sega*, which one does not dance, but "rolls," a fairly accurate description. All these young girls, and some seemed young indeed, were vigorously shaking, and rolling it. As the evening wore on, the dances grew a tad faster and some young men in the audience grew a lot raunchier. There we were all piled up on top of one another—sleeping babies with their mouth open on their mothers' shoulder, young men standing and shouting, old women nodding.

When the show was over, after everybody had filed out, the place became a discotheque and readmission was another twenty rupees. Since the owner's two daughters wanted to dance, their mother suggested that we go back inside and stay for a while. There was a lot of palaver between my hostess and her friends, as they obviously did not know what to do with me. But it was out of the question that I go back alone to the guesthouse at midnight, so I agreed to stay and went back inside with them. I had clearly become something of an encumbrance, and I tried to make up for it by paying everybody's admission.

Only a few essential vehicles were allowed on the island, and my hostess had spotted a friend's official pickup and was hoping to get a ride back, so we had to wait for the friend to turn up, which he did, but not until some three hours later. After ten minutes of the disco, I went into the washroom and stuffed toilet paper in my ears. It reduced the volume to an almost bearable level, but did nothing for the beat. There was nothing much to watch either, because the dancing had little to do with the real *sega*. The crowd was all very nice and tame and only soft drinks were served. Apart from a drunk who had been rather noisy during the previous show and who kept inviting me to dance (each time, he was tactfully removed by bystanders), nothing much happened. I was so tired and had such a headache that by the time the friend finally turned up around three in the morning, I was barely stirring. Poor pampered creatures, those Canadians, must have been the general opinion, as we bounced up and down in the back of the pickup among the deep ruts of the so-called road.

The following morning, the owner served me breakfast and we had a friendly chat. She showed me the little grocery shop she kept in the back. Like many of the women I met, she worked very hard, and I had to admire her gambling spirit and her faith in having very likely indebted herself to the limit to start a guesthouse in the middle of a forest on an island known mostly for its beaches. I paid my very reasonable bill, sincerely thanked her for her kind hospitality, and promised to pass the word around.

Guesthouse *La Citronelle*, La Digue

I then walked back to the harbour where I had a wallow in what must be the most beautiful water in the world. I did not have time to explore the famous beaches, but the water near the harbour where I paddled among the reefs was absolutely marvelous and somewhat to my embarrassment, I caught myself saying *aloud,* "This is heavenly!" After a sandwich at a little beach café farther down the road, I could not resist another swim in front of the extraordinary black granite projections, like fortresses in the sea, seemingly coming out of nowhere.

The little harbour in La Digue

After having been away for nearly two days, I found two new faces in Madame's breakfast room: a very large, tall, and cordial American who lived in Mauritius, a businessman probably, and a young Englishman, a recent Cambridge graduate on his way to a very small island to study birds for six months, and already feeling homesick. All Madame's guests had by then spent at least two or three weeks together and were on very amicable terms, but I knew only Lucy's name. Then the American, Jim, did something very American: he asked us our names.

Until then, I had only known the others by function and origin: the Italian Doctor, the Graves Man from Nairobi, the South African First Aid Instructor. It is very likely that their names had been mentioned before, but having a notoriously bad memory, I had forgotten them. Now that I actually knew the people, their names became meaningful. Suddenly, the Italian Doctor became Marco. The Graves Man from Nairobi perhaps became Sebastian, but I would not swear to it since I never understood him very well, and the South African First Aid instructor, Neils. I looked upon them all differently now that they were all properly labeled.

It was my last morning, and I sat on the low wall outside the Sun Rise Guest House, my bag at my feet waiting for M to arrive and drive me to the airport. Marco came and sat beside me. He was leaving for Kenya the next morning, an attractive, gentle, and restless young man with very blue eyes, who looked like a romantic hero. He said how he constantly thought of Africa when he was in Rome and how he pined for Italy when he was in Mombasa. How he missed people wherever he was. Few feelings are as contagious as nostalgia, and I started missing them all: him sitting beside me, and Lucy who had moved to her own place a few days earlier, and Madame's lovely garden, and Mahé, and those few weeks.

Sitting on that low wall in Mont Fleuri, my feet in their sandals stretched out beside Marco's, my heart was a little heavy, as before every departure—departures from elsewhere that is, since departures from home, especially departures at dawn, only create expectations. Another departure, I thought, then another arrival, out of so many. Perhaps because of Lucy, or even Marco, I had been briefly on the edge of the expats' world, and had sensed the intense seduction of deliberately belonging nowhere and only leaving the barest of footprints behind.

Indeed, I needed to make a fast break from these *"mélancolies du voyage,"* as Flaubert calls them, those wistful feelings of distance and abandonment. So, still sitting beside Marco, I was mentally already on my way to London where I would be shopping at Harrods food department the next day, for an Epicurean picnic in my hotel room, a transition before arriving three days later in Vancouver, where the Seychelles would soon be a quickly fading memory.

Chapter Nine

Abroad in a Bubble

Few types of travel feel as artificial as attending an international conference, particularly if one of the intentions in attending had been to get a flavour of a new country.

These meetings and conferences soon develop a culture of their own. This culture is never quite the same, since so much depends on the location, the purpose, the size of the conference, the discipline (although this is perhaps the least significant factor), the previous degree of interconnection of the attendees, the nature of the entertainment planned by the host organization, the degree of involvement of local participants, and their willingness to provide a welcoming environment.

I can certainly look at my own experience to decide which I believe to have been successful conferences and which have not. For instance, the Learned Societies Meetings (the "Learneds") that I sometimes attended were more in the nature of a Friday-night-after-work, at a pub, but still talking shop and gossiping. What contributes to define the nature of a conference, good or bad, is highly individual and almost intangible. We can naturally remember those details that we can use for gauging the general mood and outcome, but so much of it is personal that I would think twice about attempting its study.

What I propose, however, is to reflect on the extent to which travel opportunities provided by international meetings reveal local conditions.

Do we leave with the impression that we could describe upon our home, even superficially, the people we visited, their hopes, their fears as individuals and as citizens, the influence of their history on their daily life, their cultural concerns, the country's economy and its everyday impact, the part of reality and mythology in their worldview? This is probably too much to ask for, since how many of us can even truly say that we understand that about our own compatriots? However, it is one of the fallacies of travellers, and probably more so of travelling anthropologists, to assume they should be able to do so.

What we may feel instead, is that the knowledge we acquired is purely bookish—acquired even before leaving home, and reduced to what we might have heard or read, without any personal exchange or experience that might make us feel we understood something of the land. Simply put, did we speak to a single person on the street, beyond asking for directions?

I consider here two meetings I attended, two years apart, one in Thailand, the other in Venezuela. They could not have been more different in scale. The first, an enormous conference at the Open University in Bangkok with possibly hundreds from almost every continent, and the other in Caracas, consisting of no more than two dozen people from North, Central, and South America, with one very specific goal: the creation of a cooperative organization to support education and a training at a distance.

The first was anonymous, even if we occasionally met people we knew. The second was almost intimate in its comfortable exchanges. Yet, both conferences shared a single and important characteristic. When we left, few of us could have said they had learned what the average Thai and the average Venezuelan thought or did.

At both conferences, the wall of protection around us, the foreigners come to visit, had served to isolate us from any local reality. This was doubly so in Caracas, where our protectors were themselves protected. In Thailand, we were given a fictionalized version of the country, drawing upon its most arcane and hieratic mythology. In Venezuela, we only rubbed elbows with the wealthy, since we were expected to be mostly familiar with a life of social privilege.

The two representations were equally distant from the life of ordinary people and neither illustrated the realities of their daily experience. So, both countries, using diametrically opposite means (exclusion through pageantry and alien folklore in one case; attempted inclusion through presumed familiar wealth and advantages in the other), unwittingly achieved the same result. In both cases, having seen much, we left knowing little more than when we had arrived.

A *Farang* in Bangkok
1992

The flight from Vancouver to Hong Kong had been interminable, and made even worse by being pestered every hour or so by my neighbour on her way to the washroom: two sharp pokes of her index finger, a scarlet talon, at right angle into my thigh. She was elderly and her daughter, in the window seat, had fallen asleep as soon as we had taken off. At first, I had attempted a small smile, which had not been returned, and during the fourteen-hour flight, we did not exchange a single word. Just her two pokes, a scrambling of seat belt, earphones, book, and blanket on my part, and the whole exercise in reverse some ten or fifteen minutes later.

As we bumped along rather roughly, I briefly wondered whether her hand might be the last human touch I would feel, if I grabbed it in solidarity (a species kind of thing) while we plummeted down into the South China Sea. But would she let me? No, and, anyway, she had her daughter at her side.

This was a Cathay Airlines flight and most of the passengers were Asian, many quite elderly, which made the choice of entertainment rather odd. Twelve hours into the flight, after three full-length films, a *Blackadder* episode suddenly appeared on the screen. I looked around me but most people were asleep. Those who were awake did not make me think (but perhaps it was just the famously inscrutable Asian face) that the Blackadder's sarcastic British wit, Elizabethan to boot in that particular episode, offered much interest or cultural relevance.

In Hong Kong, my seat companions and I parted without a glance. I have sat beside my share of nail biters (literally, I mean, right down to the agonizing pulp), or nonstop snifflers, regular as metronomes, but this one was simply contemptuous of those around her, and my regular gymnastics through the night were never acknowledged. My own particularly source of irritation to my neighbours is heavy sighing, for which I apologize to those I have victimized during many flights.

There was a two-hour wait before our flight for Bangkok. The airport was full and all the seats in the tightly packed area were occupied. I watched several businessmen with their impeccable dark silk and cashmere suits and their slim briefcases, as Western as all get out, but their ethnicity given away not so much by the Asian cast of their features as by the inability of their Chinese hair to comply with short European cuts. Otherwise, they could have been in London, New York, Hamburg, Paris, or Rome, perhaps a little more elegant than most. They stood trim and slightly built for the most part, their smooth faces patient and calm, ready to travel the world. Then, abruptly disappearing from sight among the other passengers, a few would squat for a while, resting on the balls of their feet in the age-old and sensible waiting posture of Asia and Africa.

※　※　※

Bangkok was quite incomprehensible to me. One of the guidebooks I consulted there (Cadogan Guides) describes it as one of the liveliest, friendliest cities in the East. Visitors are charmed. Testimonies abound. "It's unique," tourists are said to proclaim, "it is the kind of place where you can arrive and feel at home right away." Others, apparently, have compared enjoyment of the city to an acquired taste for strong cheese: all the exciting components of "heat, noise, pollution, and mind-numbing traffic," overwhelming at first, soon become only so many attractive features of the incomparable charms of Bangkok.

I am still puzzled about the cheese comparison, but I certainly accept that I did not stay long enough to go past first impressions. One of those, for instance, would have involved watching whole families, toddlers and all, perched on scooters or motorcycles and weaving their death-defying way in fearsome and fume-laden traffic in the most ingenious configurations and balancing skills outside a Chinese circus act.

So, what would have been the second impressions? That people were poor, adaptable, resourceful, and courageous? I already knew that, but seeing them risk their life and that of their small children through dire necessity would never have constituted for me one of the "charming" aspects of Bangkok.

On the drive from the airport, I was particularly intrigued by those small shrines in evidence in front of houses along the highway. I looked for information about those shrines in bookstores near my hotel. Unfortunately, whatever books I found were concerned with larger, touristic aspects of the country. From the bus, the shrines appeared to be colourful, often gilded miniatures of the larger ones seen elsewhere. Maybe they were something entirely different, but I could find nobody to enlighten me. It was in Vancouver several years later that I discovered they were Spirit Houses, traditionally located on a sunny, northeast corner of properties, but in fact, they are found just about everywhere in Thailand, from apartment balconies to shop windows.

I had no experience of large Asian cities, and felt extremely out of sorts there, my mind and body at a loss to recognize anything. A combination of unusually numbing jet lag, heat, pollution, foreign sounds and smells, created one of the most unfamiliar environments I had ever experienced. The only thing I ever recognized from my forays into Vancouver's many Thai restaurants was that delicious food—a combination of Chinese and Indian cuisines with perhaps some memory of Portugal and Indonesia thrown in. Every one of my taste buds saluted in passing the spicy flavours of ginger, tamarind juice, garlic, and chili, and appreciated the delicate lemon grass and the ever-present artery-clogging coconut milk.

The conference was held at the Sukhothai Thammathirat Open University, which was at some distance from our hotels, the latter scattered in many areas, but all very likely "downtown," assuming there is even such a thing in those enormous cities, several million strong. Buses collected us in the morning and returned us at night, but anything in between left us in the hands of taxi drivers, who did not usually understand the simplest directions given in English. Even written instructions in Thai did not always help. Because of being so remote from everything and being both asthmatic and very tired, I did not see as much of hot, polluted, complicated Bangkok, as I definitely should have.

Of what I should have seen in that most complex of cities, I particularly regret not having visited the fruit and vegetable markets. Those marvelous fruit of Thailand were often seen in various combinations on our table in the restaurants or in the dining hall of the university, but what a treat it would have been to see them gathered in large baskets, their colours and aromas blending in the shade of a market stall. Such a display would probably be unrealistic, since these fruit very likely ripen at different times of the year, but there would have been enough at any time to give a feeling of glorious abundance.

I already knew some of these exotic fruits, of course, since Vancouver, with her very large Asian population, has ample supply of them. But I had never seen the famous durian (a large spiny fruit with a strong foul smell), nor the golden pillow *(mon thong)*, nor the *rambutan,* red on the outside, white on the inside, and juicy looking, nor the very large, in fact the largest of Thai fruit, the jackfruit.

I even tried to found out their Thai names, not because I would ever hope to remember them—and to what end—but because knowing their names was the tiniest attempt at coming to terms with a miniscule part of a language so alien that every single word, spoken or written, will always remain a mystery to me.

Yet, I may have a miniscule linguistic connection with Thai. The term *farang,* used to refer to all Westerners travelling in Thailand, is doubly appropriate for me since it is generally accepted to be a derivation of the Thai word for French, *farang-seht*, which is how *français* is pronounced here. I surmise that transliteration of the Thai language is problematic at best and always a complicated endeavour for linguists with its many contradictory claims and for tourists on a brief visit, the language is definitely mysterious and alienating.

As everywhere in the world, any effort by foreigners to utter the odd word of courtesy is always well received, but it is a language that finds absolutely no echo in my linguistic repertoire. My retention span is seldom longer than three or four seconds and no effort of concentration would improve it significantly. Moreover, it is a tonal language, and I have no ear for nuances: being tone-deaf in Asia is not an asset.

We were in Bangkok during the *Loi Krathong* festival held on the night of the full moon in November. As custom required, I made a wish and floated on an artificial pond (theoretically, it should have been a free-flowing river), my own *krathong*, a little crown of flowers with its small flickering candle resting on an intricately and cleverly folded banana leaf and symbolically carrying our worries out of sight.

Launching our *krathongs*, Bangkok

Loi Krathong is a charming festival, but even in the middle of it, I felt little affinity for either the place or its people. I was surprised at the negativity of my feelings, being usually somewhat more open-minded. Everything seemed fake to me—as I am sure it was, since the whole display was put on for our benefit, as well as the elaborate dances performed for us—and contributed to my intense feeling of disconnection. It even came through in what would normally have given me the greatest pleasure, such as the floral masterpieces displayed at the banquet, carried in great pomp, and placed on each of the long buffet tables.

Carrying the centrepiece to the head table, Bangkok

But all I could see were the long exhausting hours, the extraordinary manual agility, and artistic talent devoted to creating such ephemeral beauty. Rather than admire a culture able to produce such generosity, all I could feel was how alien it was. What was displayed for us was at once very beautiful, numbingly foreign, and I thought, unabashedly touristic.

Preparing the centrepieces for the banquet

My sense of being disconnected combined with the remaining jet lag, the fatigue, and the heat, which was intense, reached its peak while looking at the beautifully costumed and made-up female dancers performing at the end of the banquet given in our honour on the second night. In an exhausted daze, almost a mirage out of reality, I gradually stopped seeing them as the women they were. With their round childish faces, their frail shoulders and narrow hips, the heavy make-up hiding their expression and leaving only the pretense of a compliant and smiling softness, they did not look in the least like women, but rather like girl dolls or some of those very precocious child actresses who leave you uneasy. Although they were beautiful, quite ravishing in fact, I found them troubling and confusing.

Traditional dancers welcoming us to the banquet

I was staying at the Central Plaza Hotel where the beds were emperor-size and the orchids freshly replaced every day in the bathroom (the generous rates given to the conference attendees made such luxury possible). One evening, three Canadian colleagues and I decided to meet in the hotel lobby at seven and then go out for dinner. I arrived almost an hour early to indulge in some serious people watching. Hotel lobbies are not as interesting as market places, train stations, and large international airports, but they can do in a pinch.

I had worn beige linen pants and a dark blue cotton shirt with long sleeves, no make-up, and had a very unattractive haircut. I was so unobtrusive as to be invisible, or so I thought. However, not entirely, as it turned out. After hardly more than five minutes, a clearly embarrassed young man wearing a hotel crest on his blazer, whose mother or perhaps even grandmother I could have been, discreetly approached me and asked whether I was a guest at the hotel, and if so, would I be kind enough to give him my room number.

It took me a few seconds to realize that any woman alone, seemingly loitering in a respectable hotel lobby in Bangkok, had to be screened, even if she was a long shot from looking like a prostitute. I suppose it takes all tastes. After all, there was the famous *unijambiste* near Montmartre at the turn of the last century who, by all accounts, had many admirers of her peg leg and did a rather brisk, if specialized, business. So who knows, devotees of dowdy elderly European women with ghastly haircuts may have been rampant in Bangkok.

One day, the university had organized a tour for us, and I was assigned to a bus packed with Swedes, Australians, and Canadians. We boarded at noon. I had been sent back to my room to change my decent-looking trousers for a skirt, since we were going to visit temples, and I had been publicly chastised for almost keeping the bus waiting. When we were finally all on board, we sat and waited. We waited for another half-hour, the reason for the delay being that the companion bus had to be filled with its South East Asian and Latin American contingent before both buses could leave. Who knows why the division had occurred in this odd manner: north-south orientation—the Australians being seen as northerners—or fair-dusky skin? It would have been interesting to learn what guidelines had been used.

When the folks in the other bus had at last been rounded up, both buses were on their way, and we were given our lunches that had been waiting by the idling engine all that time. While a bit concerned with the obvious lack of refrigeration, or at the very least, air-conditioning in we expected that some clever Thai food, traditionally designed to the heat, would be served. But we were each handed a paper bag containing a hamburger, french fries, and a bottle of Pepsi, all at the same tepid temperature. Most of us abstained, and the few who did not were occasionally glanced at with some interest to see when their composure would start to change.

There had already been, after the wonderful (those anonymous little pancakes!) and benumbing outdoor banquet I have mentioned, a large number of casualties to food poisoning. Some had been quite severe, and there had even been rumours that cholera was responsible for the decimation of our ranks. This was confirmed when a colleague of mine had himself checked by his doctor upon his return to Vancouver. Several presentations had to be cancelled, and many more were read by people charged with the task at the last minute and unable to answer questions at the end of their reading.

Cholera, among the well fed and healthy, is not the devastating scourge it is among underfed and weakened populations, but it is very unpleasant nonetheless. I had no symptoms, but my old friend M from the Seychelles, was severely impaired and briefly hospitalized. We had only met once before this debacle, but long enough for him to tell me that his dogs had eaten the biscuits I had sent with the appearance of the canine equivalence to religious fervour.

Our two buses arrived at a little square beside the Grand Palace, where we saw parasitic orchids exotically growing on every tree. We left our buses, our stomachs rumbling with hunger, our minds boggled, and our eyes overwhelmed. We visited the Temple of the Emerald Buddha and the singularly Versailles-like Grand Palace with its slightly incongruous Thai touches.

How much can the mind take in as the body passes on the double through centuries of grandiose monuments erected to passionate or serene deities—with certain undertones of fierce nastiness? (What were those frightening, gilded *garudas*?) It was simply too much for most of us. I now look at postcards and photographs and can only recollect passing details, square inches of beauty lost in the vaguest impression of bejeweled grandeur, Mother of Pearl inlays, glass mosaics, viridescent blue-green shards of light, and stucco embedded with multicolour pieces of porcelain. A marvelous jumble of sights, each deserving time and reflection, not seen at the ridiculous pace imposed upon us at the time.

The Grand Palace, Bangkok

On the way back, our two buses made the obligatory stop at a very large jewelry and silk shop. Exhausted by the heat, the pace of our tour, what we had just seen, and by then very hungry, we obediently poured into a cool Aladdin's cave, an inner sanctum of jewels, silks, and carved ivory. One display case after another exhibited endless rows of rings, bracelets, necklaces, and loose gems, wide expanses of every possible precious and semiprecious stones. Unless one were passionately fond of jewels, this repetitive abundance would soon become extremely tedious—and some of us did find it rather tedious.

However, I must admit to having been strongly attracted to the small carving of a lucky fisherman, a joyful, almost cocky look on his face, his precisely detailed catch on his back, and each fish scale beautifully carved. Without Canada's ban on the import of ivory, which I otherwise wholeheartedly support, I am not sure I would have had the principles and fortitude to resist my desire to possess something so cleverly beautiful.

There was something wonderfully unexpected in that store, as well. Scattered among the jewelry display cases were huge aquariums filled with exotic fish infinitely more colourful than any precious stone. It was a truly breathtaking sight, judging by the entranced look on the faces of some of the visitors, and I particularly remember a woman, a freckled blonde Scandinavian from our bus, a head taller than most, whose mouth simply would not close.

It did not strike me as being such a clever feat of marketing on the part of the management. Their stones could not possibly compete with those flashes of fins crisscrossing the water like so many dashes of rubies, sapphires, or emeralds shining in the luminescent water, only so much redder, bluer, and greener than the gems on offer, and unlike them, vibrant with life.

I went later, on my own and more quietly, to do some shopping and bought a few yards of that sumptuous Thai silk, whose manufacture had been resurrected after the Second World War by the American Jim Thompson. His later disappearance from the porch of his house in the middle of the night has been carefully nurtured by touristic folklore as one of those Eastern mysteries never to be solved. Speculations abound about his fate, and it would be somewhat of a letdown to find out that a tiger on the prowl had simply found an unexpected supper.

Like other good tourists, I had succumbed to the lure of the Twenty-Four-Hour-Suit, with its concurrent ethical question. Yes, indeed, we could imagine those poor people—mostly women, we assumed—working night and day in cramped and ill-ventilated quarters and receiving slave wages, but it did give them work and they would be worse off without this work, so what to do? My own suit, ordered from a shop located in the hotel, was delivered to my room at four o'clock in the morning, just two hours before my departure, not accidently perhaps, considering its fit.

I also had a linen jacket made. For this error, I had no one to blame but myself. I had seen the same jacket being tried on by a six-foot-two, gorgeous, blond-haired, Lufthansa pilot and had been much taken with both. The fact that I am five-foot-one, not a gorgeous blonde-haired woman, and that I had soft curves where he had hard muscles, had not struck me as relevant at the time.

Actually, what I discovered with my two jackets is that the only concession made by the Thai tailor to switching from male to female clothing was the simple reversal of buttons from right to left. Otherwise, the shoulder pads, sleeves, darts, etc., were identical for both genders. They were too ill fitting to wear, and I am not sure that the Salvation Army in Vancouver was able to put them to better use than I did myself. In Hong Kong, the following week, I saw infinitely more elegant versions of this instant costuming, but at several times the cost.

❦ ❦ ❦

After Bangkok, returning to Hong Kong was almost like going home, a feeling that was certainly confirmed by the fact that almost every cab driver or small merchant I spoke to had a relative in Vancouver. "His name is Ng (or Lee, or Wong), do you know him?" they asked, for to the swarms of humanity who live in Hong Kong, Vancouver must look like a large village, and I could probably have said yes safely.

The weather also made me feel at home—everything was enveloped in mild gray softness. The sound of Cantonese voices, while not really endearing to those who do not understand them, was also far more familiar than the equally incomprehensible Thai voices. However, neither gray, nor soft, nor familiar, were the constantly shifting and teeming crowds, which even late at night, consumed street life in Kowloon, and certainly did not feel like any street scene I knew in Vancouver. Hong Kong is known to be a noisy and busy city, but it was actually far busier and noisier than I had anticipated

Having decided to stay an extra day on my own, I had found a very small, triangular room in a Kowloon hotel, not luxurious but respectable. Trim young men, part of the hotel staff, would plaster themselves against the wall to let me pass in the corridors with a respectful "Madame." Such greetings made me feel a notch above my usual self.

In fact, I found everything about Hong Kong superficially pleasant. It is not that I was willing to overlook the leprous walls of the buildings I could see from my hotel window, which oozed poverty, overcrowding, and all sorts of other mental and physical miasma. But the misery I could see and the greed I could guess defeated me to the point where they were not, so to speak, my business.

I visited two shops and both experiences were what shopping should be: courteous, charming, delicate, and more civilized than any other shopping I have ever done. The first stop was at a jewelry store; the reason I had not bought any jewelry in Bangkok was that the sheer number and weight of things had overwhelmed me. So in Hong Kong, I went looking for small gifts. The owner and I discussed, among other matters, the benefits of higher education. And every Christmas for the next ten years, I received from the ISE Jewellery Co. Ltd., my first card of the season.

The other was a small antique shop. When the owner came towards me, I mentioned immediately that I could not afford anything in his store and just wanted to look around. Rather than return to what he had been doing when I came in, he gave me a lesson in Chinese art. Delighted to find out that I spoke French, he elaborated at length on the *période rose,* his favourite, and the others, *verte,* and *noire.* Then he explained the significance of the rooster, when I showed him a bowl similar to the one we had at home.

He spent nearly an hour with me, teaching all along. I could do no less, upon leaving, than buy the cheapest thing in the store, which he assured me I did not have to do. It was a humble and rather rough looking nineteenth-century storage jar with a little wooden lid, a coral-red glaze porcelain from the Ch'ing Dynasty with barely discernible temple dogs, which is a long description for what the receipt stated to be merely a bit of "household porcelain."

Certainly, those two episodes with the antique dealer and the jeweler took away from the limited amount of sightseeing I had planned on doing, but I remember them with more pleasure than seeing yet another building or another vista across water. Hong Kong is reputed to have one of the loveliest harbours in the world, along with San Francisco and Sydney, but

Vancouver, mountains on one side, ocean on the other, is also a favourite of nature in this respect, and I did not really miss the sight of Hong Kong harbour.

I ended my short stay in Asia by taking afternoon tea at the Peninsula Hotel, that old bastion of what were for some the good old days. My order of tea and three crumpets required two people to carry more silver, china, and linen napkins than our family has inherited from two grandmothers and one great-aunt. In that singularly ludicrous decor, I felt perfectly at home, particularly if I closed my eyes to the people around me, who were far too elegant, far too superbly Chinese to feel at all familiar.

In the cab taking me back to the airport, the driver ("Do you know my cousin who lives in Richmond?"), a very affable man, tried to interest me in some sort of instant scheme (the details of which I did not really understand then and have forgotten since). When I explained that his fare would consume my remaining HK dollars, his contempt was as broad as his affability had been earlier. We drove on in unfriendly silence.

In Vancouver, upon my return, I was sometimes asked about Thailand and Hong Kong. I spoke of the latter easily, since it had stayed vividly in my mind, thanks in part to the two shopkeepers who had made my brief visit quite memorable, and to a sense of familiarity, I felt there. As for Thailand, I did not say very much and mostly showed photographs, my own from the Grand Palace and elsewhere, some from colleagues, and others taken by conference photographers at the banquet. It is quite likely that these photographs gave a reasonable facsimile of what I should have seen in Bangkok—may very likely have seen, actually—but somehow evoking for me the same vagueness I had experienced there, since what I could recollect was mostly groupings of images, vignettes, impressions, rather than a coherent narrative of my visit.

Of the conference, particularly considering the disruption created by the cholera from which several presenters had suffered—and that had resulted in delays, rescheduling, or cancellations—I mostly recollected that everything was too big, too disconnected, too confused, and even too alienating. Quite simply, there had been far too much of everything and so much of it had been far too unfamiliar.

The Compounds of the Rich
Caracas, 1994

"They couldn't get her rings, so they cut off her fingers." "Two Canadian women were attacked there last week." "Since you have a few days to kill before your meeting, why don't you spend them in Mexico City? It's much nicer, and you'll be safe." Such was my send-off to Caracas.

I like Mexico City, particularly those long walks with one eye always on the potholes, and so much tackiness, but also so much nobility, beauty, and history, and two days there sounded like a delightful break in an otherwise heavy schedule. However, my asthma having worsened considerably since my last visit, I felt reluctant to test the combined effect of altitude and pollution on it.

I weighed the prospect of rushing with asthmatic breath around Mexico against hiding timidly in a Caracas hotel room, and decided there could perhaps be something between the two. I am not, as a rule, unduly worried at the thought of cut-off fingers or other reasonable acts of violence aimed at divesting me of my possessions (random and gratuitous violence is another matter entirely). I never wear jewelry, do not carry a purse that could be easily grabbed by motorcyclists, my clothes are inexpensively drab, and I am overall rather discreet.

However, we have to recognize that we experience what Claude Lévi-Strauss, the French anthropologist, describes as "instant wealth" as soon as we arrive in certain countries, and this wealth, while very modest by our standards, is nevertheless perceived as substantial elsewhere. Caracas would be no exception, but I did not see why it would be different from, say, Havana or Guadalajara, where I have felt perfectly safe in the past.

I arrived at nearly midnight and was greeted by a bearded young man, a graduate student or a minor university functionary, and his very pretty wife whose cheekbones proclaimed strong Indian ancestry. It was a long drive to the Residencia Hilton, where I was booked, where my colleagues were also presumably staying, and where the meetings would take place. However, the night manager took one look at me and sent me to the much nicer Caracas Hilton across the street without a word of explanation.

The following morning, the day manager called to explain that my relocation was a promotion by the Hilton and apologized that it had not been made clear to me the night before. He also offered to move me back, if I wished. I did not think that being across the street would make much difference, so I decided to stay, not realizing how inconvenient it would turn out to be, as no one would allow me to walk even that short distance alone in the dark after dinner. Something else I had not realized was that there was no direct and easy access from my side of the street across the very busy boulevard to the Residencia and that getting back and forth required a brief detour often across rubble of an apparently abandoned construction site next door.

Caracas is not a city where the visitor feels particularly comfortable, and perhaps this is only due to the constant reminder by local friends and officials not to do this (at least alone) and not to go there (at least alone). Soon, a perhaps irrational feeling develops that only in groups does safety lie. And perhaps it is not so irrational after all. Bill, one of the Americans in our group, had travelled twice on the subway during previous trips to Caracas and had twice been robbed, but according to André, a French Canadian, it was still better than Bogota where robberies were usually accompanied by violence. It may be statistically indulgent to equate twice out of twice with 100 percent, but for Bill it will never be otherwise disproved since he is unlikely ever to take the subway in Caracas again, at least alone.

I saw very little of Caracas and almost nothing of the rest of Venezuela during the week or so of my stay. My memories, apart from a quick tour of the city on my own, are a blur of banquets, clubs, and the sometimes-overwhelming Venezuelan hospitality that never agrees to receive anything in return, all against the backdrop of the surrounding hills of poverty.

I should also mention that we worked very hard, since it was not easy to conduct meetings in four official languages (although the Brazilians soon agreed to speak Spanish and the single French Canadian English), with several North and South American countries represented and common goals having to be defined. Despite everyone's goodwill, it was not always smooth sailing.

However, from the time I walked into the room on the first morning—a last minute substitute for someone unable to attend, not knowing what or whom I would find—I realized that every unknown face in the small group standing by the door warmly smiled at me and I immediately had the oddest and probably unfounded feeling that I was among friends.

The extraordinary hospitality we were shown masked to some extent the even more extraordinary financial conditions our hosts faced, and even managed to make these appear, if not normal, at least not as oppressive as they actually were—which shows how isolated from everyday reality we were.

❦ ❦ ❦

Caracas is a long city, a spine stretching east to west and surrounded by houses cascading from the hills, more often than not the *casas brujas* of the slums. Since I knew I would have little free time to spend looking and walking around the city, I went on a bus tour on my second or third afternoon. There were only three of us in a large bus, a Spanish-speaking American couple from New York on their honeymoon and me. In such cases, where to sit is not always self-evident. The three of us bunched together behind the guide or me at a discreet distance from the couple, yet not so far as to force the driver-guide to shout or for me to seem unfriendly. Those details always concern me.

We first drove to the centre of town and then got out to walk around. We followed our guide into a particularly dismal souvenir shop whose manager looked uncannily like him. Plaza Bolivar, dominated by the Liberator's equestrian statue, was very fine indeed. Pigeons barely got out of our way as we walked by, people rushed or lolled about, and we photographed some wonderful and enormous trees whose name the guide did not know.

There were a few tourists around in pairs or in small groups. Some were tall and fit-looking, mostly blond and probably American or German, looking very efficient in their modified fatigues and comfortable shoes—in sharp contrast with the neat, even natty local men, and the incredibly tight jeans of the young women. Others were there too, conforming more to the stereotypical picture of ordinary tourists wearing droopy T-shirts and baggy shorts. Both groups carried cameras.

I had heard about the finicky concern of Venezuelans of both sexes with their appearance and of their frequent recourse in relation to other Latin American countries to cosmetic surgery, and I must admit to having looked at them more carefully than I might generally have done. Many impressed me with their stylish clothes, and for women, their impeccable make-up, and hairstyles. Many were extremely beautiful, and whether naturally or with a little help, I thoroughly admired them and the effort implied behind each presentation.

Our trio went inside a cathedral, where our guide's ministrations were unexpectedly taken over by a very old man, also a visitor, but intent on imparting his knowledge. He cackled a lot while gumming his words (he had not a tooth left in his sardonic wrinkly mouth) as he led us through the details of the side chapels. He pointed to an unfinished painting of the Last Supper, insisting the painter had been too permanently drunk to complete it.

In another chapel, he laughed at the sloppiness of the house painters who had let whitewash dribble and splatter on another mural when the ceiling had been recently repainted. Despite his sometimes-amusing gossip, which all pointed out somebody's incompetence, I liked the sober cathedral and its austere chapels.

It was a nice contrast to the Mexican churches I was used to, still gilt-ridden even after all removable gold had been taken away so long ago. My latest church visit, barely two months earlier, had been to the wonderfully fussy, neo-Gothic *Basilique Notre-Dame* in Montréal. It could not have offered a more vivid contrast with its astonishing altar, almost a miniature cathedral within a cathedral, the extraordinary richness of its chapels, the tormented dark wood sculptures of the pulpit, as if plain, bare, unattended wood would have offended God, the same God celebrated here so much more austerely.

We walked afterwards by Bolivar's house, several times rebuilt and now a museum, but it was closed that day. An arrogant statement by him, on a plaque nearby gave me pause. The plaque bears the words he apparently pronounced after the destructive earthquake of March 26, 1812: *"Si se opone la naturaleza lucharamos contra ella y la haremos que nos obedezca."* (If nature opposes us, we will fight against her and force her to obey us.)

Obviously, liberations have never been accomplished by mealy-mouthed, lily-livered, no-gut-Nellie's, and after all, what else could he say to rally around the terrified and devastated Venezuelans used to believing he was indomitable? For so he was, for a time at least, only to be rather shabbily treated later. A local writer describes him as "hounded by jealousies, ill with tuberculosis, and almost penniless," before having to retire to private life.

A statue of José Martí caught my eye. Knowing in what respect he is held in Cuba, I asked the driver about his significance for Venezuelans and he said it was merely "a decoration." The American couple (she was of Cuban origin and he Mexican) mentioned that there was also a Martí statue in New York on the Avenue of the Americas, but it did not elicit much reverence there either. I could see that if her parents had left Cuba during the revolution, Martí would not necessarily be one of her personal heroes.

We then walked through rather handsome official buildings with patios reminiscent of Old Spain.

Particularly fine examples of courtyard and fountain, Caracas

Finally, we drove off to one of the surrounding hills amid vegetation of the most incredible array of reds and pinks. There were also the ubiquitous, brilliant scarlet poinsettias at the end of bare branches, the usual golden salmon and deep pink bougainvillea, and a variety of unknown flowering bushes. Some had creamy, waxy bunches of flowers on thick branches and laurel-like leaves, others much smaller and with pretty gentian blue flowers, all found among clumps of extremely thick bamboos.

Those gardens belonged to the houses of the rich: embassies, well recessed in privacy, residences of important and wealthy men. We noticed fiercely serrated lines of broken bottles cemented into the top of garden walls that looked like the aftermath of a vicious bar brawl. We saw upscale apartment buildings displaying Babylonian-like gardens hanging from balconies in a profusion and exuberance of colours. These colourful balconies were in fact the ironical mirror image of the tenement buildings across town whose own shaky-looking balconies were filled with equally colourful laundry hanging to dry in the sun.

As we left the bus, I slipped a tip to the driver, feeling rather sorry for him. There had been only three tourists, some delay due to the American couple's desire to buy some records and then briefly getting lost during which the driver had panicked a little, our inertia in his relative's store, and the apparent boredom of it all for him. Unfortunately, instead of doing the obvious and taking a reasonable percentage of the tour fare, I went inanely through the complicated exercise of figuring out the tip in Canadian dollars, converting it into American currency, and finally into bolivares. Back in my hotel room, I recalculated the whole process, since somehow, it had not felt quite right, and the guide's thanks had noticeably lacked warmth. I then realized my intended generosity had amounted to less than a dollar.

※ ※ ※

Whatever glimpses the tour had provided, it had revealed very little of the city. Since the rest of my stay was devoted to the loftier pursuits of experiencing a more elegant and self-contained lifestyle when we were not working, I actually found out little more about Caracas than whatever I had seen on the tour. I had no sense of how people treated one another or what going to the market would be like, although I knew the economic situation was a disaster.

Even watching television did not tell me very much. There were some rather ordinary soap operas, although I had anticipated stronger stuff and had looked forward to watching *Por Estas Calles* (Along These Streets), which a Mexican newspaper had recently reviewed as "spotlighting social ills" and about which the United States Information Agency had asked "Soap Opera or Subversion?" Maybe it was only shown in the afternoon when I was at meetings, or maybe it had been cancelled.

The news usually reported a lot of violent and sometimes gory crime. One particular news program dealt at some length with a project encouraging young children to turn in their toy guns and other make-believe lethal weapons, with pious words pronounced by politicians, social workers, police officers, and the children themselves. Then, a turn of the dial often produced the worst of American television violence.

A local programmer was also fascinated by the Bobbitt case, and since Lorena Bobbitt was Venezuelan, the focus was mostly on her. *"La Castradora, Víctima o Criminal?"* they asked, but I cannot remember what the popular verdict was. Then, this being the 1990s, there was the ubiquitous Mr. Bean.

Briefly walking downtown on my own, mostly looking at monuments, parks, and statuary in public places, I had the sense of being in a well designed city but no longer a prosperous one with too many abandoned construction sites, one of the largest right beside the Hilton. There are cities in the world where, after a few hours, you know you could be happy living there, but it is uncertain what makes you think so. A good meal in a pleasant restaurant? Friendly chatter while waiting at a bank to cash travellers' cheques? A vista from a particular angle, which stirs something in your unremembered past? A peaceful stroll in a shady park with children playing? The city's depiction in a film? A book? Perhaps simply a pair of comfortable walking shoes, a propitious turn at an intersection, a balmy day?

For whatever reason and based on whatever fallacy, these cities do exist (Boston and Québec, for me on this continent) but Caracas was not one of them, even if I cannot remember having met with more kindness and generosity anywhere else than from Venezuelan colleagues—a remark perhaps unfair to the equally warmhearted Cubans.

It should not come as a surprise, then, that my most pleasant memories relate to generous meals and banquets given in our honour and private clubs visited, and as I consult the notes I took at the time, this is amply confirmed.

◊ La Hacienda, an Argentine restaurant with the appropriate decor of gauchos and pampas. Commenting on my Spanish, the fellow who picked me up to drive me to this restaurant said, "We Venezuelans speak the best Spanish, because we have no accent." Then, almost in the same breath, he went on to say that every region of the country speaks differently.

I am sitting between Bill the American, and Antonio, a Venezuelan. Across from me are Antonio's son and future daughter-in-law. She has magnificent black eyes, black hair, thick eyebrows, a red mouth, perfect complexion, and she is extremely charming. She is respectful, too, certainly enough to make me feel respectably old. She studies languages. I praise her to Antonio, realizing too late that I should have praised his son more.

The son of another man sitting at our table is going to Europe next year and intends to run with the bulls in Pamplona. "Savages," mutters another Venezuelan, who obviously has a low opinion of the Basques, at least in that respect. We talk about bullfights. He has never seen one, and when I tell him of my husband's enthusiastic discovery of them in Mexico only a couple of months earlier, he looks thoroughly disgusted.

I then mention my own introduction to them as a teenager through Blasco Ibañez' *Sangre y arena*. Nobody has heard of it, and the conversation is not going anywhere. I feel like a dinosaur. However, I feel vindicated, if not younger, when on a later occasion, mentioning this to Armando, another of our Venezuelan hosts, he exclaims, "Blasco Ibañez? Vicente Blasco Ibañez? My father used to read aloud from his books when I was a child." Regretfully, he does not think that anyone reads them anymore. But he is wrong. The book is not entirely forgotten, at least in its Hollywood version. Only last week the English title, *Blood and Sand* appeared on a crossword puzzle defined as "Valentino's bullfight flick."

From Blasco Ibañez, we go on talking about some aspects of Latin American literature, and I express my reluctant sense of seduction at some of the works: the myths are not my own and disturb me, as does the alien landscape. My neighbour's wife leans over, and perhaps misquoting, refers to Alice's inability to understand what she does not understand. A charming woman, this wife, Floridian by birth. They hold hands after dinner as they listen to the speeches, their two sons (one dark, the other fair, both well mannered and handsome—and bored, I would think—sitting by her side.

After finishing our avocados the size of small cantaloupes, filled with shrimp and unfortunately drenched in Thousand Island dressing, my neighbours are served slabs of meat on slabs of wood. An American woman and I ordered *mero*, a local fish, which Antonio tells me is the best and proves it by reciting the apparently well known adage, *Del mar el mero, de la tierra el cordero*. Obviously, I have to agree with folk wisdom, but while the fish is probably otherwise very nice, the beef-loving Argentines do not know how to cook it. I look at the other woman, who grimaces discreetly.

I suddenly realize that Antonio, a very nice man, indeed, kind and thoughtful, is also somewhat in his cups and has returned to his obsession: the current economic situation in Venezuela and the frightful inflation rates. Obviously, he agonizes about the uncertainty he and his children face. Antonio, when sober, does not talk about such things, but they reemerge as soon as his defenses are down. It is difficult to know what to say. However sympathetic we may feel, it is obvious we do not really know what it is like, and we will soon be gone and far away from Venezuela's problems.

Only two days after my return home, I read of an arrest of eighty-three bankers and executives charged with fraud, criminal association, and other crimes stemming fro m the collapse of Venezuela's second largest bank, *Banco Latino*. At least 10 percent of the population banks there, and the oil industry, the country's largest business, had tens of millions of dollars frozen in its accounts.

Notes from Elsewhere

At another restaurant, lunch is specially prepared for us: paella, cooked in a gigantic flat pan, and Sangria, served in most generous quantities. I sit at one end of the table with Profesora X, a senior administrator at the university, and a journalist who has interviewed our group during the press conference before lunch. The other seats beside and across from me are empty and I am in effect accidentally isolated within their private corner.

Soon, they are both intensely absorbed in a spirited conversation and totally ignore me, but since I have good manners and this is a formal meal, it is too late for me to sit elsewhere. Lunch goes on and on, and I remain silent, like an old-fashioned child who only speaks when spoken to.

After awhile, the meal now mostly over, I decide it would no longer be rude to go and sit beside others for coffee, given the late hour and my complete invisibility. It is exhausting, rather humiliating, and very hard on the cheeks to keep on looking alert, half-smiling as courtesy commands, while being ignored. Profesora X, as if sensing my mood, turns towards me, puts her hand on mine, and says in Spanish, "I'm sorry you don't speak Spanish." "But I do," I reply mildly.

Her embarrassment is not entirely honest, because when pressed, she manages well enough in English. And on my side, I am not entirely honest either, since my Spanish would not have easily permitted me to participate in such a long and technical conversation, even assuming I understood the context. Tomorrow night, she will host a dinner for us at a private club. She kisses me as she leaves. She smells delightful.

Hugs and kisses are commonly exchanged as greetings and farewells, the only exception being among Americans and Canadians, even—and perhaps particularly—the women among us. We nod and smile at each other, as we would at home, and warmly embrace our hosts and Southern colleagues when we arrive and when we leave. There is nothing affected in that: hugging them feels natural because that is what they do among themselves, hugging each other would not. I am not even sure we shook hands when first introduced upon arrival.

At the Izcaragua Country Club, a magnificent hacienda in the old style and on a grand scale. The rich *estancieros*, the ranching families, were obviously very rich indeed. Unfortunately, we arrive at night and can only see a very small part of the extensive grounds. The hacienda proper, now a club, is truly a masterpiece of spacious and airy architecture. Rooms, one after another, some taking a sharp turn to start a new enfilade at right angle. There are glossy floors, tile in the more rustic rooms, and fine parquet in the main reception halls. Heavily beamed ceilings with a tight configuration of varnished bamboo. Marvelous breeziness throughout; small patios scattered in odd corners (in one I recognize a lacy pomegranate tree from its unripe fruit), and little terraces and balconies we need to hang onto while craning our neck to see the full moon almost directly above since we are after all very close to the equator. The furniture is sparse and of good European stock of the last century.

In one of the smaller rooms, I find displayed on a desk some photographs of the family who originally owned the estancia. From the cars, I would judge they were taken sometime in the 1920s. The family, a few children in jodhpurs, adults posing and smiling, all look surprisingly fair, and nothing, except some adobe archways on the property and the faces of a few servants, nothing really speaks of Venezuela. This family belongs anywhere, at least anywhere the rich and fortunate people gathered after the Great War. I am curious about them, but do not know whom to ask. My local colleagues are as unknowledgeable as I am, and Antonio can only tell me that it costs US$50,000 to join this club.

After taking our time walking and looking around we gather for dinner in one of the larger rooms, glassed in on two sides, with a small inside balcony on the far wall (too small for musicians, which is the first thought that comes to mind). The table is set for thirty people, but a good number of them do not show up. Almost as many young men in gleaming white uniforms loom, ready to cater to our needs. The room is so large that we could easily dance around the enormous table, should we wish to do so.

Our little group at one end, with a few empty seats between the others and us, consists of André, the French Canadian; Antonio, the Venezuelan; Manuel, a pleasant Mexican; and me. Farther along, the others struggle, little islands of common interest and shared jokes slowly forming. I am trying, with little confidence, to remember what language we spoke when away from the working sessions: probably some Anglo-Spanish comfortably adapted to our various levels of competency.

❧   ❧   ❧

We were invited to spend our last day at the Club Puerto Azul. Some attendees have already gone home, and I will miss the nice Chilean woman. The drive lasts about an hour and a half. We are delayed because traffic has been reduced to one lane under one of the bridges.

My American neighbour, who took a cab through the same route yesterday, says the cab driver told her that many of the people who live in the slums along the side of the hill do not have running water, and since they have been tapping the city water pipes, the constant leakage had undermined the foundations of the bridge.

We then drive through the rather pretty little port and vacation town of Macuto, and glimpse two trucks parked in the main square, one full of very yellow bananas and the other of very red tomatoes. Indeed, everything has the usual look of a tourist's postcard, a look one cannot escape from in these countries: blue water, blue sky, white cruise ships anchored in the bay, brightly dressed people, baskets full of ripe fruit—all looking so lovely and colourful. How could people not be happy and carefree here?

We arrive at what is obviously the gate of a compound. Our driver goes to talk to some official-looking person and the bus is sent to another gate where an unsmiling young man in a paramilitary uniform climbs on board. Two days earlier, we had been asked to provide our passport numbers, and both Canadians and Americans had thought the precaution and security somewhat exaggerated. We present our passports and the young man's examination is anything but perfunctory. Although two Venezuelan members of the club escort us, each passport number is checked against the number already on the guard's list, and each face is scrutinized and carefully compared with its photograph. We would certainly not dare joke that passport photos often make us look like serial killers.

We finally get in the compound, disembark, and after a short time to decide on a place where we would all meet again later, we are let loose and free to wander. Immediately, Bill and I see the reason for these unusual security measures: it is a children's paradise. We have to agree that it is a long time since we have seen in our respective countries little children safely walking about on their own. Naturally, parents and maids are not far away, but the anxiety North Americans know so well when children disappear from their sight for a moment seems quite absent here.

Most families own an apartment in the club, and others rent in nearby buildings, spending either the weekend or a longer holiday there. Built nearly forty years ago (this is why Armando can afford to be a member. His father bought a membership in the days when it was still affordable, and Armando has inherited it from him), the club has since grown to enormous proportions and is designed to cater to the needs of the entire family. I toy with the idea that one could move here as a toddler and end up ninety years later playing bridge on the veranda, never having found the need or the inclination to leave.

I have never seen such a place. When staying at Las Hadas near Manzanillo (the white resort—part-Disney World, part-Middle Eastern fiction—where the movie *10* was filmed), we were told that the meandering pool interspersed with islands was the largest on the continent. Having now seen the children's pool at Puerto Azul, I start having my doubts. Young children splash and play in this pool, which in some places is very shallow and in other places chest-deep to a small adult (my size) holding a child and teaching him to swim. Flowering shrubs cover the little islands, and a wooden bridge links the largest one to the "mainland."

Nearby, the playground has everything a small child might think necessary to his entertainment, all painted in bright primary colours. Slightly older children might also participate in the general aerobic class held at sundown when it gets cooler and where they happily display their uncoordinated moves, as if some essential translation between what they see the instructor do and what they reproduce themselves requires an uncommonly long delay.

If a little more adventurous, they can swim in the Playa Tranquila where not even a ripple mars the surface of the water. If they prefer swimming pools, there are two of them: a largish one and an Olympic-size one with three diving boards of various regulation heights. For surfing, there is the ocean beach where, twice during our day there, the lifeguards forced everybody out because of the undertow. Whether this move was justified or not, the lifeguards' watchfulness must give club members a constant feeling of safety and of getting their money's worth of attention.

Teenagers and adults also have a billiards room, a bowling alley, several tennis courts, and an outdoor movie theatre with an overhanging roof. Much older adults have a well appointed area for playing cards and meet in sitting circles.

While there are many places where one can eat in the main building, a large cafeteria and a few formal dining rooms, food can also be bought during the day from small huts scattered throughout the compound, each specializing in certain foods. Near us is a hot dog stand, which we ignore in favour of another offering chicken, coleslaw, and *ayaquita*, cornmeal cooked and served in a corn leaf, and very similar to the Mexican *tamale*. We each buy our own food, and it is remarkably inexpensive.

Speaking of food and the good smells about, the only jarring notes in this earthly paradise are the emaciated cats lurking behind nearly every bush, all-ridged ribcages and loose skin and keeping at a scrupulously cautious distance. Two American women and I, no doubt true to form, put chicken tidbits at a well measured distance, far enough to inspire trust and ensure safety, and close enough for us to see the outcome of our munificence.

Seduced, not so much by the lavish facilities as by the concept of a place solely designed for the wellbeing and safety of the whole family, we have perhaps forgotten the walls carefully watched by guards. We eat and swim and snooze, and swim some more, separately or together, the day totally given to *far niente* and slowing down before going back home the following day.

Returning from the beach, my hair matted in unattractive salty ringlets, a large sloppy T-shirt over my bathing suit, baggy at the seat, I spot our group now reconstituted and gathered around something. It turns out to be an enormous white birthday cake wishing me *Feliz Cumpleaños, Monica*. I had mentioned to someone, *à propos* of food, the excellent meal to which I treated myself at the Hilton yesterday for my birthday, and here is the reward for my indiscretion. What they may have seen as loneliness—something their hospitality and kindness could not accept—had in fact been extremely restful and enjoyable for me. A decent and peaceful dinner and a glass of wine in the excellent company of Jack Aubrey and Stephen Maturin in one of the many O'Brian's books I often read while travelling during the 1990s.

Antonio serenades me, his eyes mere slits of glee on his pleasant pudgy face, *"Cumpleaños, cumpleaños feliz, Que deseamos a tí,"* he sings, and Manuel, the handsome Mexican, gives me hug. A bird with a black mask and a pale yellow beak, named by its call, "Cristo fué," sings in a tree above our heads; the bright flight of a parrot zips by between the trees. Paradise in a fortress.

I am given a knife to cut the round cake, and in the only way I know, insert the tip at the centre, ready to slice through one radius at the time. Antonio's wife grabs the knife from me and does it *properly,* making another smaller circle inside the cake, and cutting slices from each part of this newly formed ring. What is left is the small centre, the plain round part; obviously, those wanting a second helping are undeserving of the fancy icing around the edge.

Usually unsure of my domestic skills, being the type of person who cannot even peel potatoes in somebody else's kitchen, I wonder whether I have been doing it wrong all these years. I look at Norma, the blonde American woman who observes the procedure with interest; it is also new to her and I am reassured.

By evening, we board the bus and drive again under the bridge undermined by the stolen water of the poor. We are tired and gritty, with sand in our sandals. Saying good-bye, Bill kisses my hand and André my cheek, and it feels like the last day at summer camp.

The two clubs we visited cater to the tastes and needs of the wealthy, the Izcaragua Club the more elegant of the two. But they are not a rarity in Caracas. Looking at the business pages of the local newspapers, I saw shares being bought and sold for these two clubs, but also for at least a dozen more of such havens for the rich. In a city where violence, poverty, and crime are rapidly growing, it is understandable that the wealthy would be anxious to protect their vulnerability by creating such compounds and enforcing the exclusion of all others, save for those allowed in to serve and wait upon them.

※ ※ ※

Very early the following morning, I drove off as the sun started touching up the hills around the city, the *casas brujas* tightly pressed together showing their pleasant colours: the warm adobe, the cool splash of white, and here and there the delicate blue panel of, perhaps, a door. With a single bare light bulb in front of each house, the scene was charming at a distance, much like a naive painting. There was something very Merry Christmassy about these poor neighbourhoods seen from the air-conditioned luxury of the Hilton taxi taking me to the airport.

My last impressions of Caracas at the Simon Bolivar Airport were as impersonal as my first had been during the tour. It would have been nice to witness an airport scene revealing something about people: family reunion or separation, perhaps, something equally unguarded and meaningful. But none of that occurred.

I can truthfully say that I had no idea how the average Venezuelan behaved, having only met the rich and their servants. And the guide I had shortchanged. Although, this is unfair, as generalized statements usually are. My colleagues there, while mostly well to do by local standards, were also average in that they demonstrated kindness, anxiety, impatience, rudeness (though only once to me), courtesy, concern for the future, love of their children, and hospitality towards strangers.

After going through the over-zealous security (my bag was X-rayed three times, I was frisked twice, and went through one electronic checkup before being finally admitted to the departure gate) and having some time to spare, I stopped at a restaurant near the American Airlines first-class lounge. It had red tablecloths and was decorated with those large, tumescent, phallic-looking cacti, which Antonio had coyly told me were called *palos de la felicidad*. The restaurant appeared expensive, but I thought a last taste of that wonderful orange juice would be well worth the expense, so I went in. The juice definitely came out of a can and had a hint of fizz about it. The warm water for the tea came in a plastic container, and much later arrived a cup and a bag of *Canaima té*, then finally some hot milk. The duchess of York must have inspired Venezuela's approach to tea. Interviewed at length by a Venezuelan newspaper the week before, Fergie is reported to have said, "As long as it's hot and wet, and goes the right way …" But my tea was not even hot.

I did have my tiny spontaneous glimpse of Caracas, after all. Downstairs, across the vast expanse of shiny floors, a very large and hairy rat scurried. After a false entry into a shop, it emerged again and turned quickly around a corner, and disappeared from sight. The nonchalant men in uniform leaning against a counter looked on and one of them suggested, amid the good-natured laughter of the others, *"¡Es un conejo!"* (It's a rabbit!)

Chapter Ten

From Barcelona to Biarritz
1994

John was in Amsterdam and I in Vancouver and since we wanted to go to Spain that particular summer, we decided to meet in Paris and take the night train to Barcelona. After the usual confusion of wrong streets, wrong turns, and wrong buses, we found we would still have four hours to spare between Charles de Gaulle airport where John had met me and Gare d'Austerlitz, from where we would leave, so we decided to "do" the Louvre. Which we did in about two and a half hours (the Egyptian antiquities, at least) and threw in Notre-Dame for good measure.

Notre-Dame was quite as wonderful as I remembered it, and wanting to share with John something of that wonder, I kept pointing out to him stained glass windows, particularly the famous *rosaces*, which he was perfectly able to notice on his own. However, I must have felt at some subconscious level that since both the *rosaces* and I were somewhat French and Catholic of sorts, I was better equipped or qualified to admire them.

But since I did pretty much the same thing in Spanish churches, it is possible that I deem myself more "artistic" than him. My artistic comments, actually, do not go much further or deeper than uttering with an inspired expression on my face, "Oh, *look* at that!"

John was studying a notice board at Notre-Dame announcing a religious music recital, which we might have attended had we stayed in Paris, while I noticed on the same board a mention made of a priest ("Today Father So and So") who was available for the "sacrament of reconciliation and dialogue." Two simultaneously thoughts popped into my mind. First, how generous and understanding of the church to offer reconciliation, what a lovely word that was, and how appropriate for most of us lapsed yet searching souls. Second, I did not know that reconciliation and dialogue were also a sacrament; neither was listed as one when I went to catechism. However, who was I to argue with either clergy or dogma on the hallowed grounds of Notre-Dame?

Then I realized I had seen him without knowing who he was. Father So-and-So, the Dialoguer. He was difficult to miss actually, sitting slightly to the side of the tourist throngs in a well lit, glassed-in alcove, looking marvelously peaceful. I remembered him reading, but John, when consulted later, rather thought he was looking down at his folded hands and meditating—more likely, saying his rosary and waiting for a soul to reach out to him.

He looked beautiful, patient, compassionate, and I almost felt a tug of temptation at the thought of what must be truly the best homecoming of all: rejoining the fold, becoming the famous errant sheep for which the rest of the flock has been set aside, the cause of heavenly rejoicing. But I wondered what he did when someone came? Surely, they would not stay in the spotlight, appropriate to attract attention and prospects, but otherwise unthinkable for the type of very private exchange intended. So, what did he do? Were there drapes to be drawn for privacy?

In the middle of the night, in my upper berth, half-dozing, and lulled by the motion as the train clickety-clacked its way towards Spain, I realized what had been lurking in my mind all that time: Amsterdam. Those other seekers of attention and customers, in their small well lit rooms and absorbed in their more or less innocent tasks for all to appreciate and assess (I remembered a domesticated blonde knitter in a rocking chair), which is probably why, in the middle of Notre-Dame, I had thought of draperies being discreetly drawn rather than the skimpy black curtains of an old-fashioned confessional.

In all fairness to the church, what else could they do? The problem was the same: to advertise services by establishing the right atmosphere and creating a need the passerby might not otherwise have known he had. Whatever the needs and products sold, sex and fantasy in Amsterdam, or acceptance and reconciliation in Notre-Dame, the range of marketing techniques available must be rather limited.

By the time the sun was up, we became drawn into the countryside, so dry on the landside, so blue on the seaside, so Mediterranean all around. Between Cerbère (nearly at the border, perhaps guarding something) and Figueres (Salvador Dali's birth and burial place, and as is less well known, the birthplace of Narcis Monturiol, the inventor of a Catalan submarine, the *Ictino*) where we must have left the coast, what a charming landscape it was.

Cerbère, Portbou, Llança, Flaça. A little cove, some fishing boats beached there in what seemed to be the centre of the village. "No sign of glaciation," said John, and "We are not used to such relief." (I believe his knowledge of physical geography to be about as extensive as mine, so I did not pay too much attention.) White walls, red clay, blue windows, a touch of green here and there, and little villages cascading from the hillside into the tiny harbours. Once-pink towers now muted to a soft grayish patina; still skies of the deepest blue. Hints of retaining walls scrambling into the hills, some already so overgrown and eroded that their presence had become only a hint, like some handwritten imprint left on the second page and only seen in a slanting light.

Along the coast, just around the border, I could almost guess at the heady smell of garlic as I imagined it frying around shrimps and tomatoes. I could guess as well the sound of Catalan voices as might be heard greeting, arguing, and calling to one another by the little harbours. It was all there, the stuff holidays are made of. So why didn't we just stop there and be done with it? I, at least, knew I had truly arrived when we stopped in Portbou to change trains.

I no longer travel as I once did, getting off as soon as the train, the bus, the car stopped where the air was fine, the sound of voices and birds light and gay, the trees shady, the dogs benign, the cats appropriately sly, and the people courteous. But John's own longing is for what the next turn of the road will reveal. And the next after that. He would keep on with the caravan while I stopped at the first oasis. So on to Barcelona we went, and then to Madrid, and other places. And it was very fine too. However, the first impression, the first sense of true arrival lingered like the faint regret of small promises unfulfilled.

When we arrived in Barcelona, *la Gran Encisera* (the Great Enchantress, as nearly two centuries ago the poet Joan Maragall called his native city), I was well prepared: native French speaker, getting comfortably by in Spanish, seven years of Latin, and a hectic year at university studying Italian, Portuguese, and Old Provençal. I could imagine myself being a whiz at Romance languages, and no doubt, Catalan was my cup of tea. It had started at the train station, *"Accés-Vies." "Paquexprés,"* then along the railway tracks, some slogans, *"Libertat míria cadenas," "El bilinguisme no existeix," "Catalunya en catalá,"* all looking at once familiar and foreign, like misspelled Spanish.

By the following morning, I was reading street signs, then menus, then flyers, then brochures, and by evening, I was reading the newspaper. I understood it through a form of linguistic osmosis, a bombardment of accurate semantic grasps coming from two or three directions at once. I thought Catalan one of the most exhilarating languages I had ever encountered, because not knowing a word of it, having never before seen a single word in print, I understood it. It was like being given the key to the city.

My reading prowess resulted in uncontrollable glee and pride of accomplishment on my part. How I must have bored my patient husband, who is definitely not a linguist, with my constant exclamations, word recognition, self-satisfaction, and endless explanations of the similarities between French, Spanish, and Catalan, and how it is also spoken in the French province of Roussillon and in the independent enclave of Andorra.

On and on I went, didactic—one might even say pedantic—to the end. For a bitter end, it turned out to be after all. As soon as the first Catalan mouth opened and the first Catalan word came out of it, it was as if the key to the city had only opened the Tower of Babel. I understood not a word. Not on the first day, nor on the last.

So my lesson learned, I resorted once more to speaking Spanish and things went more or less well, although I may not have been very good at following directions. One evening, looking for a tapas bar recommended by our hotel, we found ourselves in the *Barri Xines,* known in other parts of Spain as *Barrio Chino.* The streets became very narrow and dark. A drunk was pissing against a wall. Then, a little square came into view, a small church at the end. There was an air of poverty and roughness about the whole area, and we decided to give up our quest for those particular tapas (after all, it was not as if tapas bars were a rarity in Barcelona) and returned to a more familiar neighbourhood.

❧ ❧ ❧

"Il y a une espèce de honte d'être heureux à la vue de certaines misères," wrote La Bruyère in seventeenth-century France, an age and place where such feelings of shame at the sight of poverty and misery were the exception rather than the norm. On the Ramblas, the five short broad streets that combine to form a wide and lively avenue, a number of men posing as statues stood in odd postures and even odder costumes, "bizarre and infrangibly silent," as Robert Hughes described them in *Barcelona.*

When I first saw the human statues, I felt almost paralyzed with shame, on both their behalf and mine. I had seen my share of begging, but never in such form. Most of the time, I feel embarrassed at my wealth in poor countries, but with some heartbreaking exceptions, I manage the trick described by Charles Lynch, a Canadian journalist exposed to the appalling poverty of Brazil, which is "to put your social conscience on hold and relax ... as tourists do."

On the Ramblas, this relaxation of conscience was impossible. Most beggars, all men, stood on small platforms, usually a simple upended box or crate. Some were costumed and made-up as traditional clowns. Others depicted famous personages with various degrees of success. One Don Quixote, for instance, painted silver all over, gave a wonderful impersonation of what book illustrations have shown us. His thinness, his narrow beard, his exalted look, his clever costume, his leaning on a lance, all perfect and corresponding exactly to the Don Quixote most of us have in mind.

Others were less clearly identifiable. One may have been a conquistador. Another may have been a centurion, covered with bronze paint and wearing a headgear made of the short bristles of a broom head attached to an upside-down kitchen sieve tied with a string under his chin, and wearing a rough tunic over long underwear.

Quite poignantly, or perhaps less imaginatively, another had simply painted his face and wore a white shirt and black pants: not a white clown, but an ordinary man with a blanked-out face. A few had, leaning against the box on which they stood, a sign explaining their circumstances. One, for instance, stated that he was fifty years old, had been working for thirty years, was now unemployed, and reluctantly had to resort to begging. He was hungry, he added, almost as an afterthought.

This went far beyond my experience of begging. For one thing, I felt it was an atrocious way to make a living—assuming they did, and I had no way of knowing. There were after all a number of foreign tourists as well as cruise ship passengers walking up and down the Ramblas, so it was quite possible they earned enough to make ends meet, or maybe they had another job during the week.

I thought it atrocious because of the absolute physical exertion they must have endured, as they did not move at all for very long periods. Frozen in their position, they waited. The centurion leaned forwards, all his weight resting on his forward thigh. When a tiny girl, sent by her parents, gave him a small coin, he bent to talk to her, and then changed positions leaning on the other thigh. This happened occasionally, and each time, he switched legs. We left him one Sunday morning early, before the heat of the day, to find him again in late afternoon, still leaning in almost perilous balance.

Being statues totally dehumanized them, yet at the same time emphasized the vulnerability of their humanity for it is not in the human nature, nor in the human anatomy to be so immobilized for such long periods. Unlike those in other countries who pester, harass, and annoy, these beggars stood, as a totally mute and reproachful testimony of the injustice of fate, and one simply could not argue with the silent statement they made.

I found Spanish beggars among the most difficult to accept. In Madrid, a week or so later, we saw another form of begging that seemed to take precedence over the statues of Barcelona. There, they were penitents, or at least I took them to be inspired by such quasi-religious images: men kneeling on the sidewalk, their eyes lowered for hours at a time. I knew the pain such a position could inflict, having once joined very briefly a file of kneeling Mexican pilgrims inching their way toward the altar on the cold marble floor of a church to judge the extent of the sacrifice performed. It is extraordinarily painful, particularly for someone who, like me, has slightly knobby knees.

What troubled me most about those particular beggars was not so much the pain they endured—which must have been considerable even if there were unseen pads under their knees, or the total dejection and hopelessness the posture revealed or implied—but how they put us, the passersby, the rich, the untroubled, in a position totally incommensurate with the reality of our ordinary status. Such position (humbly kneeling, head lowered, almost a pre-beheading posture) is only assumed in front of a deity, a malevolent ruler, or an executioner.

⚜ ⚜ ⚜

John and I did a lot of walking and sightseeing in Barcelona. The city is the home by birth, culture, or adoption of famous artists such as Joan Miró, Salvador Dali, and Pablo Picasso, as well as the equally famous Barcelona Football Club, Barça, but one cannot think of Barcelona without evoking Antoni Gaudi and the sheer madness of *El Templo de la Sagrada Familia*.

La Sagrada Familia, started in 1901 and still unfinished with spires 100 metres high, dominates the skyline of the city. "Owned" by the *Asociasión Espiritual de Devotos de San José,* it was intended to be an expiatory church, the first of many, planned by Gaudi. So important was it deemed to be that Pope Leo XIII gave special financial assistance through the granting of indulgences, blessings, and a substantial return of funds routinely given to the Vatican by the *Asociasión*.

A Catalan poet called it "the Cathedral of the Poor," and in 1905, it officially became the New Cathedral of Greater Barcelona. Paul Theroux reports a story first told by Colin Tóibin (the Irish writer living in Barcelona) about a visiting bishop who wondered why the tops of the towers, which one could not see from the ground, had been decorated. Gaudi answered, "Your Grace, the angels will see them."

Gaudi had completed little more than the west facing Nativity facade when in 1926, a trolley bus ran over him and he died. He had already radically changed the original plans, which called for the neo-Gothic style, and adapted them to his vision. Unfortunately, most of his sketches and plans were destroyed during the Civil War, so a lot of the later construction has been guesswork about what his ultimate conception had been. The work that has since continued in earnest after such difficult beginnings will eventually depict biblical mysteries in the same art nouveau that inspired Gaudi.

La Sagrada Familia has often been described in less than positive terms and George Orwell was no more uncharitable than many others were when he described it as "one of the most hideous buildings in the world." It has also been described as "that enormous penitential church seemingly made of candle wax and chicken guts," and it pains me to write that there may be a hint of truth in the image. It is a favourite of Japanese tourists, whose financial contributions are accelerating the completion of a roof. But it will continue to be for some time still a work in progress.

Totally seduced by Gaudi's eccentricities, we saw as much of his work around Barcelona as we could: his Casa Vicens, his Casa Milà, also known as *La Pedrera* (pile of rocks), his Casa Batlló with its five stories of undulating shapes, its curvaceous balconies, its ornamental street lamps, its complicated furniture. Naturally, we also went to the famous Parc Güell, with its mind-blowing mosaic work, described by Sacheverell Sitwell as "at once a fun fair, a petrified forest, and the great temple of Amun in Karnak, itself drunk, and reeling in an eccentric earthquake."

Notes from Elsewhere

John on a mosaic bench at Parc Güell, Barcelona

I would not presume to attempt a description of the work of Gaudi and do it justice. There are numerous books on the subject, written by people better qualified to address the topic. And, better still, there are numerous books of photographs, where every curve, every mosaic tile, every piece of tortuous wood or flowery wrought iron can be appreciated and enjoyed in detail.

While taking the sights in and around Barcelona, we found ourselves spending the day in the pretty little town of Sitgès, on the *Costa Daurada,* about forty kilometres from Barcelona, barely twenty minutes by a fast train. It had the usual holiday props and trappings to charm us: blue sky and sea, golden sand, promenade along the beach, brilliant geraniums in profusion, boutiques full of regional pottery and craft, ceramic street signs and their naive designs, and seafood restaurants redolent with garlic.

An ornate facade in Sitgès

    Many couples were male, since Sitgès is well known for being frequented by homosexuals. As I looked at the parade—parade is perhaps the wrong word, since there was nothing ostentatious about it. Just men walking two by two going about their business, very likely the choice of a restaurant where to have lunch, but still being a "parade" in the sense of people walking back and forth and being watched by other people sitting at the terrace of cafés looking at the world go by. So as I looked at the parade, I could not help noticing how handsome and beautifully matched some of those young men were. I clearly recognized the point of a line from a *Seinfeld* television show to the effect that gay men probably choose their partners based on similar builds and tastes, thus doubling their wardrobe in one fell swoop.

    Coming into Barcelona, we had seen from the train the small farmers' fields, with rows of rank artichokes and tomato plants tied onto tepees of small bamboo frames, a preview of what we would find at the market. Very soon, we found our way to the *Mercat de La Boqueria* off the busy Ramblas.

Robert Hughes, in *Barcelona,* described *la Boqueria* in almost elegiac terms, being to Barcelona what the *Les Halles* were to Paris. This is not how it struck me, but we kept going back to it all the same, for markets are both the soul and the belly of their cities, and it requires several visits to do them justice.

It was not, or so I found, one of those self-indulgent markets where everything is so perfect, elegant even, and offered in what almost looks like excess. No, it was a little untidy, with things sticking a bit underfoot, and the displays were certainly not artistically composed. However, it was a nice market, an honest one, with beautiful fruit and vegetables, rich and ripe, ready to satisfy any penny-pinching and fussy shopper.

There were few surprises, as markets go, except for the fish section with its abundance of salted cod, whole shops devoted entirely to it and perhaps still coming in part from the disputed fishing banks of Canada. As I bought our fruit, cheese, and bread, I was so well treated with such good humour and patience, sometimes called back to retrieve the small coin I had mistakenly overpaid, that our tiny daily purchases of four apricots or tomatoes, and two thick slices of cheese became one of the small pleasures of the day.

Our last vision of the market was at seven o'clock on the morning of our departure as we walked by a crew of street cleaners pushing their orange carts and brooms. Their heads were turned in the same direction and they were laughing. We looked too and saw what amused them. It was a middle-aged prostitute, fat, her blonde raffia-dry hair teased solid, her enormous loose breasts clad in a flesh coloured T-shirt resting on her thick waist, her short skirt baring hugely sturdy calves and most of her thighs. She was leaning against the wall of our favourite little pastry shop, a corner shop with both facades covered with floral mosaics flecked with gold and the date 1820 showing in small tiles above the door.

Sometimes, it is easy to lack charity. Looking at her—shapeless, middle-aged, and tired—all I felt was that she looked all *wrong* against that charming and very expensive little shop with its *Belle Epoque* flair. I thought she appeared inappropriate, and that she should have been plying her trade instead in the disreputable Barri Xines, not in this respectable part of the Ramblas near the Liceu Metro, right near the market that would soon be opening.

※ ※ ※

So off we went by train to Madrid. If Barcelona had been Gaudí's outdoor museum, Madrid for us meant the Prado, and particularly for me, Goya. I loved the toothy grins, the vibrant colours, the coquettish parasols, the well-turned masculine calves in their white hose, the pearly texture of the skin, and those charming little dogs. Much of what we saw was very well known—from the upsetting *Caprichos* to the two lovely *Majas,* clad or otherwise. Yet, seeing them in the reality of a museum rather than reproduced in a book was a shock, and we were deeply moved by the actual sight of what we thought we already knew.

One would think that court painters would be accommodating or flattering when depicting their famous patrons. Such courtly, and perhaps courteous, attempts at disguising the truth did not seem to be the rule in Spain, as could attest all those full-lipped, supercilious, dull, inbred aristocrats, obviously related through some flaw in their genes.

In front of the *Family of Charles IV,* an older woman with a grating voice was talking to two young American tourists. She was of a type often seen in museums—although one meets them everywhere, they are most noticeable and irritating in museums. She was telling the two young women that it was well known that the king had accepted all the children as his own, although everyone knew they were bastards, and that the queen was not good in bed, and he could not stand her.

The American girls laughed, asked questions, and happily went on their way, while the woman wandered, looking for another prey. Actually, I suppose such people are useful as an antidote to the so-called Stendhal syndrome, the affliction that causes the artistically overwhelmed to faint at the sight of yet another masterpiece.

Finally, we found ourselves in front of what I had been eagerly waiting to see, *Las Meninas,* where Velázquez depicts the little blonde *infanta* in all her finery, attended by the two eponymous maids of honour. The remarkable structure of the painting, the obvious and hidden pairing of characters, the reflected images and dualities could hold one's attention for a long time—even without being familiar with Picasso's own *Intérieur ou les Ménines* to echo some of its enigmatic composition, and even without much knowledge of artistic conventions.

※ ※ ※

While staying in Madrid, John and I decided to take a side trip to Toledo. A travel agent suggested that we join a one-day guided tour, drop out in Toledo, stay as long as we wanted, and then rejoin another tour on its way back to Madrid. It all sounded reasonable, and we soon found ourselves driving through the golden stubble of wheat and barley fields of the Mancha, their scattered giant thistles as fierce looking as John Wyndham's *triffids*.

These were the very fields perhaps where Don Quixote, lance at the ready, mounted on Rocinante *(rocín antes,* the nag leading the way), roamed in pursuit of his dreams with Sancho Pança trailing behind on his donkey in faithful, protective, somewhat cranky service. Suddenly, we saw the Roman aqueduct and our tour of Toledo had begun.

Our good luck was such that our guide turned out to be a scholarly middle-aged man, soberly dressed, gentle in manner, and soft of speech. His English was poor but his Spanish so beautifully modulated and clear that it did not matter. John seldom listens, anyway, usually relying on me to pass on vital bits of information.

Thus, we went through the ancient city of Toledo, and our guide made the most of an impossible task since Toledo is truly a marvelous place to visit, but this must be done at leisure. As we were staying on after the tour, we realized we would have to return later to see at our own pace what we had rushed through that day.

So, we visited with too little pause for reflection la Catedral Primada de Santa María de Toledo, dominating the city and its Treasure Room, of which John and I saw little, so transfixed were we by the three tomes of the Saint Louis Bible. Although presented by the French king in the thirteenth century, the illuminations were as fresh as if they just been painted, so finely, so beautifully, so lovingly and reverently made as to leave one in perfect awe. We rushed to the sacristy to see El Greco's portraits of the *Twelve Apostles*, and in front of their sad, tormented, almost demented-looking faces, it was not difficult to believe that, as legend has it, madmen from the local lunatic asylum had served as models.

We then trotted off to the Church of Santo Tomé where the details of the architecture paled in comparison with *The Burial of the Count of Orgaz*. I thought I was well prepared for it, but I should have known better after the shock of seeing the paintings of Goyas and Velázquez at the Prado the previous week.

It is a famous work, familiar in reproduction, but seeing it for the first time is truly an astonishing experience. Our guide dutifully and simplistically pointed out the contrast between its two parts. The lower part, composed in a "Spanish portrait style," depicted indeed El Greco's contemporaries in the most detailed sixteenth-century costumes of black suits and white ruffs, their severely subdued looks somehow not quite reflecting the dramatic events taking place above their heads, where the painter, now inspired by the "Italian style" gave vent to his religious imagination.

We went briefly into the *Monastery of San Juan de los Reyes (los Reyes* being the Catholic Monarchs, Isabella of Castile and Ferdinand of Aragon), originally a Franciscan convent built to celebrate their victory at the battle of Toro. We admired the lovely arches and contemplated, hanging from its facade, the heavy chains of the Catholics freed from the Muslim jails of Granada when Isabella reconquered the city. In other words, we willingly did as we were told.

We saw much evidence of the surprising superimposition of faiths and artistic styles merging pell-mell with churches becoming mosques and synagogues built by Muslims. The cathedral we had first visited had been built on the site of the Great Mosque, which itself had replaced a small Visigothic church. Above the bridge of San Martín, the church of *Santa María la Blanca,* a former synagogue stormed by a mob at the very beginning of the fifteenth century, stood close to the former little mosque now called *El Cristo de la Luz,* lovely and built on the foundations of another Visigothic church—all the result of several centuries of that most civilized Spanish approach to former religious cohabitation: *la Convivencia.*

We were told about the Moorish *mudéjar* architecture, the *Isabelino* Gothic style. In fact, we were told far too much, particularly those of our group who would not stay in Toledo to continue their tour. Much of what we saw was reduced towards the end to bits and pieces of impressions. The three that remain fresh in my mind were:

- pear tree carvings, as hard as marble under the fingertips, as fine as ivory, as smooth as silk;
- two rare little statues of the Virgin in the cathedral, the one above the pulpit smiling sweetly, the other showing in profile a slightly swelling belly; and
- the two organs facing each other, one neoclassic, the other Gothic, with the same size, the same function, but a profoundly different voice, as we heard them the following day at the end of Mass, responding in pious exaltation to yet a third organ, the oldest one, out of sight.

There were several other tours beside ours in the cathedral, particularly coming through the central portal, la Puerta del Perdón. In fact, we kept bumping into one another at doors and through narrow passages, waiting for our turn in long files like disciplined children, alert for the blue flag or the red straw hat waved by our respective leaders to rally their troops.

Our dignified guide was the exception. He had nothing to brandish and simply relied on our willingness to observe him and follow his lead. His soft cultured voice could not compete with the louder tones of the others; what we lost in quantity, we probably gained in quality, but we could not always hear it.

Our companions appeared to be of many nationalities, although we never spoke with anyone except during lunch when we talked with our immediate neighbours, two Norwegians who had extended their business trip to Madrid to visit Toledo. Our conversation was quite similar to the tour itself, covering far too much ground in too little time, stretching from the reluctance of Norway to join the European Common Market to the World Cup then in full swing (Norway had just tied with Mexico).

Most noteworthy of all was a French couple, although I hesitate to use the term couple, so far apart were they. Or, at least, he kept apart and walked far ahead of her. One only knew they were together, because every so often, she hailed him from a distance, some six or seven people separating them. *"Regarde, Jacques!"* or *"Tu the rappelles? On a déjà vu ça à …"* They appeared well matched, though: in their fifties, reasonably attractive, well dressed, sensibly shod, and widely travelled, one would judge from the endless comparisons she drew to other places they had already visited.

The guide showed us *El Transparente* in the cathedral with its baroque marble cherubs so incongruous in the Gothic surroundings and explained that the sun shone at noon through a hole cleverly pierced in the roof to illuminate during the elevation the altar located on the other side. *"Tu the rappelles, Jacques, en Egypte?"* she said. *"C'était la même chose pour l'autel de Râ!"* Later, as we approached El Greco's *Apostles* in the sacristy, *"Regarde les mains, Jacques! Avec le Greco, il faut toujours regarder les mains."* She was right, of course, and I dutifully looked at the hands and the elongated fingers, wonderfully prehensile, each with a life of its own, and charged with incipient osteoarthritis.

It was rather sad to see her try so hard, when he was so evidently unwilling to share anything with her. Although, at one time, he did condescend to speak, and in front of a portrait of Charles I, explained to her (and to us, since they were still somewhat apart) that Cisneros, the archbishop of Toledo and the King's Regent, had also been in charge of the Inquisition in Castile and León. *"En somme, un Monsieur pas très intéressant,"* she concluded through pursed lips and with the slightly censorious tone of voice the French do so well, yet very pleased to be addressed directly.

The following day, John and I revisited Toledo on our own. It is a wonderfully cramped city, built and rebuilt so many times by so many people of so many faiths, all using the same little space allowed by the natural constraints of river and elevation. It is also a city of contrasts, which came from several centuries of accommodations and compromises.

Notes from Elsewhere

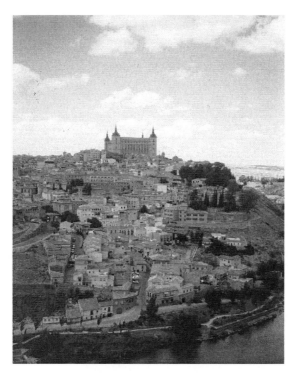

Toledo and the Tagus

As we walked up and down the narrow streets, it was difficult to miss the shops that sold knives, daggers, and other blades, all decorated in the famous *damasquinado* style, where the handle of the well-tempered steel was originally enchased with precious stones. This style, for which Toledo has been famous for centuries, is yet another reminder of the Moorish occupation of Spain.

We saw ever-present architectural contrasts between the solid traditional brick and stones and the delicacy of their decorative motifs. Underfoot, bricks and small stones polished by constant use were matched elsewhere by something more subtle, such as the ornate tiles below the narrow balconies, barely visible from the street under the wrought-iron braces that supported them.

Looking at the thick walls, the forged iron grates on the windows, the heavy iron doors often reinforced with iron strips, and always studded with the heads of enormous nails, we wondered what was to be found beyond the blankness of those mute defences, whether oases of peace and greenery or squalid quarters.

Dutifully absorbed in the religious and historical past of a city that knew her symbolic value and never doubted her favoured status as the heart of Spain, we probably missed many common signs of ordinary modern life. But they were definitely there: a baby peering beyond a heavy door incrusted with the grime of at least three centuries and well trained to crawl no farther than his doorstep. Or the sounds of a television coming from behind age-old walls, or beside a charming little church, the *Iglesia de la Virgén de la Gracia,* a homemade sign bearing a stern warning of dire reprisals to those SWINE who leave their garbage on the sidewalk.

Above, in the lowering sky, oblivious to the passage of time, swallows swooped elegantly as they had no doubt done since God knew when, crisscrossing one another's path with the precision of a well-rehearsed acrobatic team.

One of Toledo's narrow medieval streets

In order to return to Madrid on the third day, we rejoined the same tour but with a different guide and took up where we had previously left off, at the Hospital de Tavera, now a museum. John sat outside in the shade, "museumed out" and happy to be alone with his book. We were taken to see the former residence of the Dukes of Lerma with wonderful tapestries so finely restored in patches and some of El Greco's last works.

The climax of that visit was, of course (but it came as a surprise to me who had never heard of it), Diego de Ribera's famous and strange portrait of Magdalena Ventura, a hormonal freak shown with a mature man's heavily bearded face and the large, smooth, pink bosom of a nursing mother. A pamphlet produced by the museum explained she had grown a beard and mustache at the age of thirty-seven. She had seven children, three before the beard, four after. In the painting, she is suckling her last child, born when she was fifty-two.

I was not really as shocked by the male-female duality, a myth as old as time, as by the obscenity of an old body still giving birth—also an old myth, illustrated in the renewal of the seasons, for instance, but unpleasantly personified here. Obviously, I am not a great supporter of modern science's progress in these obstetrical matters.

But it was time to return to Madrid where, as good tourists and newcomers to Spain, we continued going from museum to museum, feasting on gazpacho and judging the Madrilène paella to be generally inferior to the one in Barcelona. But in the end, afflicted with the heat and the pollution (a combination of car exhaust, people smoking, and the sandblasting of so many buildings), we left for Biarritz.

※ ※ ※

On that Spanish trip, from Paris, to Barcelona, to Madrid, with side trips to Toledo and Segovia, then on to Biarritz, we rediscovered trains as the great source of pleasure they can be and the wonderful relief from flying. The sight through the windows, the people met, the small scenarios unfolding, the slower pace, all seemed most civilized.

Soon after leaving Madrid, we started seeing some changes in the colours, particularly noticeable in a small subdivision where groupings of traditional slate roofs stood glumly among newer roofs of vibrant apricot-pink tiles, much like surly nuns or parish spinsters escorting pretty and cheerful young girls on a field trip.

The bright colours continued on the land: wild roses of a white and delicate pink, brilliant poppies, deep yellow gorse, wild mustard, white yarrow. Among the fields, crisscrossing low walls painstakingly made of flat stones climbed uphill, meandering out of sight, speaking of hard work and a harsh way of life.

About an hour and a half northwest of Madrid, was the medieval city of Avila with its ramparts showing in the distance like a perfect sand castle. We could see storks roosting on treetops among fields of poppies. Then subtle changes occurred in the countryside, gradually becoming more mountainous and dry, and with endless stone walls, sometimes topped with barbed wire. The railway tracks were bordered by little clumps of dazzling poppies; farther on, on top of a hill, a fort with crenellated ramparts and round towers looking uncommonly new and unconvincing.

In the enormous old cemetery of Valladolid, visible from the train, stood the stern army of black and white crosses among the gaudy homage of glass bead and plastic flowers forever bright. In a small field, a docile sheep seemed to be either led or watched over by a small donkey.

By Burgos, the countryside had changed once more with treed hills and green fields, and showing above the rusty brown wagons at the station, we saw the gray lace outline of the cathedral's steeples. Everywhere, little hamlets of pink brick, each with its own church, sometimes a mere stone's throw away from one another. Each brightly coloured image looked like a page from an old-fashioned picture book, charming and conventional, framed by the window.

Inside the train someone was whistling, "Begin the Beguine," very well, with beautifully modulated tremolos in the right places, but I could not tell where the whistling came from. I thought probably from somewhere ahead, not very far. But it was only the face that betrayed the source (not straight ahead as I had thought, but somewhat to the side), an old man in a silk shirt. I knew he was the whistler by the fixity of his stare and the rigidity of his face; nothing showed, and he whistled through nearly clenched teeth, lips barely parted.

Then he switched to a *paso doble*, which I recognized but could not name. Suddenly, the whistling stopped as it had started, for no apparent reason, except perhaps a tune in his head, a tune that was now irritatingly stuck in mine.

Two seats away from him, an elderly woman with thin lips was holding a basket on her lap, her hand moving slyly within. Soon a head emerged and I thought it was a smallish dog, but as the shoulders followed, I realized it was a grossly inflated cat. The woman's tight lips parted indulgently, her eyes at first anxious and furtive, soon relaxed as no one appeared to object. Noticing my sympathetic interest, she even smiled at me, her hand now overtly stroking Pussy.

Suddenly, a hiss and a well aimed swipe, all claws out, put an end to the affectionate display. Reddening with embarrassment, the woman smartly slapped down the basket flap, almost catching Pussy's nose in the process. I made a point of not looking at her afterwards, having too often been mortified myself by the public behaviour of stubborn children and unruly pets.

Across from us, an American couple, small-town college, or university folks without a doubt, a guess soon confirmed when they engaged us in conversation. They were appealingly alike: blond, tall, bespectacled, eager, and as we discovered, naively nice. They had been attending a language course in Madrid and were obviously anxious to tell their tale, and quite an unpleasant one it was. They were attacked in the elevator of their hotel in Madrid. "Oh, please, tell them, Bunny! Or may I?" They may well have been newlyweds still, so courteous were they with each other and so flirtatious with little side glances exchanged and tiny gasps as each contributed his or her share of the story.

He showed the nick on his neck where a knife had pricked him. She told of kicking the two men and yelling for help, not having realized that the men were armed, and holding a knife to his throat. Warming to their tale, they explored the unthinkable possibilities and told of the complications with various offices and travel agencies, as all their tickets and some travel documents had been in her bag that was stolen. But they still had their money, as there had only been fifty dollars in the stolen bag.

Rather pleased at this point (and perhaps they needed this retelling to be reassured again that it had ended well), he hinted that they might well have fifty dollar's worth of story to tell back home. Still, it was a nasty experience, and they performed very well, quite bravely, their thirst for travel apparently unquenched by the incident.

Outside, the landscape had changed once more, and back we went to our passing picture show, as our two Bunnies went to sleep, their fingers loosely entwined, tiny puffs soon escaping softly from their parted lips.

At some point, judging by the graffiti, we must have entered Euzkadi, the land of the Basque nation, a land of tempestuous history. It is one of the Spanish provinces that for years have vigorously called for self-determination—although the others, Catalonia and Galicia, have more or less now resolved their differences with Madrid. All suffered bitterly during the Spanish Civil War. The nationalist forces bombed Barcelona in December 1935, and if nothing else is known about the Basques, the small village of Guernica will be remembered, bombed out of existence in April 1937 by the Franco government, assisted by the Germans.

José Antonio Aguirre, the first Basque president, passionately sought autonomy for his country. Under Franco, he first took refuge in Paris, but soon fled to South America during the German occupation of France, to return once more to Paris a the end of the war in 1945.

By 1959, ETA (*Euzkadi Ta Askatasuna*: Basque Fatherland and Freedom) became the rallying call. Under the aegis of ETA, the fighting arm of Euzkadi, the half-century-long history of the violent struggle continues, either terrorism or freedom fighting depending on the point of view.

Although Spain granted full amnesty in 1977 to those who laid down their arms, other militant Basques soon picked them up and the fight never really abated. Whereas ETA mostly speaks for the Spanish side, the French Basques are openly sympathetic to the cause and provide assistance, some legal, some not.

Their history is as old as Western civilization, as the Basques may have inhabited the area since the Stone Age. With the arrival of the Romans, it is presumed they came down from the hills to trade with them. By 850 AD, the Kingdom of Nafarroa, centred in Pamplona, came into being, covering modern Navarre and the three Vascongadas. Historically, physically, culturally, linguistically, the Basques, whether Spanish or French, from Bayonne to Bilbao, are definitely a people apart.

※ ※ ※

Biarritz, just across the border on the French side, is at the heart of the French Basque country. It appeared a frivolous little town full of tea and pastry shops and many tourist attractions. Biarritz once played a historic part in hosting a meeting between Napoleon III and Bismarck, where a decision was made that France would support Prussia's anti-Austrian politics.

Since there was no strategic benefit for holding the meeting there, one suspects the reason for such a choice was that the French emperor could not tear himself away from the pleasures of the sun, the sea, and the parties Eugénie was so fond of giving in her E-shaped (for Eugénie) seaside residence.

I make the empress Eugénie sound frivolous—which she was, at least until 1870, definitely a woman with an excessive taste for dresses, jewels, and travel—but she was far more interesting than the role she played in the development of Biarritz into the resort it has since become. After a dull period of French history she revived a sense of pride in luxury, architecture (with her close association with Baron Haussmann, the architect Garnier of the Paris Opera House, and Ferdinand de Lesseps of the Suez Canal, which she officially opened), and the renovation and embellishment of the castles of Compiègne and Pierrefonds. A great admirer of Marie-Antoinette, she made the French court, once more, the place to be in Europe.

She died in 1920 on a visit to her native Spain and is buried in England, the land of her exile, together with her husband Napoleon III and her only and beloved son who died tragically in the Zulu wars alongside British troops. A patriot at heart, she lived long enough to see the Allies victory in 1918 and the reconnection of Alsace-Lorraine to France.

Under its frills, Biarritz has a far more rugged history. Fishing in the treacherous Bay of Biscay and much farther afield, as well as whale hunting, had long been part of the hard life led by its small, muscular, dark-haired men with a singing accent. Before Biarritz was "discovered," those men left, their faces grim with the long months ahead and their even grimmer harpoons stored away, from the little cove of Port Vieux, now bordered by tapas restaurants. To honour and protect them, Empress Eugénie had a small Virgin erected that faced the sea.

I had acquired along the way (particularly felt while walking down from Montjuïc in Barcelona) some as yet undiagnosed stress factures on both feet, which made walking painful, particularly on a hilly town. So leaving a thankful John behind, I opted to do my sightseeing from the *Petit Train*, an embarrassingly quaint touristic contraption, not a train at all, but a hooting, tooting little engine nevertheless, pulling two toy wagons through the city.

We started near the water, went quickly uphill where, cheek by jowl, stood the former secondary residences of most of Europe's former emperors and empresses, kings and queens, princes and princesses.

The little train conductor spoke French with a heavy accent, perhaps Spanish. In the background ran an ongoing tape of a cultured woman's voice giving in musically refined tones a commentary of the history of Biarritz. One heard for a few moments about the origins of the touristic waves that had made the wealth and fame of the town. From what I could gather, adding the bits and pieces barely overheard since the voice came and went, the earliest discoverer of Biarritz' potential as a future tourist Mecca may have been a sister of either François I or Louis XIV, who compared the little port to a "gem that only needed the lapidary's skill to make it shine properly."

However, the town did not become popular until Eugénie and Napoleon III started its amazing vogue, attracting all the crowned heads of Europe. A second wave occurred during the reign of Victoria. While she did visit the town, it was mostly the Prince of Wales and his retinue who patronized it. A third wave seemed to have consisted mainly of the Duke and Duchess of Winsor and their friends in the postwar era.

Finally, Biarritz has now become a tourist spot for ordinary visitors who seem to enjoy it as much as their titled precursors did. Extensive refurbishments were underway during our visit to get everything ready for the opening of the season, just two weeks ahead. They were completing the construction of a large conference centre in an attempt to lure a new type of visitors. The current wave was obviously well on its way, but one did not feel that Biarritz would ever achieve the same elegance as in the past.

The exquisite female voice intoned, *"… des bals masqués donnés par le Marquis de Cuevas auxquels étaient invités …."* I never did find out what glitterati had attended the Marquis de Cuevas' famous masked balls, or what rich American wives of impoverished scions of the Italian and French nobility had danced the night away. The driver had stopped her in mid-sentence to urge us to look at an "English house" to the right and to a "Russian house" to the left. *"Très yolies, très yolies."* He did not pronounce the soft French *j* and called the empress *"Euyénie."* His excited voice kept interrupting the melodious historical facts.

We finally arrived at the light house, and he urged us to walk up to it, *"Très haut, très haut, mais très yoli"* while the voice continued to describe the lighthouse, forty metres from the ground and eighty metres from the sea. He also assured us that on a clear day we could see Bayonne and Saint-Jean-de-Luz and sometimes even Bilbao, across the Bay of Biscay.

At the foot of the lighthouse was a solar clock, where one's position (as indicated by the date marked along an axis facing north) and one's shadow pointed to the solar time. We were quite excited, for it worked. We kept on trying and it kept working, every time! Why had we expected it would not? Perhaps the mechanism was too simple to seem trustworthy.

The train exuded diesel fumes that came by waves and were trapped under the canopy as the driver braked and accelerated frequently. It was also extremely hot, and I was glad when the tour was over. While it provided little sensible information beside the one we could barely hear, it certainly gave a good view of the town.

The port town was indeed very pretty, now a centre of hydrotherapy, apparently good for everything from convalescence to postpartum recovery to general stress and obesity. At some point, someone must have had a stroke of horticultural genius, for the most glorious hydrangeas abounded. Along the hills facing the bay, in public parks, and private gardens, it was the flower of choice. Every shade of pink and blue and many in between, delicate pastels and sturdier hues, they mixed and blended in charming abandon, blooming among the tamaris.

We stayed three very quiet days in Biarritz, walking around a little, even attending an outdoors Big Band concert one evening, to John's delight. There was a hint of summer in the mood, with children dancing to the music and parents watching them with indulgence and pride. Perhaps because of the music, it all felt easygoing and a little old-fashioned—in the way of some of Jacques Tati's films.

When the time came to leave, we went one last time to our favourite market to buy the makings of sandwiches to eat on the train. We called it *le Marché du Jardin Public* since it opened on a pleasant little park with shady benches, although it must have had an official name. Markets not only offer a very sensual experience, but also are natural definers of cultural identities and this one was undoubtedly French to the core.

At the fish section, it would have been impossible to forget that the Atlantic Ocean was barely a breath away. So many varieties of fish left me once more frustrated by my ignorance, as I could not even match the few names I knew with what I saw. I went back the following morning simply to ask the name of a flat fish I had seen the day before, gray and covered with orange polka dots: a *carrelet*.

I also saw a woman buy a *merlan* (my dictionary calls it a whiting, a name that evokes a pallid and bland flesh, so unlike the taste I knew, pan-fried golden and crispy-skinned), a fish I recognized immediately and even remembered how it was always served in my childhood: biting its own tail like a dog with fleas. Now I saw how it was done: the fishmonger put the tail into the fish's mouth and bopped it smartly on the head with a wooden mallet, the jaw snapping shut and the fish now forming a perfect circle ready for the frying pan.

In the next section, fruit and vegetables almost made me laugh because everything was so true to form. They were all there: tiny fragrant wood strawberries, green and purple figs bursting with red flesh, fat and freckled apricots, velvety peaches, and so many others, all exactly ripe and ready for the table. A few stalls over, we passed displays of many mushrooms, the air full of their damp earthiness. Then it was the turn of the fat purple eggplants, dark and glistening, as smoothly sensual as African slaves in a Sultan's harem, and the delicate tenderness of the tiniest new potatoes, barely a fingernail worth.

Three feet away from them were the many shapes and shades of lettuce, one charmingly names *doucette,* and many others unknown all equally wonderful, but particularly, those quite girlish and frivolous with their curly blonde mops, the *frisées,* perhaps?

On our two visits, it was the same heady, mouth-watering experience, and I was filled with envy of those who visit daily that living museum of fruit and vegetables; these *charcuteries* of all conceivable meats; these *patisseries,* with their bejeweled and glazed fruit tarts in luscious little rows. By the door, dozens of varieties of flowers kept in deep buckets by the florist, the scent overwhelming, and the very essence of the Garden of Eden.

As we pulled out of the station, there at last was the first sign I could understand since the graffiti vernacular had switched from Spanish to Euskara, the Basque language. Like Turkish, Magyar, or Finnish, it is one of those ancient languages Europeans do not readily understand, and I had been frustrated by my incomprehension. But this message, both numerical and metaphorical, was easy to grasp as it proclaimed its hope for the unification of the four Spanish and the three French Basque regions. It read:

"4+3=1"

Chapter Eleven

So, What Next? Cruising to Narragonia?

The secret of a good old age is simply an honorable pact with solitude.

—Gabriel García Márquez,
One Hundred Years of Solitude.

A few days after returning from an "experimental" cruise— would we like it? We had no idea, yet we are getting older and our former way of travelling may not be suitable for very much longer—I read in our local newspaper about a study in a recent issue of the *Journal of the American Geriatric Society*. The geriatric physician in charge of the study, Dr. Lee Lindquist at Northwestern Memorial Hospital in Chicago, suggested that cruise ships could soon replace nursing homes for older people who enjoy travelling and have good cognitive function, even though they may need help bathing, feeding, dressing, or getting around. (I am drawing here from the newspaper article, not from the actual report, which I have not read, being interested here in the concept rather than the details.)

The scientist was quoted as having addressed this particular message to Canadians: "You could do the snowbird concept, but on a ship ... Theoretically, all they would have to do is buy the ticket and go." I found the speculative description of old people, probably in possession of most of their faculties, aimlessly cruising the Caribbean for years at a marginally higher cost than being kept in a nursing home or an assisted living facility, quite arresting.

There were also other advantages than the financial ones, even if not mentioned in the article. For instance, the emotional relief to children and grandchildren from the guilt of having to put the oldsters away: Grandpa would not be in a home, he'd be *cruising* ....

It would not be the first time either that surplus people would be relegated to ships, and Victorian England had her share of those infamous hulks, where either regular prisoners or convicts awaiting transportation were lodged on disaffected craft. More recently, with mixed feelings and mixed reviews, the practice was revived with the *Weare*, a US vessel bought in 1977 to ease overcrowding in Her Majesty's jails. Anchored near Weymouth, she served as a prison, but closed down eight years later.

But those hulks were disaffected ships, while older people would actually be meant to continue cruising on perfectly serviceable ships equipped with all modern amenities.

Dr. Lindquist appears to believe that loading the country's superfluous bodies on a form of merry-go-round in the Caribbean would be a solution to the problem of what to do with *them*. Not so much (since we must be honest) the superfluous as the unwanted, the undesirable, who do not always want or desire one another either.

Or was the geriatric research perhaps inspired by a fairly common medieval practice, well known to the physicians of the day, which consisted in packing off local lunatics (or even simply the indigent and unemployable) in carts, giving them a symbolic shove, and leaving them to fend for themselves, hoping that others would assume responsibility. Those carts were called "ships of fools."

Those ships of fools have haunted human imagination since their more or less formal appearance at the end of the fifteenth century. Starting with Sebastian Brant's *Das Narrenschiff* (1494), a whole stream of symbolic and moralistic literature has flourished, focused on the *stultifera navis*, the ship with her cargo of fools, sailing away toward Narragonia, the Fools' Paradise.

Many contemporary illustrations depicted the dreadful lot of those thus abandoned, adding to the horror of the vision they evoked. Brant's book had been illustrated with daunting woodcuts by Albrecht Dürer, then at the beginning of his career, and the most famous ones, from Hieronymus Bosch's in *The Ship of Fools,* appeared at some time between 1490 and 1500.

On and off, fools kept appearing in literature, their voyage always a metaphor for life. Films became another medium to interpret it, such as Stanley Kramer's film *Ship of Fools* (1965), based on Katherine Anne Porter's novel. More recently the Spanish movie, *Viaje a Narragonia* (2004) in which 101 fools representing all vices and follies, but also artists rebelling against a society they decry for its materialism, sailed for Narragonia, and who knows, a paradise all their own.

Perhaps I am overreacting to what some might even think an elegant solution to a growing problem. I do not even preclude the possibility that this overreaction may be due to my age and my personal sense of what an uncertain future might hold for us. However, there is nothing wrong with vested interests and personal biases when considering potential options. In fact, they are sine qua non components of the process of considering and deciding on one's own fate—if one is lucky enough to be able to do so.

If older people enjoy cruising and choose to spend long periods at sea, who am I to object? Many of them do, and it is good they find pleasure in doing so. What concerns me, however, is the *formalization* of the process and the finality it implies.

Nobody said it would be easy at the end. Essays, novels, poems, all speak of the thirst for evanescent wisdom, the fear of solitude, the yearning for lost loves, the decreasing strength and ability, the sore joints, the groping memory, the search for words, the loneliness, and so on. Some believe we outlast our natural lifespan and should not linger too much beyond three score and ten—or whatever the modern calculation of a lifespan might be.

In traditional societies, when old people hindered the survival of the group for which nomadic mobility was of the essence, when they became a drain on minimal resources and competed with children for scarce food, when they were no longer able to contribute to the well-being of all, it was time for society to deal with them according to the rituals in place.

Whether those societies were essentially hunters or farmers, all their members had a role in upholding the integrity of the group. For a while, they could still perform some tasks deemed to be the purview of the elderly, such as the all-important transmission of traditional knowledge and tribal wisdom, tales, and songs, as well as child-minding, which freed adults for the more onerous tasks, and those functions served to extend their usefulness to the group.

But when, at last, they could no longer fulfill this role, when their physical and mental condition would render them not only useless, but actually harmful to the commonwealth, feeble old people were picturesquely reported in common parlance to be sent "up the coconut tree" (to see whether they could still make it, I presume) or in other parts of the world abandoned on an ice floe (sometimes volunteering for it as a selfless gift to the clan).

The solution does not always lie in ships of fools, coconut trees, or ice floes. A Japanese legend, for instance, tells of *Ubasuteyama,* The Mountain of Abandoned Old People, where they were sent when they became too infirm to be self-sufficient. Once there, they could expect *ubasute* or death by starvation. The legend, based on a harsh history of famine and dire needs that haunts Japanese memory, has been used as a motif for an award-winning film, the *Ballad of Narayama.* Whatever the means used, they are mostly intended to displace the elderly who have lost their useful purpose from the community of active and productive people.

It would be untrue to write that the elderly have no longer a useful function, even in our disbanded societies. It is not uncommon for instance, in times of economic hardship, to see troubled families rescued by grandparents, who are sometimes more financially secure and more emotionally grounded than their children are.

Their knowledge and experience are also often recognized professionally, mostly in a passing manner, but recognized nonetheless, such as when old tradesmen are encouraged to pass on their forgotten skills to young apprentices. Old intellectuals and artists, even after they have stopped writing, composing, teaching, or painting, are still respected. One could certainly find many examples of old people's waning participation in everyday life.

However, there is little doubt that currently, as a group, their greatest contribution to society and the economy is of a different nature. There has been a noticeable change in older people, who are now in better physical shape and live longer than they once did. Many more are also financially independent.

The combination of means, leisure, and reasonably good health makes those in the middle-class the focus of interest and target to purveyors of services designed to address and satisfy their needs and tastes, or even to create them when not at first recognized.

Those in their so-called golden age have indeed become a genuine source of income for people involved in the extensive and growing industry of keeping them alive and amused. They suddenly find themselves in the midst of a new whirl of activities: medical tests, arthritis centres, obesity treatment, massage therapy, dementia workshops, fall clinics, etc.

Cruises are already a part of this effort to cater to their amusement, an effort also tailored to their disposable income. So we seem to have now come to the culmination, the formalization, the institutionalization of those elderly cruises into permanent floating, long-term, extended-care facilities. But, come to think of it, upscale nursing homes and their facilities are already very much like landlocked cruise ships, and in Canada at least, the caretakers are already mostly from the Philippines (as are often the cabin crew on cruise ships).

I will leave it to others to speculate on this prospect. The list of those potentially involved in planning for it is long: sociologists, anthropologists, economists, urban planners, gerontologists, geriatricians, philosophers, theologians, nurses, physiotherapists, immigration specialists, etc., and a good source of income we will be for them too. Indeed, the list is long and will probably get longer.

The core of the problem, at least in industrial societies, is partly a cultural one. As Bernadette Puijalon, a French anthropologist, points out in a documentary on geriatric care, we inherited from ancient Greece the ideals of physical beauty and strength. Thus, we conceive of human life as a rise from helpless infancy to beautiful and strong maturity and decline thereafter into a new state of helplessness, which we are not shy of calling second childhood and see it as a state of near-imbecility. The process takes the form of a semicircle with two opposite and fragile bases: infantility and senility. It is only of late that the second base, that of old age, lasts for as long as it now does. The Greek/Western model perhaps only made sense when life was shorter and the schema was balanced.

In some other societies—and Professor Puijalon refers particularly to West and East Africa—the life span is seen as a progression of ascending steps. So, if an old person is deaf because of his advanced age, it is said that having experienced all the degrees of life, he has reached such a high level that he can no longer hear our voices way down below. These societies do not deny the obvious biological losses of old age, but they attempt to compensate for them with a different psychological and cultural mapping.

There is another consideration, one we are all too familiar with, one which is illustrated by the notion of shipping old people on endless cruises as a last resort (please, ignore the pun), simply because we do not know what to do with them. The point we should also make is that the present generation has accomplished an extraordinary feat of longevity, since we can now tell our young children, "No, you are not going to die, and neither are Mom and Dad; it's only when you are very old, like Granny and Granddad, that you do."

Instead of celebrating this wonderful victory, the postponement of death, we turn it into a problem, one of the social and economic problems of the graying developed world. We wonder who is going to pay for these pensions, as people outlive their retirement by two or three decades. Here, too, the list of questions and concerns is long, but can be succinctly described as the physical, economic, and emotional burden of having to look after weakening and decaying bodies and minds for much longer than we had previously thought we might have to do.

The latest developments in cruise ships show that by 2013–2014, new mega-ships will serve up to four thousand passengers. A picture in our local newspaper gives an artist's rendition of the Norwegian behemoths: rows upon rows of cabins on seven decks. I have visions of passengers in the early stages of Alzheimer's trying to find their way home to their own door, one of several hundred identical ones. Or those afflicted with early dementia staring at their virtual portholes with HD cameras showing them what is not actually there.

❦ ❦ ❦

Is this an option John and I should even entertain? Should we start packing while waiting for that last call, "All aboard for Narragonia!" I intend to take a closer look at what life might be like on this merry-go-round. It will only be a dry run, of course, and probably no more significant than the gesture of those politicians who spend one night at a homeless shelter in the full knowledge that their next night will be in their own comfortable bed and that even if their pockets are empty for that night, the next ATM machine is around the corner.

We have decided to go to the South Pacific in September 2011, more particularly to French Polynesia, with a few days in the Hawaiian islands. It will be a thirty-four day voyage, fifteen of these days at sea, left to our own devices and that of the ship's facilities hoping to be somewhat sustained by what proximity to other passengers may offer. If all else fails and John and I get absolutely no inkling of what a more permanent arrangement of this nature (who knows? Maybe years of it) might actually be like, at least we will have seen a little of Bora Bora and Papeete, dreams from my French childhood, and will do some serious swimming in a warm ocean.

In the meantime, for some of us it is perhaps worth ureflecting on our past journeys to sustain us with our memories, to look back with affection at our former selves and treat them kindly so they will make better companions for us as we continue to travel.

At the beginning of each of our journeys, particularly in our youth, most of us were off to El Dorado and whatever wonderful future fate had in store for us. We were Ulysses, Jason, and Aeneas on their quests. We were every explorer in search of fame, knowledge, and fortune. We arrived many times at various forks on our path and took the one that inspired us, whether we believed in a fatalistic Islamic *mektoub* or whether we thought we really had a choice to determine our future.

Things often petered out, we made the wrong decision, or we lost our youth and our purpose. Or worse, we may even have become bored. We look back and think, "That's life, after all," and may even wonder whether it has all been worth it. Those hardships, those sorrows, and the difficult days, were they evened out by the joys, the surprises, the unexpected laughter—both in life and on the road?

To give us heart, it is also appropriate to remember those who lived so intensely on their travels, in sometimes appalling circumstances. The Isabella Birds, the Dervla Murphys, and so many others, defying all the obstacles they met on their way, who found in travel the unexpected inner resources that enabled them to transcend their ordinary lives. But those were unusual characters, and while admiring them and honouring their feats, I must admit to having little affinity with them.

I prefer some ordinary conclusion, more in the nature of Ben Johnson and James Boswell's after completing their 1773 tour of the Hebrides, a tour taken "in close-partnery." Boswell relates:

> I have brought Dr. Johnson down to Scotland and seem him into the coach, which in a few hours carried him back into England. He said to me often that the time he spent in this tour was the pleasantest part of his life, and asked me if I would lose the recollection of if for five hundred pounds. I answered I would not; and he applauded my setting such a value on an accession of new images in my mind.

A simple and elegant conclusion I would like to adopt. The accession of new images in our mind is the great and never-ending gift of travel, particularly if one is lucky enough to share it in close partnery. Naturally, this also applies to life's progress.

About the Author

Monique Layton lived in Morocco, France, and England before settling down in Vancouver, British Columbia, and has travelled extensively. At university, she studied romance languages, comparative literature, and cultural anthropology (PhD 1978). She has published in a variety of disciplines.

She is married to John, who manages to put up with her many so-called projects: quilting, translations, miniature furniture, etc. They have five children and eleven grandchildren.

After spending the last six years of her working life at Simon Fraser University, she is now retired.

Bibliography

Anguita, R. "America latine crece y ahora busca el equilibrio." *La Vanguardia Revista*, (June 15, 1994): 4.

Avery, Catherine, B., ed. *Classical Handbook*. New York: Appleton-Century-Crofts Inc., 1962.

Barr, Patricia. *A Curious Life for a Lady. The Story of Isabella Bird, Traveller Extraordinary*. London: McMilland and John Murray, 1970.

Bedford Sybille. *A Visit to Don Otavio. A Traveller's Tale from Mexico*. London: The Folio Society (Introduction by Bruce Chatwin), 1980.

────── *As It Was: Pleasures, Landscapes and Justice*. London: Sinclair-Stevenson, 1990.

────── *Jigsaw: An Unsentimental Education*. Berkeley, CA: Counterpoint, 2001.

────── *Pleasures and Landscapes: A Traveller's Tales from Europe*. Berkeley, CA: Counterpoint (introduction by Jan Morris), 2003.

Bertolina, Daniel, and Catherine Viau, *Marhaban Bikoum*. Documentary film, co-production Canada-Maroc, le Studio Via le Monde Inc., 2010.

Black, Ronald, ed. *To the Hebrides, Samuel Johnson's Journey to the Western Islands of Scotland and James Journal of a Tour of the Hebrides*. London: Birlinn Ltd., 2007.

Branch, Hilary. "Venezuela. Where the Andes Meet the Caribbean," in *South America* (Guidebook), 1990.

Brenan, Gerald. *South from Granada*. London: Hamish Hamilton, 1957.

Butler, R. W. "Alternative Tourism: Pious or Trojan Horse." *Journal of Travel Research,* (Winter 1990): 49–45.

Chatwin, Bruce. *In Patagonia*. London: Jonathan Cape Ltd., 1977.

────── *The Viceroy of Ouidah*. London: Jonathan Cape Ltd., 1980.

────── *The Songlines*. London: Jonathan Cape Ltd.1987.

────── *Anatomy of Restlessness*. New York: Viking Press, 1996.

Chetwode. *Two Middle-aged Ladies in Andalusia*. London: Century Publishing, 1985.

Cocker, Mark. *Loneliness and Time: British Travel Writing in the Twentieth Century*. London: Secker & Warburg, 1992.

Cohen, E. "Lovelorn *farangs:* The correspondence between foreign men and Thai girls." *Anthropological Quarterly* 59(3) (1986): 115–127.

Cohen, Stanley, and Laurie Taylor. *Psychological Survival. The Experience of Long Term Imprisonment*. New York: Pantheon Books, 1972.

Curzon, George Nathaniel. *Tales of Travel*. (1st edition, London: Sidgwick & Jackson. 1923). Reprinted with an introduction by Peter King. London: Hodder & Stoughton, 1986.

_____ *Travel with a Superior Person*. London: Sidgwick & Jackson, 1985.

D'Amore, L. Tourism. "The World's Peace Industry." *Journal of Travel Research*. (Summer 1988) 3: 56–60.

Davies, Robertson. 1994. "Getting There." In Constance Rook, ed. *Writing Away. The PEN Canada Travel Anthology*. 56–60. Toronto: McLelland & Stewart Inc., 1994

Dickens, Charles. *American Notes for General Circulation*. London: Chapman and Hall, 1842.

Doria, Edmée. *Sur les Pistes du destin*. n.p. 1976.

Dydynski, Krzysztof. *Venezuela*. Lonely Planet Publication, 1994.

Eden, Emily. *Up the Country*. London: Virago Press, 1983.

Editorial Escudo de Oro, S.A. *Gaudi's Barcelona*. n.p., 1994.

Gorbatchev, Mickhael. "Why Cuba's Time Has Come." *The Globe and Mail* (December 7, 1994): A13.

Eichler de Saint John, Maryse, Nelly Ardill, and Christian Bossu-Picat. *Island Homes*. Artistic Production Seychelles. Singapore: Eurasia Press, 1989.

Elliangham, M., S. McVeigh, and D. Grisbrook, D. *Morocco*. London: Rough Guides Producers, 1998.

Fussell, Paul. *The Norton Book of Travel*. New York: W. W. Norton & Company, 1987.

Garrigue, François. *Maroc enchanté*. Paris: Artaud. Collection Le Monde en Image, 1966.

Gilbert, Martin. *In Ishmael's House. A History of Jews in Muslim Lands*. Toronto: McCleland & Stewart, 2009.

Gilmour, David. *Cities of Spain*. London: John Murray, 1992.

Gonos, G., V. Mulkern, and N. Poushinsky, "Anonymous Expression. A Structural View of Graffiti." *Journal of American Folklore,* (1976) 89: 40–48.

Gordon, F. L., D. Talbot, and D. Simonis, *Morocco*. Lonely Planet Publications, 1998.

Govier, Katherine. *Without a Guide: Contemporary Women's Travel Adventures.* Toronto: Macfarlane Walter & Ross, 1994.
Hanbury-Tenison, Robin. *The Oxford Book of Exploration.* Oxford: Oxford University Press, 1993.
Harris, Walter. *Morocco That Was.* London: Eland Books, 1921.
Ibarz, J., and A. Maeguez, A. "Gonzçez defiende estados fuertes y democraticos y condemna la corrupciùn. Fidel, del caqui a la guayabera." *La Vanguadia,* Barcelona. (June 15, 1994): 3.
Jackson, Michael. *Prisoners in Isolation: Solitary Confinement in Canada.* Toronto: University of Toronto Press, 1983.
Keesing, R. M., and F. Keesing. *New Perspectives in Cultural Anthropology.* New York: Hold, Rinehart and Winston, Inc., 1971.
Kennedy, Sylvia. *See Ouarzazate and Die. Travels through Morocco.* London: Scribner's, 1992.
Kurlansky, Mark. "The Basque History of the World." www.rambles.net/kurlansky_basq99.htlm.
Layton, Monique. "The Ambiguities of the Law or the Streetwalker's Dilemma." *Chitty's Law Journal,* (1979:27) 4:109–120.
_____ *Street Women and the Art of Bullshitting. The Oral Culture of Drug Addicts and Prostitutes in Vancouver.* Webzines of Vancouver, 2010.
Lévi-Strauss, Claude. *Tristes Tropiques.* New York: Atheneum, 1974.
Mauss, Marcel. *The Gift. The Form and Reason for Exchange in Archaic Societies.* New York: W. W. Norton, 1980.
Morris, Jan. *Spain.* Penguin Books, 1982.
_____ *Among the Cities.* New York: Viking Press, 1985.
Morris, Steven. Britain's Only Prison Ship Ends up on the Beach. *The Guardian.* (August 12, 2005).
Murphy, Dervla. *Full Tilt: Ireland to India with a Bicycle.* London: Dutton, 1965.
_____ *In Ethiopia with a Mule.* London: John Murray, 1977.
_____ *Muddling though Madagascar.* London: John Murray, 1985.
de Nadaillac, Laure. France, *que fais-tu de tes vieux?* Documentary film. *Télévision Française,* Canal 5. 2007.
Nash, D. 1981. "Tourism as an Anthropological Subject." *Current Anthropology.* (1981:22) 5: 451–481.
Newby, Eric, ed. *A Book of Travellers' Tales.* London: Collins, 1985.
O'Brian, Patrick. *Post Captain.* New York: W. W. Norton & Co., 1990.
d'Ormesson, Jean. *Presque rien sur presque tout.* Paris: Gallimard, 1996.
Orwell, George. *Homage to Catalonia.* London: Secker & Warburg, 1938.

Raeburn, Michael, ed. *Homage to Barcelona. The City and its Art. (1888–1936)*. London: Thames and Hudson, 1986.

Reimer, Phil. "Ship-building Spree Floats More Fun." *The Province*. (October 31, 2010): C7

Robinson, Jane. *Wayward Women. A Guide to Women Travellers*. Oxford: Oxford University Press, 1990.

———— *Unsuitable for Ladies. An Anthology of Women Travellers*. Oxford: Oxford University Press, 1994.

Rugoff, Milton. *The Great Travelers: A Collection of Firsthand Narratives of Wayfarers, Wanderers and Explorers in All Parts of the World from 450 B.C. to the Present*. New York: Simon and Schuster, 1960.

Russell, Mary. *The Blessings of a Good Thick Skirt. Women Travellers and their World*. London: Collins, 1988.

El Saadawi, Nawal. *My Travels Around the World*. Zed Books Ltd., 1989.

Sartre, Jean-Paul. *On Cuba*. Westport & London: Greenwood Press, 1974. (Originally published as *Ouragan sur le sucre*, 1960.)

Smith, Frank. "Catalonia Gets Tough." *The Globe and Mail*, (August 20, 1994): D4.

Stendhal. *Mémoires d'un touriste*. Paris: Le Club du Livre Sélectionné, n.d.

Theroux, Paul. *Riding the Iron Rooster. By Train Through China*. New York: Random House, 1988.

——————*The Pillars of Hercules. A Grand Tour of the Mediterranean*. New York: Fawcett Columbine, 1995.

de Ugalde, Martin. "A Short History of the Basque Country." www.buber.net/Basque/History/shorthist.html

Wood, Katie, and Syd House. *The Good Tourist*. London: Mandarin Paperbacks, 1991.